- Ernest Augustus, Duke of Cumberland and King of Hanover — *m.* — Frederica of Solms-Braunfels
  - George V (deposed by Prussia in 1866) — *m.* — Mary of Saxe-Altenburg
    1. Ernest Augustus, Duke of Cumberland — *m.* — Thyra of Denmark
       1. Ernest Augustus, Duke of Brunswick
       2. Marie Louise
       3. Alexandra
       4. Olga
    2. Frederica — *m.* — Alphonse of Pawel-Rammingen
       - children
    3. Mary
- Augustus, Duke of Sussex
  - (illegitimate)
    1. Augustus d'Este
    2. Augusta d'Este
- Adolphus, Duke of Cambridge — *m.* — Augusta of Hesse-Cassel
  1. George, 2nd Duke of Cambridge
     - (illegitimate)
       1. George Fitzgeorge
       2. Adolphus Fitzgeorge
       3. Augustus Fitzgeorge
  2. Augusta — *m.* — Frederick William, Grand Duke of Mecklenburg-Strelitz
     - Adolphus Frederick
     - . . . . . and others
  3. Mary Adelaide — *m.* — Francis, Duke of Teck
     1. Victoria Mary (May) — *m.* — George, Duke of York
        1. Edward
        2. Albert
        3. Mary
        4. Henry
     2. Adolphus, 2nd Duke of Teck
     3. Francis
     4. Alexander, Earl of Athlone
- Sophia
  - (illegitimate) Thomas Garth
- (and others)

- Alfred, Duke of Edinburgh and Saxe-Coburg — *m.* — Grand Duchess Marie of Russia
  - Alfred
  - Marie — *m.* — Frederick of Roumania
    1. Carol
    2. Elizabeth
    3. Marie
  - Victoria Melita — *m.* — Ernest Louis, son of Princess Alice
    - Elizabeth
  - Alexandra — *m.* — Ernest of Hohenlohe-Langenburg
    1. Godfrey
    2. Marie
  - Beatrice
- Helena — *m.* — Christian of Schleswig-Holstein
  1. Christian Victor (Christle)
  2. Albert
  3. Helena Victoria
  4. Louise — *m.* — Aribert of Anhalt (marriage dissolved)
  5. Harold
- Louise — *m.* — John, Marquess of Lorne
- Arthur, Duke of Connaught — *m.* — Louise Margaret of Prussia
  1. Margaret
  2. Arthur
  3. Victoria
- Leopold, Duke of Albany — *m.* — Helena of Waldeck-Pyrmont
  1. Alice
  2. Charles Edward
- Beatrice — *m.* — Henry of Battenberg (Liko)
  1. Alexander Albert
  2. Victoria Eugenie
  3. Leopold
  4. Maurice

a simplified family tree
showing the ancestry and connections of
QUEEN VICTORIA
with
her children,
grandchildren,
and great-grandchildren
at the time of her death in 1901
(a broken line indicates illegitimate descent)

The Widow of Windsor

BY THE SAME AUTHOR:

As TYLER WHITTLE

BOTANY AND GARDENING ESSAYS

Some Ancient Gentlemen
Common or Garden
The Plant Hunters

FICTION

The Last Plantagenet
(a biographical novel about Richard III)
The Young Victoria
Albert's Victoria

FOR CHILDREN

Spades & Feathers
The Runners of Orford
Castle Lizard
The Bullhead
The Birth of Greece
The World of Classical Greece
Royal and Republican Rome

As MARK OLIVER

FICTION

As Though They Had Never Been
A Roll of Thunder
Luke Benedict
Feet of Bronze
Young Plants & Polished Corners

FOR CHILDREN

Five Spinning Tops of Naples

THE WIDOW OF WINDSOR

Tyler Whittle

HEINEMANN : LONDON

William Heinemann Ltd
15 Queen Street, Mayfair, London W1X 8BE

LONDON MELBOURNE TORONTO
JOHANNESBURG AUCKLAND

First published 1973

434 86486 2

Printed in Great Britain by
Cox & Wyman Ltd
London, Fakenham and Reading

to

Eleanor and Alick Bell

AUTHOR'S NOTE

Though a fictional treatment, *The Widow of Windsor* is entirely faithful to the known facts. No character has been invented and nothing has been deliberately distorted or omitted simply to make the writing easier or to suit a preconceived idea. The few small liberties taken to bridge gaps in the documentary evidence lie always within the seemliness of historical probability.

T. W.

PART ONE

1

The night sky over Osborne House was rent with lightning. It lit up the park again and again, and it showed the trees bending under the wind. Two firs had been partially blown from the ground and were heeling over, resting at an angle against their neighbours. Several Austrian pines had been snapped. Holm oaks and cypresses and hollies, their branches forced together into a dense mass, were battered by gust after gust. Even the leafless trees were shaken. Only the yews and the wide-branched cedars on the lawn breasted the gale. The noise was tremendous. The wind whined and howled and shrieked. There were fusillades of hailstones. Sullen rolls of thunder swelled on occasions into deafening claps.

Though it was close to midnight Andrew Toward, the Ground Steward, was in his office at the rear of the building. He had not yet attempted to go to bed. Nor could he. The storm was a threat to Osborne and to the creation of his master the Prince Consort who now lay dead at Windsor. He felt it was his particular duty to keep watch. The park worried him less than the house. The most precious exotics were tubbed and already under winter cover and the younger plantings were staked and protected. The rest would actually benefit from a good blow. It would sort out the weaklings and root prune the others. But this was by far the worst storm in all Mr Toward's experience at Osborne and he could not help being a little anxious about the Italian-style flag tower. In the flashes of lightning he looked up at it critically from his office window. It was tall and undeniably elegant but too slender, he feared, to withstand excessive pressure, and it was built on a rigid principle. To be safe it ought to give a little, and beneath it were the Queen's private apartments. . . .

He wiped away the steam his breath had made on the chilled

glass pane and rebuked himself for being overfanciful. The tower was firm enough. It ought to withstand anything save a direct hit from a thunderbolt.

He went to put more coals on the fire. It glowed brightly and there was no trace of smoke being blasted back down the chimney. Ordinarily it would have given Mr Toward great satisfaction that the new revolving, zinc cowls were working so well, but they were a reminder of the Prince Consort who personally had designed them. Remembering that his master was dead and had been cut off in young middle age made Mr Toward miserable. He took a cane chair to the window embrasure and sat there to keep watch until the storm blew itself out; to watch and remember the dead Prince, and his poor bereaved widow eating her heart away with grief in those rooms below the tower. Poor Prince. Poor Queen.

All save one of the rooms at Osborne had the entwined initials *V* and *A* above the doorway. The exception was the door of the smoking room above which there was the single letter *A*. There the Gentlemen of the Household were waiting to greet the Duke of Saxe-Coburg who, according to a courier sent ahead, should have reached Osborne some hours before. Doubts were expressed that the commander of the royal yacht would chance crossing the Solent in such weather but as long as there was a possibility they were under an obligation to sit up.

Two gentlemen were playing chess. Three more, the Lord in Waiting, the Master of the Household and an equerry, were sitting beside the fire talking in louder tones than usual because of the storm. And, at a writing table, sorting through papers, were Colonel Sir Charles Phipps, the Privy Purse and General Grey, unofficial Private Secretary. Under normal circumstances they would not have been working at this hour, but in the hiatus which followed the death of the Prince Consort, a volume of extra responsibility had devolved on them. Formerly his servants and friends, they now found themselves in the wider service of the Queen. His equerries had also become hers, and even his valets, dressers, jägers and other body servants had been transferred to her service. Both Phipps and Grey could understand her motives for absorbing the Prince's Household en bloc into hers. They were prepared to serve her to the best of their ability.

The papers sorted and checked, they were laid aside. Then Phipps, circumspect even when a storm prevented conversation in a normal voice, wrote on a sheet of writing paper for the General's eyes only 'P of W – N.C.?'

Grey's face clouded. The Prince of Wales' affair with an actress, Nellie Clifden, had been brought to the Prince Consort's notice barely a month before and had upset him a good deal. Both Phipps and Grey appreciated that a young prince, training at his first military camp, was very likely to give way to pressing temptations, but his father, so strictly self-controlled that it was rumoured wrongly he was passionless, had found it difficult to understand. Though already unwell, he had gone up to Cambridge himself to talk to his son, and not long afterwards his illness had become mortal. The dreadful result was that the Queen now partially blamed her eldest son for her husband's death and could hardly bring herself to look at him, and the bewildered twenty-year-old Prince of Wales, already conscience-stricken because secretly he did not feel the loss as much as he knew he should and because once or twice he had caught himself feeling thankful that never again would he have to meet those cold, penetrating eyes which accused him of sloth and greed and inefficiency, was in an agony of remorse.

Grey scribbled beneath the query: 'Abroad, as the P.C. planned, as soon as possible?'

Phipps nodded in agreement. He balled the paper and walked over to throw it into the fire. Then he and Grey took leather chairs and warmed themselves at the blaze of logs.

From time to time as they waited for the Duke of Saxe-Coburg they joined in the desultory conversation by the fire, but it was merely out of politeness. Each had his thoughts in the past, on the good days with their master before his health gave way. It was a great sorrow to them both that he had been cut off at the early age of forty-two before he had had time to win the affection of the people. Lord Orford's celebration of his death with bonfires and a banquet because yet another foreigner was well out of the way had been offensive and eccentric, but only an extravagant extension of what many people were thinking. Though shrewd politically, exceptionally gifted as an administrator, with a keen aesthetic sense, and a lovable nature as Phipps and Grey well knew, the Prince Consort had never been popular in England. Poor Prince. Poor Queen.

The Clerk of the Kitchen was still up and at his desk. This was chiefly because he was frightened of thunder. It petrified him, and unless he could keep a part of his mind occupied with something else the constant noise hypnotized him into a shaking coma of terror. On hearing the first rumble he had decided not to go to bed and to get on with his orders and accounts.

His little room, hemmed in on all four sides by a corridor and a storeroom, the pantry and the kitchen, and dimly lighted by a fanlight over the door and a high window of frosted glass which let directly into the kitchen, was one of the failures in the overall design of Osborne. But with the passing of time the clerk had grown fond of it. He found it comfortable and warm. As he wrote copies and lists and receipts and orders he enjoyed the savoury smell which came in from next door and the companionable sounds of cooking – the frizzling of roasting meats, the bubbling of coppers, the hiss of gas jets and stoking noises, the clatter of dishes and pots, and the jangle of spit chains. And though poky, there was just room for the shelves of ledgers and kitchen blue books, the Master Cook's table and chair and set of drawers, and his own high desk and stool.

He perched there that night, thankful for the rooms and the corridor which surrounded him because they diminished the rumbling of thunder. With ear plugs fitted it was still further reduced. Only the worst claps made him catch his breath with fright. Otherwise he was able to get on with his work, always heavy as Christmas approached, and this season doubly so because, not knowing and being unable to discover the Queen's wishes, a wide variety of alternative arrangements had to be made in order to suit whatever she might decide.

Christmas at Osborne already had its own carefully observed traditions but how far, if at all, they would be followed this season was something no one could decide. In three days the Prince would be buried. In four it would be Christmas Eve. The Chef and Master Cooks at Windsor had already roasted and sent the massive baron of beef for the Osborne sideboard. Generally it was decorated with the Queen's and the Prince Consort's initials in grated horseradish. What, this year, should be done? Should the beef appear at all? An unanswerable problem, the Clerk decided, his pen rapidly noting alternative kitchen procedures for submitting to the Master Cook and through him to the Master of the Household. Being Welsh and young and emotional he felt very keenly the gloom which lay over everyone. When he saw from a note left by a storeman that a consignment of confectionery had arrived that morning from Germany, he felt it even more. Without the special sweetmeats and *lebkuchen*, a type of gingerbread topped with almonds, Christmas at Osborne would not be at all the same. But could they be served as bonbons this year without causing a great deal of pain? The Prince who had first introduced them from his homeland was dead at Windsor. His widow was breaking her heart in her apartments below the Flag Tower. Poor Prince. Poor Queen.

Jane, Lady Churchill, Victoria's permanently resident Lady-in-Waiting, sat in the Osborne drawing-room with the Princess Alice. They, too, were waiting anxiously for the Duke of Saxe-Coburg, and neither would admit to the other that she feared he would not, could not, arrive that night.

Princess Alice was quite unaccustomed to the weight of care and responsibility which had suddenly come upon her and she needed her uncle to take from her some of the load. Lady Churchill realized this but she herself could do little to help. Though very close to the Queen, and she was, perhaps, Victoria's most intimate friend, neither ever forgot the relationship that stood between them of sovereign and subject, and, in her present state of nervous collapse, the Queen needed an equal to advise her and rally her with encouragement. Lady Churchill believed the most useful thing she could do in the present crisis was to set an example in the household of unruffled calm, that and to mother Princess Alice who from every sign was quite worn out.

It really was no wonder because through the worst of the Prince Consort's illness Alice had been the rock on whom everyone depended. She had made decisions for her mother and the family. She had even consoled her father's desolated body servants, bidding them dry their tears as long as their master lived and there was some hope. And she herself had nursed him tenderly, feeding him and giving him medicine, singing his favourite hymns to him, reading to him from *Silas Marner* and *The Warden*, calming him in delirium, soothing his anxieties, softening his angry outbursts, and encouraging his simple religious devotion with her own; making his death in the Blue Room at Windsor no less dreadful but more dignified and comfortable. Ever since she had done her best for her distracted mother, sleeping in her bedroom, soothing her after paroxysms of crying, indulging her fancies to keep everything as it had been in her father's rooms. It was she who helped hang a wreath of evergreens and his photograph above the bed in the Blue Room. It was she who collected the fresh flowers her mother had strewed on the bed each day. It was she who passed on the order that his clothes were still to be laid out and hot water still regularly carried to his apartments for bathing and shaving. It was she who, at her mother's urgent beseeching, arranged for the castle photographer to take a family group, all dressed in jet mourning and gazing at a bust of their father on a flower-encircled plinth. And it was she who, seeing how things were, took her brother the Prince of Wales on one side and instructed him to keep out of their mother's way for the time being.

It was no wonder she was tired, and, at that moment, though the drawing-room was well screened and they were close to the fire, she was shivering with cold.

Lady Churchill recommended a hot drink. It would warm her and ultimately soothe her to sleep.

Alice thanked her, but she merely drew the India shawl closer round her shoulders and held out her small fingers to the fire. She longed to be soothed to sleep, and to sleep soundly and deeply, but as long as her bed was in her mother's room she could do no more than catnap in case she was needed. She did not mind the sacrifice as long as she could make it. The least self-centred and possibly the most good-natured of all the royal children, Alice would do anything in her power for her broken-hearted mother. When she sobbed and cried in the night Alice's heart ached for her, though it was worse when she was silent. The nightlight burnt too low for Alice to see her in the great square bed but in her mind's eye she saw her sorrowing silently, her face puckered up in misery, the tears rolling soundlessly round her cheeks to trickle in salt drops onto the coverlet. In her arms she held her dead husband's nightshirt. Within reach under the covers was a cast of his hands so that occasionally she could touch them. Alice believed she could understand. Her own love for Louis of Hesse had only just begun to burn, yet already it burnt so brightly that the thought of losing him was intolerable. Her mother's love was twenty-one years older. How awful her pain must be.

Lady Churchill saw a cloud settle on the princess's face. Instinctivly she took her hand and pressed it. Sorrow blanketed Osborne far more than the storm which raged outside. Poor Prince. Poor Queen.

Emilie Dittweiler, one of the Queen's two dressers, sat in her room which gave on to the passage outside the royal apartments. The Queen had already gone to her bedroom, not to rest or prepare herself for sleep, but to sit on a sofa before a beech-wood fire and wait for her brother-in-law. She had instructed Emilie to leave both doors open so that they would be in close touch. She could not bear to be alone and, as Princess Alice had gone downstairs to take her place at the Sovereign's Dinner, someone had to be within easy call. Emilie supposed that the silver bell on the Queen's bed-table or the bell cords by the fire and bedstead would have summoned her just as speedily but, with the doors closed, the Queen would have felt cut off. Poor widow. Emilie grieved for her, sitting upright on that sofa thinking of her dead husband and sorrowing.

From time to time she slipped out of her room, unlocked the wrought-iron grille which barred the corridor, and went to peep into the royal bedroom to see that all was well. The Queen seemed to be oblivious of the storm. Emilie herself could not help starting when there was a particularly sharp thunderclap or dazzle of lightning, though at Osborne she always felt safer than at the other royal palaces. Several times she looked towards the grand staircase. Soon, she hoped, someone would come to say Duke Ernest had arrived. But when Stephen Maslin, the Queen's Page, appeared, it was only with a message from Lady Churchill. If the Queen was resting and comfortable, Princess Alice would remain in the drawing-room for the time being in order to welcome the Duke.

Emilie said yes the Queen was quiet and she was sitting before her fire, but she was strung up, tense. 'It is this waiting for Duke Ernest. And the storm.'

Maslin said he would tell Lady Churchill. Then, on his own account, he asked if the Queen had shown the least sign of recovering from her distress. There was a great fear in the Household and amongst her servants that she could not survive the onslaught of grief, that she would succumb, literally, with a broken heart, or lose her wits.

Emilie was not given to say a word to anyone about her mistress but she made an exception in Maslin's case. He had served the Queen's mother, the Duchess of Kent, for thirty-five years, and since her death only a few months before he had come into the royal service as Page of the Backstairs. It gave him a special place in Emilie Dittweiler's estimation and enabled her to confide in him as she could or would with no one else.

They talked in the doorway of her room.

She told him it had been wise to move from Windsor. Some advisers had been against it. While the Prince Consort lay above ground, his body washed and scented, carefully and lovingly groomed and dressed in full uniform and orders by his valets Löhlein and Maget, they believed the Queen would stay at Windsor. But her uncle, King Leopold of the Belgians, had quickly advised her to leave for Osborne. He had been right, said Emilie. Since the Queen had gone down that morning to Frogmore to choose a site for a fresh mausoleum close to her mother's she had seemed less strained. And the physical business of moving from Windsor had done her good. But what she really needed, confided Emilie, was a close relation to whom she could talk.

Maslin raised his eyebrows at this. The Queen had her children and her ladies. No one could have done more than Princess Alice, and Princess Victoria was due to arrive soon from Prussia.

'Of course.' Emilie made an impatient gesture. If Maslin did not realize that the Queen was less motherly than most women she had no intention of informing him. In any case, to her way of thinking, daughters married like Vicky or engaged as Alice was, were not much of a comfort to a bereaved mother. The Queen's elder sons were of even less use. Prince Alfred was already a sailor and usually away from home, and she had no cause to love the Prince of Wales just at present. Temporarily they were in charge of things at Windsor. As for the remaining children, they were still young, from Helena and Louise in the schoolroom down to baby

Beatrice in the nursery. Emilie best explained the Queen's need to Maslin by saying that, apart from her aunt by marriage, the Duchess of Cambridge, there was no one in England to call her Victoria any more and she found the loneliness intolerable. The King of the Belgians would be in England for the funeral, and so would her half-sister, Princess Feodore, but now, at this very moment, she needed the companionship of the Prince's closest relation.

Maslin cocked an eye. The Duke of Saxe-Coburg? Even discounting half the tales of the Duke's wildness he was still an unsavoury brother-in-law and Maslin believed the Queen knew all about him. She could wear tactful blinkers whenever it was necessary, but she saw and heard and knew a great deal more than her courtiers or ordinary people gave her credit for.

He was about to say this when Miss Skerrett appeared, a tall and stately lady dressed in unrelieved black from head to toe as a tribute to the Prince Consort whom she had greatly admired. Her place at Court was enigmatical. Technically as First Dresser she had supervision of the Queen's Wardrobe. In fact her self-chosen office was to make everything as comfortable as possible for the Queen and, being something of a blue-stocking, she was unofficial royal ambassador to the worlds of art and letters. On account of her sharpness she was held in awe by the Maids of Honour and by a majority of the royal servants.

'Emilie,' she snapped, rattling seven or eight ebony bracelets, 'why are you not attending on the Queen?'

Maslin began to explain. He was quickly silenced.

'Go about your business. Go. Go.' said Miss Skerrett. He went at once. Miss Skerrett continued: 'Emilie, I have come to tell her Majesty there are lights down at the jetty. It is believed they have made the crossing to Cowes, and the gentlemen are gathering to greet his Serene Highness in the hall. . . .'

She was stopped by an immense thunder clap followed by a long sullen roll. Involuntarily in their fright Emilie and Miss Skerrett seized each other's hands. Then, as the noise began to die, Miss Skerrett disengaged herself with a rattle of bracelets, and simultaneously they both heard, from the other side of Emilie's door, the insistent ringing of a bell.

. . . . .

Fortunately the hall entrance was sheltered between the two wings of Osborne House. Even so, the footmen had a struggle to manage the doors as the Duke of Saxe-Coburg and his gentlemen struggled in from the storm. With them came a shriek of wind and the smell of sea spray, and, before the doors could be closed, all sorts of débris had been blown into the house. Scattered over the floor were sand and gravel, leaves and twigs and pine needles; and a tuft of heather, wrenched bodily by the wind from the Scotch garden outside, was blown on to the large group of statuary below the staircase.

The Duke looked wretched. Ordinarily his complexion was bad and after the wild crossing he was yellow. And despite the fact that he wore a thick travelling cloak he was drenched to the skin. The formalities were hurried through so that he could change and recover his composure before being received by the Princess Alice who would take him to the Queen.

But he had no opportunity.

A little cry from the head of the staircase made everyone look up. The Queen stood there flanked by Emilie and Miss Skerrett, both of whom looked put out. Her chalk-white face was in sharp contrast to the drabness of her weeds. Her hands were outstretched to her brother-in-law.

Phipps and Grey exchanged incredulous glances. As he was a reigning sovereign, protocol did permit the Queen to welcome the Duke in person, but, under the circumstances, it was hardly to be looked for. Nor, clearly, did the Duke himself expect it for he appeared to have no idea of what he ought to do. Making up his mind, he bowed slowly and made for the staircase. But by that time the Queen had run down the stairs herself. At the foot of the staircase she threw herself into his arms and broke into a passion of weeping.

She did not admire Ernest of Saxe-Coburg. She did not even care for him. And he was wet through and travel-stained and bilious-looking. But he was her darling Albert's brother. 'Oh, Ernest!' she sobbed into his neck. 'Oh, Ernest! Oh, Ernest!'

2

When the funeral was over and done and the Prince Consort's body laid temporarily to rest in the Windsor tombhouse – now renamed the Albert Memorial Chapel – and the order given for its walls to be lined with costly marble and its roof crowned with copper, the Queen's uncle Leopold went down to Osborne with other members of the family.

He was appalled when he saw his niece. Her appearance and manner showed the extent of her misery.

To begin with he said very little, thinking it wiser to let her weep and talk. But her talk became so rapid and wild that he was gravely concerned. He recalled her disproportionate grief on the death of her mother only nine months before, when a rumour had run through the courts of Europe that the Queen of England was as mad as her grandfather George the Third. Albert had saved her from that. Gently but firmly he had made her pull herself together. Now, at the age of forty-two, the loss of her beloved husband seemed to be threatening her reason.

Directly after his first conversation with Victoria King Leopold sent for Sir Charles Phipps and General Grey. Then he sent for Lady Churchill and Miss Skerrett. Last of all he talked to Victoria's half-sister, the Princess of Hohenlohe.

Feodore was more candid than the others. Neither she nor Victoria were coy or prudish. Without embarrassment they could discuss such things as breast-feeding and opening medicines, and Feodore made it plain to her uncle that Victoria's feeling of desolation was undeniably aggravated by the approach of her change in life.

It explained a good deal and King Leopold was vastly relieved. Now his course was clear, to make her face the future.

This was not at all easy. So far she had refused point blank even to contemplate living without Albert. She was convinced that soon, thankfully, she would rejoin him in death. But her uncle had greater influence on Victoria than anyone alive. He urged her to pull herself together. Albert himself would havc wished it. He reminded her of her firm resolve that his wishes and his plans should be her law. Duty was a word he had hallowed and, as long as she lived, she had a duty to her children, her family, her friends, her ministers, and her subjects.

He was partially successful. Certainly, before he returned to Belgium he had persuaded his niece to look at her bereavement from a different viewpoint. He gave her a will to live and a purpose for living. Ever after, when considering a problem or making a decision, she would invariably look at pictures or a bust of Albert as if to see whether or not she had his approval. But the pain seemed to be no less. In fact, as the days passed, and each new morning was one more without Albert, it seemed to increase. The anaesthesia of shock was passing. One of her greatest helps immediately after Albert's death had been the suspension of belief that anything so terrible could possibly have taken place. As her frozen nerves thawed out, her desolation was pitiful to see. It was a testing time for everyone at Court.

Without exception her ladies showed they really cared for her. Lady Augusta Bruce, her resident Woman of the Bedchamber, believed in squaring one's shoulders to affliction. She had been Lady-in-Waiting to Victoria's mother and now she served the Queen well by talking frankly about the Prince Consort's illness and death. Facing each grisly detail instead of refusing to contemplate it helped Victoria regain her sense of proportion. And she was helped to be less self-centred in her grief by the Duchess of Athole who confided in her the secret that her own husband had an incurable cancer. The Queen was horrified. A bare three months before the good Duke had welcomed her and Albert to the Athole country, giving her a white rose as the ancient tribute of the Lords of Athole to their sovereign. He had been indefatigable, attending her personally at the crossing of a ford in Glen Tilt, up to his waist in water, holding her pony's bridle, and urging on his pipers who played them across the foaming river. And now this dear, good friend was doomed. Quite often, when the realization of her own loss began to engulf her, Victoria sent for the Duchess so that they could share each other's trouble. Lady Churchill best helped her, and was a brake on her tendency to be over-morbid, by being as normal and leading as ordinary a life as possible. Her world broken to pieces, Victoria needed to rebuild on the unchangeable pattern and continuity which Jane Churchill ensured. Then there was the other Jane amongst the Queen's ladies, the Dowager Marchioness of Ely, a widow herself and therefore in a special position to understand and console. And Miss Skerrett proved her devotion to the Prince Consort by taking every opportunity to praise his virtues, and the rattling of her ebony and black onyx jewellery was a welcome sound to Victoria because it always heralded an hour's conversation or more on the merits of her beloved Albert.

Alice continued to be her mother's chief support, acting as intermediary between the Queen and her ministers. It was Alice who, when her mother refused to attend a Privy Council, suggested a workable compromise. The Queen should be in one room with the door open while Mr Helps, the new Secretary to the Council, sat in the next room with three Councillors. As each item was read out it was approved by Mr Helps on the Queen's behalf. It was Alice, too, who bravely urged her mother to take a little exercise and try to see more of her courtiers. In this she was unsuccessful. Complaining that her limbs were as numbed as her spirits, the Queen suffered from overwhelming lassitude. It had happened once before when, as an unmarried young Queen, she had felt unable to face up to things and for a time had refused to ride out or dance or even walk if she could avoid it, and only with the greatest difficulty was she persuaded to get up in the morning and bathe, and allow her maid to brush and dress her hair. Bereavement now made her equally careless of her appearance, save that she was determined to wear widow's weeds for the remainder of her life, and she claimed it was too much for her to walk out in the fresh air, or see more than one person at once, or get up for breakfast, or invite visitors and members of the Household to the Queen's dinner. People, she said, should not expect it – and certainly not her daughter Alice who ought to understand....

Alice was advised by Lady Churchill not to persist. The Queen would overcome her lassitude in time. But Alice felt it as a failure, and she felt it, too, when she failed to persuade her mother to look more kindly on her brother Bertie, the Prince of Wales. The Queen was firm. She could not, she said. Even the sight of him made her shudder.

3

The Prince of Wales was twenty and exceedingly good looking. In one sense he had had a lonely childhood, only meeting those grown-ups and children who were specially selected by his father. And he had been unable to cope with the nursery and schoolroom regimen laid down for him. After struggling to meet his father's idealistic hope that he should be as wise and as talented and as good as he was beautiful, he had one day given up the attempt. After that he had simply tried, not very effectively, to keep up appearances. His father had refused to admit defeat. His elaborate programme of training for the future sovereign of England had several times been adapted and modified, but without much success. The boy intended to have the character of Galahad with the wisdom of Merlin conspicuously lacked both. Nor, concluded the Prince Consort wryly, did he even possess the force of personality to be a Mordred. Bertie was simply weak and self-indulgent: a bully, greedy, sensual, vain, and with a boisterous, childish sense of humour his father found unamusing. Moreover he was deceitful and Janus-faced, being charming in society and thoroughly unpleasant to his valet in private, tormenting him by throwing wax on his livery, water on his linen, tearing his ties, and rapping him on the nose. To a cultured man of sensibility like the Prince Consort, such loutish behaviour to a servant was deplorable.

Victoria had been largely indifferent to Bertie as a child except that, in his stubbornness and wilfulness and fits of nervous and unmanageable temper, she saw him as an unwelcome caricature of herself which she was determined to correct. On several occasions she had, literally, rolled up her sleeves and smacked him herself. When his needs were brought home to her, as for example when it was recommended he should have a playmate of his own age at Osborne, she did something about it, and admitted to the holiday circle Mr Gladstone's son, the inimitable William Henry;

but otherwise she preferred to see little of him. He agitated his dear father, and therefore he agitated her.

Bertie was not completely aware of his parents' feelings. He was so much less intelligent than either of them that he could not readily analyse anything. But, after his father's funeral, it became more and more plain that his mother wanted him away from Court. She asked pointedly when he was returning to his establishment at the White Lodge in Richmond Park.

Alice told him why; that, in his deathbed delirium, the Prince had raved about his son's disgrace and so their mother held him partially to blame for the tragedy.

Bertie was thunderstruck. His father had assured him that his mother know nothing about Nellie Clifden. He had said so plainly in his private lecture in the library at Madingley Hall at Cambridge; sitting there, hunched and tired and obviously ill, talking endlessly about family disgrace and personal purity. It was his last picture of his father, and he felt a little ashamed now because afterwards, when he was safely out of the range of those unnerving grey eyes, he had thought the lecture a great joke and Nellie a fine strapping girl, and his father's piety ludicrous. He asked Alice how his mother could possibly know about Nellie Clifden. For that matter, how did she herself know about the scandal?

Alice was short with him. Naturally she knew. Everyone knew from St Petersburg to Lisbon. The news had reached England from abroad. And though no one had actually told her, she was quite aware of what had happened. As for their father's pretence, it had been for Bertie's sake, so that he could meet his mother again without feeling ashamed of himself. It had been a kindness. But of course his mother knew. She was the Queen and she had to know everything which concerned her eldest son and heir.

Bertie gaped.

When Alice had left him he sat in the window embrasure and thought over what she had said. He blushed scarlet at the thought of his mother knowing what Alice had not shrunk to describe as 'all the disgusting details'. But then shame was driven out by anger that she should think he had contributed in some way to his father's death.

But even anger did not give him the necessary courage to confront his mother. In many ways he found her even more formidable than his father. She was little and she was stout and, in her fresh widowhood, apparently as vulnerable as an opened oyster or a crab turned on its back, but there was something about her which defied accurate description and which he found too alarming to challenge unless he was very sure of his ground. This time he was not sufficiently sure.

He considered asking his Governor, General Bruce, to speak to the Queen, but he quickly abandoned the idea. The General was a kindly and dapper Grenadier Guardsman and brother to Lady Augusta Bruce in his mother's Household, but he was too old, too removed from his generation, to understand a young man's position and would not present his case with any conviction. Lady Churchill might have made a better advocate because she was closer to the Queen than anyone, but her sympathetic interest in the Prince of Wales had been noted and frowned on two years before. It was a pity that his brother Alfred had already returned to his ship. Probably the Queen would have listened to him because she was quite unaware of Alfred's own gallantries. Alice could do nothing. Being unmarried she technically knew nothing about the scandal. But there was his elder sister Vicky. . . .

On a number of occasions he had stayed with Vicky and her husband Fritz in Prussia. They got on well. Twice they had defended him against his father's criticisms that he thought of nothing except clothes ('Even when out shooting he is more occupied with his trousers than with the game!'), and that he was stupid ('Usually his intellect is of no more use than a pistol packed at the bottom of a trunk if one were attacked in the robber-infested Apennines.'). On the contrary, they said, they had found him amusing and communicative, and he was made very welcome. Fritz had responded to his charm, and Vicky had arranged for him to meet, as if by accident, the Princess whom he hoped to marry, Alexandra of Denmark.

Bertie generally wrote a dull sort of letter, heavy with false heartiness and studded with clichés in parentheses, but his very confidential letter to the Crown Prince of Germany about his present dilemma was anything but boring. As he was expected to, Fritz passed on the message to his wife Vicky, and she was shocked by her mother's attitude. Fritz appealed by letter to his mother-in-law. Victoria was cross. It was a family matter, yes; but typical of her worthless son to involve other people. She replied forcefully through Vicky:

I never can or shall look at him without a shudder.

Then Vicky herself appealed. She pleaded with her mother to be more understanding and sympathetic.

Victoria felt wronged. Bitterly she replied:

All you say about poor Bertie is right and affectionate in you; but if you had seen what I saw, if you had seen Fritz struck down, day by day get worse and finally die, I doubt if you could bear the sight of the one who was the cause; or if you would not feel, as I do, a shudder.

Vicky persevered. She went on trying to persuade her to be more forgiving, but she met with little success. And nor did an old friend of the Prince Consort who assured the Queen that only Albert's great purity had caused him to take his son's fall so very much to heart. A less pure father, he said, would have minded less. Victoria was not disposed to change her mind, and she became icy with disapproval when he claimed that the Prince of Wales had merely commited a youthful error which very few young men escape.

It was at this point that Sir Charles Phipps broached the matter of the Prince Consort's plan for the completion of his son's education. It had already been arranged that he should leave in the spring for a tour of Palestine before engaging himself to marry Princess Alexandra. There seemed nothing against putting the plan forward. If the Queen wished, the Prince of Wales could leave within a month.

Victoria leapt at the chance of getting him out of the country. It was announced that the Prince of Wales was to travel in the Near East for several months and would be leaving at the beginning of February. General Bruce would be in charge of the itinerary. Canon Stanley, an expert on the Holy Land, was to be uprooted from Oxford to act as his chaplain and cicerone.

It was in discussing the Prince of Wales' tour that Victoria had a first brush with her ministers. She would not see them personally.

They must advise her through Princess Alice or her late husband's confidential Private Secretary, General Grey. Her ministers would understand that grief had prostrated her. She could not and would not conduct affairs as before. She was to be consulted on all matters, but would remain invisible.

The Cabinet decided this would not do at all and the Foreign Secretary was selected to remonstrate with the widowed Queen.

It was a good choice. Lord John Russell had lately been created Earl Russell and moved to the Peers, but he was still best known in Parliamentary circles by his nickname Finality Jack. Short in stature, and blandly pompous in manner except when affronted and then he became as scratchy as a cat, he had never got on well with Victoria. Oddly, considering the Prince Consort and her hero Wellington had also been small, she preferred big-boned men with what she called open faces. Russell's face was sharp and shut, and she suspected, rightly, that as a doctrinaire Whig he lacked respect for the House of Hanover. Indeed he did. The oligarchy of great landed families had his whole support. Royalty did not awe him in the least, and he was in precisely the right mood to rap the Queen over the knuckles. She had just complained of not having seen, or been consulted about, two dispatches sent out by the Foreign Office, and, at the same time, with infuriating inconsistency, had written to him:

> *The things of this world are of no interest to the Queen, beyond the satisfaction she must experience if Peace is maintained and this country is in prosperity: for her thoughts are fixed above.*

In a sententious letter he contrived to fix her thoughts below. Her duty, he reminded her, was to co-operate personally with her ministers in order that the business of government could proceed. It could not satisfactorily be conducted through third parties. Her privacy and deep mourning had been respected by the Ministry for more than a month but it could not be continued indefinitely.

Victoria did not care for the lecture. If he had not expressed the view that the late Prince Consort would himself have wished it, she would not have been so easily persuaded to abandon a declared position. But Uncle Leopold added his voice to Russell's, and, looking to the bust of Albert for approval, Victoria consented to change her mind. With a great effort she would lay her personal feelings and health on one side, and receive her ministers personally.

Lord Palmerston the Prime Minister decided that it was his duty to go down to Osborne and see her. It was a sacrifice. He would suffer agonies from his gout on the railway journey and get no more relief from his physicians than an order to take less high food and wine – a vexing direction to a gigantic meat-eater and claret-drinker for the best part of seventy years. And, at the end of it all, she would not be pleased to see him. She seldom was. This was surprising as he had the height and the open face the Queen admired, and could still be accounted a good-looking man. But though he had served her well, if boisterously, in foreign affairs, and though he was brother-in-law to her dear Lord Melbourne of fond memory, she had never really got over his lackadaisical way of going about things and his deplorable reputation as a gallant. Being really a relic of the eighteenth century he was bashfully proud of the latter himself, and so, certainly, were the British people who had voted him to power at the last election less because of his merits as a statesman than because he had just won their hearts by fathering a fine bastard boy at the age of seventy-five.

As he had feared, Lord Palmerston's journey was uncomfortable and exceedingly painful. And his audience could hardly be accounted a success. He was something of a dandy and, inadvertently, he had overlooked the Queen's decision to wear full mourning for ever. As a result, with his whiskers freshly dyed a deep sorrel colour, and dressed in brown topcoat, pearl-grey trousers, green gloves and aquamarine studs, he glittered in that sombre Court like a healthy perch amongst lugubrious bream. But he was not easily embarrassed, and Victoria, though at first visibly startled, soon collected herself, and she was moved by his obvious sincerity when he spoke of England's loss as well as hers in the tragic death of the Prince Consort. After that he touched on foreign affairs and in particular on the American Civil War in which, on the whole, the English supported the South but refused to commit herself officially. Then he approached the topic which had really brought him to Osborne, the Prince of Wales.

He noticed that the Queen's manner at once altered.

As tactfully as he could, he informed her that in the country there were unfortunate rumours she and her heir were not on the best of terms.

They were not rumours, she said, interrupting him; that is, if rumours were generally exaggerations or falsehoods. They were facts. She and her heir were on very bad terms. She told him why.

Palmerston deprecated the whole thing. 'Not good for the country, Ma'am, to see squabbles in high places.'

'This,' she said, drawing herself up, 'is not a squabble, Lord Palmerston. It is merely that whenever I see my son, I recall his contribution towards the cause of his father's death.'

'Typhoid, Ma'am,' dared Lord Palmerston, 'comes chiefly from bad drains. And you'll recall the Prince himself was in a way about the drains at Windsor.'

'I do,' she said. 'I recall as well the dilatoriness of the authorities in putting his recommendations into effect.'

'A disgrace, yes; and caused a tragedy, Ma'am. But it exonerates the Prince of Wales.'

The Queen flushed. 'You will agree that if he had not behaved so disgracefully at the Curragh Camp, his father would have had no need to go to Cambridge? You will agree that it utterly exhausted a man who was already tired and that it therefore fatally weakened his resistance to the disease?'

Women, thought Palmerston, were not usually so logical. To avoid an argument he agreed. As it was important to the Queen for the Prince of Wales to leave the country, that was sufficient for her ministers. They were quite satisfied.

'It irks me dreadfully to see him idling here,' said Victoria. 'He is better away.'

They settled to their usual discussion as to who should pay for this lengthy expedition; the Prince himself, or the fund salted away by the Prince Consort from his son's revenue, or the Queen, or the country.

The Prime Minister changed his weight from one foot to the other. They were hurting so much that he had to bring the audience to a swift conclusion and was therefore amenable to almost everything the Queen proposed. Then he told her that the Ministry thought well of the Danish match proposed for the Prince of Wales and that, if it could be satisfactorily arranged, the sooner he was married the better. Once more he commiserated with the Queen, kissed her hand, and backed painfully from the room.

Outside in the corridor his secretary was waiting with a chair.

4

The Lords in Waiting were political nominees but selected always with regard to the Queen's wishes, and were at Court in turn like her Maids of Honour and those of her Ladies and Women of the Bedchamber who were not in permanent residence. A new peer arrived at Osborne to go into Waiting and something he said at the Household Dinner on his first evening there caused an instant and profound silence. It was nothing much, merely that out in the world people were being critical of the Queen's ten-week seclusion far away from the centre of government. From the silence it caused he judged this was not at all appreciated and he was quick to disassociate himself from it. He had merely repeated, he said uncomfortably, what the world was saying.

'Then the world,' said Sir Charles Phipps with unusual warmth, 'is wrong-headed and heartless and may go to the devil.'

It was a token of the strength of feeling in the Household and amongst the royal servants.

Those who knew the Queen best were aware that she was not affecting a part, nor was she giving way to hysteria. She was genuinely broken by the loss of Albert. Therefore they defended her when it was suggested that she ought to move herself to Windsor for the greater convenience of her ministers, and they disagreed when critics said that she was being ill advised to stay in her bolt-hole at Osborne. They could well understand why, for the time being, the Queen chose to hide herself away.

Probably she was best understood by her eldest daughter Vicky who travelled from Germany as soon as she could. Vicky adored her own husband. Realizing how often she had failed to give him attention in little things, and how often directly or indirectly she scolded him for habits which she did not quite like, she could appreciate her mother's present remorse for having done exactly the same to her husband. Victoria now bitterly regretted having stayed up reading novels when Albert had wanted her to go to bed, and for having told him not to bolt his food, and to hurry out of the dining-room with his gentlemen, and not hang about over the fire. These items – tiny pebbles to those who did not know – were great boulders in Victoria's memory and her daughter understood. She could understand the renunciation of pleasures they had shared and her decision not to wear a *décolleté* dress again because there was no one any longer to murmur in melodious German how beautiful her shoulders were. And though each, in their voluminous correspondence, had commented on the shock to the system to which an ignorant young bride is exposed, both recognized and appreciated the importance of physical love in a happy marriage. Vicky delicately touched on her mother's sad state in a letter to Fritz:

> *She always sleeps with papa's coat over her and his dear red dressing-gown beside her, and some of his clothes on the bed. Poor mama has to go to bed, and has to get up alone – for ever. She was as much in love with papa as though she had married him yesterday. Mama so longed for another child.*

She realized, of course, that her mother had never really cared for her children until they were well out of the schoolroom, and even then she only saw them on specially selected occasions, but it was part of her longing for Albert to want his children and the youngest, Beatrice, had a specially honoured place in her feelings. Intelligently Vicky brought the child forward, a four-year-old, still called Baby, who early in life had fallen into the way of making memorable statements. She was carried by her sister to the Queen's bedroom before breakfast and played happily all over her mother remarking: 'What a pity it was I was too little to be at your marriage.'

Bless the child, thought Victoria, how quaint she is, but how very, very sad it all is.

Vicky persisted in distracting her, not too obviously which would have vexed her, but with a careful balance between agreeable and disagreeable topics. On the disagreeable side were the plans for Alice's wedding to Louis of Hesse that July, and Bertie's hoped-for marriage to the Princess of Denmark in the following year; but, as Albert had decreed them, they should take place despite her own feelings. And, also on the disagreeable side, was the necessity, so Vicky assured her, of going temporarily to

Windsor at the beginning of March – not only for the sake of Lord Palmerston's gout but also so that there could be another photograph of Papa's daughters gathered about his bust, a complete one this time for Vicky would go to Windsor too.

On the agreeable side was the Queen's changing view of the Prince of Wales. Time had quickly healed. He left in low spirits on February 6th, and once out of sight she felt more kindly towards him. She heard of his kind reception in Vienna by the Emperor Francis Joseph and then of his reception by the Empress of Austria in Venice. This news prompted a delightful conversation with Vicky about the shocking eccentricity of the Empress, a spendthrift, footloose Wittelsbach with a passion for mental health, sea voyages and Homer, and who travelled perpetually about Europe as Countess Hohenembs. It was the first piece of royal gossip she had enjoyed since long before Albert's death, and it did her a great deal of good. The next news of Bertie was that he was on his way to Cairo and had stopped in Albania to shoot wild pigs. By then she thought of him, and spoke of him to Vicky, as her dear boy. It was always to be the same with them. Seeing each other irregularly and for short intervals, and generally with a few hundred miles between them, they got on well enough. But thrown by circumstances into each other's presence for any length of time, he began to irk her terribly, and he became confused and troubled by her far superior intelligence.

Also on the agreeable side were talks about mausoleums. Mother and daughter shared an unusual taste for bright and fairly modest tombs. They studied the subject with some care; deciding that that of King Mausolos at Halicarnassos, with Ionic columns, cellar, ramp, sepulchral chamber, and a host of marble sculptures painted red and blue, was too elaborate altogether; that Hadrian's in Rome was too sombre and squat; that the damp, crepuscular vaults which studded Middle Europe were dingy and unhealthy; and that modifications, like Uncle Leopold's skilful use of Princess Charlotte's summerhouse as a mausoleum, were ingenious but really hardly suitable. Something which banished gloom was called for. It was a conclusion which must have mystified those who did not know or who forgot that the Queen herself expected to die very soon and enjoy the bliss of being reunited with her husband. The mausoleum more than anything decided Victoria to go for a short time to Windsor while Vicky was still in

England to see the site she had chosen and advise her on its construction.

Though her visit to Windsor was very short it was appreciated by her ministers. Uncle Leopold wrote to say it was an excellent thing. Later, when she had regained her strength, she should think of going to Balmoral, perhaps even to Coburg, and on the way she must visit him at Laeken. Victoria immediately felt betrayed. The world might not know how broken down she was, how close to a break-down, but Uncle Leopold ought to do. She would have written a chilly reply but for Vicky's persuasions. He was simply trying to be cheering, she said, nothing else. Cheering! The word was out of place in Victoria's present world. She said good-bye to her daughter who was returning at last to Germany, and went back to Osborne. There she made her will, set her affairs in order, and waited hopefully for the end.

Disappointingly it did not come.

She was surprised and a little vexed by her stubborn good health, and by the fact that far from declining she was becoming daily more energetic. She would have admitted it to no one – not even to herself – but she felt a little better for the change. Vicky's visit had been most beneficial. Her lassitude petered away because she was too vital a woman to drift aimlessly for long. She accepted a strong hint from her Uncle Leopold that it was in the interests of the throne to associate herself even more closely with the government of the country. Lord Palmerston and his Whig friends were, to some extent, men of honour, but amongst the Liberals in their party there were Radicals. If she cut herself off too thoroughly, the firebrands might decide they could do without her altogether.

From that moment the Queen needed no persuading to sit at her double desk and attend to state affairs. She became busier than ever in her life. All Albert's work – his sorting through and selecting of state documents for her attention – was now hers alone. She worked endlessly, sitting up sometimes until two in the morning, refusing any sort of aid; personally signing commissions, for example, though the Horse Guards and even her reactionary cousin George of Cambridge, the Commander-in-Chief, said a stamp manual would do as well.

A month before she would have believed that so great a load of work on top of her crushing sorrow would have drained her health. Even now when one of her courtiers unwisely mentioned the possibility of a change of government, she alarmed him terribly by clutching her head and crying: 'My reason! My reason!' And she sent a message to Lord Derby, the Leader of the Conservatives, to say that if he attempted to drive out Lord Palmerston, to whose ways she was accustomed, he might in the process deprive his sovereign of her life or her sanity. Fortunately the moment of danger passed, and Lord Derby was not called upon to make a decision, and Victoria became less and less prone to such exhibitions of hysteria.

Physically she was robust again. She actually thrived on her work. It did her good. Her longing for death modified as well. Apart from the essential sinfulness of it, there was the point that if she did die now Bertie would succeed her, and she had the firm opinion that, despite the care taken over his training, he was as yet so totally unfitted for the task that the throne would topple. Everywhere there were republicans and freemasons and socialists and conspirators who met in what her Home Secretary called 'unabolishable clubs', and they would drive Bertie from his throne without a qualm. Then all Albert's work would be destroyed and wasted. For his sake, therefore, she had a duty to sustain her health and energy and carry on the business of government.

At bottom it was for Albert's sake, not for the country's good. For the second time in her life she could not endure her people, and not only the mob which she had always pitied and mistrusted – the crowd of wretches, misled by agitators, made ugly and stupid by exploitation and poverty and ignorance – but also the vast mass of her subjects. A long time before they had held her responsible for a disgraceful episode at Court, and, from duchesses to guttersnipes, they had shown their feelings. She had shrunk from them then. She disliked them now because she would not deceive herself any longer. She knew that they had never appreciated Albert. Blind to all the good he had done, from duchesses to guttersnipes they had shunned him simply and solely because he was a foreigner and cleverer than most of them. 'The Pauper Prince' they had called him, and 'the German Professor', and 'Nose-poker', and even, mockingly, 'Lovely Albert'. Once in a black depression he had confided their hateful names to her and she could never forget this. Nor, at the moment, could she forgive.

Her feelings deeply hurt, her nerves raw and her heart sore, Victoria did not think she could ever bring herself to like her people again, not in the old sense of mothering them as she had, without being patronizing, her soldiers in the Crimean War. For the present she would simply rule them in the way Hallam prescribed and she had learnt with Albert in the first years of their marriage; and she would make certain that, whatever their feelings, the people of England should never have an opportunity to forget her husband and that they should learn to call him Albert the Good.

Albert's aims politically would be hers; his reforms at home and his strategies for the peace of Europe her chief concerns. Memorials of every kind should be visible reminders of his worth. She and her Ladies-in-Waiting would wear deep mourning for all her remaining years. She would live privately in as secluded a fashion as her position permitted. His children's children should all bear his dear name. His birthday and death-day and their wedding day should be solemn and compulsory anniversaries in the dynasty they had made together.

Victoria's mind was made up, the pattern set which, apart from small particulars, was to remain essentially the same for ever. The mould of the Widow of Windsor was cast.

5

Alice's wedding at Osborne was sombre.

Her husband Louis was heir to the small grand duchy of Hesse and was rather poor. Therefore the sort of trousseau Vicky had had two years before to take to Prussia, and which comprehensively had included two drawersful of sponges and galoshes as well as pearls and diamonds, would have been out of place. The Queen was firm about this. It would be wrong to show Louis up. Hesse-Därmstadt was a small Court, scarcely larger than the household of an English earl, where amongst other oddities dinner was eaten in full rig at the unfashionable hour of four. She warned Alice that the ordinary decencies of life might be expected in such a place, but no luxuries; therefore ostentation on her side of the family would not be fitting. But, she continued, as this was a love-match and not a dynastic marriage, presumably Alice would not mind?

Alice did not mind in the least. She was suffering a reaction from her father's illness and death and her mother's suffocating gloom and dedication to hard work. No caged bird was so eager to fly away. And she dearly loved Louis. For him she happily accepted a reduced trousseau and a wedding which under the circumstances was less grand than a Princess of the Blood might reasonably have expected.

Unhappily, three days before the ceremony, the already grey atmosphere at Osborne House was further darkened by news that the Prince of Wales' Governor, General Bruce, had died.

Immediately the innermost cell of the Queen's confidants at Court was plunged into the deepest gloom. Victoria herself was deeply distressed because the General had been a devoted servant and friend – 'a second father to our dear child' – and she had depended on him a great deal. And poor Lady Augusta was distraught. To lose a brother so soon after her beloved Duchess of Kent and the Prince Consort was overwhelming, but she bore herself bravely when they packed her off to her family for the funeral.

Against this dark background the marriage took place. It had to. Relations had been gathering at Osborne. They could hardly be sent back again, said the Queen, her unhappy voice tinged with regret, and they would have to put up with it all. . . .

Alice bore this with equanimity. Louis, too, was patient and charming, even when he found himself subject to a careful scrutiny by his alarming mother-in-law-to-be who declared she noticed 'a lack of refinement' in him, and his raffish military friends must be kept away from her daughter in Därmstadt.

July 1st came. The Queen noted in her Journal: 'Poor Alice's wedding-day . . . more like a funeral'. A bidden guest, Dean Wellesley of Windsor, held exactly the same view. Resembling his uncle the Duke of Wellington, in manner as well as looks, he called it devilishly woe-begone.

Almost everyone then cried, even the Archbishop of York, and Mr Prothero the local clergyman, and the bride's sailor brother Prince Alfred who sobbed broken-heartedly through the service; and the *sub fusc* colouring, the gentlemen in black and grey, the ladies in violet and grey, were entirely in accord with the prevailing mood of disaster.

The Queen was at the centre of everything. Throughout the ceremony she sat in an armchair close to Alice, and she cried less than most people had expected. Afterwards she dined alone with the bridal pair in the gruesome setting of the Hove Room where the chairs, tables, mantleshelf and all other furnishings and decorations were constructed of the antlers of stags killed by the Prince Consort, and talked mostly about the death of General Bruce. Then mournfully she saw them off for a three-day honeymoon in the neighbourhood, and had herself driven over to visit them on the second day.

Alice was very happy with Louis but, for her mother's sake, she tactfully wore a long face. It seemed to satisfy the Queen. She wrote to Vicky, who, close to being confined with her third child, was not at the wedding, that Alice looked serious and much older than Louis who was, in fact, six years older than she. But then, in view of what the poor, dear girl had just gone through, it was scarcely surprising.

Finally Alice gave an undertaking that she would return to England for a visit in the autumn, and if she was blessed with children she would come to Windsor for the births, and she was seen off for Därmstadt and what her weeping mother described with astonishing thoughtlessness as 'the painful drop in her comfort and station'.

Out of her cage, and with the man she loved, Alice was too good natured to take exception to anything that was said or done to make her marriage cheerless.

Victoria bemoaned the wedding because it was a poignant reminder of her own. Yet she found the gathering of her family for the occasion very comforting. Plans were made for another assembly in Coburg that autumn and she was glad of the opportunity to talk to Duke Ernest who disliked the idea of Bertie marrying a Dane. By no means as intelligent as Victoria, he found himself outwitted in Albert's game of family politics. But she would not press him to agree. Not yet. There would be plenty of time in Coburg later in the year. Plenty of time. For the moment she set about the sad business of finding a suitable replacement for poor General Bruce in the Prince of Wales' household.

Bertie had returned from his tour of the Near East a very

different boy. It had been an interesting and instructive trip: sightseeing from luxury steamers on the Nile; listening to Canon Stanley preaching in the ruins of a Roman temple in Syria; growing his first beard; visiting the Holy Places; shooting crocodiles, quails, owls, vultures and lizards; collecting botanical specimens for pressing and sending to his sister Vicky in Prussia – altogether wholesome and good for the fining down of his character. So the Queen was assured. She did not believe all of it. Never ever did she believe all that she heard about the Prince of Wales, neither the best nor the worst of it. But undoubtedly they were on better terms than before he left. But General Bruce's sickness and death had darkened the tour in retrospect. Contracting a fever in Palestine, he had become so very ill on the way home that Colonel Phipps had been sent out to take his place. And soon after he was dead. He would be difficult to replace.

Having taken advice, Victoria decided that as Bertie was close to twenty-one he should have a Household Comptroller and Treasurer rather than a Governor. He agreed very cordially. He also agreed with her choice, General Sir William Knollys, although he was a veteran of Wellington's Peninsular campaigns and there were forty-four years between them. But not long after he had a serious quarrel with his mother.

The Curragh affair still hung over his head. Not, though, on his conscience. On his tour he had written ribald letters to his Cambridge friend, Lord Carrington (of whom his mother did not approve – 'so *fast!*'), who kept women, Nellie Clifden amongst them, in much the same spirit as he kept a stable to hunt the 'Drag'. Yet he had a natural bashfulness about everyone and anyone knowing of his escapade, and he did not like it when his mother suggested that, because rumours were circulating through the courts of Europe, his future mother-in-law ought to be told the exact facts by the British Ambassador's wife. Reluctantly he felt he had to agree because the marriage might have stood in peril if she heard a more inaccurate and colourful version, and he really wanted to marry Alexandra of Denmark. But he objected strongly when the Queen said that his new Comptroller, as the person closest to him in his household, should also be told about it.

For the first time since he had been an adult he lost his temper in his mother's presence, and with her.

Furiously he asked why she persisted in rattling the skeleton of his one indiscretion, why she vetted his choice of friends and his chosen way of life, why she refused to let him help with her heavy burden of work, and why she never ceased to criticize all his actions however small or large. His handsome face suffused with blood, his shoulders shaking, his hands clenching and unclenching, he told her he could not tolerate being kept in curls and small clothes and made a fool of before his own gentlemen and servants. . . . Then he stopped short; not by an exhibition of wrath which was possible in any Hanoverian if sufficiently provoked, and in his mother's case a rare and terrible thing; nor, as perhaps he might have been, by an impassioned plea from a bereaved widow, isolated by the splendour of her rank and position, to pity her state; nor by an angry appeal for his respect and obedience as her son and subject; but by an apparently disinterested and very chilly stare. He realized, suddenly, that she was analysing his inadequacies, picking him to bits, and in a way feeling sorry for him. It was intolerable. It drove him to make a brief but sufficient apology for his loss of temper, ask her permission to retire and get away.

Sir William Knollys was informed of the Curragh affair, and, far away in Scotland where he had gone to sulk, the Prince of Wales made a slight show of independence by declaring that Birk Hall, the house bought for him by his father and in which he was staying independently for the first time, did not really suit him and he planned to sell it. His mother's reaction was characteristic. She calmly bought Birk Hall from him and added it to the growing Balmoral estate, and told him to make use of Abergeldie, a grace-and-favour house, which had a slightly frenchified atmosphere and would no doubt suit him better.

6

That year Karré, the royal courier, was exceptionally busy arranging the Queen's journeys.

Technically the responsibility devolved upon great officers of State, but it was Karré who did the work. It was never easy.

Organizing the Queen's progresses so that carriages and trains and royal yachts and packets made faultless connections demanded very high powers of administration. And to his ordinary duties were added others caused by the Queen's personal foibles. She liked to be surrounded by the familiar, and certain items had to be transported from place to place. Getting them there and on time to be ready for use was his responsibility. Bed furniture, ponies and dogs, special carriages, and a large number of books, keepsakes and souvenirs had to be transported with the wardrobe and kitchen luggage. Then, though she loved speed and had been a dashing rider as a younger woman, she had an inner fear of railways, and Karré was obliged to make special arrangements for the protection of the track wherever she went. Men were stationed at half-mile intervals beside the railroad; a precaution which, for journeys to Scotland alone, cost her Privy Purse somewhere in the region of £5,000 a year. Now, suddenly, after the marriage of Princess Alice, she showed a restless foot, and, in order to maintain the maximum seclusion, had decided that in future she would travel chiefly by night. Karré was obliged to make new and unusual arrangements, and this time without the help of Miss Skerrett who had always collaborated with him to make sure the Queen was comfortable.

Miss Skerrett had left the Queen's service. She had promised the Prince Consort to stay on for a year after giving notice of her intention to retire but, when the time came, she did not know how to broach the matter without causing the Queen distress. The anxiety upset her and this, though it was unfortunate in one way, did solve the problem. She became so seriously indisposed that Dr Jenner told the Queen she needed a long and thorough rest. Concerned for her poor Skerrett, Victoria insisted that for her own sake she must retire. They would, of course, keep in touch both by letter and visits, but her old friend owed it to herself to lead a more peaceful life. Miss Skerrett was pressed to agree and chose to go just after the wedding of Princess Alice, an appropriate twilight time. Though both felt it after so many years, they bravely made light of their parting, Skerrett rattling ebony bangles and shaking jet ear-rings and saying henceforth she would lead the life of a literary anchoress.

Soon after Skerrett's departure, the Court moved to Balmoral.

This was the beginning of an energetic tour which tired everyone's stamina except, it appeared, the Queen's.

It took courage to face Balmoral, where every single feature reminded her of Albert, but after a little while she found the place more soothing than Osborne or Windsor. There was the relief of being with simple, sensible Scotch folk who had the gift of being forthright without being impertinent: people like old Mrs Symons at the village shop, and Grant the head keeper, and the ghillie John Brown who led her pony and looked after her so well. She believed that, very probably, in the same situation, the English would have been either obsequious or over-familiar. The Scotch and the Germans made the best servants. Albert had always said so.

Dr Macleod, her Scotch chaplain, showed shrewd and practical sense when he took her to visit a poor woman on the royal estate who had been recently widowed. There he left them in each other's arms to weep together as two bereaved women, not as sovereign and subject.

Fortified and refreshed by this visit Victoria travelled to the continent, once more adding to Karré's administrative difficulties by travelling incognito as the Countess of Balmoral.

At her uncle's palace at Laeken she met, by previous arrangement, Princess Alexandra and her parents. Victoria was not especially taken with Prince Christian. She sensed his nervousness and decided that he needed stiffening with a little responsibility. It was as well the Great Powers had chosen him to succeed to the throne of Denmark. Kingship would alter him, and, as the present occupant of the throne was divorced, debauched and drunken, and the sort of scandalous monarch Victoria could not abide, so far as she was concerned the sooner he succeeded the better. Princess Christian was more of a character, the sort of forceful woman who could cause trouble. It was as well she had been officially informed of the Curragh affair or she might have been difficult. But Victoria's chief interest was, of course, for Bertie's intended fiancée.

Albert had chosen her from a short list; therefore she was to be favoured, and there was no denying her beauty, but Victoria was a quick appraiser of young people's potentialities and for a fleeting, horrid moment she doubted if the girl had sufficient intelligence to manage Bertie. Her small degree of deafness was also a handicap.

These minor doubts aside, the Queen was sufficiently impressed and was glad to go on to Coburg where she heard that the Prince of Wales had proposed marriage and had been accepted. She informed her brother-in-law Duke Ernest of the engagement with considerable satisfaction, particularly as he flushed red and then quickly turned yellow again, a sure sign that he was put out. However she repented of mortifying him, and barely mentioned the matter again for the rest of her visit.

Out in Coburg she saw her old counsellor Baron Stockmar, and was gratified by his real distress at Albert's death. He told her he was sure to die soon himself. He felt old and wretched and longed to see his dear prince again. It would be a consolation. Meanwhile if he could help her he would do so. She was non-committal. It was better so. He had served her well. But, as he said, he was old, too old now; and his judgement had gone awry. Before he died she felt forced to confide in Vicky 'how impossible it is any longer to rely on his advice.'

While she was in Germany Victoria also saw, and for the last time, her old governess who had played so large a part in her life until two years after her marriage. Baroness Lehzen looked even older than Stockmar. Her dry skin was shrivelled like that of a tortoise, her eyes dull, her breath still redolent of the caraway seeds she loved to chew. The Queen was moved. But not greatly so. Even the most poignant moments and situations were blunt compared with the sharp pain of her mourning for Albert. Skerrett, Stockmar, Lehzen had all once belonged to the pantheon. Now they had fallen.

Victoria returned to England; thence, for the second time that year, to far-off Balmoral; and afterwards she went to spend a few weeks alone at Osborne and at Windsor with her future daughter-in-law. Lord Melbourne had told her years before that betrothed royalties are better kept apart and ignorant of each other's conspicuous faults until they marry, for they have plenty of time to adjust themselves afterwards. Victoria thought it sage advice and she sent Bertie off in the royal yacht on a Mediterranean cruise.

To begin with Alexandra was uneasy. She could not help showing her resentment at the thought of being in England on approval, like a chicken in a poultry market, to be squeezed, prodded and given every test of quality by an exacting middle-aged lady. Once she realized this, Victoria put herself out to be charming. Only a few were privileged to know how dazzlingly charming she could be. Instantly she caught Alexandra's affection, and held it, despite many difficulties, over the following years. She asked if she might call her by her family name of Alix, and, as gently and considerately as possible, she instructed the girl in what would be expected of her in England. In a short time she was captivated by her future daughter-in-law:

> *She is so good, so simple, unaffected, frank, bright and cheerful, yet so quiet and gentle that her* umgang *soothes me.*

She still doubted, though, if Alix had the wit to manage Bertie. It was a great pity. He would always need firm guidance.

7

The royal wedding of the Prince of Wales and Princess Alexandra in March 1863 was as spectacular as Alice's had been simple.

Victoria's nerves would not permit her to take a visible part in the ceremony in St George's Chapel. Hidden from most eyes under a specially constructed covered way, she and her ladies crossed to the Chapel and there observed the proceedings from above the High Altar in the darkness of Catherine of Aragon's Closet. Victoria's cap and weeds were relieved by the ribbon, badge and star of the Garter and a miniature portrait of the Prince Consort framed in diamonds and worn as a brooch. She and her little court were a study in *chiaroscuro* compared with the magnificence of the scene below.

Beyond the altar rail were the clergy, the bishops in ballooning lawn, and scarlet cuffs, rochets and chimeres. And below stretched a sea of colour, the Knights of the Garter in their stalls, the Yeomen of the Guard, state trumpeters in cloth of gold, heralds in glittering tabards, gentlemen in frogged and accoutred uniforms of scarlet and blue and white and kendal green, the ladies in full Court dress blazing with jewels.

The Queen scarcely looked down. When she did she disliked

meeting the inquisitive glances of the guests below. One of the guests she recognized as Mr Disraeli, the leader of the Conservatives in the House of Commons, because he had such a very dramatic, oriental appearance, with long, oiled ringlets, olive complexion, a massive domed forehead and coal-black eyes. Victoria was shocked when she saw this eminent parliamentarian raise a quizzing glass to peer at her, and she gave him such a look that he quickly turned away. But then, despite herself, the Queen could not resist looking quickly at Mrs Disraeli, an object of extreme fascination because she was a re-married widow and twelve years older than her husband. But it was only a glance. Her attention was drawn by a flourish of trumpets and a peal from the organ, and her eyes misted with tears as she recognized a chorale composed by her beloved Albert, and above the singing of the choir burst the thrilling high notes of Jenny Lind.

After the service the Prince of Wales led his bride to their wedding breakfast. Thirty-six other royalties were present, but not the Queen. She ate a solitary and silent meal in her own apartments, busy with her thoughts.

Most of her thoughts were morose. Inevitably the wedding had reminded her of her own, and all the sad associations had crowded back. And, although she had cause for gratitude in that eight of her children were at that moment safely under her roof, inevitably she thought of the one who could not be there. Alfred her sailor son had caught typhoid and was now convalescing in Malta. She was deeply troubled about Alfred. The Greeks, having got rid of their unsatisfactory king, had elected him to the throne, but Albert had decreed that Alfred was to succeed his childless uncle Ernest as the sovereign of Saxe-Coburg, and she had refused to allow him to accept the kingdom. Perhaps this had unsettled him because suddenly there was evidence that he was misbehaving in exactly the same wild way as his elder brother, mixing with fast people and forming liaisons with the most disreputable demi-mondaines. If serious scandal were to be avoided, he would have to be married off without delay. Only for this was Victoria grateful that Albert now lay in the beautiful mausoleum she had built, at the cost of £200,000, at Frogmore; he would have been heart-broken to see his second son also take the wrong path of self-indulgence. Perhaps being herself a Hanoverian, with many of the same high appetites, and having had such extraordinarily wicked uncles, she was better able to understand her sons' indiscretions than poor Albert would have been. Not, though, that she would excuse them. They must learn self-control and reform themselves and try to be a credit to the memory of their father. Bertie and his bride especially must not be frivolous and must set a good tone in society. Because she was now virtually cut off from her subjects it would be their responsibility.

Quite unaware that his mother had made so solemn a resolution on his wedding day, Bertie took his bride to say good-bye before they left for a formal three-day honeymoon at Osborne. She unbent a little to him, and was loving to Alix, complimenting her on her poise and dignified manner during the marriage ceremony. She presumed, she said – emphasizing her own isolation from the event – that everything had gone well? Very well, replied Bertie, except that Vicky's elder boy Willy had prised the cairngorm from his dirk and thrown it across the choir, and when rebuked by his Uncle Arthur had bitten him in the knee. The Queen was shocked. It seemed somehow rather irreligious, and must have been very painful for Arthur; but, then, Willy was a curious child. Only the day before he had hurled a lady's muff out of a carriage window, and he was given to calling his father's gentlemen by uncomplimentary names. She promised to see to Willy herself, and later she would go down to the Mausoleum to find a little peace and quiet and pray that their marriage would be blessed.

The Prince of Wales' wedding had been a superb spectacle but the arrangements for transporting the bridal pair down to the railway station were far from satisfactory. On the way they were mobbed by a crowd of Eton boys. It was not pleasant to see the young gentlemen scrag the policemen on duty and swarm to the doors of the carriage, roaring and hurrahing and screaming. The Princess smiled wanly, but she was alarmed. The Prince, conceiving it prudent, bowed solemnly to the leader who shrieked once or twice and then drew off his ranks so that the carriage could proceed. In future years that same chubby-faced schoolboy was to be a considerable nuisance to the Prince. His name was Randolph Churchill.

Non-royal guests found the post-wedding breakfast breakdown in arrangements even more aggravating. There was a great crush.

Lord Palmerston's gout was far less painful, but he did not appreciate having to travel in a largely unsprung third-class compartment on the special train back to London. Nor did the Duchess of Westminster who, festooned with half a million pounds' worth of diamonds, felt out of place in the third-class. The Disraelis found themselves pushed into the corner of a carriage. But Dizzy refused to be put out and made a joke of it. All the way to London, looking more oriental than ever, he sat on his wife's lap.

8

In the following months there was much to depress the Queen.

The Prince of Wales was her chief anxiety. She did not approve of his constant running after entertainment. Nor did her first enchantment with Alix last very long. She and Bertie initiated a London season so brilliant that it surpassed all others. Balls, routs, banquets, breakfasts, theatre and opera parties, fêtes champêtres, receptions, race meetings, river parties, assemblies and formal ceremonies succeeded each other in a glittering stream. Victoria looked out from her seclusion at these demonstrations of worldly exuberance and did not care for them in the least. Bertie had been dedicated by his father to higher things. But, though she sent for him and told him so, it made little difference.

Soon she was equally anxious about her son Alfred. He was on shore leave from the Navy and evidently was losing his heart to his sister-in-law. Victoria was aghast. She did all she could to keep Alfred away from Marlborough House and she discussed plans for his early marriage.

After that there was a family quarrel about the disputed duchies of Schleswig and Holstein. Vicky, because of Fritz, supported the Prussian claim to these territories; Bertie, because of Alix, supported the Danish claim. The Queen herself was more in favour of a third claimant, largely because Albert had favoured him. Lord Palmerston was not a great deal of help. Only three people, he said, had ever fully understood the historical conundrum of Schleswig and Holstein. One was the Prince Consort, and he was dead. Another was a German professor, and he had gone mad. The third was himself and he had forgotten all about it. In the end England supported the Prussian claim which delighted Vicky and made Bertie very angry and rude and noisy.

The Queen was affronted by her eldest grandchild, Willy, who behaved boorishly on a holiday in Scotland. She tried to make excuses for him. He had a withered arm and a crooked neck, and he suffered a great deal at the hands of German medical men. But he was altogether too bellicose, and she found it difficult to forgive him when he declared shrilly that she and all his English relations were *Stumpfnase*. The Queen of England pug-nosed indeed! It was as well that only the family and a few confidential servants had any German.

But by far the worst of Victoria's lowness was caused by an increasing conviction that the dead had no consciousness of this world. With all her heart she wished to believe that Albert knew all she was doing and saying and thinking, that he was constantly aware of her, that they were in close touch. But her doubts grew and strengthened and cast her down terribly, and it was not until she met with a carriage accident in Scotland that her doubts began to dissolve once more.

Alice had returned to England, as she had promised, to have her first baby at Windsor, and afterwards she joined her mother at Balmoral. On the day of the accident they had driven out for a picnic luncheon with Helena and they were on their way home. Brown, of course, was with them. In his way he was becoming indispensable. And Alice's black boy, Willem, was there as well. It was past twilight and quite dark and there were frets of mist in the ditches. The carriage lamps were alight, but the coachman seemed to have difficulty in keeping to the road and the nearside wheels slipped from the metalling and jolted over the rocks and gravel at the roadside. When this happened a second time Brown held up a lantern to light the way. Meanwhile Victoria sat back trying to work out whether the coachman was ill – he was certainly old – or whether he had been at the whisky in the luncheon basket. In view of the fact that he had been much altered lately, she decided that Dr Jenner should be asked to examine him when they reached home.

At that precise moment the carriage began to tilt. Alice and Helena abruptly stopped talking. The Queen gasped in dismay.

The seat slowly slipped from beneath her. She tried to snatch at a strap for support as the carriage jolted on to its side.

There was confusion. The horses were down and kicking. Alice was crying out. The little black boy screamed.

Then Brown was raising her in his arms. She felt sick and dizzy. He was panting and repeating again and again: 'The Lord Almighty have mercy on us! The Lord Almighty have mercy on us!'

Though for far too long Victoria had failed to take care of her health, and though she had landed heavily and painfully on her head and had dislocated her thumb, she still had great resilience. In no time at all she was telling Brown to leave her and do something with the thrashing horses, and no sooner had he and the coachman cut the trace and got them to their feet again than she was helping to rescue her daughters. Their clothes had to be cut and ripped free from the smashed carriage. After that she examined Brown's knee which he had hurt in jumping off the carriage and she decided it needed massaging with spirit. But the picnic basket had gone on by pony pannier and all the black boy could find in the carriage was a bottle of claret. This had to do service as a drink for them all, and for washing her own bruised and grazed face and her thumb, and for rubbing Brown's knee.

Helena was dazed and crying until the Queen sharply told her to dry her eyes. But Alice recovered almost as quickly as her mother. When the coachman went off for help, she made a sort of tent with plaids over the side of the carriage so that they would all be warm and dry.

After the excitement the Queen felt very low. It was at moments like this, she said, that she most missed her beloved husband, and she would not be consoled when Alice tried to comfort her. She was sure, she said, that Papa had watched over them. But the Queen shook her head. The dead, she murmured, had no consciousness of the living. It shocked her daughters into silence. But contradiction came from an unexpected quarter. In his forthright Scotch fashion Brown told the Queen she was mistaken.

She bridled a little. 'No one can be certain.'

'I am,' he replied.

Then she remembered Brown's gift of second sight. She remembered, too, that Highlanders were gifted with other occult powers. She questioned him closely.

His replies were guarded and when the Princesses tried to draw him he dried up altogether. But the little he had said affected the Queen. She found herself impressed by his certainty.

In the days which immediately followed Victoria felt more and more reassured. Her spirits rose. The accident had been an unpleasant experience but she regarded it as a small price to pay for the renewal of the comforting belief that she and her beloved Albert were not entirely cut off from each other. After that carriage accident, now that her belief was revitalized, Victoria found herself better able to carry the burdens of widowhood. Thereafter she faced problems with a new boisterousness, although the unexpected could still shock her.

Barely a month after the carriage accident when the Court had moved south again, Lady Augusta announced her engagement to Mr Stanley the clergyman who had been Bertie's cicerone in Palestine. Victoria was appalled. She almost regretted that she had actually brought the two together, and had only recently rewarded him for his service by appointing him Dean of Westminster. It seemed, she remarked stiffly, an odd way of showing thanks for his preferment to steal away one of her most particular friends.

She poured out her troubles to Uncle Leopold:

> *My dear Lady Augusta, at* 41, *without a previous long attachment, has, most unnecessarily, decided to marry (! !) that certainly* most *distinguished and excellent man, Dr Stanley! ! It has been my* greatest sorrow *and trial* since *my misfortune* I *thought she* never *would leave* me!

Dr Stanley was a little alarmed that, quite unwittingly, he had as it were poked a stick into a hornets' nest. He was a retiring, unworldly scholar who knew more about Ur, Ai and the Cities of the Plain, than the vapours of widowed ladies, but he neutralized the Queen's hostility by his great tact and delicacy of feeling.

Lady Augusta had great percipience. She sensed, rightly, that the Queen felt betrayed and that, at the same time, she knew she was being unreasonable. As tactfully as she could she undertook to come into Waiting at regular intervals. Secretly she was glad for the Queen's sake that she had dealt a blow at the establishment of a group of women at Court who were devoted to the perpetual remembrance of the Prince Consort.

The Queen's frost slowly thawed. By Christmas she could think of Lady Augusta without showing annoyance. And then a fresh trouble pressed upon her which drew her attention right away from the Deanery at Westminster. Her seclusion became at last a subject of outspoken, public comment.

One day she was shown a copy of posters which had been attached by night to the railings outside Buckingham Palace:

These

COMMANDING

PREMISES

to be

LET or SOLD

in consequence of the late
owner's declining business

The Queen was incredulous, thunderstruck, and outraged in turn. The Stanleys' offence was nothing compared with this, nor with the insolence of those journalists who wrote that the time had come for her to put her mourning aside and live in the public eye again. They impertinently claimed that, in the struggle between grief and duty, a sovereign was not like a private person. As an invisible office worker, a stamp monarch, the Queen was depriving her subjects of th epageantry they loved; and by remaining in mole-black weeds she was depressing the trade of hosiers, dressmakers, milliners and drapers.

'Drapers!' she exclaimed when this claim was brought to her notice; and again, in startled wonder: 'Drapers!'

Sir Charles Phipps wrote a long letter to Lord Palmerston at her dictation. She made it plain that she considered it was his responsibility to explain the facts to the people; that although she was not suffering from any detectable organic illness, she was far from strong and so constantly worn out with an immense amount of business, and that her physicians had advised her to avoid Court ceremonials and State occasions. Would Lord Palmerston please release these facts into Society, she asked, so that ultimately they might filter down to the cellar levels where journalists pricked their ears.

Palmerston accepted this curious commission without question. It was given out that on medical advice her Majesty's activities were restricted.

But this did not prevent those who had a vested interest in clothing putting out a rumour that she was going out of mourning. The newspapers caught the story and puffed it. The Queen was enraged. She decided that on this occasion she would have to defend herself. In her own hand she wrote a denial for publication in *The Times*. It was an unsigned statement but the Queen's inimitable style proclaimed her authorship. In her heart she despised *The Times* which she hated for its cruelties to Albert, but she recognized its special distinction which, as she remarked to Lady Churchill, was like that of the supreme villain amongst the forty thieves, and she had to make use of it. It was imperative to state openly that she had not the least intention of putting aside her weeds.

> *This idea* [she declared in her letter] *cannot be too explicitly contradicted.*

There were other pricks and stings.

All the royal children were present at Coburg for the unveiling of a gilt bronze statue of their father, but Victoria detected too much joy in the reunion, too much noise; excited shouts from the little ones, and chatter, chatter, chatter amongst the grown-ups. It struck her as inconsiderate, thoughtless. She said so and noticed some of them exchange quick glances as if to say 'Mother again!' This hurt.

Then, on the way home, in the comfortless and eerie Castle of Kranichstein, she inspected Prince Christian of Schleswig-Holstein who had been proposed as a suitor for Helena. He looked, she thought, like a bald sheep, and he had neither money nor prospects, but he was prepared to live permanently in England so that she would not be deprived of Helena's company. He would do. Having made up her mind the Queen was exceedingly put out when the Prussian press, of all unspeakable things, mocked the engagement announcement.

Already vexed, she was not best pleased to return home and find the country in a crisis because of cattle disease, and the government doing very little about it. With the maddening lack of concern of great Whig land-owners, her ministers explained that no one could alter the eccentricities of Divine Providence. Nor, said Lord Palmerston, should a mere mortal try.

Victoria confided in her uncle, King Leopold, that gout was making the Prime Minister irascible, and it was no wonder. He was rising eighty-one and destroying himself with his high living. At a recent dinner the Speaker had witnessed him manage two plates of turtle soup, cod with oyster sauce, pâté, two greasy entrées, a platter of roast mutton, a thick slice of ham, and half a pheasant. Victoria was fond of food herself. Potatoes and pudding could make her eyes sparkle. But she was dismayed by the thought that the government and safety of her kingdom depended to such an extent on the strength of Lord Palmerston's digestion.

But Victoria's greatest anxiety, as ever, was caused by her son and heir. It was well she had been resolute in her decision to deny him access to secret papers for he proved to have an extraordinary lack of discretion. He was also mixing with the most disreputable people and when Alix had a prematurely born son Victoria was convinced it was because of the flightiness of her pleasure-loving existence. She took so little care of herself. Never afterwards could the Queen bear the sight of ice-hockey because it was while watching Bertie play the game that Alix began her labour and only just reached Frogmore House in time. There had been no preparation. Nothing was ready. What a scandal! And the baby's head was as small and as pointed as its mother's. The Queen doubted if there was anything inside it at all, and, if Jane Churchill wanted the truth of the matter, his bulgy pug eyes betrayed a look of idiocy.

Bertie's refusal to accommodate her wishes about the names he and his son would use as monarchs was in line with his rebelliousness in visiting the revolutionary Garibaldi who was staying in London. He knew she wished him not to. And later when, once more against her wishes, he and Alix took the baby to Copenhagen and kept him there long after the time they had promised he should be returned to England, she took the cap off her indignation and wrote to insist the baby be sent over at once. She also rebuked Bertie for not travelling incognito which, in the present delicate state of affairs in Europe, was politically necessary. His reply was impertinent. In a rage she sent a curt order that as he could not travel incognito, he was not to return through France as he wished to do. With sour reluctance he did as he was told, but quarrelled disagreeably with his brother-in-law Fritz.

The next flare-up between them came as a result of a report that the Prince of Wales was encouraging younger and poorer men than himself to gamble for high stakes and, according to Lord Palmerston, he was already drawing on his capital to meet his own gambling debts. His mother decided that this time he merited a semi-public rebuke. She protested through Colonel Phipps and the Prince of Wales' Comptroller. To Lord Palmerston she said: 'My uncles! He is an awful resurrection of my uncles!'

Palmerston agreed. But quietly. He was less himself than usual. Not only did he feel physically unwell, but the burden of existing in a world becoming increasingly alien to his likes and ideals was burdening his spirit. He found nowadays that he could almost envy President Lincoln who had been shot in a box at the opera, and, with the Civil War behind him, had been cut off at the height of his career. He went down to Brocket, his brother-in-law Melbourne's place in the country, to rest his soul as much as his gouty limbs in the low-ceilinged library and the rose garden where there was a sundial of worked stone.

The Queen was informed of his illness. It worried her. It worried her particularly when she heard that the Prime Minister's appetite had gone, that his whiskers were undyed and showed white for the first time, that Lady Palmerston had been found weeping silently when she thought no one observed her. In a letter she expressed her concern to Uncle Leopold. Somehow, life without Lord Palmerston was unthinkable. He had always been there since the day she ascended the throne as a girl of eighteen. And she broke down and she cried when the news came from Brocket that he had died.

Sorrow like this put her own troubles into proportion. She could see now which were pricks and stings and which were something worse. She had never really liked Lord Palmerston, she told her uncle, but she had become used to him, and missed him dreadfully.

King Leopold was sincerely sorry for her and he sent his consolations. But he himself was in the tightening grasp of a mortal disease. Eventually her ladies told the Queen. She had to know, but she could not believe them. Her uncle dying? All her life he had been there to guide and help, comfort and love. It could not be true. Jenner was sent to Brussels, but he could do nothing. The Queen's half-sister Princess Feodore came quickly to Windsor to be with her. Because, unhappily, it was true. Uncle Leopold was dying.

He died on 10 December 1865 in his palace at Laeken in the greatest pain.

9

A singular fruit of the carriage accident at first dusk on a rough road near Balmoral was that John Brown the ghillie moved south with the Court. He was given the title of Highland Servant to the Queen.

A bare handful knew the reason why Victoria wished Brown to be in continual attendance. Some thought she was indulging in a romantic whim; others that she had an eye for a fine figure of a man. The real reason was chiefly hidden. The little Brown had said to convince her that the dead were aware of the living had made the Queen long to hear more. He was reluctant to add anything. But she was determined. She especially wished to know about his own powers. She was prepared to take trouble and practise an unusual patience to draw the truth out of him.

Eventually she was successful, and what he told her seemed to open marvellous possibilities.

Victoria had always been superstitious, interesting herself in predictions, collecting charms and lucky talismans, and in keeping off the evil eye. She had also shown a marked interest in the practice of spirit rapping when it was brought to England by the Fox sisters in 1848; she had actually tried table-turning, though only, she professed, as a game; and she had listened breathlessly to the French Emperor Napoleon the Third who, long before on a private visit to Osborne, had curled and uncurled the points of his waxed moustaches as he talked endlessly of the occult. Albert had not approved and had attempted to move the conversation to a less galvanic topic, and, failing that, had tried to discredit the Emperor's claim with science and reason. People, he said, simply did not float in and out of windows in a recumbent horizontal position as it was claimed for the Scotch magician and medium Daniel Dunglass Home, and though he admitted the existence of telepathy he doubted the truth or the value of anything else taught by the spiritualist movement. Afterwards he had told Victoria that it was in her own interests not to overheat her imagination by listening to such rubbishy stuff. It could so easily unsettle her nerves. Obediently she had listened, but now she wondered if she ought to disregard his advice. What did her feelings, even her nerves, matter in comparison with the chance, however remote, of getting in touch with him? And it appeared that this marvellous blessing could be effected by Albert's old servant, John Brown. . . .

Though by nature impulsive, the Queen schooled herself to be cautious. She sent privately for Miss Skerrett to ask her advice. She was certain that Lady Churchill would have been cynical, Lady Ely shocked, and Lady Augusta baffled. Miss Skerrett, on the other hand, had always shown a certain sympathy towards her interest in superstitions and the occult. And Miss Skerrett did not let her down. She arrived at Court looking a picture of health and eager to be of service. Doors usually left open were closed. The Queen and Miss Skerrett talked in the strictest privacy.

A week later Victoria plucked up the courage to ask the Dean of Windsor to call on her.

Dean Wellesley had a unique value as her spiritual adviser: he blended respect with firmness and, if the occasion demanded, he could be exceedingly candid. This she found refreshing after the platitudes of those of the clergy who, out of nervousness or toadying, told her what they thought she probably wanted to hear. And she was absolutely sure of him, unlike those who, though apparently scholarly and wise, sometimes had the subtlety to conceal the fact – even from themselves – that their lips were framed by hearts which longed for stalls and mitres.

Nevertheless she was still exceedingly nervous when, by appointment, he called to see her on a humid July afternoon. She was not even comforted as usual by his extraordinary likeness to his uncle the Duke – a man to whom the English royal family had taken their troubles as naturally as the Bourbons sought out Dominican confessors. He would not, she feared, have much good to say about spiritualism.

She was right.

In the same crisp, staccato talk of his uncle, he was scathing about spiritualism whether as a religion or as a philosophy – 'Which is what, Ma'am, its adherents arrogantly claim.'

He saw from her expression how important it was to her. Thereafter he was more gentle. Spiritualism, he said, was perhaps permissible – if it was treated lightly, as a game, or regarded solely as a scientific experiment. A good deal, he said, depended on the medium; inevitably a person of influence and therefore, in the case of a queen, of supreme importance.

The Queen was frank. So was the Dean.

Then she said something which surprised him. Was it wrong, she asked, that her desolation had decreased a little in the past months? It truly was but a little, yet the partial lightening of her heart gave her feelings of guilt as well as of pleasure.

The Dean begged her permission to pace about a bit. He walked to the window and back again, to the window and back again. He was wondering why a widow, feeling her loss *less* keenly, wished to make use of spiritualistic means to communicate with her husband. Then he decided that, whatever the reason, it ensured the Queen would not allow herself to be deceived nor put upon. He also detected a discreet question – was she being faithless to her husband by accepting the loyalty and friendship of another? It was a question he had answered a number of times to widows trying to adjust themselves to a new way of life, even to a second marriage. Honesty made him tell her that a decrease in constant sorrow did not signify loss of affection; in fact, a settled mournful resignation was a more lasting proof of affection than acute grief.

She thanked him and the conversation glided to other matters – the health of Mrs Wellesley, the Dean's rose garden, two vacant stalls, the deplorable state of Europe. . . .

From that date, amongst the Queen's luggage wherever she went was a small portmanteau of close wickerwork and buffalo hide. There were two keys to its intricate lock; one sealed in an oilskin pouch and kept, in case the other should be inadvertently mislaid, in the permanent keeping of the Privy Purse. The other was always in the Queen's possession, or, on rare occasions, was attached to Emilie Dittweiler's bunch of wardrobe keys. The portmanteau was only opened in the presence of certain people, and its contents were a closely guarded secret. They were an ivory pencil holder with leads in a screw-capped ivory tube, and a heart-shaped planchette board with a hole for the pencil at the pointed end and, at the other, supports on well-oiled, brass casters.

On infrequent occasions a sheet of cartridge sketching paper was laid on a small table and the planchette placed in position. Hands were then laid lightly on the mobile board and the pencil marked the paper with hieroglyphics, letters, squirls and patterns.

Sometimes the resting fingers were long and white and slender and belonged to the cynical Lady Churchill; sometimes they were Emilie's, the right hand easily identified because of the blue thimble marks on the longest finger; sometimes they were heavily jewelled and short and stubby and royal; but almost invariably they were a man's fingers, wide, toughened with work, the nails overshort, their quicks discoloured, and the first joints dotted with sandy hairs.

John Brown did not care for this special employment; though it gave him a particular importance he did not value it. With his fingers on the planchette he actually felt less significant as a person, and, having an independent spirit, he disliked giving himself into the power of something unknown and uncontrollable. In every way he sought to dissuade the Queen from making these painful experiments. Her first eagerness was subdued. Brown's evident distress took away from her own pleasure. Though she longed to consult Albert whenever a fresh problem arose to baffle her, she forced herself to be more and more self-dependent.

The poet Robert Browning had a profound mistrust of spiritualism. His adored wife had lost her wits in this one respect, putting her high intellect and reasoning powers to one side and falling into the control of unscrupulous or bigoted protagonists of the occult. His revenge on the chief magician, Mr Home, had been an invective in verse 'Mr Sludge the Medium', but nothing could ever compensate for the damage done to his wife. Sometimes he actually believed that, allied to her invalidism and nervous weakness, her unbalanced faith in spiritualism had in some way contributed to her early death.

And now he heard that the Queen herself was becoming interested in the same hated pseudo-religion.

He was much concerned, not because he had any depth of feeling for the monarchy as an institution or for Queen Victoria as a person, but because of the Crown's influence. The Queen's interest in the occult would be slavishly copied by many others. It was a critical situation. Fortunately he was acquainted with Dean Stanley and, recalling that the Dean's new wife had been one of the Queen's ladies, he took himself quickly to the Deanery at Westminster and poured out his anxieties there.

It was as well that Lady Augusta happened to be at home for her husband's instinctive reaction was one of horror and she was able to convince him and Mr Browning that the Queen had too much hard practical common-sense to allow herself to be taken in. If the rumours were true, and she was indeed endeavouring to be put in touch with her dead husband, she could be depended on to be more sensible than most women in the same position.

Nevertheless, urged Browning, the rumours were rife. The cult would quickly gain adherents. Something had to be done.

The Dean explained Browning's interest to Lady Augusta. She sympathized. But she pointed out there would be no chance of an official denial on such a controversial matter. It was an unhappy impasse.

While the Dean was at the bell-pull summoning a servant to show Mr Browning out, Lady Augusta quietly advised him to meet rumour with rumour. Let him and his friends put it out that, far from approving of spiritualism, the Queen held it in ridicule. Jesuitical, yes, she whispered, but it was for the protection of sillier widows than Queen Victoria. She added in a louder tone for her husband's benefit that she would herself ask for an audience and see what could be done. The poet thanked her, detected a tiny conspiratorial movement in her eye as he said good-bye, and went away marvelling.

Lady Augusta saw the Queen privately and explained Mr Browning's anxieties. She found Victoria very disposed to listen. In fact learning self-dependence had moved her to reconsider the whole subject. Of late she had arrived at the conclusion that Albert would really wish her to use her initiative in cases not covered by his expressed wishes or example in the past, and there was no denying that she felt far, far closer to him in the Blue Room at Windsor or in any of the special places dedicated to his memory than in the artificially contrived atmosphere of a seance. No more than Brown did she really care to be at the mercy of an uncontrollable power, and she suspected that the planchette was not unlike laudanum in that the less it was used the less it was required.

Mr Browning's warning merely served to fix a resolution which had already been made, that the portmanteau of wickerwork and buffalo hide should simply be in reserve for the rare and special occasions when its contents might be used in a spirit of scientific enquiry. But she did not say all this.

Beyond the briefest of assertions that neither Lady Augusta nor Mr Browning had cause for anxiety, Victoria dwelt largely on the exasperating impossibility of keeping anything secret. Long-nosed, wide-eared housemaids and footmen were the trouble, and nothing nowadays could be done about unreliable domestics.

Then the subject was changed altogether, the bell rang for tea – just as Lady Augusta liked it – and they talked of poetry. Mr Browning's, confided the Queen, was too prolix and complicated. She far preferred Mr Tennyson's.

10

Had he wished, the Queen's Highland Servant could have made unscrupulous use of his position and of his powers as a medium, but his ambitions were those of a Scotch crofter and very simple. He wanted security and an honourable place and the satisfaction of giving good service both for himself and his brothers. And this he had. Being in a post of great responsibility and great privilege in the Queen's permanent entourage, his highest ambitions were already satisfied.

At the heart of the Court were Lady Churchill and Lady Ely, and the dressers, Emilie Dittweiler and Annie Macdonald. On the periphery were Maslin the page, and the Prince Consort's senior valet Löhlein. The latter resembled his dead master in many, many ways, and, because the old Duke of Saxe-Coburg had been a notorious philanderer, it was presumed that Löhlein was really Prince Albert's half-brother. From the time Brown went south he was a part of this small and exclusive circle and Löhlein took him under his protective wing, teaching him protocol, and warning him always to avoid arousing jealousy.

It was a lesson Brown found difficult to learn. He disliked the suavity of the Household and called it humbug. And he would have no truck with the servants who at first patronized him and giggled at his kilt. It was an attitude not calculated to make him the best-loved person above or below stairs at Windsor or Osborne. But no one underestimated his influence or his power.

The Queen appeared to be totally blind to the fact that the permanent attendance of an unattached, rough, but good-looking Scotchman, a few years younger than herself, with undeniable physical strength, a Viking beard and china-blue eyes, was liable to be misunderstood. Lady Ely decided it was her duty to advise caution. She had an excellent opportunity when the Queen behaved with surprising lack of discretion on a visit to the widowed Duchess of Athole at Dunkeld. Marching through wet heather had drenched Brown's kilt and this chapped and cut the back of his knees. Victoria made her concern very obvious. She at once sent for a doctor, and, later on a drive out with her hostess, made poor Brown's legs the chief topic of conversation all the way from the foot of Craig y Barns round Cally Loch through Cally Gardens and round the three Lochs of Lowes. Lady Ely determined to speak out. That evening she took an extra glass of wine at dinner and then, in the privacy of the Queen's rooms, she mentioned that the Duchess had shown some surprise that a servant's legs should cause so much concern. But either the Queen failed to understand the import of her cautious hint, or she preferred to ignore it, for she merely laughed, made a slight, inoffensive joke at the Duchess's expense, and continued as before showing an indiscreet interest in the affairs of her Highland Servant.

The inevitable happened.

Before long there was whispering. There were covert smiles. Thin trickles of gossip began to seep into society like poison into a fresh well. The ghillie was soon known as King John, and the Queen of England was called Mrs Brown.

The gentlemen of the Queen's Household became seriously concerned. Public attacks on the debauchery of George the Third's seven sons had been commonplace, but that had been at a freer, far more bizarre time. Now the world was narrower. The puritanism which had slept since the Lord Protector's time was awake again; its pruderies and prejudices re-established. Phipps and Grey knew this. It was the jibe of republicans that courtiers were popinjays who thrived in an inward-looking society and knew nothing of the world, but though this might have been true at some of the courts in Europe and the Orient it was not true in England. Since the Prince Consort's death the Queen's gentlemen saw themselves as her only protectors and they kept themselves informed on anything which might be of service to her. They realized that the Evangelicals with their Non-conformist auxiliaries had great power. Were they displeased they might even shake the throne itself; and, as a woman, a queen, a mother and a widow, Victoria was in so exalted a position that the faintest breeze of scandal about her had the force of a raging gale.

Colonel Phipps, feeling his age and the weight of his responsibilities, advised the Queen that her reputation stood in danger.

At first she was amused. Then she was incredulous. He was greatly relieved. He knew she could never have deceived him by such a show if there had been anything to hide. When the full significance of what he had said at last sank in she flushed crimson and tears gathered at the corners of her eyes. She wiped them away and said it was dreadful that people should think her unfaithful to Albert. The slandering of her own reputation mattered much less to her. There had always been gossips, she said, and self-righteous ones were sad fudge better ignored.

Phipps actually found his own fears for her being soothed away. He was told not to worry. She preferred to keep to a course which she knew was right and which certainly would have been approved by her husband. As a lone widow, sometimes the cynosure of all eyes, she needed the close attendance of a strong dependable bodyguard like Brown, and she was certain that right-thinking people would take no notice of the scandal.

Phipps doubted it, but he admired her courage and he highly respected her obvious innocence and he said no more.

Unhappily this was their last interview. Not long afterwards, at the beginning of 1866, he was taken ill and he died. Victoria was very distressed. Another and particularly precious link with Albert had been broken. The Colonel had been so faithful and good to her. She was glad that through his daughter Harriet, the Phipps family would still be connected with the royal Household.

The Master of the Household, Sir Thomas Biddulph, was appointed to the Colonel's place as Privy Purse, and the Queen took the opportunity to beg Lord Russell to make General Grey her official Private Secretary. It was astonishing, she said, that although her ministers each had a private secretary and Russell, as Prime Minister, had two, she officially had none. But Lord Russell, with his dislike of innovations and his barely hidden scorn for Hanoverian sovereigns, did not oblige, and Grey was made joint Privy Purse. To encourage him the Queen brought on his nephew-in-law Colonel Ponsonby who had been Albert's equerry and great friend. Since the Prince Consort's death he had been stationed in Canada but now had returned to command the 1st Battalion of Grenadier Guards. As an equerry he regularly came into Waiting and, already standing high in the Queen's confidence, he was soon equally high in her regard and affection.

Uncle and nephew between them now strove to contain the growing scandal centred right at the heart of the Court. The lower servants were never permitted to look at or to address the Queen. They melted out of sight at her approach and, as she was usually preoccupied with family or state affairs, she seldom noticed their existence, and perhaps, without realizing it, she might occasionally have been indiscreet before them. The new Master of the Household instituted a thorough investigation into those of the servants who looked after the royal apartments in all the Queen's palaces and houses, and a few unreliable ones were transferred to other work. But it was like plugging a fen bank with sandbags against spring flooding. The whispering behind hands became open murmurs. The newspapers were alerted.

Mrs Prothero, wife of Canon Prothero, Rector of Whippingham on the edge of the Osborne estate, took great pleasure in her flower garden. She was an individualist and a pioneer in that she did not care for the fashionable bedding-out plants and exasperated her head gardener by insisting on deep beds of perennials and biennials. She further enraged him by refusing to let him keep them tidy. Dead heads had to be left, fallen petals unraked, withering foliage uncut. It shamed him, he said, and the other gardeners before the village, but Mrs Prothero liked these things and he could do nothing about it. She even tended many of the flowers herself. The staking of delphiniums, daisies and hollyhocks was always her chosen task, and she was a great weeder – wearing for the purpose a pair of grate-blacking gloves and kneeling on a special hassock which lived in the kitchen so that it would be regularly dried out by the range.

One afternoon Mrs Prothero was busy in the hollyhocks which grew plentifully beside the drive gate when someone called out to her from the lane. It was a youngish man in a billycock hat. This he raised as he inquired in a town voice if he had the pleasure of seeing Mrs Prothero.

Ladies caught unawares wearing grate-blacking gloves and with dried bits of hollyhock in their hair generally found themselves at a disadvantage. Not so Mrs Prothero who thought nothing of her appearance because she noticed immediately that the youngish man's eyes were not on her but on the hollyhocks. And she had barely time to confirm that she was Mrs Prothero before he was congratulating her on the magnificence of the Rectory hollyhocks. It was not simply polite enthusiasm. He appeared to know what he was talking about.

From that one thing led to another. He also had a particular liking for perennials, and said that his sister, who lived in Upper Norwood, was a painter of flowers; more than that, she was an embroiderer in fine silks of her own plant designs copied from nature.

Mrs Prothero was enraptured. He was neither a parishioner nor by his dress and manner a gentleman. Nor had he been introduced. But Upper Norwood was respectable enough. He was invited into the garden and led to the glasshouses, and such is the camaraderie amongst gardeners and plant collectors that they had toured the gardens and gone into the Rectory to see Mrs Prothero's own sketch book before she realized she did not even know his name.

When she asked he momentarily replaced his billycock, removed it again and placed it against his heart as he introduced himself.

'Smith, Madam. William Smith. Shortened by my sister in Upper Norwood to plain Bill. Not difficult to remember, Mrs Prothero, and, in these topsy-turvy days, we with the elegant names of Smith, Jones and Brown are on the up and up.' He nodded in the direction of Osborne House.

Mrs Prothero smiled. She was a good, even saintly lady not at all given to tittle-tattle and never before had she discussed other people's affairs, least of all those of her husband's most august parishioner. But the droll Mr William Smith had such a quaint way with him. . . .

Some time later when he had gone on his way and she was back amongst the hollyhocks, snipping and tying, weeding and loosening the soil and still smiling as she thought of her amusing visitor, the effect he had created began to steal away. It was like losing the euphoric feeling induced by a second glass of champagne, and when at last she faced reality Mrs Prothero was aghast. She went indoors to find her daughter Mildred. She dared not, simply dared not, tell her husband yet.

Mildred Prothero was a practical girl. It was better, she said, to know the worst. She instituted tactful inquiries and discovered gradually the awful extent of her mother's indiscretions.

Yes, a youngish man in a billycock hat had made a scratch dinner at an inn on the outskirts of East Cowes and had asked the way to Whippingham Rectory. And, yes, he had talked for quite a time to an old man who until two years before had been the Rector's head gardener and who had been delighted to have an appreciative audience. Generally no one would listen to him but this visitor from London had been so keen to learn all that he could about plants and trees and Mrs Prothero's particular favourites. Kindly he'd given him a beer and a shilling – as he ought, added the publican who supposed that gentlemen in billycocks who worked for the London newspapers were rich as Rothschilds compared with a parson's pensioned gardener. . . .

The realization that she had been beguiled and had chatted so comfortably about the Queen and her excellent Highlander to an unknown journalist froze poor Mrs Prothero with horror.

Never afterwards could she enjoy her hollyhocks.

Press agents were equally assiduous at Balmoral. Windsor and Buckingham Palace were hemmed in by troops of Life Guards, but the Queen's private houses where she liked to live as ordinary a life as is possible to a reigning monarch were more easily approached.

The innocent doves who, on one pretence or another, tried to draw the estate workers, or old Mrs Symons at the village shop, or even on one occasion, the Minister at the Manse, turned out to be vultures – with all the ugly manners of those unattractive scavengers. They hardly learnt a thing to the Queen's disadvantage. Even when offered substantial bribes the estate workers and crofters would not pass on cracks about the Queen, and the Minister was so hostile to the journalist who saucily claimed the public's right to certain information that his people feared he would attack the man physically. As for Mrs Symons, she derided the newspaper men at the top of her voice with such offensive words as haverels, duddy betherels, pawkie puddocks, drouds, gowks and grumphies, said she'd not have the lady of Balmoral back-bitten, nor good John Brown, and on one never-to-be-forgotten occasion she scorned words and, deciding that action was more just, she boxed the ears of a journalist from Aberdeen who was pretending to be something else.

Nevertheless, from disloyal sources or, more probably, from imagination, certain stories were culled and appeared in the provincial newspapers and in the weekly London journal *Punch*. They were directed solely against Brown – at his prominence at Court, his taciturnity and his 'inordinate indulgence in whisky', but the innuendoes were brazen.

The Queen's reaction was surprising. Normally a forceful woman and given to hysterical bouts of temper, she appeared to remain quite calm. She strongly resented the gossip, the smirching of Brown's reputation and, by inference, her own, but she had made up her mind to conceal her feelings. To show her hurt and anger would be to play into their hands and she would give them no satisfaction at all if she could possibly avoid it. The same barbaric people who had failed to appreciate her beloved Albert, and who had never attempted to understand her sorrow as a widow and her longing for privacy and seclusion, were now snapping at her honour and calling in question her domestic purity. And all she would give them for their trouble, for their cruelties and sarcasm, their short-sightedness and their self-righteousness was a cold smile. Nothing else. The uncertain, nervous, dithery, passionate creature who had leant so heavily on her husband had

had to learn self-dependence. Under her cold exterior Victoria was still raw with pain and sickened by their callousness, but all she showed publicly was a supreme indifference. In private, on the other hand, she could be devastatingly angry.

General Grey caught a glimpse of the fires below when, in duty bound, he told the Queen that scandalous rumours had spread abroad. The *Lausanne Gazette* had published a report of her marriage to Brown, and the British Minister at Berne had lodged a formal protest. For a moment she was speechless with anger, quite beside herself. But she was furious with her Minister because he had lowered himself to the level of the press. A spiteful copy of this report found its way into a London paper, but this moved her not at all. Her message to the Foreign Office concerning ministers abroad assuming responsibilities which were not theirs was a document so trenchant that even that normally placid place was put into a flurry.

The Queen showed another aspect of the same dark rage to her eldest son.

She disapproved profoundly of his friends – a flashy lot, and she deplored his personal self-indulgence, his vanity and irresponsibility and his ostentation, and, above all, his greed which had already blasted his good looks and earned him the nickname of Tum Tum; but, realizing his shallowness and inadequacy, and secretly feeling partially to blame for them, she had tried her utmost not to interfere with his private life. She would even defend and support him in public, so long as his behaviour was not spectacularly churlish and dishonourable. Now it seemed to her he was being caddish.

Alix had been ill with rheumatic fever for a long time, and so seriously that her mother the Queen of Denmark had been at Marlborough House for two months. Even now, five months later, she was only just able to be wheeled out into the garden and, in addition to the affliction of her deafness, she now had an unbendable knee and a permanent, disfiguring limp. And for months past, though at first sorry for his wife, the Prince of Wales had shown himself incapable of the least form of self-denial, and had neglected her shamefully.

His mother sent for him to tell him so. 'Your conduct has been shameful,' she told him. 'Utterly shameful.'

The Prince began to bluster. She cut him short by asking witheringly if he had no self-control at all; and, before he could reply, she went on to say that by gratifying his love of pleasure so publicly at race meetings, supper parties and shameless meetings with demi-mondaines, he was insulting to his own wife.

'She is the Princess of Wales and the Queen's daughter-in-law. I will not permit her to be held up to ridicule and contempt.'

The Prince lowered his eyes. Neither physically nor morally was he very courageous but his mother had made him angry. He wanted to sound nonchalant but his voice trembled with emotion as he advised her to check the sources of her information. Were those who had traduced him to her entirely reliable?

The Queen was about to say authoritatively yes, they were; but, by now in proper control of his voice, he quickly added: 'For you know how little faith one may have in rumours – either circulated by word of mouth or by newspapers.' His eyes narrowed and he looked at the ceiling. '*Punch*, for example, or *Tomahawk*, or the *Elgin Courant* or the *John o' Groats Journal* or the *Lausanne Gazette*. . . .'

His voice trailed away, not because his memory was failing – for this sort of thing he had an excellent memory – but because his tongue was suddenly dry. There was a palpable atmosphere in the room which frightened him. He looked down at the floor again. The silence was broken by his mother ringing the silver bell on the table beside her. Without another word he was being dismissed.

Involuntarily he panicked. He believed he had seen every aspect of his mother's anger from aloof coldness to hysterical fury but this majestic disapproval was a new experience. It was terrifying. The massive weight of her anger seemed to charge the air about her. He longed to find the courage to speak a word, but it was too late. The double doors of the drawing room were opened behind him. He put out his hand to take hers and kiss it. Then, two inches away, he stopped. She had made no movement towards him and he dared not touch her.

Lifeless, gorged and heavy with rage and hurt, refusing to speak or move or look at her son, she heard him back away from her and leave the room.

Victoria's nerves had barely recovered from this disastrous interview – and her son's uncouth and saucy reference to the John Brown scandal was something she would find very difficult to forgive – when the Prime Minister and the Commander-in-Chief begged for a private audience and broached the very same matter.

They were not particularly suited to the task. Lord Derby who had been Prime Minister since the Conservatives won the last election was a brilliant orator and eminently civilized, but he never forgot he was a Stanley, and in manner he was close, laconic and grand. He was too blasé altogether to get on with his sovereign. George, Duke of Cambridge, then Commander-in-Chief, was Victoria's cousin and she had always been fond of him. Indeed she had gone out of her way not to be censorious about his liaison with a polka-dancing actress who gave him three healthy Fitzgeorges, and it was gratifying that a member of the family should be at the head of her army. But, though amiable, he was becoming as bluff and blunt as his deaf old father had been, and she could not believe her ears when in his tactless, jolly fashion he told her that at a coming military review it would not do for her Highland Servant to be seen on the box of her carriage.

Lord Derby put in a word of agreement.

Unhappily it was only a word. The Queen found it a hard pill to swallow unsugared by the polite phrases of regret which royalty expects. Her brow became thunderous. Would they please explain themselves, she asked.

They did, or they tried to; the Duke of Cambridge becoming more and more bluff and worldly and incomprehensible, and the Earl of Derby stiffer and stiffer. Between them they conveyed the unwelcome news that because of gossip the Horse Guards and the Cabinet had decided that if Brown appeared in public with the Queen there might be an incident. At best he would be pulled from the box and set upon. Whatever happened the dignity of the crown, the army, and the government would be impaired.

Victoria gasped at their impudence. And then, suddenly, the full volcanic force of her fury overflowed.

For a moment the Earl of Derby forgot he was a Stanley. He had seen many displays of Hanoverian tantrums: George the Fourth, black-faced in an apoplectic rage, his voice a bellow; William the Fourth, his patience teased beyond endurance, gobbling incoherently like a turkey; but the Queen's passion was fiercer than that of either of her uncles. Derby had never heard anything quite like it. Involuntarily he took a step backwards as though to protect himself a little from her rage. As for the Duke of Cambridge, he simply gaped at his cousin, then pulled himself together, closed his mouth, and stood to attention with his head bowed while the storm raged on. It was impossible to take in all she said. The spate of words was tremendous, and anger had thickened her normally clear voice. But the general sense was unmistakeable, and certain expressions and words thundered through the rest like cannon fire . . . calumnies against a defenceless widow . . . tricks sufficient to break a woman's heart . . . persistent disloyalty of ill-disposed people . . . panic when there should be steadiness . . . public resentment of her natural wish for privacy . . . insufferable insolence . . . malevolence . . . slanderous gossip . . . abdication. . . .

The force of her passion made Victoria feel faint and as she steadied herself in her chair she recalled Lehzen's warning of long before – that people would doubt her reason if she gave way to tantrums. It enabled her to control her rage. By a huge effort she brought it under and subdued it. Then in a cold, decisive voice she thanked Lord Derby for his official advice. It proved, she said, his personal interest in her welfare because none of her previous prime ministers had ever interested themselves in the palace servants. And she was equally grateful to her cousin. It was kindly of him to spare some of his valuable time as Commander-in-Chief to the consideration of who should and who should not ride on a carriage box.

As it happened, she concluded, they need not have troubled themselves because she had made up her mind that no change should be made under any circumstances. She smiled. At the coming military review, she said, the Queen's Highland Servant would be in his accustomed place on the box of her carriage. She held out her hand to be kissed.

When they had gone Victoria went to her private sitting-room and sat at a desk to write a memorandum for her Household. In the first line she spluttered apart a steel nib as she gave a brief account of what had occurred and commanded the support of her gentlemen and equerries –

> . . . *to prevent her being teased and plagued with the interference of others, and moreover to make it* completely understood once *and* for all *that her* Upper Highland servant *(whether it be Brown or another, in case he should be* ill, *replaces him)*

belongs to her outdoor *attendants on State as well as private occasions. The Queen will not be dictated to, or* made *to* alter *what she has found to answer for her comfort.*

There was an impasse between the Queen and her advisers. Her decision was irrevocable.

An untirely unlooked-for and shocking event far away in North America broke the deadlock. There was a rebellion in Mexico. On 19 June 1867 the Emperor Maximilian, younger brother to Francis Joseph of Austria-Hungary, was shot to death by a revolutionary firing squad; his skull, skin and hair sold off in lots as souvenirs; and his Empress, Victoria's first cousin, sent raving mad. The English Court went into mourning. The military review was cancelled. Lord Derby and the Duke of Cambridge made private resolutions never to expose themselves again to the full wrath of their sovereign.

By the sheer strength of her character the Queen herself broke the back of the John Brown scandal. It was never completely killed, but thereafter it did her very little harm. Point blank she refused to discuss it any longer. Her friends, she said, did not require an explanation, her enemies would not believe one.

It was certainly true of her friends who, seeing how much comfort and happiness Brown brought her, were thankful that his psychic powers had served to introduce him to a post he filled with such excellence.

His ordinary physical presence was a great reassurance to the Queen. People had mostly forgotten the attempts on her life when the Prince Consort had been there to protect her. In her time she had been shot at by a half-witted pot boy, a cold-blooded agitator, and a hunchback; and, though less mortally dangerous, she had suffered the worst fright when a retired, martinettish army officer had jumped up beside her carriage and belaboured her with a cane. Always she had striven to wear a mask of imperturbability but they had been terrifying episodes all the same, and with Brown close to her she felt safer. She liked his protective strength, and the fact he was so dependable, never taking a holiday, never taking time off, was a further comfort. He was always there. And obviously he had a great affection for his royal mistress.

No one at the centre of the Court made a special fuss of Brown, but they never ignored him. They were shocked when, as sometimes happened, he forgot himself and called his sovereign 'woman', but on reflection they realized that it did no harm and they respected his integrity and his scrupulousness in not taking advantage of his unique position.

The Queen's closest confidante, Lady Churchill, was privileged to know precisely why she valued Brown so much. He offered her a degree of informality and, in a Court where protocol was precise and rigid, it was a blessing and a relief for the sovereign to have a servant who was entirely unshockable and discreet. There were no oh's and ah's from Brown when the Queen asked for whisky instead of tea, or when she smoked cigarettes on picnics to keep away the midges. Then there was his forthrightness. He had no need to flatter, and was an honest, outspoken man, without a trace of the humbug Victoria detested.

For these special qualities Victoria was prepared to understand and forgive his failings. Men, she said, had to have some failings because perfection was out of the question, and she surprised Lady Churchill by admitting at long last that even the Prince Consort had had imperfections. She affirmed that, considering the amount of work he had to do, it was natural for Brown to be short-tempered on occasions and to take refuge in rather more whisky than was good for him, and she readily covered up for him when it was obvious he had been at the bottle. On one occasion he did not appear after luncheon to take his seat on the carriage box for her afternoon drive. Colonel Ponsonby was dispatched to see what had happened, and he, finding the Queen's Highland Servant incapable of getting downstairs let alone of riding on a box, returned to jump on the box himself and the drive proceeded. Neither he nor the Queen spoke of the matter again. On another quasi-public occasion Brown swayed a good deal and then fell flat on his face. Without hesitation the Queen said she also had felt a distinct earthquake tremor. Just as Victoria expected complete loyalty from her friends, so she was prepared to be completely loyal to them without distinction.

With all the force at her command, Lady Churchill supported the Queen's friendship with Brown. She recognized that it was, of course, an unusual relationship but she was positive in herself that even if sometimes the Queen amused herself by entertaining the idea she would never have dreamt of giving herself to Brown physically as scandal said. She was proud of his good looks, and she liked to have a man about, but, apart from the fact that by now she had completely subjected her body to the discipline of widowhood, her feelings for the Prince Consort had been profound and nothing could have moved her to be unfaithful to him. Then, and this was something on which she and the Queen were entirely agreed, though the world seemed to have overlooked it, there was nothing very romantic about good Brown. Nothing romantic at all.

PART TWO

1

On a warm July morning in 1867 the Queen sat breakfasting outside the Tea House of wood and splatter-work at Frogmore.

A table and a serving table had been set out on the grass in the shade of two holm oaks. Silver breakfast dishes had been brought down from the Castle in a pair-horse fourgon, warmed in the little kitchen attached to the Tea House, and carried out one after the other by liveried servants. A Scotch dairymaid brought fresh butter and jugs of cream and milk from the dairy near by. The Queen's collie Sharp lay at her feet and growled at everyone who approached. Brown had recently nursed him through a serious illness and he now had an uncertain temper, but whenever he showed signs of snapping she would poke him with the end of her parasol or with the toe of her shoe. She was obliged to poke him several times when the royal pipers filled their bags and marched in and out of the trees playing tunes. No more than the English servants did Sharp enjoy Scotch music in the forenoon. The Queen, though, liked it immensely and not only while she ate her porridge but right through the meal.

That morning her appetite was excellent. Deciding it was too warm for porridge, she enjoyed a plateful of Frogmore strawberries instead. After that she helped herself to a sliver of ham and then to a piece of smoked haddock before she ate her invariable breakfast dish – two lightly-boiled eggs from a select strain of White Dorkings.

The meal finished, she sat back to enjoy the morning air and the scents of roses, and sun-warmed laurel leaves, and a delectable sweetness which told her that the pineapple pits not far away had been opened and that some of the fruits were at exactly the right stage of ripeness.

Half an hour later the dishes and tables had been cleared, the pipers dismissed, Sharp had been taken off for exercise by Brown's brother, Hugh, who was now Royal Kennelman at Windsor, and the Queen herself had crossed the little lake which lay between the Tea House and the Mausoleum and had paid her daily visit to Albert's grave.

The royal round had begun.

On such a day Victoria found her routine work less wearisome. Because no July day in the British Isles was ever quite without a breath of wind, and dust and blown-about papers were a vexation, Brown recommended she sit at a table indoors. But she decided against the Tea House. It had a leisurely, relaxing atmosphere and the flying swallow painted at the centre of the ceiling was always a distraction. She went instead to the special room in the head gardener's house which was set apart for her use. It also contained a bird, but this was a stuffed cockatoo and could be put to one side of the room and, though the french windows opened on to a stone-circled pond with a fountain and golden orfe, she could turn her back on the view and attend to her papers. It was a less enervating place altogether for business.

On the table before her Brown placed her pen box, standish, folding desk and a quantity of black-edged writing paper as well as the locked dispatch boxes and a tray of the morning's correspondence. There were two unopened family letters, and a large pile of others already minuted by General Grey. At the top, so that it should immediately catch her eye, was a letter from Downing Street. In wordy, nervous language the Prime Minister begged that the Queen would postpone her intended departure for Osborne for three more days. Pinned to it was a minute from General Grey to say the Chancellor of the Exchequer wished for an audience that morning. Would half past eleven o'clock be suitable? And where should it be?

As was intended, the promise of a visit from Mr Disraeli somewhat mollified the Queen's vexed reaction to Lord Derby's letter. She sent word to the Castle that the time was suitable and she would see the Chancellor in the Queen's Room in Frogmore gardens.

In the past months, despite an initial revulsion because he was an Italian Jew by blood and because he had once helped to topple her old friend Sir Robert Peel from power, the Queen had found herself intrigued by Mr Benjamin Disraeli. To judge by reports, time had quietened his ebullience and his outré taste. She recalled Lord M. telling her of Disraeli paying calls in a black velvet coat, scarlet waistcoat, gold-embroidered poppy-coloured trousers, and jewelled rings worn on top of white kid gloves. He now dressed more soberly as befitted his position, but there was still a little something about the cut of his coat, the large pearl at his shirt front, and the way he used his single eye-glass which showed the firefly had not lost all its brilliance. In no time at all she had decided he was impossibly romantic, essentially an artist and not at all suitable for high political office. As quickly she discovered that though he was a highly skilled novelist he was also a shrewd statesman.

Seeing the Queen's interest and having a high regard for Disraeli, Lady Churchill said that no one in England had such a sense of fun, and, while he was cynical about some things, he had a sense of breathless wonder about others. A heady mixture of Puck and Bryon was how she described him.

It intrigued the Queen still further.

Soon he had been at Court more often than his office as Chancellor could possibly require. So, on occasions, had Mrs Disraeli, the elderly re-married widow who had caught Victoria's interest at the Prince of Wales' wedding. Both were out of the ordinary. Mary Anne was seventy-six and her Ben was sixty-three and, while political enemies said he had been saved from financial shipwreck by a timely marriage, it was clear that, like her own, their marriage had cemented into something beautiful and enduring. They adored each other. With a naturalness Victoria found very comforting both could talk about the Prince Consort and understand her loss because they knew about love. They lived in it all the time. Odd, both of them, but valued friends.

Without making a formality of it Disraeli was continuing the Queen's lessons in political science and affairs which no one had dared or troubled to carry on after the Prince Consort's death, and he had the patience and the manner to listen as well as to talk, and was prepared to give advice and sympathize with her private family disasters.

Recently they had been heavier than ever. To everyone's horror Prussia had waged a seven-week war with Austria and, winning it, had proceeded to seize the lands and revenues of those who had been allies of her enemies. The result was a painful family upheaval. Princess Alice was on the losing side. Her husband's Grand Duchy, already small, was made minute. Hanover was lost, the Queen's cousin George the Fifth deposed and his private fortune sequestered. The King of Saxony, suzerain to the Duke of Coburg, was also driven out and the Princess of Wales' uncle, the Landgrave of Hesse-Cassel, lost everything he had.

In reviewing these calamities Mr Disraeli had been a reservoir of understanding and good advice. He was equally consoling in more intimate family troubles. He understood exactly when the Queen confessed her anxieties about Vicky's children. Willy especially was a worry. In compensating for his physical deformities he was consistently rude and cocksure about everything. Mr Disraeli was privileged to read an entry the Queen had made in her Journal about the young prince:

> *May God preserve him, and may he grow up good, clever and liberal-minded in his views, worthy of his beloved Grandpapa, who was so anxious about him, and that he should not grow up into a "conceited Prussian".*

The Chancellor polished his eyeglass and, asking permission to be candid, said the sentiments were understandable, but he feared Prince William was already a conceited Prussian and would require watching by his grandmother.

Victoria admired his honesty as much as his perspicacity and she found his sympathy very consoling when poor Vicky lost her most recent baby Sigismund. It would be a very good thing, said Mr Disraeli, if Princess Vicky could be got over to England for a time. Politically it had been impossible for almost three years. He would look into it.

Even the stupidities and gadding about of the Prince of Wales which so jarred on the Queen's nerves somehow seemed less trying when Mr Disraeli called him Prince Hal and in his lovely soft voice declaimed appropriate passages from *Henry the Fourth, Part One*.

Now, because Lord Derby had no intention of risking his sovereign's displeasure any more, Disraeli was appointed the Cabinet's spokesman whenever a personal approach seemed likely to answer, or when matters of fine delicacy had to be discussed. Nothing could have been more satisfactory to all parties. The

Prime Minister was relieved of an onerous duty. The Chancellor of the Exchequer, who had a high regard for the Queen, could enjoy being in her company. Victoria herself was assured that instead of being bludgeoned into accepting unpalatable recommendations she would be charmed into them by odd Mr Disraeli with his sallow parchment skin and beady bright eyes.

She was not, though, so sure that she would allow herself to be charmed that morning. At the recollection of Lord Derby's preposterous proposal her blue eyes became a steely grey, she pressed her lips together, and her round chin set into marble obstinacy.

If anything an hour and a half's hard work stiffened her resolve. But it began to weaken the moment Disraeli arrived and kissed her hand, and asked permission to walk up and down between the prospect of golden orfe and the stuffed cockatoo so that his tired circulation machine, agreeably started up by the walk from the Castle in the wake of surely the longest-legged footman in the royal employ, could continue to chug beneficially for a little time longer. It was excellent for a constitution somewhat damaged, though he trusted not irreparably, by an old-fashioned liking for Madeira and seedcake and a very modern one for Chablis, foie gras and Egyptian ortolans stewed in brandy. . . .

'Mr Disraeli,' cut in the Queen dryly, 'is it your plan to put my head in such a whirl that I am in no fit state to discuss Lord Derby's letter?'

'Ma'am!' exclaimed the Chancellor, a splayed hand on his heart, the other screwing his single eyeglass into place, his tone registering astonishment that she could believe him capable of such trickery. Then with a sudden smile, a change of voice, the smoothing of his great forehead which had crumpled into anxiety like glaze cracks on a toby jug, he admitted it. 'But, of course, Ma'am. Although nothing was said, I believe, about my purpose for requesting this audience, you have rightly connected it with the Prime Minister's anxiety that the Sultan's state visit should be honoured by the sovereign. And so anxious is Lord Derby,' he continued, 'that combined with his gout – which, with the examples of Lords Liverpool, Aberdeen and Palmerston before him, he might have known was a special pitfall for First Ministers of the Crown – he is cast into a frame of mind which could only be called melancholy. . . .'

'Mr Disraeli,' interrupted the Queen for a second time.

'Ma'am, I beg your pardon. The rebuke, though unspoken, is deserved. Mrs Disraeli, Ma'am, has had occasion to say that when nervously inclined I go on so. I should not, Ma'am. I should not go on so.'

'Nervously inclined?' repeated the Queen, half alarmed, half incredulous.

He nodded, or rather let his head fall. 'Exactly,' he murmured. He begged her patient understanding of his present difficulty. He polished his eyeglass and let it dangle and spin from his forefinger like a jewelled pendant. Naturally, he said, he was nervous because duty obliged him to persuade her to undertake something she found so objectionable. Did it lie within his power he would not dream of pressing a Queen for whom he had such a profound personal respect, but in the tussle between inclination and duty his service to her as a minister rather than as a friend had to be paramount for England's sake....

Victoria was not in the least taken in, but she was charmed. She played his own astute game, saying that, although it would involve special and expensive arrangements, in view of the situation she would agree to receive the Sultan at Osborne.

From below lowered eyelids she peeped at the Chancellor. He was stifling a sigh. His skin seemed to look sallower, more tortoise-like. With long, thin fingers he touched the tip of his sparse imperial beard. 'Ma'am,' he said at last. 'I am aware, and the English people are aware, of what Osborne House means to you. It is your home, built to the Prince's design and decorated and furnished as the centre of your family life. To be invited there is, in effect, the highest personal privilege you could offer the Sultan of Turkey and his subsidiary the Khedive of Egypt.' He hesitated. 'But I fear, I greatly fear, that their political advisers, being orientals unversed in the politenesses of western courts, will expect their masters to be received by the sovereign in the capital....'

'I shall not go to the Palace,' said the Queen decisively.

'Oh!' For a moment he looked non-plussed. 'It pains me inexpressibly to press the matter, Ma'am; but in France where the Sultan and the Khedive have been for the Paris Exhibition, they were personally received by his Imperial Majesty.'

Victoria was not impressed. She was extremely fond of the Empress Eugénie who was to be her private guest that month at Osborne, and the Emperor, though flirtatious, was undeniably attractive as a man; but she knew that he was also a political adventurer, a gambler in national enterprises, whose latest hare-brained scheme of establishing a Mexican Empire had cost Maximilian his life and poor Charlotte her reason. By a movement of her lip – it could not be termed a smile or a sneer – Victoria conveyed the impression that, so far as she was concerned, the actions of the little Corsican's nephew bore no relation whatever to those of a Queen of England by lineal right. She picked up the letter. 'Lord Derby did mention it,' she said. 'But I believe you have forgotten that he did not actually specify London. There you are.... Windsor *or* Buckingham Palace.'

Disraeli took the letter and solemnly read the last few lines.

'You are right, Ma'am; and I think maybe your choice is a good one.' He began to eulogize Windsor, truly the seat of the Royal Family as Buckingham Palace could never be. The Sultan and the Khedive would be sensible of the Castle's historic greatness, and so forth....

It was only when she had sighed and sighed again and regretted the necessity to postpone her departure and had grumblingly agreed to wait at Windsor that she realized Disraeli's cleverness. But she was not angry. Like the skilful drawing of a tooth it surprised more than pained her. And, really, he was so amusing. Nevertheless she took the opportunity to warn him that alterations in her plans did cause her great nervous strain. And she was much disheartened by the public lack of understanding of her difficulties. She had forced herself to open Parliament once, and she had had small levees and Drawing Rooms, and she had paid a formal visit to an industrial centre in the Midlands, but people had no idea what these appearances had cost: the apprehension, her timidity, the welling panic, the dreadful isolation, the longing to shrink away from the hundreds of eyes. Even the recollection of it was enough to make her voice break and tears appear at the corners of her eyes.

Immediately Disraeli was solicitous. 'If I may, Ma'am, advise you?' he murmured. 'And as a devoted servant and friend, shedding my chancellorship now that our formal business is concluded?'

'Please, Mr Disraeli, I should greatly appreciate it.'

They had a frank conversation and in the end it was decided that Dr Jenner should be sent to the Prime Minister to give him the facts about her health. She also wrote a reply to Lord Derby's letter for Disraeli to take personally to London.

'With all respect, I would recommend you to be entirely open,' he urged. 'Say with your pen exactly what you have said to me.'

Victoria did her best. The pen raced over the black-edged paper and on to the second sheet.

The Queen is almost driven to desperation by the want of consideration shown by the public *for her health and strength, and she foresees ere long a* complete breakdown *of her nervous system. She really believes that unless she were crippled by rheumatism or gout, or something which absolutely* prevented *her walking, people would worry her until she sank under it!*

'Excellent,' murmured Disraeli when she read this out loud. 'Strong but to the point.'

She had not yet finished. She underlined the fact that she worked and drudged from morning to night weighed down by responsibilities as Queen, widow and mother, and added:

Often she had wished that the time might come when she could go to that world 'where the wicked cease from troubling and the weary are at rest'.

'Poetic,' exclaimed Disraeli.

When the letter was done, sanded, and sealed with a wafer, for the Queen still disliked using envelopes for letters sent by private messenger, Disraeli pocketed it, and bowed to take his leave.

'But Mr Disraeli,' said she in dismay. 'Will you not take luncheon with me?' She smiled. 'It is probably too late at this hour to command stewed Egyptian ortolans, but there will be something – beef or mutton, and a pudding. And we could ask the confectionery cook if a seedcake could be sent up.'

He bowed. 'Ma'am, I have a dreadful passion for beef and will gladly accept your kind invitation.'

Then, at her suggestion, he gave her his arm and they walked out into the garden, round the pool of golden orfes, and promenaded in the glasshouse where exquisite and delicate roses were specially grown. He soothed away the memory of her *crise de nerfs* by talking of the Paris Exhibition, the marvellous reconstructions – the Roman catacombs, an Inca palace, the palace of the Swedish liberator, Gustavus the First, the seaport at Antwerp, and an Egyptian temple complete with a two-thousand-year-old, black-fleshed mummy; and amongst the marvels on display, a curious piece of American furniture called a rocking chair, the products of a remarkable substance known as petroleum, a new feather-weight metal called aluminium so precious that a dinner service made of it had been ordered for the Tuileries, and a German steel cannon which fired exploding shells, each shell being the weight of six brawny Life Guards. This last made Victoria gasp. How, she wanted to know, could such a weight be got into the air. Mr Disraeli confessed that he had no idea – 'But you know the Germans, Ma'am, inventive, scientific.' He went on to reassure her that like the Prince Consort's Great Exhibition of 1851 it was hoped that the present show in Paris would bring people together in brotherly amity, and when she pointed out that almost on the exhibition site an attempt had been made on the Tzar by a disaffected Pole, he rapidly glossed it over – 'A failure, Ma'am, of course. Excitable exiles can't shoot straight. No one hurt save the French Emperor who thought he'd lose Russia's friendship and had dyspepsia.' And Disraeli emphasized the good work being done for England by the Prince of Wales who, as always in his beloved Paris, was at his jolliest. The *Chefs de Protocole* depended on him more than anyone else to give a lead and, being a great collector of uniforms, he was absorbed in examining the huge variety displayed in Paris from the dazzling White Cuirassier uniform of the German Chancellor, Bismarck, to the magnificence of Algerian Spahis, French chasseurs with green plumes, turbaned Zouaves in red and blue, grenadiers in high shakos, light infantry in yellow-striped tunics, and the medley of colour and metal worn by artillery men, cuirassiers, carabineers, cavalry scouts, lancers and hussars. . . .

Mr Disraeli's colourful descriptions and his soft, musical voice, combined with the sweet scent of roses and the warmth of the glasshouse, made the Queen feel quite heady. To shake off the feeling, for Victoria never allowed sentiment or sensibility to overwhelm her common sense for long, she changed the subject. She wanted, she said, to know all about her guest, the Sultan.

Anyone other than Benjamin Disraeli might have paused for a moment. Not a great deal was known about the worm-eaten

Ottoman dynasty, and it would not do to paint an accurate picture of Abdul-Aziz, despot of the Bosphorus. His father had been considered an enlightened Sultan but really the only piece of western progress to penetrate Turkey during his reign was a four-poster bed. Abdul-Aziz himself was typical of a prince brought up by the harem under the subversive influence of such exotic functionaries as the Keeper of the Parrots, Chief Nightingale Keeper, Master of the Girls and, most powerful of all, the chief black eunuch called Guardian of the Gates of Felicity. He knew exceedingly little about anything and was neurotic, impotent and, some said, quite mad. Mr Disraeli did not hesitate. Ignoring these startling facts altogether, he told the Queen that a Sultan's life perforce was wrapped in considerable mystery but that he had succeeded his brother according to the quaint Ottoman laws of succession six years before, and had shown an unexpected and touching feeling for the victims of a cholera epidemic which had decimated his capital. And then, rapidly, he went on to talk of something else until it was time for luncheon and he could indulge his dreadful passion for beef.

Unhappily there wasn't any.

'Ma'am,' he protested when the Queen wished to order a joint from the kitchens. 'I overlooked to say that I also have a quite alarming fondness for boiled fowl.'

There were two on the sideboard.

2

All the Queen's children grew fond of Benjamin Disraeli.

Princess Beatrice, still called Baby, though by now she was a schoolroom miss of ten, set the fashion in the family by referring to him by his Parliamentary nickname of Dizzy. Not that she would have used it to his face. She was far too correct and old-fashioned and even quaintly referred to herself in the third person as Princess Beatrice and her mother as the Queen. Her brother Leopold, always full of mischief despite his lifelong invalidism because of haemophilia, was less respectful. Generally he called people by a combination of initials; his mother for example was H.B.M. and Bertie the P of W. But, as he solemnly remarked, Mr D was his name for his tutor, the Reverend Mr R. Duckworth, and to call Disraeli the C of E would be open to misunderstanding. In any case he might change his cabinet post and become something impossibly long like the President of the Poor Law Board. He would have to be plain Mr Dizzy. And plain Mr Dizzy was very content to be so. Leopold and Beatrice loved him, and they loved Mrs Dizzy too. The four of them would go to raid the Osborne fruit garden, Mrs Dizzy doing heroic work under the strawberry nets with the crook of her parasol while the others picked and picked and picked. Then, replete, they would sit on the steps of the Swiss Chalet and Dizzy would tell stories. The Queen was privately amused when Leopold informed her that Mr Dizzy was as good as a kirk minister for telling grisly stories about the devil, and still more so when Baby remarked with great accuracy that the Chancellor smelt beautifully of hair pomade and sealing wax.

Prince Arthur was devoting himself to a military career and trying to follow in the footsteps of his godfather the Duke of Wellington. More than any of the other children he resembled his father, and the Queen was determined to keep him on the straight and narrow path of virtue. His governor was instructed that his appearance must be ordinary – that he must not have a centre-parting nor lounge about with his hands in his pockets; that at all costs he should be kept away from stage doors and race meetings and the Marlborough House set; and that, as an aid to self-control in all things, the temperature of his rooms should never be allowed to exceed sixty degrees. All this was done and, to the Queen's intense satisfaction, Prince Arthur showed no signs of following his elder brothers' wicked ways. But it seemed unlikely, on the face of it, that such an orthodox seventeen-year-old should be able to get on with so bizarre a creature – half gad-fly, half fire-fly – as Mr Dizzy. Instinctively at first he was shy, but he was quickly disarmed. Dizzy had sat under Wellington to learn politics and had shared his preference for a country landowning aristocracy to the new focus of power where fortunes were made by the nabobs of industry. He passed on to his serious godson the best of the Duke's ideas, and a necessarily expurgated account of his adventurous career. It was odd but true that, though everyone knew of Prince Arthur's devotion to the Duke, no one had troubled to tell him very much about him. Disraeli on Wellington was by no means a Boswell on Johnson but it was infinitely interesting to the Prince. He became Dizzy's strong supporter.

Princess Helena was as orthodox as her brother Arthur and she, as well, was slow to approve of Mr Disraeli's special place at Court. But time showed her that under the flamboyance there was a great deal of hard practical wisdom and even more of kindness in his make-up. Since her recent marriage, Disraeli had gone out of his way to be kind to her and her husband. Poor Christian took a long time to settle in England. When Schleswig and Holstein had been seized from his brother the family had fled into exile carrying with them rose-trees and doves as well as furniture from the ducal palace; and it was a sign of his nostalgia that he had brought cuttings of those roses to strike in the gardens of Cumberland Lodge, his new home in Windsor Park, and two of the doves to breed in the pigeon loft there. Dizzy understood this homesickness and did his best to help wear it away. And while a good many people considered Christian as a comic opera sort of princeling, a figure of fun chosen for Helena because he was tame enough to do as he was told and live in England to keep the Queen company whenever she wished for it, Dizzy had the advantage of a closer and truer sight of his worth. Realizing he was horridly alarmed by the force of his mother-in-law's personality, he underlined to the Queen Prince Christian's qualities of gentleness and good heartedness and his talents as a plantsman and landscape gardener which, with his love of shooting and hunting and his warm domesticity, would assuredly have endeared him to the Prince Consort. Victoria was impressed. She made Prince Christian Ranger of Windsor Park, began to notice the distinct beauty of his sapphire eyes rather than his baldness and plumpness, and she ceased to bark at him even when he was at his most irritating. Princess Helena was not slow to realize what she and her husband owed to kind Mr Disraeli. They were not ungrateful.

Princess Louise now nineteen years of age and longing to be married was very sensible of Dizzy's charms because he so exactly appreciated her position. He knew she was the most artistic and creative of all the royal children, and possibly the most romantic, and that it was a torment to her to be marriageable at a time when the only available suitors belonged to petty German royal houses. In his mind's eye he saw her as a helpless maiden imprisoned in her tower by boredom and the dread of a loveless marriage, and he gave her to understand he would cheerfully be her St George. Louise, austere and royal, smiled serenely. The thought of dear Dizzy as a knight in armour bearing down on a green dragon in her defence was delicious. She loved him for it.

Disraeli saw little of the Queen's two married daughters Vicky and Alice. What he did see he liked. Both were what he called the tomato bottlers of womankind, capable nurses and bandage rollers in war, sale of work and charity ball organizers in time of peace. His respectful admiration for them was reciprocated. Vicky was a shrewder judge of her mother than the other children and, with Lady Churchill, she understood that for the satisfaction of her romantic feelings her mother looked to Mr Disraeli rather than dour John Brown. She was relieved that Mr Disraeli was as level-headed as he was romantic. Alice was delighted that poor Mamma had such an understanding minister, and Dizzy sent a contribution to her work for unmarried ladies, several gold coins in a velvet purse stitched by Mary Anne.

Too cut off from the Court and too blasé to come very much under the spell of Mr Disraeli, the Queen's elder sons nevertheless realized their obligations to him. And in his presence neither was quite able to resist his affectionate manner of addressing them as 'Dear, dear Prince', nor a statesman who wore an eyeglass and frockcoat with such distinction.

Despite the Queen's plans and his growing reputation as a roué, Prince Alfred, Duke of Edinburgh, was still unmarried. He did not mind in the least, and it was Disraeli who persuaded his mother that, as he was next in succession to Saxe-Coburg, the selection of a suitable bride ought not to be hurried. It was never uttered but quite understood that anyone with so liberal a supply of wild oats was perhaps wise to sow them before marriage rather than afterwards. The Prince appreciated Dizzy's good offices in this delicate matter. He was also grateful for his help when the Queen found out that on foreign service he had been in the habit of flying the Royal Standard and accepting honours as a Prince of the Blood rather than as a captain in the Royal Navy. She was very angry indeed, but she would have been angrier still had it not been for Dizzy's moderating influence.

The Prince of Wales had the same reasons for being grateful.

Disraeli frequently softened and sometimes deflected altogether the majestic bolts aimed at Marlborough House.

A few were fired at the Princess of Wales. Something ought to be done about Prince Eddy. As second in direct succession to the throne he was particularly important, and he needed to be taken in hand. Though not blessed with brains he must be taught to use the few he had. This was Alix's especial responsibility. Further, Alix ought not to be so violently against the Prussians. They behaved badly, of course, but in a large family it was important to maintain the appearance of friendly relations. And Alix should not be seen knitting, nor permit overfamiliarity, nor lie in bed all morning so that her husband had to breakfast alone.

But the heaviest and hardest bolts were hurled at the Prince of Wales. He deserved them all, and one in particular. Because Alix was still badly crippled after her rheumatic fever and the doctors advised the baths at Wiesbaden, Bertie accompanied her there for a two-month cure. But within days he was bored and was slipping off to enjoy the rakish society of Baden. Stories circulated from court to court – the gist of them being that once again the Prince of Wales had publicly shamed his wife by neglecting her. When she heard the report Victoria was so extraordinarily angry that she wrote to Bertie's Private Secretary to say something must be done. The poor man replied that he was powerless. 'In no points will His Royal Highness brook interference.'

Disraeli went to work. He had little respect for the Prince of Wales. He was too callow, loud, and indifferent to other people's feelings. But he did admire his tolerance of Jews. In fact, with the exception of the Rothschilds, the Jews in the Marlborough House set were not the sort he would have chosen to present to Mary Anne; but though Anglicized, Christianized, and the Semitic mysteries in him pumiced away by western culture, Disraeli yet had a blood loyalty to his race. To the traducer of Jews he would be hard. To a friend of the Jews, like the Prince of Wales, he was prepared to be helpful. And, besides all this, there was the primary consideration of the Queen's distress. It hurt him to see her so hurt by her son's behaviour, and he wanted to reconcile them.

When the Prince returned to England, his face aglow because of some lucky coups at the gaming-tables and apparently unaware of the pain he had caused to everyone, Mr Disraeli saw quite a lot of him. Their talk was never profound, but the Prince was glad to find this new family friend so understanding. Disraeli bolstered his diffidence, and encouraged into growth the affection which the Prince had always had for his mother when she was not being too cross or regal. He also emphasized the Prince's good points to the Queen and begged her to think more leniently of 'Prince Hal'.

She so far responded that she sent for Bertie, saw him at Windsor, and showed she forgave him for his most recent lapse. As is the maternal way, she managed to persuade herself, and perhaps him, that the doctors shared some of the blame for being so unwise as to propose Wiesbaden in the first place. Both were deeply touched. They had forgotten how much they loved one another. The Queen wrote to Vicky:

> *Really dear Bertie is so full of good & amiable qualities that it makes one forget and overlook much that one would wish different.*

Mr Disraeli the reconciler was not a self-deceiver. Peace had been made but it was only temporary. No undertakings had been given or required. They would fall out all their lives, but it was desirable that they should see each other's qualities from time to time.

As for the Queen, she was sincerely grateful.

So was the Prince of Wales.

3

The first Home Secretary in Lord Derby's ministry had proved uselessly indecisive. Faced by a riot in Hyke Park he had done nothing but wring his hands and burst into tears. His successor Mr Gathorne Hardy was a wool nabob from Bradford and had a very different manner. Already he had won popularity by his firm attitude to any form of anarchy and his stolid refusal to panic. It was all one to him that, soon after his appointment to office, the acme of all subversive literature was published by a German Jew exiled in London under the title of *Das Kapital*; and that a dubious lot of revolutionaries calling themselves the International met for a congress in Lausanne; even that, much closer to home, the Irish firebrands were astir again. It was said he was a great taker of secret precautions, and this gave to the Home Office an authoritative air, a new security, which it had lacked for a long time.

He soon had the Queen's approval. She liked his spirit. He grew to like hers.

When it was recommended that Oxford, the potboy who had tried to shoot the Queen on Constitution Hill in 1840, should be released from a criminal lunatic asylum, the Home Secretary himself expected her to raise a strong objection. But she did no such thing. With a turn of phrase she had learnt from Lord Melbourne long before, she said that if twenty-seven years in a criminal lunatic asylum had not tamed him nothing would. She had Brown to protect her and she presumed that, in any case, Oxford would be beguiled to go abroad? Oxford was. He went off to Australia to be a housepainter where, said the Queen, with a rather surprising lack of tact towards her colonial subjects, he could not possibly do any harm.

The Sovereign and Home Secretary were entirely in accord about Ireland. The Queen had been told by Wellington himself that the Irish, confronted by any sort of problem, either fought like the devil or despaired, and she was firmly of the opinion that the vast majority were both unreliable and false, and took in sedition with their mother's milk. Gathorne Hardy agreed. The poet Shelley, he informed the Queen, had gone to Dublin in a mischievous spirit to foster their rebellion against England, and even he – the visionary and revolutionary – had publicly admitted that the Irish were impossible and irresponsible, and ingrates who believed that the only thing more ridiculous than an Englishman was an Englishman who loved Ireland.

But when, after the disastrous potato harvest in 1867, the Irish carried their violence into England, the Home Secretary became concerned by the Queen's spirited refusal to regard the matter as at all grave. He went to call on Mr Disraeli. Would the Chancellor, he asked, kindly speak to the Queen. He was not an alarmist. Yorkshiremen seldom were. But he was concerned about his responsibility for the Queen's safety. He had warned her, on a reliable report, that the Irish might attempt to kidnap her at

Balmoral, but she had paid little attention. On his own initiative he had arranged for a detachment of the 93rd Highlanders to be sent over from Aberdeen, and extra police had been detailed for duty at Balmoral, but all the Queen would say to her Household was: 'Too foolish! Too foolish!'

Disraeli was silent for a minute or two when his guest finished speaking. Then he said solemnly, 'Here, Hardy, we have a problem of great complexity. . . .' He broke off. 'Permit me to offer you Madeira?'

He poured two glasses. When they had both drunk a little he held up his glass and looked through the amber-coloured wine, saying as he did so: 'You, too, I understand, have been threatened?'

Gathorne Hardy shrugged. 'A Home Secretary is the natural target for malcontents.'

'And any fears you have you hide, and take adequate precautions?'

'Yes, I suppose that is so,' replied the other with a smile. Then his expression altered. 'You consider the Queen is doing the same?'

'I do not know,' said Disraeli. 'To be frank, in either your position or in the Queen's I should be less able to conceal my fears. Secret societies revolt me, be their members tongsmen or Jacobins or communists or these ribbonmen of Ireland, and revulsion perhaps exaggerates my dread of falling into their hands.' He drank more wine. 'I envy you your Roman scorn for hole-in-the-corner *lèse-majesté*.'

The Home Secretary stirred in his chair, grunted, and finished his Madeira. There was the faintest trace of pink on his cheekbones.

'I say all this,' continued his host, 'because I am inclined to believe that the Queen's reaction to the threats of a secret society is more in line with mine than with yours. And if this is so,' he added, 'it would be out of the question to unnerve her further by labouring the point.'

'I see,' said Gathorne Hardy. 'Her sang-froid has misled me.'

'No, no, no, no,' cried Disraeli immediately. 'It is not sang-froid. To say "Too foolish! Too foolish!" in the face of such threats gives the appearance of sang-froid, but really it is splendid, heroic bravery.' He put the glass down. 'Because you have responsibility for the Queen's safety, and should be aware of the exact truth, I feel obliged to break a confidence and tell you something of what I know.'

'You may be sure . . .' began the other, but he was cut short.

'Of course, I appreciate that I may rely on your discretion. And you, I know, will accept that the reliability of my information, though the source cannot be named to you, is nevertheless impeccable.'

Without elaboration he told Gathorne Hardy about the Queen's dread of mobs. The isolated attempts on her life had terrified her but none had had a lasting effect. It was the mob she had grown up to fear – the rick burners, the reform rioters, the militant chartists, the Fenians – the amorphous, ignorant, violent, unrelenting pack who, given the chance, would, she was sure, tear their sovereign to pieces. And to this fear was added one other.

Disraeli went to a small cabinet and took from a locked drawer a plaque done by Wedgwood on a bright blue jasper background. It showed a head in profile, bewigged and wearing a wreath of bay leaves, and above it a crown with a motto attached, the two words HEALTH RESTORED. He handed it to Gathorne Hardy.

'George the Third?'

'Indeed, yes,' said Disraeli, nodding. 'A plaque made to commemorate his recovery from the first attack in 1789. Probably you will have some sort of recollection of his death in 1820 at Windsor? Being, I judge, ten years or so older than you, and a young man at the time, my own memory is very clear. I recall it exactly, as though it were yesterday, or this morning – the sighs, relief all round. Poor mad creature, they said, his day was done.' He took back the plaque and studied it through his eyeglass. 'And whenever she is in an excess of grief or rage, or sometimes when exhaustion combines with exasperation and frustration, our Queen remembers she is his grand-daughter.' He carried the plaque back to the cabinet. 'She is not, to my way of thinking, the least out of her mind. The old King's doctors made it plain that his derangement sprang from a bodily disease, something physical rather than mental, and the Queen's remarkably good physical health is a byword. Still, there has been talk – on occasions when she quarrelled violently with the Prince Consort, when her mother died, when she was widowed – and however discreet and watchful her attendants are the talk eventually filters through to her, and when she is low she is, I believe, haunted by the possibility of losing her wits.' He sat down again and looked hard at the Home Secretary. 'That she does not give the appearance of fearing lunacy or mobs in no way presumes these fears do not exist. And too much weight added to either anxiety can only cause unnecessary distress. "Too foolish!" she says; but I make no doubt that her heart sank when she heard those rascals might try to kidnap her.'

Gathorne Hardy spoke at last. 'I had not quite realized . . .' he began, and started again. 'She must, indeed, be a very brave woman.'

'She is,' said Disraeli simply. 'And one whom I honour and care for. I would not wish to add to her burden by emphasizing the danger in which she lies. My advice, if I may offer it, would be to give Grey all the details and the Queen the bare bones of Fenian threats. You may leave it safely to him to take care of her, and give her what warnings are necessary.'

Gathorne Hardy took this advice, and his admiration for the Queen's calm courage knew no bounds.

Sensibly she refused to dwell on the activities of the Fenians and kept herself busy. To her normal work on government business which consumed a good part of each day she added the selection of sketches and suitable passages from her journal to be printed as a record of her great happiness with Albert in Scotland. It was to be published under the title of *Leaves from the Journal of Our Life in the Highlands*. But, though she endeavoured to keep her mind off the Fenians, from time to time they obtruded and then, Gathorne Hardy noted, her coolness was exemplary.

She rose superbly to meet the crisis when, with vindictive cruelty, the Fenians chose 14 December to explode a bomb against the wall of Clerkenwell Prison. Being the anniversary of the Prince Consort's death it was a day when the Queen was quite apart, visiting the Blue Room and the Mausoleum, attending a special memorial service, keeping largely silent, seeing no one. But she had to be told of the outrage and she instantly put her own feelings to one side, dictated a letter to the Home Secretary condemning the outrage and asking the government to give her faithful and peaceful subjects more effectual protection from such atrocious wickedness; and she did all she could to show publicly her contempt for the Fenians. In a practical way she sent Dr Jenner up to London to help with the men, women and children who had been blinded and cut about and disfigured for life, and she carefully selected fruit and toys for those in hospital.

Not long afterwards when the Court had already gone to Osborne for Christmas, General Grey was so anxious for her safety that, instead of approaching her directly, he sent a memorandum for her to read slowly and mull over. In it he said that the Home Secretary, the Colonial Secretary and the Commander-in-Chief had all been warned of attempts to be made on the Queen's person – either kidnapping or assassination – while she was at Osborne for Christmas.

> *It is difficult to believe* [he wrote] *when all seems so still and peaceful that danger can lurk about the quiet woods and valleys of this island. But General Grey must repeat the expression of his honest conviction, that it is precisely in these solitary and peaceful places that real danger lies.*

He begged her to return to Windsor where there was a permanent garrison to protect her.

Her reply was typical of her determination not to alter a single plan on account of her rebellious Irish subjects. She would authorize additional precautions to be taken at Osborne, but that was all.

> *The Queen does* not *intend making any difference in her intention of remaining here, as settled, and must ask* not *to have this* again *mentioned.*

One glimmer of her fear showed through. She wrote the same day to the Home Secretary asking for the recall of Parliament so that the Habeas Corpus Act could be repealed. But it was only a glimmer, and she immediately agreed when the Ministry pointed out that such a move was really undesirable.

The day after the Duke of Marlborough arrived at Osborne with yet another and very explicit warning. He had received a telegram from Canada that eighty Irish-Americans had set out in two ships having declared their intention of murdering the Queen. Under the circumstances it would be wiser, perhaps, if she would consent to move back to Windsor. . . . But the Duke hurriedly abandoned that topic when he saw the familiar firming of her chin and a flash from her eyes. He assured her that for the next three weeks ships of the Royal Navy would patrol the shores of the Isle of Wight and troops would be sent over. Though he realized it was an imposition, he requested her not to drive out far from the house and never after dark.

That evening the Prime Minister read out a letter from the Queen to his assembled cabinet of ministers. It concluded:

> Such *precautions are taken here that the Queen will be little better than a* State *prisoner. She may consent to this for a* short time, *but she could* not *for long.*

Marlborough, who had brought the letter, scratched his head. 'She really is extraordinary,' he commented. 'If the Bog Irish were after me I'd show a trace or two of concern, believe me.'

Lord Derby raised his eyebrows. 'No trace?'

'None that I could see. And as soon as she had written the letter she changed the subject. Said Hallé was coming down to stay and had me on my hands and knees looking through music.' He took snuff. 'Incredible. Menaced by eighty damned cut-throats, she calmly sorts out piles of music on the floor with her Lord President of the Council.'

Across the table Mr Disraeli exchanged glances with Mr Gathorne Hardy.

4

Lord Derby felt it was time to go. He was sixty-nine, had crippling gout, and the weight of leading his third administration had become just a little too heavy. Then one night he dreamt of Mr Lear the artist who, years before, had drawn the beasts in his menagerie and fascinated his family with nonsense rhymes. He woke up in his curtained bed envying Mr Lear his freedom. Though so high in his profession that for a time he had been the Queen's drawing master, Lear had cut loose to follow his own inclinations, travelling here and there with a cat and three

Albanian servants, painting, lithographing, scribbling nonsense, doing what he wished. Dreaming of Lear's liberty made Derby long for his. He would like to sit about at Knowsley doing nothing and forget the Fenians and parliamentary reform, and campaigns abroad, and telegraphic cables laid across the Atlantic. . . .

There was no reason – not a single one – why he should not follow his inclinations. If he wished to resign he could.

Excitedly he sat up in bed. After a dreadfully painful attack lasting ten days his gout had become quiescent and he fancied himself better than for months past. Now was the time to go.

Waiting beyond the curtains, the Earl's valet was surprised to hear him begin to chant. It was Mr Lear's song *The Pelicans* and hardly a concert performance because Derby could not hold a key. But delight at having made up his mind to resign gave his singing great vigour.

Ploffskin, Pluffskin, Pelican Jee!
We think no birds happy as we!
Plumpskin, Ploffskin, Pelican Jill!
We think so then, and we thought so still!

And so Mr Disraeli at last became First Minister of the Crown, and enjoyed himself packing Derby off to Knowsley and rearranging the Cabinet.

As a young man he had written a novel entitled *The Duke* which had caused his father to exclaim: 'Dukes! What does little Ben know of dukes?' It appeared he knew them well, for out of his fourteen ministers three were dukes and two more were the sons of dukes.

It was February, 1868. Disraeli had arrived.

Surprisingly the Queen was just a little anxious about the elevation of her dear Mr Disraeli.

To begin with, though so liberally hemmed in by ducal support, it was the first time in her reign that a commoner had become Prime Minister, and the last two to be so, Mr Perceval in the reign of her grandfather, and Mr Canning in the reign of her uncle, had early come to grief: the former being shot dead by a crazy bankrupt in the lobby of the House of Commons, and the latter lasting only four months in office before being carried off by mental trouble and a severe chill.

And, to go on with, she was frightened that Mr Disraeli might alter, that, on kissing hands, he might take himself too seriously and lose the light touch which made him so endearing.

Quite recently, on the publication of her book *Leaves from the Journal of Our Life in the Highlands* – which, with 20,000 copies disposed of in a month, was really doing very well – he had admitted her to the confraternity of letters. 'We authors, Ma'am,' he had said, knowing full well, because she told him, that her faulty grammar had been looked over and corrected by the Privy Council Clerk with the apposite name of Arthur Helps. Hard-headed Victoria smiled at the flattery. Romantic Victoria thought it charming of him. Amused and touched she hoped that great office would not spoil his puckishness.

She need not have worried.

Right away Disraeli wrote to recommend a Mr Ward Hunt as his replacement as Chancellor of the Exchequer, describing him as a man of remarkable appearance:

> *He is more than six feet four inches in stature, but does not look so tall from his proportionate breadth; like St Peter's, no one is at first aware of his dimensions. But he has the sagacity of the elephant, as well as the form.*

The Queen blinked when she first read this, and rapidly read it through again. Later she showed part of it to Lady Churchill. They laughed and laughed together. There was no danger, said Lady Churchill, of Mr Disraeli changing.

She was right.

One day in apparent seriousness he said the time was ripe for a new prime minister; the signs were propitious.

'Signs?' repeated the Queen.

He nodded solemnly. 'Yesterday, Ma'am, the Royal Buckhounds ran a deer through Wormwood Scrubs and killed in the goods yard at Paddington. Such an unlooked for, extraordinary event I regard as a portent.'

And a week later, to the Queen's surprise, he teased General Grey – himself the son of a former prime minister and an old parliamentarian – for bribing the electorate.

'Sir!' said the General.

The Queen, shocked, exclaimed: 'Mr Disraeli!'

'He did it, Ma'am, thirty-four years ago at Wycombe. Twice he beat Benjamin Disraeli at the polls.'

'A fluke,' said the General gruffly, embarrassed by the memory of Dizzy with lace cuffs and a gold-topped cane, and wearing a pink and white favour the size of a dahlia, haranguing the crowds from the portico of the Wycombe Red Lion. 'Absolutely a fluke, I assure you.'

'On the contrary, General. I, as a radical independent, offered cheaper bread. But you were irresistible. You had a brass band. And nothing,' he continued, smiling from ear to ear, 'corrupts the electorate more than military music.'

Mr Disraeli's reports of parliamentary proceedings had always been racy. Now they were more so, the commonplaces spiced to make them more appetizing for the Queen. In describing the place hunters in the Commons he said one was most violent and bitter –

he positively raised his crest and hissed like an adder.

And he mentioned that, at the slightest opportunity, a whole team of them emerged to do battle with words:

It is a company, a troupe, like one of those bands of minstrels one encounters in the sauntering of a summer street . . . but not so fair and radiant as your Majesty's subjects at Balmoral.

There was no danger in the Prime Minister's flattery of his sovereign. It was in his Byronic style and she saw through it as much as she loved it. Giving and receiving flattery was a game both enjoyed and which neither took in the least seriously. Thin steel lay beneath the silk. Benjamin Disraeli was no toady, and Victoria respected him for it.

When she asked for preferment for Mr Charles Kingsley because he was a worthy Broad Church clergyman and the author of that moving book *The Water Babies* he refused point blank. Kingsley to him was not simply the hero of small chimney-sweeps but also a dreadful poet and the author of a viperish pamphlet which impugned the sincerity of Dr Newman. Disraeli's own religion was not robust; nevertheless he admired men of real conviction like Newman, and on no account would he give preferment to his detractor. He wrote candidly to the Queen to say the advancement of such a radical as Kingsley was not in the interests of his party. And when, at the Queen's dinner, someone spoke disparagingly of the Earl of Cardigan, once the Balaclava hero but now clearly revealed as a martinet, a bully, and a rascal, and the Queen herself had added a word of disapproval, Disraeli risked a good deal socially by speaking up for him. Lawsuits, scandals, his own bad temper and an extravagant and eccentric wife had done for Cardigan, he said, and however horrid his vices they could not entirely cloud his virtues – his generous hospitality in former years, his exquisite taste, his poise, and his gallantry as a soldier. After all it had been Cardigan who, five lengths ahead of his staff and squadrons, had led the Light Brigade right up to the Russian guns, into the battery, and out again. There was a silence at the table. Victoria, remembering Cardigan's enviable insouciance in the face of the mob's hostility, and that once she had admired his soldierly good looks and bearing, felt ashamed of her own volte-face. She was glad Mr Disraeli had defended his virtues, especially as the wretched Earl was now apparently beshrewed by a second wife who wore his cherry-red Hussar trousers as a bicycling uniform, danced the *cachucha* on the table after dinner, had herself rowed about the harbour at Cowes during regatta week dressed as a Spaniard and playing the guitar, and frequently threw Blue Minton dishes at her husband's head. She was doubly glad Disraeli had been charitable to Cardigan when, only a month afterwards, the Earl fell off his horse and died. It not being the thing to speak evil of the dead, everyone at Court was now calling him a gallant old reprobate. Only her new Prime Minister had had the courage to say it when he was alive.

Disraeli as Prime Minister appeared to take life no more seriously than Palmerston had done. Neither approved of puritans, humbugs or hangdogs. Yet Victoria found he was a rock when things went wrong. He was as indignant as she when what she called 'shameless articles' attacking her continued seclusion appeared in *The Globe*, *The Times*, and *The Daily Telegraph*. And he was solicitude itself when Prince Alfred was shot in the back by a Fenian in far-away Australia. The wound was serious but not fatal. The Fenian was executed. For his understanding and eagerness to help, Disraeli received the highest accolade the Queen could offer. She told Lady Churchill, who passed it on, that Lord

M., even perhaps the Prince Consort himself, could not have been kinder.

The compliment emboldened him to propose that, despite the Fenian outrages against her people and her family, the Prince and Princess of Wales should earn goodwill by paying a formal visit to Ireland and, if the Queen agreed, establish a royal residence there. She did not agree. Given this lead, she said, other countries might get the pretentious idea of wanting a royal residence, and it was quite out of the question. Moreover it was unwise to encourage the Prince in his constant love of gadding about.

Mr Disraeli thought it sufficiently important to persevere. The Prince, he assured her, would come to no harm. Though his list of talents was shorter than one could wish, high amongst them was an ability to get on with people and manage crowds. A formal visit from the Heir Apparent and his wife would go far to quietening down agitation. The Dubliners would appreciate it if the Prince were to be installed as a Knight of St Patrick, and he could combine public duty with pleasure at the Punchestown races because the Irish dearly loved a race-goer....

The *races*! The Queen bristled. She did not consider, she declared, the Punchestown racetrack a fit place for the consolidation of goodwill between rebels and the Crown.

She was so unusually acidulous that, if Disraeli had not been genuinely devoted to her and very good-natured, they might have quarrelled. As it was, on his guarantee that they would be well protected, and that the government would underwrite all expenses – because this, after all, was a political affair ('For health and relaxation,' she wrote, 'no one would go to Ireland') – she gave her grudging consent.

The visit was a great success.

The Irish gave the appearance of being pleased that the Queen had sent her eldest son to see them. The Princess, in some discomfort as she was carrying her fourth child, was nevertheless glad to have Bertie to herself away from the distractions of London. She found the Irish people very agreeable and the soft, water-colour tints in the landscape quite enchanting. The Prince who adored collecting Orders was pleased with his K.P., and was given an uproarious reception at the Punchestown races. Mr Disraeli, breathing deeply with relief when the return journey was safely accomplished, enjoyed recommending the Viceroy for a dukedom.

The Queen enjoyed having temporary charge of her grandsons at Osborne except when little George Frederick Ernest Albert, usually so well behaved, showed resentment at being reproved for bad manners and shot under the tea-table to reappear stark naked. His Grandmamma was not in the least amused, but Mr Disraeli was when, later, she told him about it. The deep lines at the corners of his mouth were generally turned down no matter how much his eyes danced, but the account of Prince George's strange rebellion entirely altered his grave demeanour and his face was soon wreathed in smiles.

Mr Disraeli's sense of humour served him well. It certainly helped to lighten a great deal of government business.

Part of his inheritance from the former prime minister was a war in far-off Abyssinia, originally caused it appeared because the Emperor Theodore, King of Kings and Lion of Judah, was piqued at having had no reply to a letter sent to Queen Victoria. She was equally piqued when informed of this. She always answered letters. Lehzen her governess had been very strict about it. The fault must lie with the Foreign Office. Mr Disraeli discovered that it did. Excellent. It was something else for which she could blame that odious Whig, Lord Russell. All the same, the Emperor of Abyssinia was trounced for his impertinence and Disraeli put up the victorious English general for a peerage.

A less welcome inheritance from the Earl of Derby was the Irish crisis. The royal visit was a shrewd move but the Irish expected considerably larger concessions than a dukedom for the Viceroy and an expensive, seven-day show of interest by the reigning House of Saxe-Coburg-Gotha. The Liberal opposition, split and fractured since the resignation of Lord Russell, now glued itself together under the leadership of Mr Gladstone, and proposed to solve Irish affairs by disestablishing the Church of Ireland. Disraeli would have none of it, and declared it would exacerbate as much as soothe. But in the Commons he had a minority against the united force of liberalism.

To the Queen's chagrin only a few months after moving into Downing Street he was defeated at a division. To her utter dismay he arrived at Osborne with his resignation.

She refused to accept it.

He pointed out that constitutionally he had to offer his resignation and she ought to accept it.

She asked if there was no other way.

A compromise, and not a very good one, suggested itself. Disraeli returned to London and announced to the Commons that her Majesty had declined to accept his resignation and had given him authority to dissolve Parliament for a general election as soon as public business would permit.

The Liberals jeered. Their leaders tipped their hats forward. The back benchers shouted out that the whole thing was unconstitutional. Three nights of debate followed. They abounded in invective and recrimination.

Dizzy showed a calm front. He paid sufficient attention to his critics, but four-fifths of his concentration was devoted to a fresh royal *imbroglio* which threatened to upset everyone's summer. The Prince of Wales' squalid affair with the actress Hortense Schneider had come to the Queen's ears. She had begged him to forego the London season and spend a few weeks in the country with his wronged Princess. His refusal had been saucy.

Your absence from London makes it more necessary that we should do all we can for society, trade, and public matters.

The Prime Minister saw someone else's malice behind this dagger-thrust at the Queen's seclusion; nevertheless he was becoming increasingly disenchanted by the Prince of Wales. His silliness and vulgarity were trying. It would be better, perhaps, for the Queen's nerves if she had a good holiday right away from her son and everyone else. Somewhere new and exciting. Italy? France? Switzerland? The last, where there was promise of adventure with respectability, would probably be the most appropriate. He would recommend Switzerland. . . .

It was time to speak. Very slowly, as though he were a lizard waking after a lengthy bask in the sun, the Prime Minister rose to refute the charge of unconstitutional conduct and to demonstrate two points: that the sovereign had a right to choose her First Minister, and that she had chosen him. In his buttonhole, pale against the black cloth, was a single primrose, one from a box of spring flowers gathered in the Osborne woods and sent to him by the Queen.

Witty, epigrammatic, his imagery enamelled, his tongue golden, the Prime Minister sent his followers into noisy ecstasies of loyalty.

The roof of the Chamber rang with their hurrahs when he sat down again.

The members of the Opposition were equally noisy but far from complimentary. They disliked his studied mannerisms, the apparently negligent way in which he had publicly skinned the rabbit of their moral indignation, and only in the safety of numbers dared they bait him with their clamour. Alone or in small groups they felt more vulnerable to his tongue and few men could be more cutting. On hearing that Gladstone had repeated the jibe that he was a Hebrew mountebank, he had icily described the new Liberal leader as 'Oxford on the surface, but Liverpool below,' and once he had silenced those who disdained him as a Jew by saying snappily: 'My people had been princes in the cradle of civilization for a thousand years when your Berkeleys and your Mowbrays yet wore woad.' But such bites and stings were rarely given. Generally, as after his speech on this occasion, he displayed a maddening nonchalance. He studied the ceiling while his detractors raged, polished his eyeglass, and then suddenly used it, quizzing the opposite benches for characters to be drawn into a novel he was planning. It was to be a frothy, satiric piece. The hero Lothair would be rich and young and noble; the heroine, Corisande, gentle and beautiful – a personification of the Established Church. . . .

5

Karré, the Queen's courier, was sent to look out a suitable holiday place in adventurous but respectable Switzerland. He returned with sketches and photographs and notes and, from a small list, the Queen chose to take the Pension Wallace at Lucerne for several weeks from the end of July. It was to be squeezed between her summer and autumn visits to Balmoral and though, for a part of that period, Parliament would be sitting, Mr Disraeli's new Lord Chancellor very kindly agreed there could be no great constitutional objection to the sovereign being out of the country while her Lords and Commons legislated. The Foreign Secretary, Lord

Stanley, who was the Earl of Derby's heir, would go to Lucerne as Minister in Attendance.

This completed the government's arrangements. Those of the Household were more complex.

The Swiss visit was nothing like the Queen's holidays in Germany where she had always stayed with members of her family. It had to be decided whether she should travel informally just as the Prince of Wales, for all his extravagance, generally did, or in a far more elaborate, truly royal fashion. Possibly, had the Prince of Wales not been mentioned the Queen might have chosen to travel simply, but his suspicious way of travelling about *en garçon* thoroughly upset her. She would have nothing to do with such a habit. A compromise was effected. At least one hundred royal servants would accompany the Queen, and a large quantity of favourite pieces of furniture and pictures and horses would be sent in advance. But the Swiss were not to be told the English Court had taken over the Pension Wallace. The Queen would travel incognito, not this time as the Countess of Balmoral which might be identified, but as the Countess of Kent.

The Court was ruffled by this decision. Colonel Ponsonby, who was to go out to Lucerne as equerry, grumbled to his uncle, General Grey, that the incognito would double his troubles not halve them. Baby had not quite lost her *folie de grandeur*. Under no circumstances, she told Miss Bauer the German governess, would she consent to be Lady Beatrice Kent. 'So inconvenient,' sighed Lady Ely, who would have to conceal the fact she was a dowager marchioness and therefore of higher rank than the incognito Queen. 'I rather think,' Dizzy chuckled to Mary Anne, 'that, with a kilted Highlander on the box, our dear peeress might be identified.'

The Queen was of course identified, but as much by Brown's manner as by his clothing. He treated Switzerland as a subject colony of the British Empire and insisted that the Queen's wishes be met immediately. This did not endear him to the Swiss but the Queen was patient. He was, after all, from a small Scotch village and found the Swiss no more congenial than the Germans or the English. Certain prejudices could not hurriedly be put aside. She wrote indulgently in a letter about poor Brown's 'increasing *hatred* of being "abroad".'

Apart from occasional brushes between the Queen's Highland

Servant and the local natives, the holiday passed far more pleasantly than Colonel Ponsonby had dared to hope. Certainly the Queen was happy. He accompanied her to a monastery at Engelberg where, greatly daring, they pushed open the door and Victoria found herself for the first time at a Roman Catholic service. Prince Leopold's tutor, Mr D., was acting as her chaplain and, on her return to the Pension Wallace, the Queen thought it proper to tell him of her adventure. He did not appear to find it very shocking and said courteously that he was glad she had been so favourably impressed. But he was curious about her remark that the monks' singing was particularly fine – 'Very like the chanting of the Georges'. He confessed his puzzlement to Prince Leopold. What could the Queen have meant? Was she referring to church singing in the Georgian era? Or had she perhaps once heard her uncle, George the Fourth, singing at Court? They discovered the truth by discreet questioning. Anxious to underline her indubitable Protestantism, and feeling, in any case, rather 'Scotch in religion' at that time, the Queen had preferred to avoid the controversial word 'saint', but she had been referring, in fact, to the music at St George's in Windsor.

This was but one of the pleasures in a long and exciting holiday. There was work to do of course. Those dispatch boxes, she was sure, would pursue her to Australia should she ever decide to go so far; but the Foreign Secretary was there to help, and she had time for driving out and picnics, seeing glaciers, making a successful expedition to the Furka, collecting Alpine plants for pressing with Louise and Leopold and Beatrice, trying local foods, inspecting Swiss cattle, riding her pony Sultan to the top of the Rigi – higher than Ben Nevis itself, visiting the William Tell shrine and afterwards hearing Colonel Ponsonby explode the whole story as a myth, and writing to dear Mr Disraeli, whom she missed.

He wrote often: the same sort of engaging, serio-comic letters she so much valued. They covered every topic from grave affairs of state to featherdown gossip, from ecclesiastical appointments to the reception of a new minister sent by the United States. As the Foreign Secretary was at the Pension Wallace the Prime Minister himself had done the honours by inviting the American down to his country place in Berkshire, and found him simple, well-bred, genial and very English in feeling. His only blemish was the loss of an eye in a duel –

But, it is believed, he was only a second, and a peacemaker, which makes his fate the more distressing.

6

Mr Disraeli himself was Minister in Attendance at Balmoral that autumn and afterwards he returned with a heap of presents from the Queen, two albums of Scotch views, a box full of stiffly-posed family photographs, a full-length portrait of the Prince Consort, and a Scotch shawl for Mrs Disraeli. He also brought a recollection of five days' continuous rain.

Mary Anne exclaimed delightedly over the shawl and immediately began to cosset her dearest Dizzy. It was what she most enjoyed doing in all the world. And she did it supremely well. She happily admitted her ignorance of most intellectual pursuits, and claimed that she could never recall which came first, the Greeks or the Romans, but she was the perfect wife for Disraeli, cheerful, courageous, and adept at managing their houses, servants and gardens. Still, at the age of seventy-seven, her whole purpose in life was to spare him unnecessary anxieties and spoil him. Now she begged him to rest after his journey. Mr Corry, his secretary, had been persuaded to leave all business until the next morning. Dizzy was to sit comfortably by the fire and they would talk while a little late supper was being put together.

Disraeli smiled. Mary Anne's little late suppers were famous. After long night sittings in the House he would find her waiting up for him with champagne and a string of delicacies. What would there be tonight? – whitebait, perhaps, or snipe, or grilled oysters? At least he would be spared the scourge of Balmoral, deer pudding, every alternate day as a savoury.

When the supper arrived and was placed before him his smile broadened further. Suspecting that his palate might be jaded by the wholesome but repetitive simplicities of the Queen's table,

Mary Anne had ordered less rugged dishes. Amongst the silver and glass and napery before him he saw poached scallops in a piquant sauce, grilled quails stuffed with force-meat and foie gras, and one of his favourite supper dishes, lambs' kidneys wrapped in fat bacon, sprinkled with dry sherry and ground juniper berries and roasted inside large potatoes. Just in case her intuition had failed her, and he required more ordinary fare, there was a hot boiled ox tongue with Cumberland sauce.

'Dear Mary Anne,' breathed Dizzy fondly, and enjoyed his supper a great deal.

Afterwards he took candles and lighted her upstairs. There were coal fires in their dressing-rooms and, behind a fine-meshed guard of brass-work, a fire of pear and apple wood scented as well as warmed the bedroom.

'Luxury, luxury, luxury,' cried he. The Queen's fondness for healthy coldness and her positive attachment to draughts had made his stay in Scotland trying.

Mary Anne's maid undressed her mistress, but Disraeli sent his valet off to bed and endeavoured to settle the kidneys, quails, tongue and scallops by ten minutes with a pair of Indian clubs. As he exercised he called through the door of his dressing-room, telling Mary Anne how splendidly Canute-like the Queen had been about the atrocious Scotch weather. She had literally defied the rain, taking her daily drive in downpours and enjoying picnics, drinking John Begg whisky mixed with Lithia water instead of tea, and eating cakes sent in the weekly parcel from the Windsor confectionery kitchen, while wrapped in plaids and waterproofs and partially sheltered by a trap umbrella. Her stamina, he called out, was astounding. Lady Churchill had told him of a purgatorial expedition the autumn before when all but the Queen almost succumbed to exhaustion, damp, cold and discomfort. They had gone on a visit to a shooting lodge of the Duke of Richmond, setting off in a full gale and passing through wild country over terrible roads with hairpin bends. By tea-time the gale had dropped and they had to struggle through thick mist until this gave way to pelting rain. Finally, long after the appointed time, they reached their destination only to find the baggage animals had gone astray. Unable to change for dinner the Queen had cheerfully sat down to the meal in her damp riding habit, but she felt unable to go to bed without the necessary things for her *toilette* and, though tired out, had waited up for the luggage until after two in the morning.

'Our sovereign,' he called – his voice a little muffled by the nightshirt he was dragging over his head, – 'is a remarkable woman.'

He asked permission to enter and found that Mary Anne had dismissed her maid and was sitting on a long Jacobean stool before the fire. He went to sit beside her, sniffing the wood smoke appreciatively, and toasting his toes.

'She is such a delightful compound of romance and practical common sense,' he continued. 'Her imagination peoples the glens with Jacobites all perfectly dressed and with snow-white jabots – though I took it on myself to remark that the real thing was probably very dirty and evil-smelling and would be the first to drive her from Balmoral with their busket-hilted claymores – and, at the same time, Brown tells her the servants keep too long hours, so she plans to order that ladies must be out of the drawing-room by eleven and gentlemen out of the smoking room by midnight. You may imagine that the princes will object strongly, and so will the guests. No smoking after twelve! It is like school.'

'The dear Queen,' murmured Mary Anne, who had a very real feeling for Victoria. 'So sensible and sensitive.'

'Exactly, just so, precisely. And I find her contrariness intriguing. She is not in the least squeamish. The gralloching of a deer does not upset her, nor the kill at a hunt. But simultaneously she has a touching tenderness for domestic animals.' He chuckled. 'Already she has been at Gathorne Hardy about British cruelty to animals and he, poor man, kept at a constant stretch by those abominable Fenians, hasn't the least idea of how to reassure her.'

'I believe I could tell him,' murmured Mary Anne.

'Then do, please, my love. It would be the greatest help to us all.' He sighed. 'I regret more than I can say that very soon we shall be out of office and no longer able to serve so kind a friend and so splendid a sovereign.'

'Out?' repeated Mary Anne.

He nodded. 'Inevitably.'

'Oh!' she exclaimed. She had not realized.

'It is inevitable,' he repeated. 'There is no need for us to hire an haruspex to look for portents in the entrails of sacrifices. The signs are plain to the Carlton Club, and that is enough. We shall lose the election.' For a moment they were silent. Then he took her by the hand and continued: 'It means we can return to Grosvenor Gate and go down more frequently to Hughenden, and to celebrate this gift of freedom I shall now teach you the rudiments of what, in the mists and frosts of Scotland, they call a Highland Fling.'

There and then he did so; he holding up his nightshirt so that she could see the footwork, she in her nightgown quickly catching the rhythm and copying him. True, the only music was provided by Dizzy who wailed through his nose when the bobbing tassel of his nightcap permitted it, and Mary Anne was bothered because two false curls popped from beneath her cap, and no one could describe their heavy pacing through the steps as elegant, but they both enjoyed it. It was fun to dance together in their old age before a wood fire.

But then Mary Anne faltered. She recovered so quickly that only someone as discerning as her Dizzy would have noticed it, but he did notice it, and he noticed the look in her eye. Without any fuss their Highland Fling drew to a close and he helped Mary Anne to climb into her side of the large bed.

'Leave the bed curtains open, my love,' she suggested. 'The fire flickers so beautifully.'

'Of course.'

Dizzy went round to his side of the bed, and soon, like ancient wax dolls, they were laid side by side on the feather mattress.

Not often, but sometimes, they said their night prayers together. They did tonight, and then talked in a desultory way about the coming election.

Secretly, and she would never have admitted it to him, Mary Anne was relieved that they would be leaving Downing Street. The house at Grosvenor Gate was bigger and much more convenient, and she was thankful that she would no longer be the Prime Minister's wife. She could not manage things as before. It was spreading and hurting more. And the less she had to do the longer she hoped to conceal her illness from dear Dizzy because, if he knew, he would only worry and fret.

Dizzy, too, was relieved that he would soon be out of office. It meant that he would be deprived of the right to visit the Queen almost at will, but it was vital that Mary Anne should have less to worry her. For as long as he possibly could, he wanted to conceal from her that he knew all about her mortal sickness because, if she was aware of it, she would only worry and fret.

He took her hand and pressed it. She returned the pressure.

Happy Mr and Mrs Dizzy.

One of the very last pieces of business transacted by the Queen and Disraeli as her Prime Minister was the appointment of a new Archbishop of Canterbury. Their discussion was characteristic of both. The Queen said she wished for Bishop Tait of London because the Primate of All England was naturally brought into close personal contact with the sovereign and she happened to find him agreeable. Moreover, she wrote:

> *His health, which is not good, would be benefited by the change.*

Disraeli prevented himself, though only just, from remarking that the see and province of Canterbury was not a convalescent home. He simply demurred because he considered Bishop Tait an enthusiast and he had an eighteenth-century distaste for enthusiasm. He described it to the Queen as:

> *a quality which ought never to be possessed by an Archbishop of Canterbury or a Prime Minister of England.*

But eventually he was persuaded and gave his consent and, as a *pourboire*, offered a canonry to Mr Prothero of Whippingham.

Then the Carlton Club's prognostications proved correct. The country went to the polls, including this time a large number of new voters, and chose Gladstone and the spoiling of the Irish Church, rather than Disraeli and the *status quo*.

Sadly the Prime Minister went to Windsor to tender his resignation. He had made it clear to everyone that he did not intend to retire from public life and take a peerage, but he accepted one for Mary Anne. On 23 November, 1868, she became Viscountess Beaconsfield in her own right, accepting the honour as a royal tribute to her dear Dizzy. Then she and he went to Hughenden, to laze and potter and garden and read and walk by the lake where

Dizzy kept his powers of rhetoric flexible by making speeches to the pair of swans he had named Hero and Leander.

Neither for the first nor the last time in her life the Queen felt a martyr to the obnoxious constitutional system of her kingdom, but she concealed her feelings. Mr Disraeli was no spirit to be imprisoned by retirement. She was confident that one day he would return.

Accepting the inevitable she chose to send for Mr Gladstone. Though there were radicals at his coat tails she hoped he could be reasonable and unprovocative. He had shown great feeling when she was widowed, and he was, after all, the father of William Henry who had come to Osborne as a boy to keep Bertie company and who had endeared himself to everyone by his sombre liking for beetles, slugs, toads and what he called nasties.

General Grey was sent north to Cheshire to sound out Gladstone. There he was met at the station by Mrs Gladstone in a wagonette, and received by the Liberal leader in the semi-darkness of a library lighted by two candles and a flickering fire. Together they ironed out difficulties, and Mr Gladstone consented to form a ministry. Early the next morning he travelled by train with General Grey to Windsor.

7

Queen Victoria would never have permitted her close friends to influence her in the way Queen Anne was pushed and pulled about by her favourites, but it was understood at Court that the Marchioness of Ely's special province of interest was politics and affairs, and Lady Churchill's the ordinary day-to-day domestic social round. It was therefore to Lady Ely that the Queen turned for information on her new First Minister.

She herself already knew something of Mr Gladstone's kindness and rectitude from her own observation, but most of what she had heard about him had come from one of three sources; either from Mr Disraeli who, with all his virtues, could scarcely be impartial about a political rival; or from General Grey who thought it unwise to let his tongue wander freely; or from Lady Lyttelton, once her lady-in-waiting and superintendent of the Royal Nursery, who, though her very close friend, was Gladstone's sister-in-law and perhaps prejudiced a little in his favour.

Lady Ely was under no sort of restraint, and admitted that she did not altogether care for Mr Gladstone.

'Why ever not?' asked the Queen sharply.

'He is an enigma.'

In her most matter-of-fact voice Victoria remarked that all statesmen were enigmatic. 'Stockmar used to say it was their hall-mark.'

'Lord Melbourne?' teased Lady Ely.

'Come, Jane,' said the Queen briskly. 'I was devoted to him but I'll not pretend, nor allow you to do so, that dear Lord M. was a statesman. He paid far more attention to champagne and Cicero and to me than to his office.'

Lady Ely raised her eyebrows at this plain speaking. It invited her to be as plain about Gladstone. She said that though he had the appearance of being steady and solid and dependable, really he was nervy, a dreamy castle-builder, and extraordinarily impressionable. 'And a good many people,' she concluded, 'rather doubt his sincerity.'

The Queen shook her head in disagreement. 'No, Jane. I have a nose for humbug, and so far it has registered nothing to Mr Gladstone's disadvantage.'

'I hope,' murmured Lady Ely, 'that it never will. He has, of course, many advantages – a huge fortune, a happy family, a love of religion, wide scholarship, great powers as an orator; and yet...' she paused.

The Queen looked at her steadily. 'He does not ring true?' she suggested.

Lady Ely would not commit herself so far but she admitted that hearsay painted an odd picture of him. 'He is such a conglomeration. For all his dour, demure behaviour, he thinks more like an Italian than an Englishman and while he's proud of his nickname as "the People's William" he was still enormously pleased when one newspaper proposed him as a candidate for the throne of Greece. And what a mixture of pastimes! He diverts himself with declaiming Homer and felling trees.'

'He chops them down himself? With an axe?' The Queen was astonished.

'Indeed, yes.'

'Good gracious! Can you imagine Mr Disraeli felling trees?'

Lady Ely could not. She smiled. 'They say,' she said, 'that Mr Gladstone first met Mr Disraeli at Lord Chancellor Lyndhurst's dinner-table. They were served with roast swan and while Mr Disraeli rhapsodized about its white flesh and tenderness and the delectable truffle stuffing, Mr Gladstone merely remarked that geese did not grow so large in Cheshire.'

The Queen smiled. She also felt some dismay. She asked if Mr Gladstone could possibly have been serious?

Lady Ely said nothing was more certain. Gladstone was inclined to be over-earnest.

And, on reflection, the Queen felt obliged to agree. She recalled an occasion when the Prince Consort had shown his distaste for Burlingham House by suggesting the government make it into a barracks, and, far from appreciating the irony, Mr Gladstone had sent him a carefully reasoned argument, under three headings, pointing out why it was not a practical proposition.

'One can only hope,' she said to Lady Ely, 'that he will not be too ponderous as Prime Minister.'

Lady Ely echoed the sentiment. 'One can only hope,' she repeated.

After her useful conversation with Lady Ely, the Queen was prepared to give Mr Gladstone her confidence, but only within certain limits. And from the day he kissed hands as First Minister, he was prepared to respect her wishes and accept her directions, but, again, only within certain limits. Wisely he made not the slightest attempt to replace Dizzy in her esteem or confidence and, with an excellent sense of what, under the circumstances, was very fitting, he used dispatch boxes rather than private audiences as their chief means of communication. Furthermore, in less important matters, he did not trouble the Queen directly, but only through her Private Secretary. A two-way flow of memoranda between palace and ministry was the foundation of their relationship and, in it, each warily tested the other's strength and weakness.

From the beginning the Queen made it clear she was not going to suffer being bullied as she had been by the insufferable Earl

Russell. She was firm. Gladstone's cabinet list was barely completed before he received a terse note on the two royal yachts.

> *Both are (the one broken & the other wanting serious repairs) useless & the* Queen & Royal Family *without any large ship fit to take them* even across the Channel ! !

Then an old nuisance was resurrected when a rich subject offered to provide a royal residence in Ireland. It would not do, she said. And when asked to entertain the Egyptian Khedive at her own expense at Buckingham Palace she refused point blank. Could Princess Louise dine with Mrs Gladstone and their daughter Agnes? No, she replied, certainly not.

Gladstone was not vexed. He realized the Queen was simply exercising the few muscles of power left to the Crown, and on occasions he showed the same firmness as, for example, when asked to find a cathedral stall for Prince Leopold's tutor, Mr D., whom he considered far too young and lacking in parochial experience for such preferment.

In some matters, naturally, their strong wills clashed.

He did not like it when she refused to make one of the Rothschilds a peer. Her partiality for Dizzy showed she was not in the least anti-Semitic, but she had strong views about Orthodox Jews in the nominally Christian House of Lords. Because it was important to his party Gladstone pressed the point both personally and through the Foreign Minister, but she was adamant. Sixteen years had to pass before she consented to an Orthodox Jew being given a peerage.

Gladstone was more subtly persuasive in trying to draw her from her seclusion. For some little time past General Grey, with great delicacy of feeling, had been trying to persuade the Queen to undertake more public duties. He received neither thanks nor satisfaction for his pains, merely the cold rejoinder that Dr Jenner had given contrary advice.

Grey's sense of duty to the Crown was too strong to allow him to leave it at that. He wrote privately to the Prime Minister urging him to press the Queen to make more public appearances. In his opinion, he said, the Queen was really as strong as a horse despite her talk of shattered nerves and overwork and weakened health, and she was being molly-coddled by Jenner who ought to know better. If she did not go out more often, he foresaw a rise of republicanism and perhaps the end of the monarchy in England.

Gladstone received this advice with gravity. Intrigues bred easily in the hot-house atmosphere of royal courts but he had absolute faith in Grey's integrity and his devotion to the Crown. He was not the sort of man who would ever be motivated by petty spite. Nevertheless his appraisal of the situation seemed a little hard on the Queen. Gladstone being ten years older than she, and more highly strung than almost any of her ministers, had a certain understanding of her problems. He told Grey that he himself could appreciate the Queen's weariness and shrinking of mind caused by the strain of constant, unremitting work, but he agreed that Jenner was not helpful. He agreed to try to persuade the Queen to accept more public duties but he was not sanguine of success.

The Queen was at Balmoral, enjoying a sunless but warm morning, when she received from the Prime Minister a request from the Lord Mayor of London that she open a new bridge at Blackfriars. Unwittingly he incensed her by calling it off-handedly 'a minor subject' and saying that her consent and appearance 'would give great public satisfaction'.

Although it was approved by Dr Jenner – who now had a knighthood for his loyalty – the Queen had a sore conscience about her continued isolation from the public. Naturally unaware of the Prime Minister's sympathetic appreciation of her difficulties, and already tense because of General Grey's continued insistence that she appear more often in the public's eye, this application to open a bridge touched her on a nerve. Dear Mr Disraeli had supported her when people carped at her seclusion. He had been consoling and had sent her off for a rest and a change in Switzerland. But Mr Gladstone lacked his tender heart. He wished to prise her from the shell which had grown about her since Albert's death, and display her.

In a short letter to the Prime Minister, in which her nervousness showed by the large use of abbreviations, underlinings and the use of dashes, she firmly refused.

It was unfortunate for both of them that, once committed to a course of action which he thought important, Gladstone was as unstoppable as a shell from a gun.

He instantly made a second, more insistent application.

This was the beginning of the Blackfriars Bridge affair which haunted them both for five months. Outwardly he remained exquisitely polite. Inwardly he deplored her obstinacy and self-centredness. She never troubled to conceal her irascibility.

The second appeal on a subject which she considered closed made the Queen exceedingly testy. No, she repeated, it was quite out of the question. Gladstone sent a four-line acknowledgement and said he would communicate her implacable determination to the Lord Mayor. Its brevity and coldness made her uneasy. It almost seemed as if her own Prime Minister was refusing to accept any sort of responsibility for her decision. In effect he was saying, on her own head be it. But, unbelievably, within a fortnight he sent a third appeal.

> *The Queen* [she wrote from Windsor] *is much surprised at being* again *teazed and tormented about this Bridge . . .*

and she repeated her insistence that under no circumstances would she open it in summer time. But his persistence was wearing her down. She might, she said – without promising anything, of course – drive to *see* the bridge in the autumn when it was cooler. . . .

In the end, to her perplexity and great displeasure, she found herself committed to open it in November.

Two days before the event she sent a last flutter of apprehension through those who had arranged the ceremony by talking of racking headaches and the cold and saying dolefully she hoped nothing would prevent her from being at the opening. But when the day arrived she did her duty and, to Gladstone's amazement, she confessed she was touched by the enthusiasm of the crowds who welcomed her to Blackfriars. She even approved of a baronetcy being conferred on the Lord Mayor, but added a clear warning that this particular exercise of her public duty would have to satisfy her subjects for a long, long time. She was not prepared to be prised again from her daily routine.

Apart from this acrimonious affair of Blackfriars Bridge in 1869, sovereign and prime minister got on tolerably well together. He adapted himself to be patient with her occasional inflexibility and her ostrich-like refusal to face unpalatable facts. She did her best with the formidable memoranda he sent her, though, alone of her prime ministers, he never seemed to appreciate her liking for straightforwardness, simplicity, and brevity. Even when, still worrying like a terrier at the disestablishment of the Church of Ireland, he sent her a draft bill of vast length and complexity accompanied by a so-called helpful explanation of almost equal length and quite as bewildering, she refused to despair and worked at it with a dogged persistence which Lady Ely thought admirable, Lady Churchill thought extraordinary, and Brown considered daft.

In the main Victoria and Gladstone were on good terms and were very much in accord on most matters from the regulations governing the style and size of beards in the Royal Navy and the removal from office by Act of Parliament of a seditious Mayor of Cork, to the odiousness of 'the so called and most erroneous "Right of Woman" ', and the absolute propriety of Gladstone nominating his elder son for a junior Lordship of the Treasury.

The Queen insisted that it was not only proper but highly desirable for William Henry to be given an appointment. As his father's son he ought to have an instinct and capacity for public service. Secretly it enchanted her that those whom she still thought of as children had suddenly matured and become trusted servants of the Crown. To her the new junior Lord of the Treasury would always be the small boy she had smacked for naughtiness at Osborne as though he had been her own child. And in the same government department was Lord Claud Hamilton whom she recalled as a small boy defiantly refusing to bow to her and Albert at Ardverikie. Instead he had stood on his head and demonstrated that he wore nothing under his kilt. At the time she had been mildly shocked – especially when, though reproved, he repeated the performance. Now she was much amused at the recollection though, to save Lord Claud embarrassment, she pretended to have forgotten the incident.

In his first year of office Gladstone's admiration for the Queen grew larger. Her respect for him also grew. He alarmed her by his presence when, as she privately complained, nervousness made him throw back his leonine head and address her as though she were a public meeting, but she did not hesitate to tell him her private problems. Then his manner softened and he became almost as warm and as sympathetic as Mr Disraeli. When Leopold had haemorrhage after haemorrhage at Osborne and nearly died, he troubled her with the extreme minimum of public business and was entirely sincere in his offer to do anything he could to help. When Vicky and Louise showed an interest in the hateful subject of female emancipation and the younger went to the lengths of writing to the champion of women's rights in England, only Gladstone appeared to understand her depth of revulsion and because of this she felt herself able to accept his advice not to give the matter any sort of importance by saying or doing anything at all. Then, when a pamphlet appeared in the streets entitled *What Does She Do With It?*, and she found that she was the target of an extremely offensive attack which said she was over-rich, over-paid, and over-mean, Gladstone did his utmost to squash the publication and correct publicly the gross errors it contained. And on the frequent occasions when the Prince of Wales worried her, Gladstone never failed as a source of consolation and sound counsel.

8

For the first few months of Gladstone's ministry the Prince and Princess of Wales were out of the country on a lengthy tour of the Near East. But, though far away, they still caused the Queen ample anxiety. She was not at all pleased when Vicky wrote to say they had caused a family squabble in Prussia on their way out, and very angry when she discovered that some of Bertie's less reputable acquaintances were to join the party in Egypt. She wrote to protest. He countered by impertinently suggesting that she should go to London more often. Her reply to this, he told his Private Secretary, was a 'corker', but, quite unrepentant, he wrote a second time to say they lived in radical times and the more people saw the sovereign the better.

It was unwise to defy and torment her. Inevitably it aggravated her censoriousness. She heard of him and his suite sailing up the Nile in six steamers of blue and gold, and that amongst the necessary luggage towed astern in lighters were three thousand bottles of champagne, four thousand of claret, lobsters in tanks, and closed crates of live quails. All this to the Queen was ostentation, horrid opulence, vulgar. She wrote to warn him against extravagances and especially on the way home through Paris, pointing out that there was a very strong feeling in the country against the luxuriousness and frivolousness of society. He told her not to worry, paid not the slightest attention to her warning, and arrived back in England with a brick-red face, crates of souvenirs and an Egyptian orphan to pour out his coffee, and stories of his and Alix's adventures, disguised as Mr and Mrs Williams, in the bazaars of Constantinople.

'Williams!' repeated the Queen in considerable disgust. It was not the sort of sobriquet she would have chosen herself.

No sooner was the Prince home again than he quarrelled with the committee of White's, simply because he could not have his own way about the smoking regulations, and he went off to found a less restrictive club elsewhere. Then he neglected Alix at the time she was having her fifth baby, though this no longer surprised anyone. Worst of all came a scandalous story from the Norfolk coast. Sandringham was being rebuilt on a larger scale and, for the time being, the Prince had hired a house near by. There he gave a ball for his cronies and their ladies and the Queen was shocked to hear it publicly reported that her heir had personally carried a drunken guest to bed and laid a dead seagull on the pillow beside him. Practical jokes were all very well but there were things a Prince of Wales could not do under any circumstances. She protested vigorously, and Gladstone said he hoped his radical followers would not make capital out of it. They shook their heads together over the Prince's wildness, but when he found himself in serious trouble they instantly combined to support him.

On a February day the Queen received a letter from her son. In it he told her frankly that one of his acquaintances, Sir Charles Mordaunt, was filing a petition for divorce from his highly-strung twenty-one-year-old wife and citing two of his closest friends as co-respondents. He himself had written her a number of trifling letters and had been subpoenaed as a witness in the case.

By now Victoria was resigned to her son's gallantries. The example of her uncles and her own father, the living example of her cousin George of Cambridge whose three bastards were causing him great trouble by falling deeply into debt, had obliged her to accept that philandering was as much a characteristic of the House of Hanover as the famous nose was of the Hapsburgs. She knew all Bertie's women by name – from Nellie Clifden to Hortense Schneider – and she was sure that Lady Mordaunt had never been his mistress and that his letters were innocuous. Nevertheless, read by a clever and unscrupulous lawyer in open court they could be made to sound damaging, and there was always the risk of Bertie being asked awkward questions. She at once telegraphed a reply to show her confidence in him – and wrote a letter which contained no reproval but merely asked him to be more circumspect in future. He was so surprised and touched that he burst into tears.

Mr Gladstone reassured the Queen by the sincerity of his conviction that truth must prevail. Still more reassuring was the Lord Chancellor who, having studied the letters and the case documents, declared the Prince's innocence was perfectly obvious and that as Lady Mordaunt had just been removed to a private mental home her husband's petition must fail. Most reassuring of all was the Prince's Private Secretary who said he had reason to know that the judge would not allow any improper questions to be put by the Mordaunt counsel. Still, her protectiveness was aroused by Bertie's pitiful panic as he waited a fortnight on tenterhooks for the case to be heard, and, recalling Lord M. and Lord Palmerston once cheerfully deciding to bribe or intimidate an obstreperous newspaper reporter in Windsor, she rather regretted that those useful if corrupt practices were now regarded as reprehensible.

When the day came she waited with some trepidation for news. It was telegraphed through in cypher. The Prince of Wales had suffered seven minutes' examination and had behaved perfectly. He denied committing adultery, and no cross-examination followed. Sir Charles Mordaunt's petition failed.

Later she asked both Mr Gladstone and the Lord Chancellor to write serious letters to her son and remind him of his position and responsibilities. And she herself spoke to him. She referred to the proverbs of smoke and fire and touching pitch, and she passed on Mr Disraeli's caveat that, once roused, the non-conformist conscience of the British middle and lower classes was a very terrible thing and capable of the most hideous folly.

It was a sensible warning which he remembered as he and Alix were booed and hissed as they drove through the streets of London, though his temper was badly frayed when there was an ugly scene in a theatre between hired cheer leaders in the gods and self-righteous citizens in the stalls as he and his party entered the royal box. Gradually the moral indignation dissipated itself, and at Royal Ascot, four months after the court hearing, he re-established his popularity in a characteristic way. He was hissed as he drove up the course before the races but, such is the fickle way of crowds, when a horse in which he had an interest won, they crowded round the stand to cheer him. He lighted a cigar, raised his hat to them, and shouted distinctly above the uproar: 'You seem to be in a better temper now than you were this morning, damn you!'

At the very same time on the same day his mother the Queen was supervising the clipping of her sheep at Balmoral.

9

Albert's death on that black Saturday had so broken down Victoria she had believed herself incapable of recovery, and her sorrow irreparable. Yet time did not mend so much as entirely renew. She was like a tree crushed and cut back by the shock of her loss. Thereafter she was a different person, growing shoots of nervous strength which grew larger and more serviceable as the years passed. Although it never lost its interest, death for her had truly lost its sting. But in 1870 three of her old friends and servants died, and they had been so intimately bound up in her past and in Albert's that their passing was like the ending of an era.

The first was her Private Secretary, General Grey, struck down by a seizure. Victoria had the news of his stroke at Claremont (always 'unhappy Claremont') and felt his death so keenly that she went up to London to see him on his deathbed in St James' Palace. She trembled violently to see him lying there, his bed covered with lilies of the valley, and grieved because she would never look on his face again. Her one consolation was that he had already spoken to her about his nephew Colonel Ponsonby being one day his successor. It gave her some relief to be able to appoint him without delay – and this time the office of Private Secretary was at last formally recognized and gazetted. There was a grumble of warning from her cousin George of Cambridge that the colonel and his wife were pinky radicals, but she knew that she would trust the dear General's recommendation. Through Dean Wellesley a hint was sent to the Ponsonbys that they should be politically discreet, and not once did the Queen have cause to regret making the appointment.

The second death was of Sir James Clark, the royal physician who had helped her through all her childhood ailments, all her confinements, and all her children's ailments, and – despite the fact that he had officially retired – he had done all that he could for her mother and for Albert in their last illnesses. The ordinarily close relationship between a physician and his patient had been made even closer by his understanding of her nervous troubles and his talent for mixing deference for an august patient with stern rebukes to a self-willed woman. Though he had selected Jenner to look after her she never felt he was quite as honest. The candid Victoria, who could turn a cold, appraising eye upon herself, realized that Jenner tended to agree with her too much. Clark had not. And how long he had practised. It was almost fifty years since he had attended the dying Keats in Rome.

One day, not long after his death, her Maid of Honour in Waiting was reading aloud from a daily newspaper and there was reference to the northern districts of London. At once her eyes filled with tears and she gave the little sign which told the girl to stop reading. The northern districts of London. . . . The words had made her think of Sir James, a tenuous connecting link which brought from the well-bottom of her memory a picture of him standing there talking to her faithful governess Lehzen. It had been years and years before when she was recovering from typhoid. Not only had she felt weak and depressed but she was also terribly ashamed because she was hollow-eyed, her skin blotchy and unhealthy, and her hair in ugly tufts as they had shaved her head to reduce the fever. Dr Clark had promised her troubles would be over quite soon and she would be herself again – just so long as she did as she was told. She could remember his orders now as Lehzen wrote them down : no singing after meals, exercises with Indian clubs, a standing desk to write at, extra bread and butter, and regular drives to the north of London. She had never understood why the north was so salubrious but he had insisted and every day the carriage had gone from Kensington and they had driven in all weathers through Finchley, Hampstead and Harrow. Poor, dear, kind Sir James. . . .

That same faithful governess, Lehzen, was the third to die in far-off Bückenburg. She had spent the latter part of her life dreaming of the past and putting out of her mind the unpleasant parts – that quarrels with Prince Albert had made it necessary for her to leave England, and that her beloved Victoria had sometimes neglected her in her exile. Now, at the advanced age of eighty-six, she died in a room full of royal portraits and mementoes.

No one in the world had been closer to Victoria until her marriage, and, reminded of Lehzen's self-sacrifice and devotion, she felt ashamed that she had tended to forget her. She told herself it was necessary, of course, to shed certain people as one grew older, and being out of sight had naturally put Lehzen out of mind, but some of her distress when she heard the news was because she felt she had let her old friend down.

10

The second July issue of the *Illustrated London News* in 1870 had as its frontispiece a picture of the Queen giving out prizes in Windsor Park, a peaceful bucolic scene which charmed the subscribers.

No one could have guessed that beneath a serene, smiling exterior, the Queen felt anything but tranquil. She was depressed and not far from tears, and after the ceremony drove back to the Castle where she fanned herself and drank cooled Seltzer water and went through her dispatch boxes looking for a ray of hope although she knew it was futile.

It was hot, trying weather. Already the farmers were praying for rain. Across the Channel there was talk of war. Those French Chasseurs and Zouaves and Algerian Spahis who had made the crowds clap with pleasure at the Paris Exhibition three years before would soon be rattling down the dusty roads of the Rhineland; and, though the Germans might bring into action their terrible steel cannon which fired shells the weight of six Life Guards, she was assured by Vicky that the Fatherland was in no state to go to war. Wretched Bismarck. It was because of him that

Albert's policy for a philosophical, artistic and pacific Germany lay in ruins. Albert had wanted Prussia to use her strength and resources to make a great Germany. Chancellor Bismarck preferred the contrary and used Germany's resources for the glorification of Prussia and the Hohenzollern family. This was bad enough, but far worse was his responsibility for Germany's unpreparedness. The Fatherland actually lay in peril.

In the days which followed, the Queen was beset by anxieties.

For the flimsiest of reasons the French Emperor went to war. Immediately the frivolous Victoria who had once been excited by the gaiety and sophistication of Paris gave place to the serious Victoria who recalled the Prince Consort's condemnation of the French as 'a vainglorious and immoral nation'. She was, of course, sorry for the Empress Eugénie because she had suffered so much from her husband's libidinous conduct, but otherwise she spared no sympathy for the Second Empire. The two words 'corrupt' and 'decadent' were often on her lips.

She was cross, too, with the Pope who chose to declare himself infallible and invite trouble at the very time the French garrison who protected his temporal power was called away to fight the Germans. Unless he was careful the Italian Government would move in and seize his territories, and though Victoria did not at all approve of a spiritual overlordship the Pope was a fellow sovereign. His overthrow, for that reason, was very much to be deprecated.

The Queen's children were also being vexing, quarrelling amongst themselves about the war. Bertie, who adored the lights, rich sauces and cocottes of Paris, and Alix, who never forgot her Danish origin, were outspokenly anti-German. This distressed Vicky and Alice, both of whom raised hospitals to look after the German wounded, and it even made the normally easy-going Prince Christian fret to leave his doves and roses in Windsor Park and fight for the Fatherland. So bitter was the contention that to settle it Victoria used her authority as Queen rather than as a mother. She sent the complaining letters to Mr Gladstone with a request that he speak to the Prince of Wales. The Prime Minister behaved perfectly. He explained to the Prince that England was committed to a policy of tight-roping between the two belligerents and it was essential for all members of the royal family to conceal their private sentiments. Thereafter the Queen was relieved to note that Bertie held his tongue in public even when, entirely contrary to expectations, Germany not France won battle after battle. She herself, though secretly overjoyed, maintained the same disciplined silence as the campaign brought victory to the Fatherland. Barely six weeks after the beginning of the war the French army surrendered at Sedan and the Emperor was taken as a prisoner to Germany.

Victoria was at Balmoral on her second visit that year when she heard the news and received a triumphant letter from Vicky:

> *Such a downfall is a melancholy thing, but it is meant to teach deep lessons! May we all learn what frivolity, conceit and immorality lead to!*

A trifle priggish, thought the Queen, nevertheless it would not be a bad thing if Bertie, who was roistering over the hill at Abergeldie, learnt this sort of lesson.

Dr Macleod, the Queen's Scotch chaplain, appeared to agree that the Prussian victory was divine retribution for the wickedness of Paris and the Emperor of the French. On the following Sunday he preached a thrilling sermon on a text from Isaiah:

> *Woe to the crown of pride, the drunkards of Ephraim*
> *Whose glorious beauty is a fading flower.*

On the whole the Queen was satisfied. Germany the non-aggressor had triumphed. But she did not altogether care for the fact that the ungrateful French had promptly deposed the Emperor and put Paris in a state of siege, nor that the Empress Eugénie had had to fly for safety, being smuggled out of Paris by an American dentist, racing for the coast in heavy disguise, and then begging a passage from a yachting baronet who happened to be moored at Trouville. She wrote to comfort the Empress and begged the King of Prussia to be merciful as a conqueror.

Still silent publicly, but less partisan than before, she quietly watched events.

The overthrow of established order always alarmed her, and as if to underline her conviction that deposing was a highly infective political disease, came the news she had expected from Rome. The Italian government had seized the Papal Territories. Another sovereign had lost power.

More disquieting news came from the continent. While the Parisians were so feeling the pinch of hunger that only the very rich and fortunate could enjoy a salmi of rats or a grilled slice of spaniel or joints of elephant from the Jardin d'Acclimatation, the Iron Chancellor Bismarck was breakfasting in his elegant rooms at Versailles off three hard-boiled eggs and regretting he could no longer manage the eleven eggs of former days, and dining substantially on special rations and the gifts of admirers – a huge trout pasty, Varzin wild boar with a compote of raspberry jelly and mustard, Reinfeld ham, geese stuffed with olives, roast oysters, turtles, and gamebirds seethed with sauerkraut in champagne. Soothed by gluttony he was proposing that Paris should be bombarded into submission, a suggestion which, Victoria was glad to note, her son-in-law Fritz hotly opposed.

Unfortunately Bismarck was supported by the King of Prussia and Victoria was shocked. For the first time she felt antipathetic to Vicky's father-in-law and saw him in a different light. His quaint habits of making do without a bathroom in any of his palaces, and marking the level of the wine at the end of a meal, which once she had found eccentric and amusing, she now described as unpleasing – worse, unroyal. And she was reduced to thoughtful silence when she heard that he had submitted to Bismarck's persuasions and had proclaimed himself Emperor of Germany.

Victoria disapproved. What, she wondered, would Albert have said to a King of Prussia being Emperor of Germany?

Gladstone also disapproved. It was the result, he told her, of the Chancellor's policy of 'blood and iron'.

The phrase alarmed the Queen and mystified her, but the Prime Minister's explanation was neither short nor simple. For elucidation she turned to Mr Disraeli.

Nowadays she paid no attention to the constitutional rule which prevented retired prime ministers from giving her the benefit of their wisdom. She believed it was ludicrous that the statesman and chief councillor of today might, at the whim of a voting public, be tomorrow the one person in her kingdom prohibited from giving her advice. And so, without offending the Prime Minister's susceptibilities, she had kept discreetly in touch with Mr Disraeli. What he told her now made her thankful she had done so. It appeared that far from being the innocent party the Prussians had stealthily provoked the war, and it was all Bismarck's doing. The Chancellor, said Mr Disraeli, had an ogre's appetite for power. Not content with snapping up the spoils of wars with Denmark and Austria he had deliberately schemed to crunch the bones of France. And, as Mr Disraeli explained how he had done it, Victoria was appalled by his subtle, diabolical planning.

'Machiavellian,' she exclaimed now that the scales had fallen from her eyes.

The word 'Bismarckian', Mr Disraeli prophesied, would one day carry a far more sinister meaning.

It seemed as if he was proved right almost immediately. Bismarck had his way. Paris was subjected to a month's bombardment and the French were driven to surrender. Bismarck then demanded outrageous compensation; rich tracts of territory and five milliards of francs, and he humiliated the French by ordering that German troops should march as conquerors through the capital.

Still the Queen kept silent in public.

Vicky wrote a restrained letter to deplore the animosity growing between England and Germany. Unstated but implicit was what her mother already knew: that Fritz and his humane and cultured followers had been outspoken against the harsh terms, but, being in a minority, they were powerless. Vicky ended on a cheerful note:

Count Bismarck is not eternal.

Victoria hoped not. Secretly she warmed towards the citizens of Paris and was proud of the way her own people had responded to their appeal for help. The Ministry had requisitioned Royal Navy ships loaded with Army stores and sent them straight to France. The Lord Mayor had started a Relief Fund and had been inundated with contributions. It was gratifying to know that the bombed and hungry Parisians were at last being fed.

Then, abruptly, her feelings altered. A mob of radicals and socialists seized Paris from within and initiated a new Terror in the name of the International. Victoria dreaded the contaminating influence of Communism and she had the greatest difficulty in concealing her agitation as the French looted and pillaged each other in their own chief city, firing and destroying works of art, lynching and shooting and seizing innocent hostages and making mass arrests on barely any suspicion. When she was able to master her fears she took every opportunity to show her disgust for the Commune. She received the former French Emperor Louis-Napoleon at Windsor, giving him full royal honours, and was pleased to agree to his proposal of residing at Chislehurst in Kent. While the riff-raff of Paris pursued what she considered their blood-thirsty, idiotic policies, she pretended to show some sort of confidence in the reliability and common sense of the English proletariat. She drove through the streets of London to open the huge hall built as a memorial to Albert. And though she was frightened when the Home Secretary told her there was to be a republican demonstration in sympathy with the Communists in Hyde Park, and enormously relieved when it turned out to be a fiasco, she showed a bold and scornful face throughout.

Eventually the forces of the French Government put down the disorders, but not before the Communists, in an excess of rage and spite and despair, had fired a whole section of the city, and gutted many irreplaceable public buildings, and shot out of hand a large number of defenceless hostages, amongst them the Archbishop of Paris.

11

At the heart of the Court they could see how the violent disruption of order fretted their royal mistress, and the Queen's three closest friends were not idle in trying to help her.

Their methods were different.

Lady Ely attempted to leach some of the terror out of the war and the Paris revolution by speaking of them as sensibly and as unemotionally as a good staff officer.

John Brown considered that the steady application of routine at home would dull any shock from abroad, and he kept the Queen to an even more exacting daily routine.

Both methods were helpful, but Lady Churchill's was perhaps

the greatest success. Whenever bad news arrived she allowed the Queen just sufficient time to take it in and react to it and then she distracted her with the commonplace and the ordinary, and most of all with talk of her growing family. Dwelling on her children was rarely soothing to the Queen, but it stimulated her thoughts away from France and Germany.

Her boys were the source of much anxiety as well as joy. It took all her considerable powers of detachment to look at her youngest son and realize that he was unlikely to live even half a man's span. Leopold was far too delicate to leave her and be attached to one of the professions of arms, but she had it in mind to give him a feeling of usefulness by employing him one day as an additional secretary – with a key of his own to the dispatch boxes – so that he could help her, as Albert had done, with government business. Arthur was turning out to be the most dependable of them all, a pattern of his dear father and without a trace of the roistering habits of the Hanoverians. He had a capacity and liking for soldiering and when he officially represented her he did it with dignity and aplomb, even when once received with studied rudeness by an American president. Already she had formed a plan that when George Cambridge retired Arthur would make a first-rate Commander-in-Chief. Alfred was still single and far too conspicuous in sowing his wild oats, and Bertie as ever was going his wilful way.

Girls were an even greater problem.

In the Queen's opinion the Helena–Christian experiment had been a failure and she was not pleased when Jane Churchill suavely disagreed.

'On the contrary, Ma'am, they appear to be reasonably happy.'

'I meant,' said the Queen, 'that so far as *I* am concerned the marriage has been a failure. They are no company at all. Living down in Windsor Park they might as well be in Putney or, for that matter, Pekin. And marriage has changed them. Helena drives me distracted with her trivialities, her committees and charities, her bazaars and sales of work; and Prince Christian drives me distracted by lolling about. He is a horrible loller and does little except eat and eat and eat, and shoot pheasants.' She smoothed the lap of her gown. 'I planned that they should be a comfort to me and they have failed me utterly.'

Lady Churchill pursed her lips. She was too good a friend to let this pass. Neither the words 'selfish' nor 'self-centred' were used.

No one, not even she, could use them to the Victoria of England. But they had polite synonyms. And these she did use.

As a result the Queen went into an angry sulk and barely spoke to her friends for days. But not even this prevented Lady Churchill from bravely repeating the hateful synonyms when the Queen remarked that she did not care to hear people talking about marriage in front of Baby. Baby, remarked Jane Churchill, was a baby no longer, and just about to leave the schoolroom, and, sugaring the pill as well as she could, she pointed out that it was wrong for a not unattractive and gay little princess to be offered as an ignorant sacrifice on the altar of her mother's personal convenience.

This time she earned herself a whole week's Coventry during which Victoria communicated with her in pert notes written in the third person.

Eventually the Queen broke her silence. Why, she asked, should she *not* ask this simple sacrifice from a daughter? She was alone, a widow, isolated on her throne, and needed the companionship of a close relative. The question was, in fact, rhetorical. She knew that Lady Churchill would not change her mind, but she insisted on the last word. By unspoken but mutual consent the subject was not discussed between the two friends again.

Happily the Queen had a different view about being parted from Princess Louise who, besides being the prettiest and cleverest, was also the most prickly and least congenial of all her daughters. It was not easy to live comfortably with Louise and therefore it was as well that temperamentally she was no stay-at-home. But her future presented some problems because she was determined to achieve independence through marriage.

Victoria had often worried that marriage might be out of the question. Only a very few were aware that her daughter had a physical handicap which made it almost certain she would never have children. The Queen took confidential advice on the problem. Dean Wellesley assured her that as, presumably, the Princess could consummate a marriage, it would be theologically and legally valid. Jane Churchill assured her that socially it was also valid. It was unthinkable, she said, that the girl should be barred from marriage simply because of the likelihood that she would not have children.

Still not entirely persuaded, the Queen then found herself facing another difficulty. Louise declared that she had lost her heart to the Duke of Argyll's heir and was set on marrying him. Victoria was a shrewd judge and noticed that Louise had not changed as young girls do change when they are in love. Probably, then, she was really motivated by a desire to escape from the restrictions of a single life at Court and found young Lord Lorne a not unattractive key to liberty.

Victoria herself liked Lorne. He was another of those whom she recalled as a child and who had suddenly grown up to occupy a position of importance. She looked out her old journals and was amused to find a reference to him as far back as 1847. On her first visit to Inverary she had described him as 'just two years old, a dear, white, fat, fair little fellow with reddish hair'. She also remembered him as a boy at Eton who had occasionally come to play with Bertie at the Castle. No one could take exception to him as a man. He was good-looking, talented, cultivated, rich and heir to the chieftainship of the Clan Campbell. But she guessed that Bertie would object.

He did, and vociferously, because Lorne was a subject.

Aided by Jane Churchill the Queen soon had a host of good reasons why it would not be a misalliance for Louise to marry a Duke's son. The most persuasive were that the Plantagenet and Tudor dynasties had married subjects, that Parliament would appreciate the voted dowry and pension being spent in the country for a change, and that the alternative, a German minor royalty, was not specially attractive now that Prussia had gobbled up most of their revenues.

Eventually the Prince of Wales gave his grudging consent to the engagement. Yet he was made exceedingly angry by a story circulating in the Highlands. Someone had congratulated a Campbell on the clan's great matrimonial coup and had received, for his pains, the frosty, arrogant rejoinder that it was the Queen who ought to be congratulated for having a daughter fit to marry the son of MacCailean Mor.

On hearing this the Prince's lively sense of humour entirely failed him. Ordinarily, perhaps, he could have seen it as a joke, but this touched his dignity. He was furious, and he stormed to his mother about insufferable impudence, and how galling it was that his sister, a Princess of the Blood, should be allied to such a haughty, saucy lot. She managed to calm him, but it was not easy, and she herself shared some of his indignation. For the very first time she found herself exasperated by the pretensions of the Scotch, and when Brown repeated the same story, and showed by his manner that he thought it rather clever, he afterwards wished that he hadn't.

Small touches continued to vex the Queen right up to the day of Louise's marriage. Her own superb wedding present of emeralds and diamonds was matched just a little too closely by the Argylls' gift of sapphires and pearls. Then Dean Wellesley rather oddly permitted trumpets and organ to play 'The Campbells are Coming' when the bridegroom entered St George's Chapel. And Mr Ponder, her chief confectioner, had been too ebullient altogether in his design for the wedding cake. It was the largest she had ever seen, standing five feet high and having taken three months to build, and was lavishly decorated with roses, thistles, doves and Corinthian columns, and figures representing the four seasons, and the arts, sciences, industry and agriculture.

Jane Churchill, already agreeably surprised by the change in the Queen, was further startled by her comments on the cake. *Much* too grand for a small affair like this. Much too grand. And then, peering at it closely, the Queen observed that it looked rather like the Albert Hall done over in whitewash. It was the first intimation her closest friend had had that the vast structure built to commemorate the Prince Consort was not exactly to her liking.

Not long after the wedding the Princess of Wales had her sixth child who, to the Queen's strong disapproval, was given the unlucky royal name of John. He survived only twenty-four hours. All Alix's children – and this was to be the last – were born prematurely and therefore exposed to extra risk, but she had been unusually careless and the Queen believed Bertie should have looked after her better. Dean Wellesley was deputed to censure him for encouraging his wife to neglect her health.

A certain sense of guilt and pique at his mother's interference made Bertie retaliate by writing to her:

> *I think it is one's duty not to nurse one's sorrow. . . . I shall also be glad when Alix resumes her social duties (with, of course, due care for her health). . . . Besides our social duties, which are indeed very numerous in the Season, we have also many to do as your representatives.*

This sniping at her secluded life provoked the Queen enormously. And why should they not represent her, she asked Jane Churchill? It was the least they could do.

She roughed out a bitter reply and would have made a fair copy and sent it had her friend not persuaded her to wait. It was good advice and she was particularly glad she had taken it when it became clear that her elder daughters shared Bertie's view about her seclusion. She noticed hints in their letters; broad ones from the unsubtle Vicky, finer ones from Alice, that she should get out more into the public eye.

Guessing at a conspiracy, the Queen scotched it in her inimitable way by ignoring it altogether. She was impervious to hints, polite proposals and outright appeals, invariably changing the subject.

Alice promised to come over and be with her at Balmoral that autumn and suggested that perhaps she always ought to have one of her married daughters with her through the wintertime. Victoria had once suggested this herself and had been vexed because no one had responded. Now she treated the proposition with the gravest suspicion and decided it was a bribe. She refused to answer the letter. Alice was both hurt and puzzled.

Vicky and Fritz and their family came over to stay at Osborne and Vicky spent the journey screwing up her courage to speak seriously to her obstinate mother as soon as they arrived. But her resolve foundered when she found herself being sharply rebuked for having altered the travelling arrangements at the last moment. 'So inconvenient to me, dear. . . . You know I do not care for changed plans. . . . Everything entirely contrary to my expressed wishes and advice. . . .'

Fritz advised caution and Vicky decided to wait until her mother's temper had cooled down, but this took a long time. There were brass cannons on the miniature fort outside the Swiss Cottage, and her grandchildren were for ever alarming her by firing them off at unexpected moments, and little Waldemar, to show his love for his English grandmama, laid his pet crocodile at her feet which sent her into the vapours and caused a terrible scene.

When the Queen was at last in a calm frame of mind Vicky broached the painful subject, and was brushed aside. Her mother simply would not talk about it. Not on any account, and especially as Bertie and Alix were there that day. Instead she insisted on disparaging Bismarck – marvelling that Vicky's father-in-law had seen fit to make him a prince – and she compared him unfavourably as a First Minister with her own Mr Gladstone. She still, of course, missed dear Mr Disraeli and Mary Anne, but the Gladstones had turned out more favourably than she had dared to expect. . . .

It was a safe, comfortable topic of conversation because Fritz admired the Liberal Prime Minister, and Bertie and Alix had recently become quite friendly with the Gladstones.

Alix told them that the Gladstones had a habit of singing together whenever they were feeling particularly affectionate or happy.

It was quite customary, the Queen pointed out, for couples to sing duets.

Her daughter-in-law smiled. 'But not, I think, Mama, a song quite like this.' She thought for a moment, then shook her head. 'I do not have it pat, and I did not quite catch the tune. Bertie knows it. He sings it frequently. Bertie will sing it for you.'

He did. He threw back his head and in a musical baritone he sang the Gladstones' song:

A ragamuffin husband and a rantipoling wife,
We'll fiddle it and scrape it through the ups and downs of life.

Everyone laughed, including the Queen, though her eyebrows rose at the same time. It was a surprising side of the Gladstones which she would never have suspected.

As surprising was Bertie's story that Mr Gladstone had once won eightpence from the Prince Consort in a game of commerce. She began to bristle. Albert gaming? It was unheard of. . . . And then she subsided again, because, suddenly, she had a clear recollection of Albert playing commerce for money. How strange that she had forgotten it. She could remember as though it was yesterday Albert and Mr Gladstone having an interminable conversation about the doctrine of the Immaculate Conception, but for years she had forgotten about the payment of that eightpence. Odd.

Then she smiled to herself. A discussion was well launched. There were no fears now of Vicky bringing up that objectionable subject of her seclusion. It was easier to talk about the Gladstones.

12

Ironically it was Mr Gladstone himself who next raised the objectionable subject of the Queen's isolation from her subjects. It was not because he had been influenced by her children, though naturally he was aware of their feelings in the matter, but because he genuinely began to fear for the monarchy.

The republicans had been stirred up by the deposing of Louis-Napoleon and the Pope. The Fenians too, who seized on any opportunity to discomfort England, were conspicuously anti-royal. Rumours about the Queen's parsimony and the Prince of Wales' unfitness to succeed were elaborated and enlarged. Gladstone feared the effect of such gossip. Neither the scurrilous pamphlets sold in public houses nor the regular attacks on the Queen and her Court in certain newspapers were as damaging as the every-day talk of ordinary people, and the Prime Minister was advised that there was a great deal of gossip.

Busy as he was with bills concerning Religious Tests in Universities, Ecclesiastical Titles, Courts of Appeals, Land Boundaries, the Purchase of Commissions, and the Disabilities of Trade Combinations, Gladstone began to give a great deal of time and attention to what he regarded as the Monarchy Problem.

His wife who saw familiar signs that, terrier-like, he would not let go until he had won his point, grieved for their happy relationship with the Court. It was bound to deteriorate and founder. The Queen had been close to losing all patience with him over the Blackfriars Bridge affair and this matter, she could tell from William's earnestness, was going to be even less palatable. She begged him to reflect first and deal gently with the Queen. After all she was attending far more to her public duties, and according to Lady Ely, she had been under considerable strain since the war in Europe.

William gave his polite smile which promised nothing, and with a sinking heart Mrs Gladstone realized that to him the Queen had temporarily ceased to be a woman with feelings and was docketed in the same way as the Army or drinking licences or primary education in Scotland or any other problem of the moment. She knew that his strong sense of duty would make him sacrifice all personal feelings and he would press and press and press the Queen – to her disadvantage and to his own – for the sake, as he believed it, of the country.

A suitable opportunity for raising the point was at hand. The Queen had asked Parliament to grant an annuity to her son Prince Arthur and, in the course of the debate, one critic expressed a desire to see more of the Queen. Gladstone cleverly won her approval by supporting her, saying he was sure the House was gratified by the number of public appearances she had already felt able to make that year. She wrote to thank him and, at the same time, she bewailed the press which had taken up the matter more strongly than ever.

Four days later the Household at Osborne felt her displeasure. Mr Gladstone had written to warn her that a disappointed minority both in the House of Commons and in the country was likely to cause trouble. It would be a great help in placating these ill-disposed people if she could postpone her visit to Balmoral until after the Prorogation of Parliament.

The Queen refused. She was unwell. She needed to go north on the stated day. Her nerves would not stand a postponement.

The republican press got wind of what was happening and made two sour comments, first that the Queen's itinerary was neither as sacred nor as important as the laws of the Medes and Persians, and, second, that it really mattered very little where she was at any time, but it seemed that if the country was backward enough to have a monarch she ought to be at the centre of things while Parliament was sitting and not holidaying at the public's expense north of the Border.

Enraged by this effrontery the Queen demanded that Gladstone protect her. He must make it clear that she *was* often out in the public eye and that she *was* unwell.

Recalling General Grey's insistence that much of Victoria's illness was imagined and Jenner could not be relied upon, Gladstone dared to take a risk. He pressed her, and not with the deft, light touch which might have won her over, but ponderously. He begged her to give way and remain in England.

Her shrill reaction was frightening. She demanded to see the

Lord Chancellor at once, and having made her points again and again and again, with increasing force and noise, she repeated them in a long vituperative memorandum. It concluded:

It really is abominable that a woman, a Queen, loaded with care & anxieties, public & domestic which are daily increasing should be unable to make people understand that there are limits to her powers. . . . She must solemnly repeat that unless her ministers support her & state the whole truth she cannot go on & must give her heavy burden up to younger hands.

Mrs Gladstone never directly interfered with her husband's work. Most of it, anyway, was hidden from her. But she did see this memorandum. Perhaps its high note of hysteria so alarmed Gladstone that he wanted his wife's advice, but when she gave it – that he should not insist – he did not take it.

Mrs Gladstone was appalled. William must see that this was no ordinary affair.

But William did not see. He was unenthusiastic about a compromise proposal from the Queen that she stay three days longer in England. He asked the Clerk of the Privy Council to influence her, and Lady Ely, and Colonel Ponsonby – but he got nowhere. He and his colleagues then turned to Jenner to get at the medical truth. It was like shearing with blunt clippers.

Feeling pained and worried Gladstone once more repeated his demand. By now it was more in the nature of ministerial advice than a request.

The Queen was obdurate. On the appointed day she left for Balmoral.

Politically it did not matter a great deal. No one knew of the disagreement between the Queen and her Prime Minister but it was important in that it marked the end of their cordial relationship. Gladstone the monarchist was deeply saddened. In that summer of 1871 he wrote a long private letter to Colonel Ponsonby bewailing the recent confrontation of Cabinet and Crown or, as he evidently considered it, of common sense and womanish obstinacy.

Small and meaner cause for the decay of thrones [he wrote] *cannot be conceived. It is like the worm which bores the bark of a noble oak tree and so breaks the channel of its life.*

Soon after her arrival at Balmoral Victoria had the painful satisfaction of falling so ill that the doubters, led by her own First Minister, were confounded. She was low and nervy and very much run down. An ugly and agonizing abscess, six inches across, appeared on her arm and she confided to her journal that she had not felt so ill since her bout of typhoid at Ramsgate thirty-six years before. A surgeon from Edinburgh advised lancing and instantly the pain was relieved. But no sooner had the Queen partially recovered from this affliction than she had a series of attacks of rheumatic gout which prostrated her with pain. At some times she was unable to do anything for herself and week followed week without any noticeable change in her condition.

Unknown to her it saved her from being pestered by Alice who had written a round robin signed by all the royal children begging her to leave her seclusion. When the moment came for it to be presented the sight of her mother helpless and in great pain leaning back in a wheelchair was too touching. Alice lacked the heart to add to her troubles. The round robin was torn up.

And possibly the Queen's illness saved her from too much of the Prime Minister's heavy earnestness. He came into residence as Minister in Attendance at Balmoral but she could not see him for three days after his arrival. When she did give him audience her seclusion was not mentioned. They discussed less volatile topics.

Gladstone, made over-serious by nervousness, tended to preach and be unaccommodating. She, on her part, made no secret of the fact she no longer had the same confidence in him.

In his tower room overlooking the pine plantations of the Prince Consort, Gladstone wrote to the Foreign Secretary about the lack of harmony between them. He did not mince his words.

Her repellent power which she so well knows how to use has been put in action towards me.

Uncomfortable and unhappy, he realized that an entirely new stage had begun in their relationship, and he saw no solution to the Monarchy Problem.

13

On 22 November the Queen breakfasted for the first time since her illness with those of her children who were at Balmoral. By then she was much stronger. Strangely her health had been improved by a swingeing public attack on royalty by one of Gladstone's more radical followers. It acted as a tonic. Far from being cast down she wrote an angry letter asking how the Ministry proposed to correct this seditious Member of Parliament. Revitalized by the brush, she felt better able to face things.

It was as well because that very morning she heard that the Prince of Wales had a mild attack of typhoid fever. He had been staying at Londesborough Lodge near Scarborough where foul drains had infected two servants and several house guests. Alice, who had gone to stay at Sandringham for a while, telegraphed that there was no real cause for anxiety. Alix had sent for an expert, Doctor William Gull. Everything that could be done was being done.

The message was less reassuring than Alice had intended. Already emotionally prepared for the approaching anniversary of Albert's death on 14 December, Victoria dreaded that now she would lose her son. Sir William Jenner was at once dispatched to Norfolk. As soon as possible the Court moved to Windsor so as to be in close touch with events at Sandringham.

As the awful anniversary drew nearer the Prince's state grew worse. Jenner and Gull issued bulletins by telegraph several times a day and found it difficult to give fresh news. Their predicament was noted by a future Poet Laureate in one of the most fearful couplets ever printed.

> *Flash'd from his bed, the electric message came,*
> *He is not better; he is much the same.*

In fact he grew steadily worse.

By the 27th the Queen was at Sandringham. It was her first visit there and she was not over-impressed. Though the drawing-rooms were grand and the billiard room and hall enormous, the bedrooms were pokey. She had left Leopold behind at Windsor but many of her family were already there.

Immediately she noted that Alix and Alice were stiff and reserved with one another. She soon had it out of Alix. Alice was a dear, so very efficient, and a magnificent nurse; but she was also exceedingly domineering. Victoria saw her daughter and warned her not to sergeant-major in someone else's house. It was necessary, replied Alice warmly. Alix was too vague altogether, and her deafness was a serious drawback in the sick-room.

Vexed by their quarrelling the Queen herself took command. The house, she said, was already overcrowded. No more relations must be sent for. She supervised admittance to the sick-room and received the doctors' reports. They were more sanguine than she had expected. The Prince's attack, said Jenner, was far worse than that of his father, but he had the Hanoverian stamina and youth was on his side. His breathing was causing the most anxiety. And no wonder, thought the Queen. Bertie's high living had made him over-fat and he smoked a quite terrible number of cigars each day. No doubt fright would make him correct these faults when he recovered. She would not say 'if'. In her opinion sick-rooms needed a spirit of hope as much as good nursing and she made a brave showing herself, sitting behind a screen in the sick-room, admitting the family in rotation to keep watch.

She was as surprised as she was relieved when the ghastly crackling noise from Bertie's chest subsided and his fever showed signs of abating. Indeed within forty-eight hours he appeared to be so improved that she thankfully accepted Jenner's advice that she husband her strength and return to Windsor for a time.

The day she left was Alix's birthday, December 1st. But hardly anyone thought of it. The Prince of Wales' Household was cast down to hear that Lord Chesterfield had died that day. He had caught typhoid at the same time and at the same place as the Prince of Wales.

Colonel Ponsonby did not tell the Queen immediately. Jenner had stressed that, after her illness in the autumn, she needed to be cossetted and her nerves rested whenever possible. When, at a suitable juncture, he told her the news, she faced it bravely. Comforted by messages from Sandringham that the patient's improvement was being maintained, she was at last beginning to relax. In fact, her anxieties were so soothed away that, when a message came that the Holy Father was praying for her son, she sent a brisk reply that his Royal Highness's progress was quite satisfactory. Therefore she was shocked to receive a telegram on 8 December from Sir William Jenner:

THE PRINCE PASSED A VERY UNQUIET NIGHT. NOT SO WELL. TEMPERATURE RISEN TO 104. RESPIRATIONS MORE RAPID. DR GULL AND I ARE BOTH VERY ANXIOUS.

By the evening the Queen was back at Sandringham, driving from the station through snow drifts. She went at once to the sick-room. Alice and Alix were on either side of the bed. Bertie lay there heaving and delirious. The crackling had returned to his breathing. It was louder than before. She bent to kiss his forehead and darted back as he lashed out with an arm. Trembling and close to tears she sat behind the screen to keep her watch.

That evening she dined alone in her room with Louise. Alfred asked permission for George of Cambridge to come to Sandringham. This time, though the house was more crowded than ever and stifling on account of all the windows being closed against the sharp frost outside, the Queen said yes, he might come. And Leopold and Beatrice must come from Windsor. All the family should be there.

Louise and Alfred exchanged glances. Already their mother had decided Bertie was dying and, though no one spoke of it, at the back of everyone's minds was the spectre of December 14th, the anniversary of the Prince Consort's death. Despite her recent illness Victoria showed great strength. She became everyone's rock, and she marshalled the family in a way that brooked no argument.

George of Cambridge was seriously upset. He was devoted to Bertie and Alix and was convinced that his young cousin would die. To keep himself occupied he undertook to help with the huge number of telegrams of inquiry but he was really far too agitated to sit about and, recalling that foul drains caused typhoid, he began to inspect the Sandringham sewerage system. The fug in the overcrowded, unventilated house was terrible but he found worse and more sinister smells. Princess Louise's bedroom he declared uninhabitable which, in view of the shortage of space, was very trying; and he had estate men in to investigate a smell of drains in the library. They found it was a leaking gas jet.

Both Ponsonby and Jenner did their best to calm the old gentleman because he was depressing the ladies. But he really took small notice of anyone except the Queen. She spoke to him herself and told him there was every reason for hope. Instantly he promised to wear a cheerful countenance for her sake. No one else, said Ponsonby, could have done it.

Though she dominated her family and the Household the Queen did not interfere with the work of the physicians. Nor did she quarrel with their judgements. When they announced that the sight of his wife might excite the Prince the Queen agreed, but she saw how the prohibition upset poor Alix and with her flair for practical compromises she overcame the difficulty. She instructed her daughter-in-law to crawl into the sick-room on her hands and knees so that she was invisible from the bed.

But by far the Queen's most valuable service both to her son and to everyone in that frightened house was her example of calmness. She refused to panic and was devoted in her watching, going backwards and forwards between the sick-room and her rooms, mostly sitting behind her screen, but sometimes sitting close beside her fevered son who heaved on his bed and whistled and sang and shouted obscenities and cursed and sometimes bayed like a hound.

She did her best to soothe him when he strained against his own weakness and cried out in a tremendous voice: 'That's right, old Gull. That's right. That's right. One more teaspoonful, Gull my boy. Gull. Gull. Gull.'

'Dear Bertie,' she murmured lovingly when he bellowed bawdy songs and roared out lists of racehorses and ordered from imaginary supper menus and raved about women so loudly and in such a way that even Alix could hear him and his sisters did not know where to look. His mother was quite unabashed. He was doubly dear in his weakness and abandon, and she prayed for him out loud. In a rare moment of lucidity and quiet he noticed this and she found she was hearing his prayers as she had done a long, long time before on visits to the nursery.

On December 13th the crisis was at hand. When Bertie almost died in a great fit of coughing Victoria had the screen removed. His delirium was excessive as he grew still more feverish. He frightened her by clutching at the bedclothes and trying to feel for things in the air. The dreadful anniversary which was to fall on the next day filled everyone's minds.

Poor George Cambridge could keep his promise no longer. In a futile attempt to cheer himself up he went to his room and wrote up his journal.

> *Everybody writes, everybody telegraphs, all being intent for news. The alarm and consternation and excitement in London are terrific, the loyalty displayed by the entire nation is sublime.*

But it was no use. His anxiety and grief were too much. He wept over his journal and there were tears in his eyes for hours. The other royalties and members of the households were equally despairing. The doctors were downcast. Only the Queen kept her indomitable spirit. She saw as many people as possible. To each she repeated her conviction that, though serious and alarming, Bertie's state was not hopeless.

On the 14th, the sad and awful day, she was proved right. The crisis was passed. Weak and still very ill, the Prince had survived. Typically, on regaining consciousness, the very first thing he asked for was a bottle of Bass's beer.

Five days afterwards the Queen returned to Windsor.

14

There were lavish celebrations for the recovery of the Prince of Wales and Londoners vied with one another in showing their affection for the Crown. The Queen refused to be taken in. Her deep-seated mistrust of the mob made her sceptical. Nevertheless she was still severely shaken when, forty-eight hours after an official Service of Thanksgiving for the recovery of the Prince of Wales, an attempt was made on her life.

On this occasion she was unable to put on a stoical front. Pulled down by her long illness, and by watching at her son's bedside, she showed for the first time how very frightened she was.

She had been driving out with Arthur and Leopold and Lady Churchill, and when Brown jumped down at the Garden Entrance to Buckingham Palace an unknown youth suddenly appeared on the other side of the carriage. Victoria shrank away from him and threw herself into Lady Churchill's arms, crying: 'Save me! Save me!'

Brown heard the cry, tore round the carriage, and dragged the man away. Lady Churchill, her arms about the Queen, paled when she saw a pistol lying on the ground. She straightened Victoria's bonnet and helped her compose herself.

Practised in the discreet handling of difficult situations, the equerries and grooms quickly had everything under control. The young man was removed; the Queen and her Lady-in-Waiting and the Princes handed down from the carriage.

Still shaken, her hands trembling, her face blanched, Victoria looked straight ahead and walked into the Palace.

John Brown was rewarded for his prompt action with the Queen's heartfelt thanks and an annual pension for the rest of his life. Her decision, made in the face of everyone, that Brown should always ride on the box of her carriage, was entirely justified.

She herself was also compensated for her moment of real horror. Apparently forgetting their recent dislike of her seclusion and alleged parsimony, the people made her the target of a great outburst of affection. She was sympathized with, praised, cheered, toasted and eulogized. But she had few illusions and observed cynically that the popularity of royalty in England appeared to depend on its capacity for survival. She took little pleasure in the loyal demonstrations. In her opinion, no oration was worth the awful fright of being physically attacked by a feeble-minded lout.

The examining magistrates soon established all the facts about the young man who had attacked her. He was an Irishman named O'Connor, and had had the lunatic notion of forcing her at pistol point to sign an order for the release of certain Fenian prisoners. His pistol, like that of another assailant, had been more of a toy than a weapon, and the Queen herself recognized that he had not meant to kill. But he had meant to frighten, and he had succeeded only too well. She wrote to the Prime Minister and insisted that treating this case too leniently or as contemptible would not do at all.

Mr Gladstone was entirely in agreement. So was the Lord Chancellor. But Baron Cleasby, the judge who tried O'Connor, merely sentenced him to a year's imprisonment and a whipping.

Victoria was exceedingly angry and her anger mounted when she discovered that in recent months Cleasby had been responsible for an increasingly large number of eccentric judgements and sentences. On the same day, for instance, he had given a petty thief three years' imprisonment and a man who had killed his wife by pushing her under a dray a much shorter sentence of three months. A strong letter was sent to Downing Street. Mr Gladstone wrote patiently about what he admitted were 'absurd proceedings' and 'the vagaries of Baron Cleasby'.

Secretly he was overjoyed that his Monarchy Problem had, as it were, been solved by a single attack of typhoid fever and the single act of a mad Irish boy. In his delight and relief he forgot his recent differences with the Queen, and that since her illness their relationship had been on a different footing.

He was soon reminded of it.

The Queen remained distant, chilly and obstinate.

When he proposed useful employment for the Prince of Wales after his convalescence, his suggestions were vetoed one after the other. And when Victoria announced that in April she planned to run over to Baden to visit her half-sister, and he begged her to reconsider because Parliament would then be sitting, she refused to co-operate, insisting that the visit was essential and that it must be made. Then, before he could beg her to reconsider, she spoke warningly of shaken nerves, and changed the subject to the Regent's Park Canal which, she said, was in a disgraceful state.

Gladstone was obliged to leave it at that.

It was as well that he did. The Queen again showed her singular and vexing habit of being proved right. It turned out that her visit to Baden had after all been important and necessary. Not long afterwards Princess Feodore died. It had been their last chance to meet.

Death could never again take Victoria by surprise. Now that she was in middle age and had reached the majestic and settled time of a woman's life her first extravagant avowals to Albert's memory had been greatly modified. She altered her avowal never to do anything without him and she was certain now that Albert would have approved of necessary improvements. As a result she had taken to visiting new places and had ordered a new and more convenient royal railway carriage, and a better royal yacht, and had built for herself a retreat at Glasallt Sheil some distance from Balmoral where there were no immortelles in her bedroom, merely a single bed with a headboard of peacock blue. But these were merely outward things. Victoria's faith in her husband's wisdom never diminished, and, when things went wrong, she took strength from his teaching about pleasure and duty, joy and sorrow, and his advice about not giving way to sudden grief in bereavement. Nevertheless, at the time of her half-sister's death, Victoria was already sorrowing for her dear friend and Scotch chaplain, Dr MacLeod, and she was particularly vulnerable. By tragic irony his death had deprived her of her most consoling counsellor. She had to face the bitter news from Baden without his support, and it deepened her grief. She and Feodore had been inseparable in their girlhood at Kensington and all their lives they had been devoted to each other. Thank God, she exclaimed many many times, that she had been able to visit her that Eastertide. Generously Feodore had bequeathed her the villa at Baden but she valued far more the small keepsakes and the dachshund puppy, which her half-sister had chosen for her. He was a living reminder of their last, precious time together, a deep-tan dog, already portly and with the imposing name of Waldemar.

With Waldemar on her lap she lamented Feodore in her journal:

> *I stand so alone now, no near and dear one near my own age or older to whom I could look up to, left!* All, all *gone! She was my* last *near relation on an equality with me, the* last *link with my childhood and youth. . . .*

There she paused and reflected. Her last phrase was not strictly accurate. There was always Maslin, her Page of the Back Stairs who had known her for forty-four years. Instinctively in her unhappiness she sent for Maslin and for a number of days she saw more of him than was usual. She found it did her good to talk about the old days at Kensington. Maslin understood. He sympathized. It was a comfort to have Maslin there.

But there was small respite for Victoria. No sooner was she over the worst of her grieving for Feodore than she heard Mary Anne Beaconsfield had died at Hughenden. Her end was heroic. Dying in great pain and literally of starvation because her cancer would not permit her to take or digest food, she had been brave and gracious to the last – all for the sake of her Dizzy. He was inconsolable, and his state was pathetic because Mary Anne's fortune had merely been a life interest. At one awful stroke he had lost a devoted wife and a comfortable home. Victoria was moved to tears at the thought of Mr Disraeli leaving the house at Grosvenor Gate and putting up at an hotel. She did all she could for him, but always with a feeling of helplessness. She realized she could do very, very little to help.

Victoria felt it less keenly when almost simultaneously the exiled Louis Napoleon died at Chislehurst, though what her family crudely called her 'club instincts' were aroused. Because the death of a fellow sovereign must be seen to be calamitous, even if he had been living in rather seedy exile, the Queen made elaborate preparations for Court mourning and for her family led by the Prince of Wales to attend the funeral.

It caused a mild brush with her ministers. The Foreign Secretary, Lord Granville, pointed out through Gladstone that Republican France might well object to such a formal recognition of the Bonapartes. The Queen was unimpressed. Dexterously she changed the subject. Why, she asked, did Lord Granville have the nickname 'Puss'? And when Gladstone stared blankly at her she decided he was feigning astonishment and acting cleverly and that the sobriquet must therefore have some radical and perhaps indecent significance. Once more she abruptly changed the subject. A few moments later Gladstone found to his amazement and dismay that somehow the audience had finished. Lord Granville was obliged to go to Court himself. He explained to the Queen that as an equivalent honour had not been paid to the memory of Louis-Philippe when he died at Claremont, the Bourbons would not take it at all kindly if a royal fuss was made of the Bonapartes at Chislehurst. It was the sort of argument the Queen most readily appreciated. The Bourbons mattered. For their sake she agreed to alter her plans, and she went privately to the lying-in-state and to condole with the Empress and the young Prince Imperial. With Eugénie she was natural and affectionate. No matter what statesmen said or did, she recognized the sorrow of another widow and wished to lighten it.

Then, soon afterwards, she was greatly upset to lose one of her grandsons under the most dramatic and painful circumstances.

Alice's fifth child, Frittie, had the Coburg curse and was haemophilic, and, being delicate, he was the more loved by everyone. In an awful catastrophe, while his mother by terrible coincidence was actually playing a funeral march of Chopin in the next room, Frittie toppled from a balcony and fell twenty feet into the courtyard below. His screams cut through the music. Alice stopped playing. With the screams from below she heard the cries of frightened servants. She herself rushed down and picked him up and rocked him and called out to him in a frenzy of grief. But Frittie never recovered consciousness and later died.

Trying to console her daughter helped Victoria to overcome her own sorrow and shock. She advised her son-in-law that Alice should be kept busy, saying it was a pity she did not have more formal duties in the Grand Duchy to take her mind off things. An occupied mind, she declared, saved one from falling into despair.

For once Louis of Hesse was impatient with the Queen. He recalled the shattered little figure in black at the time of his wedding, gulping down her daily diet of despair; and, though usually the most placid of sons-in-law, he was irritated to receive advice – good though it was – from such a source. But then he remembered what Lady Churchill had said to Alice, that her mother's sorrow had never been an hysterical self-indulgence which required the correction of a sharp slap, but a form of break-down caused by shock. She had been fortunate to emerge from it undamaged.

Louis' anger was softened. He wrote a polite reply agreeing that when she felt up to it, Alice should do all that she could, though he doubted if either of them would be able to overcome the sorrow at losing their beloved Frittie.

Victoria was very fond of him and considered his sentiments proper. But she was convinced it was urgent for Alice to begin distracting herself immediately. She wrote again begging Louis to keep his wife fully occupied. It would soothe her sorrow and give her a new purpose in life. She must be kept busy. She must.

15

Prince Alfred, Duke of Edinburgh, had at last found a wife. He engaged himself to the Grand Duchess Marie, daughter of the Tsar.

It pleased his mother in one sense, because for years she had been wanting him to settle down and his two previous choices had been eminently unsatisfactory; one princess lacking health and morals, and the other belonging to the Hanover family whose blindness was hereditary. But, in another sense, an alliance with the Romanoffs was not at all to her liking because of their absurd pretensions.

She bridled when the Russian court claimed that Marie, as a grand duchess, took precedence over every lady in England – including the Princess of Wales – and announced that it was quite out of the question. She took further umbrage when the Russians went on to request that Marie should be an imperial royal highness. And she was incensed when the Tsar positively refused to send over his daughter for the sort of early training Alix had had. She would have been more angry still had she known the Tsar had openly called her a silly old fool and said that the only daughter of the Romanoffs was not to be looked over like a market heifer.

The Tsarina tried to mollify both her angry spouse and the angry Queen of England. She telegraphed that she herself would meet Victoria at Cologne.

'Cologne!' stormed the Queen. 'How can I, a sovereign and a lady, make myself available all in a moment to run after her?'

Alice tried to persuade her mother. For her pains she received a withering letter. It included the sentence:

> *I do* not *think, dear Child, that* you *should tell* me *who have been nearly* 20 years longer *on the throne than the Emperor of Russia & am the Doyenne of Sovereigns & who am a* Reigning *Sovereign which the Empress is* not – what I ought to do. . . .

Having eased some of her resentment by discharging this bolt at her daughter, Victoria was prepared to be more cordial for the sake of Alfred. His fiancée Marie turned out to be charming, which was a blessing, but she did not relish the thought of the Tsar making a state visit to England after the wedding.

In point of fact, years and years before when she had been young and unmarried and he had been Tsarevitch, she had entertained him at Windsor and had lost a little of her heart to him. Then he had been so smiling, so masterful, so patient in teaching her to dance a mazurka, and he had partnered her in a *Grossvater* under the benevolent gaze of old Lord Melbourne. But now she supposed he would have changed as much as she had, and would perhaps be more like his terrifying father who had slept on straw, knouted Polish nuns, and ogled her own ladies. In point of fact, when he did revisit Windsor Victoria found him rather dull, except when he talked about India and then his eyes glowed with envy. To tease him she made a point of showing him a rhododendron in the Windsor collection which was named after Lord Dalhousie, the great annexer of Indian states and the frustrator of all Russia's ambitions on the North-West Frontier. The Tsar merely remarked that the rhododendron's yellow chalices were unusually pale.

It was a sombre visit and being forced frequently into close proximity with her royal visitor was a trial to the Queen.

'The Emperor's breath!' she exclaimed in confidence to Jane Churchill. 'His breath! It is horrid.'

Lady Churchill suggested that, being Autocrat of all the Russias, the Tsar had no one to inform him of it.

A horrid suspicion occurred to the Queen. 'Now, Jane, you must promise me, absolutely faithfully, to be frank if my breath is ever offensive.'

Lady Churchill smiled and promised she would do so, but the Queen was not quite sure. Until a month or so after the Tsar's departure she would occasionally demand to know the truth, and would test the sweetness of her breath by puffing shyly at her friend.

All in all, Victoria did not care for entertaining foreign monarchs. To begin with it cost a great deal, and no matter what scurrilous matter was printed about her private finances she felt that with so many children and grandchildren she could not properly afford to squander her income on illustrious visitors. And, to go on with, her secluded life had nourished her disposition to be shy with strangers. Therefore it was only out of a very strong sense of public duty that she was ever persuaded to greet foreign sovereigns and their envoys.

When she did, she insisted that things were done correctly. Four Burmese Ambassadors quickly discovered this when they said they preferred not to prostrate themselves in the oriental fashion at the court of a western queen. Victoria was prickly with disapproval. She claimed that to all intents and purposes she was Empress of India, and she insisted on the eastern ceremonial. Otherwise, she said, she would not receive the envoys. Hurriedly they capitulated. One after another they prostrated themselves in the Windsor Throne Room and laid a lacquer box containing gold and rubies at the Queen's feet. One of the Maids of Honour described the scene as most picturesque. Brown thought it strange. The Queen herself considered it fitting.

Receiving sovereigns themselves was never very agreeable though Victoria found herself intrigued by polygamous and oriental despots. She retained a warm memory of the visit of the Sultan of Turkey who ate little but fruit, had beautiful eyes and was mortifyingly ill at a naval review. She had clever Mr Disraeli to thank for that first taste of the romance and mystery of the East. He had shrewdly tricked her into agreeing to see the Sultan at Windsor. Now Mr Gladstone reaped the benefit. A trifle heavily he informed the Queen that the country's foreign policies in the Middle and Near East made it important for the Shah in Shah to be received in England with all the splendour and magnificence he had received in Berlin. To his surprise the Queen agreed, though she snappily asked why a Shah of Persia called himself 'imperial' and, not receiving a satisfactory reply, ordered that the title should on no account be used during the visit.

Gladstone himself wavered when the English Ambassador at Berlin spoke of the Shah being possibly accompanied by French demi-mondaines, and mentioned his habit of sitting on the carpet to dine off a somewhat *relevée* cuisine which he ate with his fingers, spitting out tough or unwanted pieces on the floor like an owl disgorging pellets. He almost threatened to withdraw government hospitality. But the Queen and her ladies were agog to see this barbarous despot, and were not a little chagrined when he turned out to be punctual and dignified. Any concubines he might have had he courteously left in France and there were no problems about table manners as at Court he ate only fruit. The Household whispered tales of burnt carpets, and young lambs being roasted whole over charcoal braziers in the Shah's rooms, but the Queen was inclined to be indulgent. He had a way of addressing her through his interpreter and Grand Vizier as his most auspicious sister of the sublime nature – which was extravagant, of course, but rather pleasant. And she enjoyed the compliment when he informed her he was having her *Leaves* translated into Persian so that he could read it. Most of all – because she had a sense of the ridiculous hidden from most people – she took pleasure in the contrasts between east and west: the Shah extravagantly kissing her photograph in public at Windsor railway station, and then doing the same in the middle of a luncheon in the Oak Room while her pipers marched up and down playing; their difference in diet, he with his iced water and chilled strawberries and forced persimmons, she with her boiled potatoes, liver-wing of fowl, and honest English duff; and the startling contrast in their appearances, the Shah in spectacles and a diamond-studded coat with ruby buttons and emerald epaulettes, and she in her large pearls, the Koh-i-noor diamond and widow's weeds. Bertie was very obliging and took their guest here and there about the place for more masculine entertainments. Having been told of a boxing match in the gardens at Buckingham Palace she raised a hand and said she wished to hear no more details. But Bertie, because he knew she would particularly like it, told her of the Shah's remark at Trentham. He had gone there as a guest of the Duke of Sutherland and, noticing the magnificence and hearing that the Duke was the largest landowner in Great Britain with 1,358,000 acres, he had gravely warned the Prince of Wales, 'Too grand for a subject. You'll have to have his head off when you come to the throne.'

The Queen went herself to Dunrobin Castle to taste the hospitality of her over-grand subject. When he heard of the project the Prince of Wales was incredulous. His mother disapproved of Sutherland. She had objected to him being on the expedition up the Nile. He was one of those friends she advised him to drop now because if he ever became king they would be an impossible burden. Sutherland was not welcomed at Court. He roistered and gambled. He was fast, he drove a curricle in the Park, took his own fire-engine staffed by noble and princely friends to fight fires with the Metropolitan Brigade, and it got to the ears of the Queen that he was connected with that scandalous story of the actress and the oyster. Yet she now proposed to be his guest at Dunrobin.

The Prince could not contain his curiosity and asked why. Her reply was simple: 'I was fond of his mother.' Then, realizing that this was rather a non sequitur she added: 'It is my privilege as Queen and woman to change my mind.'

Her son had to be satisfied with that, and, on a dull but fair morning, the Queen set out from Balmoral complete with children, household, servants and her second piper.

The journey was not uneventful and there were plenty of other things to include in the journal; eating luncheon while the train at a reduced speed glided over the wild moor of Forres where Macbeth met the witches; seeing for the first time Culloden field 'where that bloody battle was fought, the recollection of which I cannot bear'; receiving addresses at points along the route; and being given something of a shock half-way through tea when the train appeared to stop in the middle of nowhere and her host the Duke of Sutherland appeared at the window wiping grimy hands and grinning in welcome. It appeared he had been driving the engine himself all the way from Inverness.

At Golspie, where they took to carriages, the local people had put up triumphal arches which Brown freely translated from the Gaelic. She recognized one herself as it was in Lowland Scotch.

Better lo'ed you canna' be;
Will ye no come back again?

'Strange!' she murmured, 'when we have only just arrived.'

Brown frowned at such levity, or failed to see it as such. Laboriously he explained the history of the couplet. How odd, sometimes, he could be, thought the Queen, so blind to nuances and shades of humour.

But it appeared that on this visit Brown was being deliberately obtuse, perhaps to show his disapproval of travelling so far north. He took it ill when the Duke informed him that his perfectly comfortable bedroom had once been the castle prison; and when the royal party was inspecting the Dunrobin dairies and one of the rooms there was opened to reveal to the Queen a startled off-duty police guard sitting up in a bed holding the blankets to his chin, Brown said it was disgusting, disgusting. The Queen took the trouble to mollify him. It was worth it, Lady Churchill agreed. Brown in one of his moods was not a pleasurable companion.

In the shortest possible time the Queen's view of the Duke of Sutherland had undergone a transformation. She began to like him. But the good impression he made on her was spoilt by his deviousness in inviting the American explorer, H. M. Stanley, to Dunrobin. It meant that Stanley had to be presented to the Queen, and, although he had found Livingstone in Africa, neither Victoria nor her admirers cared for his self-advertisement and exaggerated boasting. Because the Duke insisted, she did see him and she presented him with a gold snuff-box decorated with brilliants. But she disliked being tricked. Sutherland had made her into a humbug. Victoria seldom if ever admired people simply because they were famous. They had to pass her own personal scrutiny first. Stanley did not succeed. She found him 'a determined ugly little man – with a strong American twang', and she was prepared now to believe the stories that, far from opposing slavery, he was brutal to Africans and kept many female slaves himself. She even took the trouble to pass on this opinion to her cousin the King of the Belgians who had large African interests. It had been a mistake to trick her into seeing the explorer, both for Stanley himself and for his patron the Duke of Sutherland.

16

In her middle fifties Queen Victoria was growing dumpier. The mode which emphasized the elegance and the beauty of Lady Churchill and Lady Ely only served to give her the appearance of a hedgehog. Years before a French sailor had mistaken her for the laundress of the royal yacht, and she still looked comfortably bourgeois. Somehow it seemed fitting that the gentlemen of her Household privately referred to her by the affectionate nickname of Eliza. She looked an Eliza. But, despite her appearance, she was more truly regal in manner than any of her fellow sovereigns.

Already circumstances were combining to make her into a living legend. There was a royal cult, led by Lady Augusta at the Westminster Deanery. They spoke of the Queen as 'the Blessed One'. Significantly the Queen's drum-major began to refer to her Accession Day as Ascension Day. Her portrait in stained glass crept into places of worship.

'Fudge!' she exclaimed when she heard of these extravagances.

Yet she never made light of what she believed was a true picture of her position. She held that royal power was her appanage by the gift of God, and she was aggravated by the English system which expressed her will through a third party, the odious People's William.

Mr Gladstone grated more and more on the Queen's nerves. His supporters claimed that his administration had initiated long-needed reforms. His sovereign's views were different. She remained courteous, inviting the Gladstones to stay at Osborne, graciously offering him a permanent residence in his own constituency of Greenwich – an offer he felt obliged to refuse – showing a perennial interest in William Henry and his family, and giving Agnes Gladstone an Indian shawl on her engagement to the Headmaster of Wellington. Yet at the same time she badgered Mr Gladstone with memoranda; complaining that the government had done nothing whatever about making the railroads safer or the services better at keeping time; bewailing the indiscreet publication of Baron Stockmar's memoirs by his sons; making so many difficulties about Gladstone's plans for a royal residence in Ireland that they had to be abandoned; expressing outrage and shock because he had written 'secret' on the draft of a finance bill sent to her – 'Does he think,' she inquired rhetorically, 'that his queen is a common bletherer?' – and castigating *The Times* 'with its usual impudence and impertinence' for seeing fit to give her a lesson on expedition and punctuality.

Gladstone, who, with the help of only two clerks, managed to write 24,000 letters a year while he was in office, rather girded at the necessity of writing so many of them to the Queen, yet he showed unfailing solicitude. Soon, he knew, his work would be at an end. Some of the Liberal legislation had not been all hat popular in the country. The momentum of the Ministry's reforming zeal was running down.

John Brown had a habit of echoing his royal mistress's opinions, or people thought he had, which almost amounted to the same thing, and he was heard to remark in loud tones that the sooner the Ministry was out the better.

Dizzy watched and waited.

He now had the air of an Egyptian mummy – serene, tranquil, impassive, inscrutable; his face carefully painted, each ringlet dyed jet-black, and only his eyes showing how much he had suffered at the death of Mary Anne. For months after her death he tried to numb the pain by constant political activity. He and his faithful secretary, Montagu Corry, made unheard-of party preparations for the next general election. Each constituency had its official Conservative candidate. A Central Office was established in London to link the constituencies. Conservative associations were formed in large centres of population, and the lower orders suddenly found themselves provided with Conservative Clubs and reading rooms.

Dizzy himself always preferred to think of England in rural terms. A benevolent Church, Crown and Landlord were he believed the true political requirements of a free Englishman. And he had a strong distaste for the fruits of the new industrialism: non-conformity, radicalism, gross inequalities, and squalid towns which grew larger and larger, slithering over the countryside like ill-set and repellent jellies. It was perverse of him therefore, but perhaps typical, that he sounded the first trumpet notes of the coming campaign at the very heart of all he detested, the cotton town of Manchester. It was then that he charmed his audience with a lyrical and stinging description of the Liberal Government.

The Ministers reminded me of those marine landscapes not very unusual on the coasts of South America. You behold a range of exhausted volcanoes. Not a flame flickers on a single pallid crest. But the situation is still dangerous. There are occasional earthquakes, and ever and anon the dark rumbling of the sea.

There was a minor earthquake at Downing Street when the Prime Minister read the Manchester speech over his solitary breakfast. He apostrophized the ham before him: was Dizzy an excursionist? Had he ever seen the coasts of South America in his life?

In the reception given Dizzy by the Mancunians he read the knell of his Ministry. But, in a sense, he did not care. He was tired, tired; and, privately, he was relieved when the Liberals' bill to settle Irish university education was thrown out in the Commons by three votes. It meant he could retire and get away from the Queen's hostility and the perennial problems of office. He would go back to Cheshire and Homer and felling trees and give up politics altogether. . . .

His plans for personal freedom were scotched by his old adversary.

So delighted that she actually chattered, the Queen begged Mr Disraeli to form a Ministry, but he begged her to be cautious. By waiting, by forcing Gladstone to go on while the carrion birds circled over his dying policies, he could ensure a longer term of office for the Conservatives. He was entirely frank with the Queen. A small sacrifice now would repay handsomely.

Victoria was persuaded and she sent for Gladstone. By her tone she let him see she had small confidence in him as a First Minister but she compelled him to resume office. For ten more months he carried on, and all the time his sovereign was less than accommodating.

Across the Treasury Bench the beady eyes of Benjamin Disraeli watched the Prime Minister's struggles. In a moment of pique Gladstone spitefully called him 'the Artful Dodger'. Not in the least put out Dizzy accepted it as a compliment. He did not, on the whole, like Dickens but he admired some of his creations, the Artful Dodger amongst them.

The end came in February 1874. Gladstone suddenly announced the dissolution of Parliament. At the following General Election the Conservatives were returned with a majority of forty-nine. The Liberals in part attributed their defeat to their unpopular Licensing Act. 'We have been borne down,' said Gladstone mournfully, 'in a torrent of gin and beer.' He had been borne down in fact by Dizzy's elaborate arrangements and he knew it. Now at last he could resign and go home to Cheshire.

If he expected a change in the Queen's attitude simply because he was leaving her service he was disappointed. She was chilling and unforgiving. In the privacy of his diary he confided that he had been treated with 'scant kindness'.

The last audience was quickly done with.

'Mr Disraeli,' said Lady Ely, Court oracle on politics, 'is turning out a dear old Whig.'

The Queen, who never did understand the two-party system, was quite prepared to believe it. Lord Melbourne had been a Whig Prime Minister with a resolute dislike of change, and so there seemed to be no good reason why Mr Disraeli, her Conservative Prime Minister, should not be a reformer at heart.

He certainly appeared to be so as he led the country squires and clergymen of his party to consider the necessity for enlarging the rights of Trade Unions, reducing the working week to fifty-six hours and making Saturday a half-holiday, and insisting on factory employers as well as employees carrying out their contractual obligations. He even interested the Conservatives in drainage. They would carry on the sanitary reforms of the Liberal Party. On resigning office, Mr Gladstone's Home Secretary had declared he could die a happy man because he had achieved the drainage of Windsor. But more than Windsor was to be drained now. 'Sanitas sanitatum et omnia sanitas,' was the new ministry's watchword.

For a while the lampooners and caricaturists refrained from calling the Prime Minister 'the Wandering Jew' and 'Hope of Zion'. Instead they called him 'England's Plumber'.

Victoria was amused.

Certain of Disraeli's reaction, she delighted her ladies by imitating his voice and style. 'I care not a fig, Ma'am, not a fig, a pin, a rap.' Then, in a brilliant imitation of Mr Gladstone, she showed how he might have reacted to being called a plumber. Sternly she denounced the public's ingratitude and its unreasonable hostility in levelling at a servant of the people such obloquy, opprobrium and vilipending contumely.

It was all so convincing that when next Mr Disraeli appeared at Court the ladies almost expected to hear him say he did not care a fig, a pin, a rap; and the mere sight of him sent one of the two

Maids of Honour into such a fit of nervous giggles that she had to leave the room. The Queen did not rebuke her. It was her own fault. She could be indiscreet with Jane Ely or Jane Churchill, but realized she ought to hold her tongue before the other ladies. She hoped sincerely that Mr Disraeli would not be offended.

He was not. At Court he was seldom offended. In her company he shone and was quite unaffected. He truly admired her shrewdness, her refusal to have the wool pulled over her eyes, her penetrating insight into people's characters, her exquisite sensibility, her ability to enjoy being sentimental without becoming slavishly so, her frank way of going about things, and her accomplishments with her pencil and needle and as a linguist and musician which would have kept her in far more than bread and butter had she been born into genteel poverty and not to inherit a great throne. Most of all, he admired her matchless dignity. His Mary Anne had left amongst her papers a letter begging him to re-marry after her death; but though he thought of it he never put it into practice. He had many women friends, all middle-aged or elderly, and enjoyed with them a close romantic association which gave him the greatest satisfaction. Chief of them all was the Queen, and now it looked as if he would have a number of uninterrupted years with the privilege of seeing her almost as often as he wished. He devised a game in his imagination. Her retreat at Osborne was a faery kingdom. There she ruled as Queen Titania and he was her faithful Robin Goodfellow eager to venerate and serve.

Though courteous always, he was never afraid to be bold. 'Ma'am,' he asked her once over the dinner table, 'did Lord Melbourne ever tell you that you were not to do this or that?' She found it both amusing and somehow touching, and she told him, yes. In the same simple spirit he talked about Mary Anne and she spoke of Albert. And he could not keep from her the pleasure of his imaginary game. One day, when she sent him snowdrops, he wrote in the formal third person to thank her for the precious gift, and confessed that he had worn them at a banquet as though they were a special order.

Then, in the middle of the night, it occurred to him that it might all be enchantment, and that, perhaps, it was a Faery gift and came from another monarch: Queen Titania, gathering flowers with her Court, in a soft and sea-girt isle, and sending magic blossoms, which, they say, turn the heads of those who receive them.

'It might all be enchantment.' Victoria found it so. It was fey, yes. But in her middle fifties with a stout figure and her feet on the ground she appreciated feyness as an appetizing, irresistible dish. Both she and Disraeli were realists and sensible and they saw no point in wishing impossibly for youth again. Victoria in the Isle of Wight was no Titania in a Faery Isle, nor could the balding, painted, parchment-skinned statesman of over seventy be considered a personification of Puck, but there was quiet contentment to be gained from dreaming. Both had imagination. Both enjoyed silent melodies and the pictures only seen through closed eyes. Both were very happy in their affection for each other.

17

Queen Victoria had a talent for conciseness. She managed to reduce Lady Augusta Stanley's lengthy description of Prince Alfred's splendid wedding in St Petersburg to three words! 'What a day!' And, for a time, she had the habit of using the concise expression 'unheard of!' to sum up the whole gamut of her feelings of astonishment or displeasure.

A press rumour that she had committed suicide was unheard of, and called for an indignant assertion that she was 'quite well'.

When an edition of Charles Greville's journal from 1818 to 1830 was published, and she saw her uncles mocked and criticized in print, her letters of protest seethed with italics, exclamation marks, and heavy capitals. It was an unheard-of impertinence!

When someone attempted to assassinate Prince Bismarck at Kissingen ('he's really another old Bonaparte' was Mr Disraeli's comment) it was unheard of!

When Beatrice was confirmed she received some sentimental verses from her French teacher comparing her to a lily and wishing her good fortune now that she was free, and this was totally unheard of! Free! Beatrice was to be the prop, comfort and companion of her widowed mother to old age, a Benjamin!

When the first volume of Theodore Martin's biography of the Prince Consort was published, its immediate success was unheard of.

When Prince Otto of Bavaria, who was considering visiting her at Windsor, rushed into Munich Cathedral during the Corpus Christi festivities, and, wearing a wide-awake and a shooting jacket, threw himself on the altar steps and made a candid confession at the top of his voice, it was quite unheard of! He had better stay at home or he might indulge his extravagant religious impulses in St George's Chapel.

And when at Frogmore there was, appropriately enough, a summer plague of frogs, that was unheard of too. Nasty, slippery, slithering things. A long time before, in the year of European revolutions, Victoria had met an army of toads swarming over the Osborne lawns. Superstitious and depressed, she had been dreadfully afraid. Now, her nerves were stronger and she lifted her skirt, and picked her way through them. They were tiny, barely bigger than bluebottles, hopping and crawling everywhere. Stoutly she insisted on having tea in the tea-house despite the fact that it was hemmed in by frogs, and she turned over the problem to her son-in-law, Prince Christian, insisting it fell within his province as Ranger of Windsor Park. The Prince came and bowed to her and turned his sapphire eyes on the host of frogs. Eventually he hit on the idea of sweeping them up. Gardeners with besoms worked tirelessly and, it seemed, endlessly to clear the lawns and gravel paths. Afterwards the Queen, Prince Christian, and the royal gardeners took advice from an expert naturalist. He wrote a solemn report. To prevent a recurrence next year of such a plague the spawn must not be allowed to hatch. Ducks were needed. He recommended Aylesburys. They were great gobblers of spawn. Victoria ordered the ducks. The whole situation was quite unheard of!

But by far the most unheard-of situation was the great to-do in Parliament about a bill to put down ritualism. There was a conflict between the Lords and Commons, internecine conflict amongst the bishops, even conflict between cabinet ministers. Such a dreadful fuss! Unheard of!

In fact Victoria's own religion was an enigma. The Lutheranism of her mother and her governess had left little mark. She had been prepared for confirmation by a robust Evangelical who considered High Churchmen as traitors to the Reformation. Then, at eighteen, she had found herself with the theoretical power to appoint bishops and give out a great deal of preferment, and, at the same time, she had come under the influence of Lord M. who had an eighteenth-century distaste for enthusiasm, frowned on too much church-going, and thought it a pity when religion was allowed to obtrude into private affairs. Albert had been sceptical, dismissing mystery as unscientific and cutting formal churchmanship down to size.

The Queen's unorthodox religion had been fired in this crucible of mixed influences. Some of her ideas were elevated into healthy principles. She disliked all forms of bigotry. Roman Catholics she thought quaint, and Dissenters vulgar, but she liked both far more than the people who said they were damned. And she refused to believe that emotional revivalism like the performances of the American missionaries Moody and Sankey provided a lasting religion. She announced it was 'not wholesome to the mind or heart'.

But she also had some very strange notions. One of her Evangelical Maids of Honour, in trying to share some of her own enthusiasm for the blessings awaiting them in Paradise, said what a joy it would be for the Queen to converse in the shadow of the divine throne with her great ancestor King David. 'Now he,' returned the Queen coldly, 'is *not* a person I would wish to meet.' And she ostentatiously refused to pay attention when lessons about David were read at divine service. It was not because of his abandoned behaviour with Uriah's wife, nor because of the unseemly things he did to the uncircumcized Philistines, but simply because in her eyes by prancing about naked in the sight of his people he had let down the monarchy. She was also convinced it did not matter in the least if she communicated in the Church of Scotland, though the Archbishop and all her religious advisers without exception warned her that it could only do harm. And then, suddenly, like the majority of her subjects when the matter was raised in Parliament, she forgot her dislike of bigotry and became violently partisan. The only salvation, she told Dean Stanley, lay in the Broad Church. She spoke of 'Evangelical trash', said that they did 'as much harm as the High Church' and called them 'narrow-minded and uncharitable'. But Romanism was worse. It poisoned the minds of the young and members of the upper classes. She was a Protestant, she said, and it was time the Protestant churches got together to resist the blandishments of the papacy. Bowing and scraping in church was unheard of. So were altar lights, crucifixes, saints, stone Lord's Tables, vestments, incense, and most odious of all, *confession* and *celibacy*. She learnt a jingle written by a passionate Protestant which underlined the particular horrors of celibacy, and she quite often repeated it.

God give her wavering clergy back that honest heart and true
Which once was theirs ere Popish fraud its spell around them threw;
Nor let them barter wife and child, bright hearth and happy home
For the hectic bliss of the strumpet kiss of the Jezebel of Rome.

Disraeli, had he been able to, would have avoided the issue. He inclined privately and aesthetically, as Gladstone did publicly and as a matter of faith, to a moderate Oxford position. But he attached no real importance to ritual. One sapient friend had remarked: 'Dizzy's attachment to moderate Oxfordism is something like Bonaparte's to moderate Mohammedanism.' To him the Church of England was an historic force of great importance which needed looking after, and generally the best way to do that was to leave it alone. But the Bishops and the Queen pushed and pushed. He was obliged to give way.

The result was as he had feared. Violent passions were influenced. Needless things were done and said. The measure went through but he made no secret of his opinion that he thought it inopportune and ill-advised.

Hearing this, Archbishop Tait made an appointment to see the Prime Minister. Heavy with displeasure, he said he was sure that on reflection Mr Disraeli would agree that ritualistic clergy needed to be disciplined. All the strength of his very powerful personality played on Dizzy like an electric aura. . . . And it made not the slightest difference. No, said the Prime Minister, and he claimed the right of the last word, he did not agree. He did not agree at all.

Nor did he shrink from letting the Queen know his opinions. She pressed that if something was not done to control ritualists the

Church would fall. He would have none of it. He would not even support her when her old friend Mr Gathorne Hardy said in public that she was not Head of the Church. She demanded a speedy retraction. Everyone knew she was Head of the English Church and of the Scotch Church. But no retraction was forthcoming and, a day or two later, having taken legal advice, the Prime Minister wrote to say Mr Hardy had been right. Right! It was unheard of! Mr Disraeli in his jauntiest style made it clear that Queen Elizabeth had waived the title and ever since the sovereign had been Supreme Governor of the Church of England; while, so far as the Scotch Church was concerned, the Lord Advocate advised that the connection of the sovereign with the Kirk was purely civil.

The Defender of the Faith kept silent after that about religion. No more was said. It was as well, decided Dizzy. He hoped the Queen would recapture her sensible dislike of bigotry. Being Titania suited her so much better than being Supreme Governor of the Church of England.

18

On an August evening in 1875, the Queen and Beatrice and Leopold were aboard the royal yacht *Alberta* on the first leg of the autumn journey to Scotland.

Victoria generally enjoyed crossing the Solent, but on this occasion Leopold was being sullen. Refusing to stay on deck, he had gone below by himself. It was too bad of him, she said to Lady Churchill. Sulking in the family always made her apprehensive and the prospect of the long journey ahead made her positively nervous. She was already worried about Beatrice who appeared to have a fondness for disreputable people. A day or two before she had been taken on a visit to the Empress of Austria who was staying at Steephill Castle so that she could see how low royalty could sink. But at the door Victoria had begun to doubt if it was really wise to present her dear innocent child to the auburn-haired beauty who neglected her hard-working little Emperor so shamefully.

The way the Empress travelled about in disguise and collected gondoliers and ate outré dishes in shady places and enjoyed low company should have been an awful warning to Beatrice. Instead she had actually enjoyed herself and shown an instant liking for the Empress. It was alarming, worse – shocking. And now Leopold was adding to his mother's troubles by refusing to understand how necessary it was for him to be careful, girding at the restrictions she was bound to impose on him for his health's sake. . . .

Victoria could not sit still as she would have liked to do and watch Spithead drawing nearer. She left Beatrice at the ship's rail and walked backwards and forwards with Lady Churchill discussing her troubles. Her friend had often been a champion of the royal children. She now tried to point out that Prince Leopold was surely more aware of his disease and the risks he ran than anyone. Might it not be a good plan, she asked, to give him more freedom? Why not a dukedom like his brothers and something to do? Why not a wife?

Victoria was opening her mouth to protest when her daughter turned from the rail:

'Mama, do come and see. There is a most beautiful schooner on this side.'

The Queen raised an admonitory finger. She did not care to be interrupted and from where she was she could already see a schooner's tall masts and billowing sails.

'I hope,' she said severely, 'she is not crewed by those dreadful people who simply sail close to stare and gape.'

'It looks,' murmured Lady Churchill. 'It looks as if she expected. . . .' Her voice tailed off.

'Mama! Mama!' Beatrice's voice was suddenly sharp. 'She is colliding with us.'

There was a crash and a tearing noise. The schooner's masts loomed over the paddle-wheel. The *Alberta* began to shake and swing off course.

The Queen, Beatrice and Lady Churchill remained motionless. Then both Maids of Honour in Waiting came running from below.

'Ma'am,' cried one. 'There is an accident.'

'A collision,' shouted the other hysterically. 'A collision.'

The Queen stood up.

'Harriet, Horatia,' she said. 'Kindly be silent. Leopold! Where is Prince Leopold?'

Colonel Ponsonby had followed the Maids of Honour. Victoria, very pale, seized his arm. It was so unlike her that he realized how upset she was. At that very moment the masts of the schooner toppled and slid out of sight.

The Queen's voice cut through the silence. 'Where is Prince Leopold?'

As if in answer he himself appeared and took her arm.

'There is no danger to anyone on board, Mama,' he reassured her.

'And the yacht?'

Colonel Ponsonby looked away. 'Prince Leopold and I will go and find out, Ma'am. She has gone, but there may be survivors.'

'And Harriet, Horatia, will you please both accompany Colonel Ponsonby?' The Queen's lips were bloodless. Without warning she sat down. Lady Churchill's arms were about her. Already Emilie Dittweiler had arrived unsummoned from her quarters. She had a bottle of sal volatile. Princess Beatrice took it from her.

'No,' said the Queen, pushing the bottle away. 'No. Listen.'

Before they had time to do as she asked she was on her feet again. She went forward and looked over the side. To her horror there was not a vestige of the schooner in sight, merely a boat hook, a spare spar and three deck chairs.

Captain Welch of the *Alberta* sent a request that the Queen should go below. Two bodies were to be brought aboard.

But Victoria hesitated. She watched as an elderly bearded man was heaved out of the water. His face was livid. Two sailors knelt to give him artificial respiration, but one shook his head at the other. It was no use. The Queen hesitated no longer. She went below.

In the succeeding twenty-four hours all the facts were brought to light. The schooner *Mistletoe* had been privately owned and, in her shipwreck, three lives had been lost. Opinion was divided as to where responsibility lay for the collision. Then the newspapers took it up. All agreed that nothing more could have been done for the survivors than had been done, but in the apportionment of blame there were pro-*Mistletoe* newspapers and pro-*Alberta* newspapers.

The Queen felt personally implicated. She insisted to Colonel Ponsonby and Mr Disraeli that she was not a mere passenger on the *Alberta*. When on board her flag was flying and she was in command. Therefore she was responsible for any fault of her officers. Realizing her distress Colonel Ponsonby wrote to the Commodore of the Royal Yacht Squadron criticizing the way people sailed close to gaze at the Queen. If possible it ought to be prevented so that any possibility of collision was avoided. Mr Disraeli, more sensibly, tried to stiffen the Queen's resolve in private but otherwise he did nothing. The coroner's verdict, four weeks later, was that the deaths had been accidental but that Captain Welch of the *Alberta* had been in error of judgement.

Victoria accepted this philosophically but she regretted very much that Captain Welch's reprimand would have to be published. She hoped, she said to the Prime Minister, that it might be avoided. He said he would see what could be done and undertook that every effort would be made to fulfil her wishes. But both he and she knew it was out of the question. Publication was inevitable. When, eventually, it was published and eight months later there was a Parliamentary debate on the matter, he did not stir up public interest by giving the matter any importance. Denied attention it flagged. Soon only a few remembered it. But amongst them was always the Queen.

The *Mistletoe* incident affected her deeply. In old age she was to admit that two of the worst moments she could remember were the death of Albert in the Blue Room at Windsor and the collision at sea in 1875. She had terrible nightmares in which the shipwreck took place again and again. She heard the rending and splintering of timber night after night, and the snap of rigging and the tearing of sail-cloth and the cries and the juddering roar of the *Alberta*'s engine. And she saw picture after picture of the collision, one snapping after the other like a torturer's lantern lecture, always ending with two, the worst, the starkest – a picture of the masts toppling and sliding out of sight, and then one of that old man's black face as the two sailors bent over him and pumped at his arms. For a time she had no heart to be Titania, barely the spirit to keep going about her daily duties; and though most of this *crise de nerfs* was hidden from her Court by her habitual mask of regal composure, a few saw it and were distressed for her.

Disraeli saw it immediately. He cast about to discover something which would take her out of herself and push the collision to the back of her mind. Only three months afterwards the perfect diversion presented itself.

The fourteenth earl of Derby, who had been Prime Minister, was now dead. His son and heir, the fifteenth earl, was Foreign Secretary. Disraeli liked him. He respected his scholarship, wit and lack of bellicosity. He had, too, a nice humility. 'The least Stanley of the Stanleys' was Dizzy's comment.

This nobleman was standing before a large open fire at the Foreign Office on a November morning when Mr Frederick Greenwood sent up his card. There was a fractional pause while Derby studied the card, but Mr Greenwood was editor of the *Pall Mall Gazette*, a not inconsiderable organ in the political world. He was invited to the sanctum so lately vacated by 'Puss' Granville where Lord John Russell had once spun his Whiggish net, and, for years and years, aided by a mere handful of clerks, Lord Palmerston had bullied Europe with his gunboat policy.

What Mr Greenwood said was brief. He told Lord Derby that the Khedive of Egypt was selling his controlling shares in the Suez Canal to France. For ready money he might be persuaded to change his mind and sell to England.

Derby himself was not enthusiastic. He was easily overawed by great entrepreneurs. Dizzy was not. He seized on the opportunity and persuaded his cabinet to agree with him. Nothing should stand in England's way, even though Parliament was not in session and the necessary finance could not be voted. He reassured his colleagues. There were advantages in being old Isaac D'Israeli's son.

Montagu Corry was sent off to see Rothschild. Being from the Prime Minister he was directly ushered into the dining-room where Rothschild was eating grapes. Corry refused all offers of hospitality. The matter was urgent, extremely urgent, he said. Disraeli had need of four million pounds on the following day.

Rothschild sucked at a grape and extracted the skin from his mouth.

'Four millions. Four millions. And your security, Mr Corry?'
'The British Government.'
Rothschild took another grape. 'Very well. You shall have it.'

Aware of the Queen's low state of mind, Disraeli played exactly the right notes to inspirit her. He refused to treat the triumphant purchase as a simple government coup, and, disdaining the Gladstonian and more normal method of reporting the business affected by her ministers, he offered the Suez Canal as a personal offering to Titania.

Mr Disraeli, with his humble duty to your Majesty: It is just settled. You have it, Madam. . . . Four millions sterling! And almost immediately. There was only one firm that could do it – Rothschild's. They behaved admirably; advanced the money at a low rate, and the entire interest of the Khedive is now yours, Madam.

It was an exotic gift which, as he had hoped, drove the *Mistletoe* disaster to its proper place in the Queen's subconscious.

Unfortunately, though, she rapidly developed an appetite for more. She wished, she said, to be Empress of India. Russia, Germany and Austria and Hungary, even China, had emperors and, until recently, so had Mexico and France. Moreover, since the Mutiny she had been Empress of India in all but name and all England thought of her as such. She made it known in political circles that she now wished for the formal title.

It made Mr Gladstone in Cheshire shake his head. He had formally resigned from the leadership of the Liberal Party, but through his friends he made it clear that this un-English idea was not a good one. The more radical Liberals were prepared if necessary to rely on the average Englishman's dislike of any sort of change and to make party capital out of it. Naturally they blamed Disraeli for his love of oriental tinsel.

In fact Disraeli had shaken his head with equal vigour. He was more than a little alarmed. The time was no more opportune to make Titania Empress of India than it was to bully clergymen into toeing the line about what they should do and wear and put in church. He begged the Queen to wait for a time while he quietly looked into the matter to see if it was expedient and feasible. To move hastily would be to make it too controversial because it was just the sort of juicy morsel the press enjoyed.

Reluctantly she agreed.

19

The Prince of Wales was going to India. He had managed all the arrangements and got himself grants towards the considerable expenses of the visit by the cunning expedient of telling his mother it was with the full approval of her Minister and telling Disraeli it was with the full approval of the Queen.

Neither was deceived, but Disraeli thought the Prince could do India no possible sort of harm and the Queen believed that if he kept a discreet tongue in his head he might in fact do good and help her towards achieving the imperial title. But Alix was not to go. Her presence would raise too many problems in a country where women were kept in subjection.

There were the usual storms about the Prince's staff. The Queen did not approve of his three personal guests. Inevitably they included the Duke of Sutherland – 'with his piper – unheard of!' Nor did she care for his plans to take a detachment of Life Guards. She stopped the last, but Disraeli advised her to give way over the rest and send her own representative with the Prince.

The Queen sent for Lord Alfred Paget – one of the beautiful Pagets and once the gayest and most handsome of her courtiers. She still had a place in her heart for him, and he still adored her. She received him in the drawing-room of her private apartments at Windsor, a sure sign of her affection.

Though no longer young he held himself well and no one at Court could kiss the royal hand with more panache. He stood back against a table of bamboo and lacquer, and he begged to know how he might serve her.

'Lord Alfred,' she said. 'I wish you to go to India.' She explained why and what she wanted him to do. 'It is for the Prince's own sake,' she finished. 'He needs looking after.'

The request was unusual and Lord Alfred felt just a little too old to go off gallivanting with a Prince of Wales – for that, as he well knew, was what would be required of him. But he still had spirit. The man who had paid a special visit to the field of Waterloo to see where his father's leg had been buried was not the sort to balk at any task, however bizarre. He did not hesitate.

'Of course, Ma'am.' He bowed. 'It will be a pleasure to serve you.'

She did not miss the point. He would do things for her which no power on earth would have made him do for the Prince of Wales. 'Dear Lord Alfred,' she murmured.

As he bowed a second time his eye caught a statuette of the Queen on the large red table behind the fire sofa. It was an equestrian figure modelled when she was little more than a bride and took him back to the days when she had led her Household in tremendous gallops across the countryside. Melbourne with his white beaver hat had always been there, and after her marriage the Prince, but the best rider of all had been the Queen.

She followed his gaze, and smiled, sharing the same thoughts.

'We are growing older, Lord Alfred,' she said softly.

'It is a privilege,' he replied gallantly, 'which is denied to many.'

So Lord Alfred Paget was added to the Prince of Wales' suite and the Prince revenged himself by having a row with Brown. It was the quickest, surest way of provoking his mother.

The year before the Prince had told Colonel Ponsonby that he refused to go to Abergeldie because Brown interfered with the shooting. It was too much, he said, for a Prince of the Blood to have his shooting creamed off by a hired ghillie. His reason was now leaked to the Queen. She was very angry indeed. Oh, the ingratitude! Dear John Brown had saved her from O'Connor, and her own children persisted in quarrelling with him.

Indeed they did. 'Brown rows' as Ponsonby called them were a feature at this time.

The royal children's hostility to Brown put the Queen into a false position. She had no doubt that on occasions he got a little above himself. Everyone did at times. But, considering his opportunities, Brown took very little advantage of his position. For a village boy – and she did not deceive herself that he was anything else – he was a remarkably self-controlled and loyal servant. But she was of the opinion that her children, with their advantages of position and upbringing, ought to be more tactful and, instead of causing trouble and demanding that she arbitrate in their quarrels, they should be prepared to put up with Brown's weaknesses simply because he meant so much to her. If they wouldn't or couldn't, and insisted on placing her in a difficult position, why then she would defend Brown even when he was in the wrong. She had the ruthlessness to realize that in the matter of ordinary day-to-day comfort he meant more to her than her children did.

Bertie was bad enough. Alfred was worse. Marrying a Grand Duchess had made him put on airs and he told his mother it was humiliating for Marie to have to greet her Highland Servant.

Ordinary politeness, came his mother's tart rejoinder, demanded that no servant be ignored; and that particular servant protected her from assassins, chased reporters over the bens to ensure her privacy, made sure she was always warm, dry, kept from danger and well looked after.

It made no difference. Prince Alfred and Brown quarrelled repeatedly. On arriving at Balmoral the Prince shook hands with everyone except Brown. Then when Brown ordered the fiddlers to stop playing, his order was countermanded by the Prince. And so it went on. The Prince at last rebelled against the quaint royal custom of putting cut-up squares of newspaper in the lavatories and he laid the responsibility at Brown's door. The Queen snapped back. How could it be Brown's fault? It had been the custom at Windsor when she was a girl. She ordered a thorough investigation into the dispute between them. The Prince would only consent to see Brown in the presence of the Queen's Private Secretary and said: 'If I see a man on board my ship on any subject, it is always in the presence of an officer.' This vulgar reminder that he was a Royal Highness and Brown was a nobody enraged the Queen. 'Balmoral is not a ship. I will *not* have naval discipline introduced into my own home.'

Alfred hit back by supporting his brother Leopold's sulky attempts for greater independence. He recommended that he be given the command of a corps of volunteers at Balmoral. And he persuaded everyone in the family to agree. Everyone urged the Queen to consent. She almost did – until Brown said the terrain was hardly suitable for a royal commanding officer with a gammy knee, and he killed the idea stone dead by warning her 'There'll be bugling here, and bugling there, and not a scrap of peace will we get for all the bugling.' That was that. Brown's advice did not endear him to the royal princes.

Vicky was no better than the rest. Being aware of her inmost thoughts through their regular and frank exchange of letters the Queen reckoned that Vicky more than anyone ought to have understood what Brown meant to her. But apparently she did not, and saw him simply as a servant, and gave her daughter Charlotte careful instructions about how to behave when she went to stay with Grandmama in Scotland. When the first greetings were done Victoria told the child to say 'how d'you do' to Brown. She did. But she would not shake his hand. 'Mama,' she said primly, 'says I ought not to be too familiar with servants.' She found herself shaken and scolded for her rudeness, and the Queen herself apologized to Brown for her grandchild. He was hurt and showed it.

Brown rows. Despite threats, Bertie did go to Abergeldie that summer and did a good deal of shooting. When he had to go south to prepare for his visit to India he called to say good-bye to his mother. Fortunately he had shot four stags that day. Unfortunately he lost himself afterwards and did not arrive at Balmoral for dinner until ten past ten. He was under some strain, but he dutifully sent for Löhlein and Brown to say good-bye when it was time to go. Löhlein he made a great fuss of. He always did, believing he was his half-uncle. But in the Balmoral hall that night his display of affection looked ostentatious. Then he simply put out his hand to Brown and when Brown said: 'God bless your Royal Highness, and bring you safe back!' he gave a grimace. The Queen burst into tears. Almost everyone believed it was because she was overwrought at the imminent departure of her son. A few, about three or four, knew better.

Brown rows. Brown rows.

It was something to get away from Balmoral on a visit to Louise at Inverary, yet even there there were looks because Louise danced a reel with Brown. And why not? Beatrice danced a schottische with a mere Campbell forester, and at home at Balmoral she herself often danced with Brown at ghillies' balls.

In fact, secretly, she was surprised. Louise was putting on airs. She complained that her husband's relations did not treat her with becoming respect. Such nonsense, the Queen thought. Louise had married into a Duke's family and that was that. She suspected that

Louise was already tiring of her handsome Lorne and lacked the self-control to hide her feelings. Poor girl. She had had no children as the doctors had feared. Poor Lorne, too. It was a pity he wasn't going to India with Bertie. He would have enjoyed it. It was a pity, she thought in a sudden gust of anger, that all her children could not have gone there. The Brown rows would die down and she could have a peaceful autumn and winter.

At divine service at Crathay on the week-end before the Prince of Wales' departure the minister uttered a long and loyal extempore prayer for his safety and ended : 'Oh, bless abundantly the objects of his mission.'

As a Scotch minister can, he got the best out of the word 'abundantly'. It echoed round the kirk.

The Queen in her box pew gave a very small inclination of the head. What was the man praying about? She doubted if Bertie had any mission, beyond the exchange of costly gifts which he would not have to pay for, the eating of sumptuous banquets, the pursuit of oriental beauties, the sticking of pigs and the shooting of elephants and tigers. Still, he might impress upon the Indians their need for an empress.

'Amen,' she said solemnly.

The prayer was answered.

The Indians declared their devotion for the Empress through the Prince of Wales. They did it constantly and with great enthusiasm. So much so that Disraeli sighed and admitted defeat. The Indians appeared to want an empress as much as the Queen wished for an imperial crown. Reluctantly he prepared a Royal Titles Bill to put to Parliament. Empress of India would be added to her style and title after Defender of the Faith. But she would not be Empress of England and her children would not be Imperial Highnesses.

Ignorant of what was being done in London, the Prince of Wales was enjoying himself. His talent for balancing the grave and the gay was never more pronounced. Appreciating the pomp of his welcome at Bombay – and no prince, except perhaps his nephew, Willy of Prussia, was as fond of ceremonial, bright uniforms and accoutrements – he also thoroughly enjoyed the illuminated arches with quaintly-styled loyal mottoes such as 'How is your Royal Mother?' and 'Tell Mamma we're happy'. And later, after holding an investiture of the Order of the Star of India on the Maidan, an occasion of magnificence seldom matched in the history of the Orient, and banqueting with equal splendour, he insisted on seeing a performance of his favourite farce, *My Awful Dad*.

'Princes of the Blood,' said Victoria when she heard of this, 'ought not to have favourite farces.'

Her representative in India had his patience tried and his stamina tested as he tottered from one junket to another, but Lord Alfred refused to be left out of anything. He considered it his duty to be present on all occasions. The Prince, he reported, was in his element and apparently inexhaustible. Receptions, banquets, balls, firework displays, race meetings, polo games, naval and military reviews, garden parties, church parades, hunts and entertainments succeeded one another in a glittering stream. The Prince was the perfect society figure and with his combination of dignity and geniality made many friends for England amongst the Indian princes. He also deprecated the insolent habit of some of the British who referred to the Indians as niggers, and he let his displeasure be known. The Queen felt bound to admit that Bertie had far, far exceeded all her expectations, and it was gratifying that, largely owing to him, she would soon be Empress of India.

For her sake Mr Disraeli had faced his critics and was steering a Royal Titles Bill through Parliament. It appeared to satisfy most people except the republicans – and the Prince of Wales who, by an oversight, had neither been consulted nor even informed about what was going on and which touched him so nearly. He wrote an angry complaint from India but Disraeli was not in the least put out. Beginning 'Sir, and *dear* Prince', he sent a bland apology saying that owing to His Royal Highness's circumrotation about the sub-continent he had not been kept fully informed of his address. This extraordinary excuse made the Prince laugh so much that Disraeli was forgiven.

The Prince was pleased, too, with the letters he was receiving from his mother. They were unusually warm and complimentary. When, to Lord Alfred's infinite relief, he at last left India, with a huge assortment of valuable gifts and a menagerie, orchids, two native A.D.C.s and a Madras curry cook, he was confident that he stood high in his mother's esteem. It was a rare comfortable feeling.

Unfortunately it did not last.

Even before he reached Cairo in the spring of 1876 the drawing-rooms of London were buzzing with what became known as the Aylesford–Blandford scandal.

20

It was March and the Queen was on one of her infrequent visits to London. She was in low spirits. At the beginning of the month her dear, dear friend Augusta Stanley had died. Though they had seen less of each other in recent years their affection had not altered in the least. And now Augusta was gone. Victoria had tried to do all she could to comfort the sorrowing Dean, but it was difficult. Her own sorrow matched his.

Everyone understood this.

Respecting her grief, people were still reluctant to intrude on her privacy, and she was left a good deal on her own both by the members of her family and by the Household. She was, therefore, rather surprised when word was brought one afternoon that the Princess of Wales desired a private audience. The matter was urgent. Might she be admitted at once?

Victoria's heart fluttered when her daughter-in-law came into the room. 'Dear Alix,' she said, raising her from her curtsey and kissing her on a cheek which was unusually warm. 'Pray be seated and I will order tea.' Remembering Alix's deafness she repeated herself.

'Thank you, no, Mama.'

'A little wine, perhaps? A biscuit?'

'Thank you, no.'

The Princess sat on the edge of a chair trying to compose herself. She made mention of Lady Augusta's sad death and apologized for breaking in on the Queen without any sort of notice.

Victoria gave her a little nod, to show that she understood, and to encourage her.

'I have come to you, Mama,' began Alix and broke off. There were diamonds of tears at the corners of her eyes. 'I have come at once because this afternoon two gentlemen called on me.'

The Queen's face tightened into a frown. 'You received them?'

The Princess lowered her eyes. 'Yes, Mama. They were Lord Alington and Lord Randolph Churchill.' Lightly she touched her ear by way of explanation. 'I believed that Lady Ailesbury had been announced and I sent for her to come up.' Again she touched her ear. 'This deafness can be a great nuisance. It misled me into receiving two gentlemen.'

The Queen smiled at her. 'There, no harm is done. Now that you have told me, I can silence any gossip.' Her round chin set firmly. 'And I shall.'

But her reassurance did not appear to comfort Alix.

'Lord Alington,' she said, 'was merely there as Lord Randolph's friend, but Lord Randolph. . . .' The tears broke from the corners of her eyes. They slid down her cheeks. 'Lord Randolph, Mama, was not a gentleman.'

The Queen gasped. She did not care for the Duke of Marlborough's younger son. He had always been a worry to his mother and, besides being that awful thing – a political adventurer, he was a star if not a planet in the Marlborough House Set. Moreover he was brash, and he had married an American, and he was for ever telling that stupid story of how as a boy at Eton he had frightened the Princess of Wales when she was being driven down to the station in her bridal carriage. Well, it appeared he had frightened her again, and seriously this time. 'Yes,' she said grimly. 'Tell me, dear. It is not difficult to believe anything of that scamp from Blenheim.'

Alix hesitated, but only for a moment. 'You know, perhaps, Mama, about the Aylesfords?'

'I do.'

Who, thought the Queen irritably, did not? They advertised their mischief so blatantly. Lord Aylesford who was now with Bertie on his way home from India, had said he would divorce his wife because she wished to run off with Lord Blandford, Randolph Churchill's elder brother. It was disgraceful.

'Lord Randolph does not want the divorce to go through. It would be bad for his brother.'

'It would.'

'And it would be bad for Lady Aylesford.'

'Yes Alex, it would,' agreed the Queen rather impatiently. 'Please come to the point.'

'It is a painful point.' Slowly and with obvious reluctance she explained that at some time in the past Bertie had been enamoured of Lady Aylesford. Whether or not it had been an innocent flirtation was beside the point. What mattered was that in an excess of love he had written a number of compromising letters.

The Queen looked up at the ceiling. 'Again!' she exclaimed.

'Yes, Mama. You know what Bertie is. We both know him so well.'

Indeed we do, thought the Queen. Suddenly she felt an urge to take a strap to him – but, even if he had been there, one could hardly claim a parental right and thrash a heavily-bearded, portly thirty-four-year-old Prince of the Blood however much good it might do him.

Alix's voice broke through her thoughts. She was saying that Lord Randolph had the letters and wished the Princess to persuade her husband to bring pressure on Lord Aylesford. Otherwise the letters would be published —

'One moment, Alix, please,' interrupted the Queen. 'I wish to have this exact. Lord Randolph threatened you with those letters?'

Alix nodded. She had stopped crying. There was a look of defiance on her beautiful face.

'In your own drawing-room?'

'Yes. He shook them at me. A packet. And he assured me that if they were published Bertie would never sit on the throne of England. . . .' She broke off. The Queen looked terrifyingly angry.

She took her daughter-in-law's hand. 'You are not to worry,' she said in the calm but strong voice which a number of people had learnt to fear. 'I shall take care of this myself by writing immediately to Bertie and giving him my full support and confidence. He has been a stupid boy and no doubt he deserves a shock to put him in his senses, but I will *not* allow that dreadful little Churchill to intimidate a Princess of Wales in her own drawing-room.'

. . . . .

The Prince of Wales was enjoying light Egyptian entertainments – quail shooting and Offenbach – when he heard that his supposed friend Randolph Churchill had shaken a packet of his letters in Alix's face. He was so angry that he instantly sent his naval A.D.C. by the fastest possible route to challenge Churchill to a duel. He undertook to meet him on the sands at Calais and teach him a lesson in manners. At Malta he received Churchill's insolent refusal. He claimed that a duel between them was impossible because the Prince was heir to the Crown, and no one, he added nastily, knew that better than the Prince. . . .

It was a great comfort to have his mother's support. To his surprise and delight the Queen had telegraphed and written her entire confidence in him. She offered to fall in with any plans he might like to make in concert with the Lord Chancellor and Mr Disraeli.

The spring was unusually fine but Dizzy still found it cold. Well wrapped in his long white overcoat he took a constitutional in Birdcage Walk. Montagu Corry was with him but neither spoke. Corry was enjoying the fresh green of the trees and the tepid sunshine, Disraeli was worrying about the Royal Titles Bill. The radicals were being difficult. He would push it through, but not without a struggle, and the Queen was clearly suffering from the hostile criticism which she tended to take as personal insults. His hide being as tough as that of anyone with long Parliamentary service, he would have to steer most of the acrimony in his own direction. Poor Queen. She already had enough burdens, and Titania ought not to be racked with terrestrial concerns.

For the moment he put the Royal Titles Bill out of his thoughts.

What, he asked, breaking the silence, were they to do about their gadabout Prince Hal?

Montagu Corry shifted his concentration from spring to this less congenial topic.

They talked for a long time, walking backwards and forwards beneath the trees. There were difficulties but, under real pressure, Lord Randolph might be persuaded to part with the letters. Then the Prince's return must be carefully stage-managed. The *mis en scène* should include a meeting of husband and wife on shipboard before he met anyone else. It would gratify the public, and still wagging tongues. To still them further the Prince and Princess should go to the opera on the first night of their return to London. They would take their two sons, a fine domestic touch. They would be greeted by society as a perfectly reconciled couple. Aylesford must, of course, be pressed into withdrawing his divorce proceedings. Ordinary separation was the civilized, gentlemanly thing to aim for and it should not be difficult to persuade him. Aylesford was a buffoon. Playing the Aylesford game in the Marlborough House Set meant that his lordship scrambled about the room on all fours while ladies and gentlemen aimed kicks and slaps at his posterior. Such a man, thought Dizzy, would be as pithy and bendable as a reed. And afterwards? The Queen was friendly with the Marlboroughs and would not wish to drive them from Court. But some sort of temporary exile seemed called for. Possibly it would be as well to make the Duke viceroy of Ireland, and as for Lord Randolph . . . well, said Dizzy, if he knew the Prince of Wales, Lord Randolph was going to be cut dead and ostracized by society for a very long time.

It all turned out as the Prime Minister and his Private Secretary had plotted under the trees in Birdcage Walk.

Everyone in the end was partially satisfied, no one wholly so, except, of course, Lord Randolph who was not in the least satisfied. For his ungentlemanly behaviour to the Princess of Wales he suffered as a social leper for the next eight years.

21

After a great deal of patient and skilful negotiation Disraeli squeezed the Royal Titles Bill through both Houses of Parliament. Victoria gladly added her royal consent. The bill became law. Henceforth she was Empress of India.

On May Day she was proclaimed. Almost at once she sent for a present brought her from India by Bertie, a copy of her own *Leaves* translated into Hindustani with covers of inlaid marble.

She valued it greatly and, with her sense of occasion, she decided it was appropriate to autograph it with her new style and title. It was the first time she had writen *Victoria R & I* and the signature was a little shaky.

Then she sent for dear Mr Disraeli who, having given her such a very welcome present as the Suez Canal, had now presented her with a vast empire. She begged him to accept a peerage. Often before she had expressed a wish for it, declaring it was only seemly that the First Minister of a Queen should be a peer. Now she added the cogent, friendly argument that the Prime Minister was growing older and he needed to escape from the hurly-burly of the Commons to the more stately campaigning in the Lords.

Disraeli hesitated. He was aware of the Queen's reluctance to ennoble Jews. Courteously and modestly he mentioned it.

She was amazed. 'But you,' she said, her eyes wide, 'are not a Jew.'

She meant it. To Victoria one was or was not a Jew according to religion.

Dizzy, with his deep consciousness of belonging, as he called it, to the children of the sun, was wryly amused by her definition. But he was also touched by her thoughtfulness, and because his old rival Gladstone would never again lead the Liberals in the Commons, he consented.

In August he went down to the Faery Isle and there Titania made him a belted earl. He chose to use Mary Anne's title, and one of the first acts of the new Lord Beaconsfield was to endorse his belief that there could be no possible harm in the Queen's desire for a retired and private life at Osborne. It gave her great satisfaction because the critics of her seclusion had recently renewed their attacks and had talked sneeringly of the invisible empress.

Dizzy reassured her. Let the press, the radicals and the busybodies say what they wished. The electric telegraph, railway expresses and an increasingly rapid postal service made Osborne sufficiently close to the centre of government. And, in any case, Tiberius had had his Capri. Why should not the Empress of India have her Isle of Wight? These, he told Victoria, were their mellow years to be savoured and appreciated.

His own pleasure was spiced when Gladstone snappily disapproved of his rival's peerage. Montagu Corry told him that the old Liberal leader had stormed: 'Earl! Earl! I cannot forgive him for not having made himself a duke!'

Dizzy's happy optimism made him see splendid vistas stretching ahead – the promise of a calm, Arcadian old age. Temporarily he overlooked the fact that he was at the centre of a political battle-ground.

Quite soon he was reminded of it.

In the field of diplomacy there was evidence of unrest. The Prussians, for example, were more above themselves than ever, and neither the Queen nor her subjects were pleased to hear that England's Ambassador had been treated like a schoolboy at the Emperor's court. Inadvertently he had arrived for an audience with a dirty face, and, there being no time for him to go away and wash, he had been seized by the Iron Chancellor and cleaned with spit and a handkerchief outside the Emperor's door. Such humiliation annoyed the English – except, fortunately, the Ambassador, who did not mind in the least, and the new Lord Beaconsfield, who translated it as a sign of Bismarck's disposition to be friendly.

Then the perennial problems of the Orient threatened to erupt again. It was understandable, perhaps. There had always been an Eastern question in English diplomacy. For a thousand years Russia had thirsted for control of the Bosphorus and she was the enemy to peace. Turkey, who blocked Russia's wishes, was the friend – but feeble, corrupt, decaying. Turkey was the dying man of Europe.

Within the short space of four months the Ottoman Empire had three Sultans. Abdul Aziz, who called himself one of Queen Victoria's oriental brothers and was a Knight of the Garter, developed eccentric tendencies. Amongst other quaint amusements, he had a habit of releasing poultry in the royal harem and there he would stalk and slaughter them amidst the screams and giggles of his concubines. He was deposed and soon afterwards slew himself with a small and blunt pair of scissors. His successor was a dipsomaniac, and he, too, was quickly deposed. The new Sultan was the son of a consumptive Circassian slave who had a morbid dread of poison, crowds and electricity, and had a passion for regattas, Sherlock Holmes, and a certain little Belgian *modiste* kept as an extra to his vast harem. Throughout Europe this Sultan was known as Abdul the Damned. Inevitably there was trouble. Ruled by such inadequate despots the Ottoman Empire was breaking up. The chancelleries of Europe watched and waited. In distant, foggy London, Dizzy – shaken from his dreams of Arcady – consulted with Derby. They wondered who would pick up the bits? Would Russia now seize the Bosphorus and threaten India and Suez and English trade? Was Bismarck sincere in his anti-Turk feelings?

There was no time for leisurely speculation.

Abdul the Damned's subject peoples in Bosnia, Herzegovina and Bulgaria rebelled, and, although raising a small expeditionary force to quell the rebels was a severe strain on the treasury and commissariat and general resources of the Turks, they managed it. . . . And suddenly, mystifyingly, Dizzy and Derby found themselves under attack; not from Russia or from any European state, but from the direction of Cheshire.

Although the leaders of the Liberals were at one with the Conservatives in their Eastern policy, Mr Gladstone was not. He rose, literally, from his sick bed to denounce the violence done to the Bulgars by their Turkish masters. His source of information was the *Daily News*, where it was stated children had been massacred, women violated, girls sold into slavery, and Christians thrown into dungeons.

Gladstone sat at his desk and wrote a pamphlet. White-hot with indignation, it was a memorable onslaught, its peroration grand:

> *Let the Turks now carry away their abuses in the only possible manner, namely by carrying off themselves. Their Zaptiehs and their Mudirs, their Bimbashis and their Yuzbachis, their Kaimakams and their Pashas, one and all, bag and baggage, shall, I hope, clear out from the province they have desolated and profaned.*

The Queen was mystified by the peroration. 'General Ponsonby,' she inquired. 'What do these peculiar words mean?'

Her Private Secretary bowed. 'They are titles of office held in the Ottoman Empire, Ma'am.'

'They sound very terrible.'

'They do indeed in Mr Gladstone's pamphlet. But I should draw your attention, Ma'am, to the fact that your Majesty's ambassador has not yet reported any atrocities.'

It cost Ponsonby something to say this. He was a doctrinaire

Liberal and devoted to Gladstone. But his duty to the Queen, to give her impartial advice, had to come first.

The Queen brightened. 'There are no official reports?'

'Not yet, Ma'am. We may hope the newspaper report was exaggerated. They often are.'

'Indeed, yes.'

Leaves had sold by the thousands, but it never came near the sale of Mr Gladstone's pamphlet. The country thrilled with horror. There were monster protest meetings at Blackheath, Piccadilly, St James's Hall, and elsewhere. Disraeli, as the official ally of Abdul the Damned, found himself at the centre of a political gale. It blew and whistled about his head. So cyclonic were people's feelings that in a Liverpool theatre where *Othello* was being played, the whole audience rose and applauded at the words: 'the Turks are drowned'.

The leaders of the Liberal Party, Lords Granville and Hartington, Puss and Harty-tarty to their followers and friends, were distinctly put out. It was understandable. On Gladstone's formal resignation of the leadership they had been voted into joint office, but the People's William had resurrected himself and was on the rampage up and down the country, speaking his head off in the Commons, and earning himself a new affectionate title. He was now called the Grand Old Man – which was all very well, but where did it leave Puss and Harty-tarty?

The Prime Minister refused to declare himself until he heard officially from the ambassador at Constantinople. He spoke of 'Bulgarian Atrocities' as though the words should be kept permanently in inverted commas, talked jauntily of 'coffee-house babble', and castigated Gladstone's pamphlet as the worst atrocity of the lot. And even when the news was officially confirmed, he still would not alter his policy.

Goaded by his insouciance Gladstone retorted that very likely the Conservatives would go on to annexe Egypt and then Lord Beaconsfield would make himself Duke of Memphis.

Dizzy replied without passion that the Government's policy was to protect India and the Suez Canal, and it was the correct one. He asked what the Liberals would have him do? Was it reasonable to avenge Bulgarian atrocities by butchery on a larger scale?

This sort of logic had no appeal to the mass of people. They continued to agitate, and Dizzy let them. He attempted to seem calm. When over-heated he disciplined himself to make private not public comments on what he regarded as Gladstone's self-interested behaviour:

> *Posterity will do justice* [he wrote to Lord Derby] *to that unprincipled maniac Gladstone – extraordinary mixture of envy, vindictiveness, hypocrisy and superstition; and with one commanding characteristic – whether Prime Minister, or Leader of the Opposition, whether preaching or praying, speechifying or scribbling – never a gentleman.*

It showed how, beneath a placid exterior, Disraeli felt the taunts and stings that he could conceive so mistaken a pen-portrait of his great rival.

It was in fact a dreadful time for the Prime Minister. He knew from his long and deep political experience that when England was afire with moral indignation it was wiser to do nothing until the flames died down, but many of the flames licked at him. And, while he burnt from public reproofs, his life was made no easier by the need to act as reconciling grand vizier to the royal family.

The Queen's children and her Household were split down the middle in their political views and this hardly made for peace. There was trouble between the Waleses because the Prince had taken up with a Miss Chamberlayne from Ohio, a young American coarsely nicknamed 'Chamberpots' by the wronged Princess. And further trouble blew up when the Queen discovered that her heir had actually set up a permanent mistress named Lily Langtry. Dizzy did his best, but the royal family made his head spin.

Then the public upheaval about Bulgarian Atrocities gave way to another which – in a typically British fashion – was almost exactly its opposite. Having been urged to thrash the Turks, Lord Beaconsfield was now urged to thrash the Russians because Russia had declared war on the Turks. Everyone was suddenly converted to his point of view. He had been right all along. If Russia won and seized the Bosphorus she would menace the Indian Empire and trade. The atrocious Turk was once more England's friend. Dizzy must trounce the Russian bear.

A popular ballad was sung the length of the kingdom:

We don't want to fight,
But, by Jingo! if we do,
We've got the ships,
We've got the men,
We've got the money too.
and then, in a rousing tutti:
The Russians shall NOT *have Constantinople*

Disraeli cynically observed that an Englishman's moral indignation was most easily dowsed by a threat to his pride or pocket. But he had been too long in politics to be astonished by the volte-face, and, besides, it was amusing to hear that a new Sunday occupation had sprung up of going to boo Gladstone's London home and break his windows.

Lord Derby was less indulgent. He was revolted by the bellicosity of the mob and, rather than risk a war, he resigned. Dizzy had to let him go, but only with the greatest reluctance. Thereafter he persevered in his policy of alarming Russia by a threat of war which he had no wish to make.

It was a diplomatic tightroping which ordinarily suited him, but it was exhausting. Under constant attack from the Liberals because he used the expression 'the interests of England', he taunted them for their lukewarm patriotism. And simultaneously he was obliged to cool the blazing heat of his sovereign's patriotism. She was exceedingly belligerent and he found it trying. Family squabbles, the unusual heat of that spring and summer, and her old dislike of the Russians inflamed her military ardour. She telegraphed or sent letters by special messenger every day, sometimes every hour of the day. She was desperately worried, she told him, that England would lose her prestige for ever. It worried her night and day.

The language, the insulting language, used by the Russians against us! It makes the Queen's blood boil!

And it continued boiling:

Oh, if the Queen were a man, she would like to go and give those Russians . . . such a beating.

She even threatened abdication, but here Disraeli felt he was on safe ground.

> *If England is to kiss Russia's feet, she will not be a party to the humiliation of England and would lay down her crown.*

Yet she actually appeared to mean it. She gave a second warning. If Russia took Constantinople she would abdicate.

'*Be bold!*' she urged him.

He was bold in the sense that, with coolness and constant good humour, he continued to give an appearance of doing absolutely nothing at all. He refused to be bullied by anyone. Even Princess Mary of Cambridge found him intractable. He found himself next to her at a dinner one evening, a formidable enough event in itself because she was one of the biggest women in England and spread here there and everywhere, but her sharp criticism of his slowness in chastizing Russia made her even more of a dragon. She goaded him to declare war for the honour of England, adding: 'I cannot imagine what you are waiting for.' But Dizzy was not to be squashed. 'Potatoes at this moment, Ma'am,' he replied deftly.

When Parliament rose he fled to Hughenden. He felt old and he felt unwell. He gasped so much when he walked that he had to sit still or use Mary Anne's pony trap. Montagu Corry made him return to London to see a doctor. The diagnosis was lengthy. The Prime Minister had asthma, bronchitis, Bright's disease, and so forth. It amounted to the fact that he was on his very last reserves of strength.

Russia won her war. She wanted the Turkish plums. Close to hysteria, the British people demanded that she be attacked. The fleet was sent to Constantinople, but it was not used. Dizzy was still biding his time and enraging everyone. He remarked that the peace terms offered by Russia to Turkey could not possibly be acceptable to the Powers. And he was right. Bismarck agreed with him. The Powers were invited to Berlin to thrash the matter out.

Travelling half-way across Europe was a dismal prospect for a man as old and as ill as Dizzy. He took with him his new Foreign Minister, Lord Salisbury, who was a Cecil and therefore, he judged, by birth a shrewd negotiator, and who had, moreover, the impressive looks of a minor prophet. He himself felt and said he most resembled a walled-up crusader. This pair of plenipotentiaries, crusader and minor prophet, took a special train from Brussels and planned their final game of bluff and double bluff, and double, double bluff with the Powers face to face.

They put up at the Kaiserhof. Lord Odo the Ambassador had explained that the British Embassy would be far less comfortable. Anything, anything, anything for comfort, said Dizzy, apparently revitalized rather than exhausted by the long crawl to Berlin. His hotel apartments were bright and comfortable and warm. There were huge bouquets awaiting him and a basket of strawberries and chilled wine and fond messages from Titania's eldest daughter. The Crown Princess was so glad, she wrote, to have Mama's great friend Lord Beaconsfield in the country. He, too, was delighted to be there. Recently, amongst his lady friends, he had instituted an Order of the Bee, that is, to each he gave a brooch fashioned like a bee. The Queen had permitted Princess Beatrice to accept and wear the order. Should he, he wondered, offer it to the Crown Princess? But he had little time in which to ponder the question and, in the event, Vicky never was so honoured, because Bismarck's secretary was at the door begging that the English plenipotentiaries should spare time for a preliminary meeting with his master before the Congress. Dizzy glanced meaningly at Salisbury. The Congress had to be carefully arranged beforehand or, of course, it could not be expected to function smoothly.

This was how it turned out.

The Russians tried a counter bluff, but Lord Beaconsfield remained cool and immovable. He went so far as to order a special train to take the British delegation away and immediately the Russians collapsed.

To threaten a war which he had no intention of declaring for months and months and months and suddenly get his way were delicious to Disraeli. He and Bismarck had quickly sized each other up and respected each other. The Iron Chancellor was struck by the force behind his frail guest. He looked too emaciated, too delicate to have such strong sinews in negotiation. Dizzy frankly admired Prince Bismarck's military directness and his way of averting disaster when things tended to go wrong at the Congress. He also vastly admired the old Chancellor's habit of sinking stout and champagne. Stein after stein disappeared at a rate that would have given any other man of his age an apoplectic stroke. And the way he dealt with a dinner at the Turkish Embassy (the best dinner, Dizzy noted, of all the embassy dinners), gobbling up kebab after kebab and gorging himself with a pilaff, was positively astounding. . . .

When the Congress ended in July, 1878, all the British requirements had been met and Dizzy had in his pocket the island of Cyprus from Turkey – another personal present for Titania.

He and Salisbury returned to a reception of flags, bands and fireworks. When their train pulled into Charing Cross station, the Prime Minister was welcomed by no less than four Dukes and, leaning on Salisbury's arm, he tottered through a double line of peers and peeresses and Members of the Commons to his carriage. General Ponsonby was awaiting him at Downing Street with a personal message from the Queen and a huge mass of flowers. Later Beaconsfield and Salisbury appeared on the balcony. Dizzy's voice came thinly after the cheering. 'We have brought you back, I think, Peace with Honour.' And as the cheering was resumed he added in an aside to Salisbury, 'Fickle, fickle lot.'

The Queen was enthralled. She admitted she had been wrong to try poor Lord Beaconsfield's patience so sorely. She was grateful for Cyprus, she said. She had heard it was a beautiful island with interesting historical associations and she hoped one day to go and see it. Meanwhile, as a token of her great regard and affection, he and Lord Salisbury were to receive the Order of the Garter. In view of his infirmities she was reluctant to ask him to kneel to receive the insignia, but it was the usual form, and if dear Lord Beaconsfield *could* manage it. . . .

Lord Beaconsfield could.

22

What a summer!

With her customary conciseness the Queen summed up that marvellous time. Mr Gladstone had once more retired, confounded and no doubt scowling, to his Cheshire cave. Her favourite Prime Minister was absolutely secure in the affection of her people, had given her an island with fascinating classical and biblical associations, and had promised that, to all intents and purposes, she would soon be Dictatress of Europe.

All this put the Queen in a sunny mood and she was unusually tolerant with the vagaries of her family. Though no fonder of Prussia than before, she gave Willy the Garter, her blessing to Arthur's plan to marry a Prussian princess, and sent a telegram of outraged horror when someone shot at the old Emperor. Neither Bertie nor Alfred would reform. They were as wild as hares and had not a scruple of self-control. But she could see that they were trying to be more circumspect, and it was gratifying. George of Cambridge, on the other hand, was kicking over the traces in a surprising way for a gentleman of his years. His sister, the enormous Princess Mary, told the Queen that he had found himself another lady. 'Another!' exclaimed Victoria. 'To replace Mrs FitzGeorge?' Apparently not. Mrs Beauclerk was in *addition* to Mrs FitzGeorge, and the Commander-in-Chief was at great pains to keep them ignorant of each other's existence. 'Impossible, of course!' said Princess Mary. 'Impossible!' agreed the Queen. She did not find it difficult to be sorry for Cousin George.

It was indeed a marvellous summer for Victoria but she was incapable of abandoning herself wholeheartedly to enjoy life. In Titania's pleasure-ground there was always a bower for tears. And so, in her Journal, while she thankfully recorded that her own dear Loosy (as she had now begun to call Louise) was off to Canada where Lorne was to be Governor-General, and that Leopold was happy with his secretaryship, and Beatrice, her Benjamin, was now twenty-one and the achieving of her majority had been celebrated by an unusually early skirl of the pipes beneath her bedroom window at Osborne, she also remembered a series of dark disasters:

> *On the 25th, the sudden death of the poor Duchess of Argyll, on June 2nd old Lord Russell died, . . . on June 1st, poor Mr Moon, of the Windsor Mews, drowned himself, on the 2nd the frightful and so nearly successful attempt on the old Emperor William, on the 12th the death of the poor king of Hanover, on* the *24th, his funeral here, . . . on the 26th the death from typhoid fever of the poor young Queen Mercedes (of Spain) and the destruction of the poor young 20-year-old King Alphonso's happiness and hopes for the future, only to be*

compared to poor Princess Charlotte's death, which quite crushed poor Uncle Leopold, and destroyed a nation's hopes.

In fact, braced by her feeling of good will, the Queen actually went to the funeral of the blind and deposed King of Hanover. She found the service less harrowing than she had expected, ('really, quite interesting!' she told her cousin Mary), and because it was the first funeral she had ever attended, it gave her a warm feeling of accomplishment.

Then, abruptly, a deep shadow overtook her. The self-destruction of Mr Moon in a royal horse-trough was one thing, the horror which overtook the family at Darmstadt was in a different category altogether.

Louis had inherited the Grand Duchy and Alice found her life less restricting. Nevertheless, in comparison with her sister Vicky, the Crown Princess of Germany, she was still by no means rich. But, far worse, it seemed to her that for some time she had been less rich in their mother's natural affection. Since Frittie's death she had had another child and was sensitive to her mother's criticism on the upbringing of children. She also felt it that she, whose presence had been demanded as her mother's prop and stay for long periods after her father's death, was no longer required. It was, naturally, good that Mama should have recovered so well. Nevertheless, she told Louis, she missed her regular visits to England. They were very infrequent now. Alice was a daughter who wanted to be wanted.

Victoria when she was being frank with herself, and on occasions she was devastatingly so, admitted that Alice in maturity had not the same attractions as the dear, sweet Alice who had so devotedly nursed her father. By princely standards she was poor, but her mother judged that she ought to make the best of things and not talk about it so much. Once when Alice was at Osborne she offered her two ponies for the children. Alice said thank you, but could she have a horse instead – one quiet enough for her to ride and strong enough to be a charger for Louis. She made it sound, said the Queen crossly, as though they could not afford a horse. When the subject was raised again at dinner and Alice begged for one horse instead of two ponies, her mother snapped no, and turned the conversation to the cooking of cutlets. After this Alice had a sense of grievance. It was aggravated by her mother refusing to allow her to stay for two nights at Buckingham Palace on her way to Balmoral. And this summer, when she and Louis had taken the children to Eastbourne for three months' holiday, she had again been refused permission to stay one night at the Palace on the way. She could not see her mother's point that it was unreasonable to require the servants to go to such great trouble for a night or two. She thought her mean despite the fact that she was paying for the three-month holiday beside the sea. The differences between them rankled. But when they were together it was different.

When Louis took the children home from Eastbourne Alice herself went on to Balmoral. She had not been feeling well. She was easily exhausted and sapped of all resources of strength. As soon as she saw her, the Queen was sympathetic. They were tenderly affectionate to one another. Far from being vexed, as Alice had feared, because she spent most of the day on a sofa, her mother was solicitous. Poor Alice, she was worn out. All differences between them were ironed out. It was a golden autumn, for mother and daughter a memorable one. Victoria cried to see her go. She was better in health, built up by rest and the care of the Queen's ladies at Balmoral, but she so obviously lacked the toughness which had once been her special characteristic.

In November the Queen was back at Windsor. Then, to her alarm, a telegram arrived from Darmstadt.

VICTORIA HAS DIPHTHERIA THE FEVER IS HIGH I AM SO ANXIOUS ALICE

Alice was not the kind to exaggerate. Her telegram meant what it said. If she was worried the child must be gravely ill. For three anxious days the Queen waited for news. Then came a second telegram.

TONIGHT MY PRECIOUS ALICKY HAS BEEN TAKEN ILL

The Queen sent for Sir William Jenner. Though he no longer travelled about with her and the humdrum work of Court Physician had been taken over by a Scotch doctor named Reid, it was to Jenner that she turned in grave cases. Would he, she asked, hold himself in readiness to go to Darmstadt if it should prove necessary? He immediately consented. Karré the courier was instructed to arrange everything so that Sir William could leave at any time.

The very next day came news that the baby, Mary, had been stricken. Then Princess Irene, then Alice's husband Louis, then their only son Ernest.

It was a disaster, a plague which looked as if it would decimate the family.

The Queen quietly got on with her work, reading and signing innumerable state papers, but whenever a fresh telegram was brought to her she closed her eyes and said a prayer before she read it. Mary, her youngest grandchild, died, and not a great deal of hope was held out for little Ernest. But the others, though they had suffered severely, were responding to Alice's constant and devoted nursing.

Remembering her daughter's frail state at Balmoral, Victoria wondered how she could possibly find the strength. It seemed that, in fighting for her husband and all the children left to her, Alice had heroic, quite impossible, fortitude.

It was illusory.

To comfort her son, who believed he was dying and was terrified, Alice kissed him on the forehead. She was infected and caught the disease herself.

Victoria broke down when she heard the news. She knew perfectly well that Alice did not have the strength to survive. She begged Sir William to go to Darmstadt. He left at once.

The dreadful anniversary of 14 December was approaching. Just as the family had gathered when the Prince of Wales had been close to death seven years before, so they gathered at Windsor waiting nervously and in silent groups for news from Darmstadt.

The Queen sat apart most of the time, regretting the differences she had had with Alice, feeling grateful for their last happy holiday together that autumn. Occasionally she went with Beatrice down to the Mausoleum. More often she slipped into the Blue Room and said her prayers where Albert had died and she and Alice had kept watch at his bedside.

Lady Churchill watched her anxiously. She was no alarmist but she realized the Queen had abandoned all hope. When the Prince of Wales had been so desperately ill she had never given such an impression. Now she was different. As Sir William was away Lady Churchill could not discuss her fears with anyone, but she dreaded that at the loss of her first child the Queen might suffer a crisis of nerves as she had done on the death of the Prince Consort.

Alice died on the anniversary of her father's death. Brown took the Queen the telegrams. Under the circumstances he was the best person to do it. There were three telegrams : two from Sir William, and one from the bereaved Grand Duke Louis.

The Queen accepted the news sensibly and with dignity. She cried a little, but in her heart she was glad that Alice's troubles were over. Alice had been like silk, spun too finely, spun right out of existence by work and strain. It was touching, she murmured to Brown, that her two dear ones were united on that day of all days. Now they all had a clear duty to care for the poor Grand Duke and his orphaned children. It was for them she ought to be sorrowing, not for Alice.

Brown wept only for his royal mistress. Never in his long service had he seen her quite like this. Poor, poor body, he was saying under his breath, poor, poor body.

But though Victoria's grief was deep, it did not master her. There was to be no break-down this time. She felt it was her duty to tell her children personally. She went to them one by one, supporting and encouraging them, holding her own sorrow in check until she could go to pray again, alone and undisturbed, in the Blue Room.

Later that same day she walked and talked with Lady Churchill. The world was poorer without Alice because she had been a good, sensible woman and there were not many about. Energetic, capable and single, never in the least haughty or proud. That had been Alice. Jane Churchill agreed. She had had rare and amiable qualities.

23

Lord Beaconsfield's ministry had a year to run. He was strongly advised to go to the country directly after the Congress of Berlin, when his personal popularity would have returned his party with a mammoth majority. But he was ill and prostrated with tiredness, and lacked the stamina to face an election before it was absolutely necessary. He proposed to wait.

Unfortunately that last year was not a happy one for England. Two unpopular frontier wars were thrust on the country: in South Africa and in Afghanistan. Dizzy began to see his mistake. Wryly he admitted it to Montagu Corry and a few confidants. But not to his sovereign. He would not add unnecessarily to her troubles by mournful prophecies of what probably would happen in the following year. Shrewd Lady Ely knew, but no one else. At Court he was the same smiling, incorrigible, dear Lord Beaconsfield.

The Queen was distracted by family concerns.

Louis and his children were invited to come to Windsor as soon as possible. There they were cried over and spoilt. But Victoria also tried to make some sort of sensible arrangements for the future. Ideally Beatrice ought to take the place of Alice, but she did not really wish to lose her Benjamin and, in any case, there was an absurd ecclesiastical canon against marrying a deceased wife's sister. Both the Queen and the Prince of Wales were eager to have the law altered in England but met with stiff resistance from the bishops. 'And they are *my* bishops!' Victoria exclaimed characteristically. This aggravating episcopal defiance destroyed Victoria's first plan. She quickly substituted another. Prince Christian could very well be left to look after himself in Windsor Great Park and Helena should go over to Darmstadt at regular intervals to oversee the upbringing of Alice's children. Once a year, of course, perhaps more often, they should be sent over to Grandmama at Osborne or Balmoral.

Barely three months after Alice's death there was another tragedy. Vicky's youngest son Waldemar – the little boy who had offered his pet crocodile to Grandmama and made her shriek – died from haemorrhages. Like so many in the family he was a haemophiliac.

Then Bertie's eldest boy began to cause anxiety; not about his health, which seemed sufficiently robust, but because of his incapacity. His tutor was writing confidentially of 'the abnormally dormant condition of his mind.' Which, in the plain language of John Brown, expressed in the privacy of a revolving tea-house at Osborne, meant he was but elevenpence and a ha'penny in the shilling. Victoria recalled her own foreboding at his birth and was horrified. Unless he improved, his succession to the Crown would be disastrous. Plans were made for him and his brother George to travel round the world, but even this evoked a pharaoh's serpent of trouble. The Cabinet did not want them to travel in the same ship, the risk of losing both at one stroke being too great and their impertinent interference, as he saw it, made the Prince of Wales very angry indeed. It was his responsibility as their father, he told the First Lord of the Admiralty, to make such decisions.

After that there was a disaster in Natal. Louis Bonaparte's son, the Prince Imperial, had asked for special permission to serve with his regiment in South Africa, and he was killed in a skirmish. Victoria felt his death keenly. So did the English nation. His body was brought back to England and his funeral was splendid. The Queen herself saw his body taken from the house in Chislehurst. Her sons and her cousin the Duke of Cambridge were pallbearers.

Then the institution of monarchy was again threatened when a lunatic waiter fired revolvers at the King and Queen of Spain. That the shots went wide barely lessened Victoria's shock and sense of outrage.

Disaster followed disaster.

Disaster at Cabal where the British Embassy was sacked and all members of the mission massacred.

Disaster in Scotland where on a stormy night the Tay Bridge collapsed under a train and seventy-odd passengers were drowned in the Firth....

All this contrived to isolate the Queen from the reality of the political situation at Westminster.

In her unofficial rôle as political adviser Lady Ely conceived it her duty to give a warning. Victoria paid some attention, but not enough. Even Lord Beaconsfield murmured a warning, but he did it so charmingly and poetically that she missed the point. To the astonishment of Lords Hartington and Granville she sent word that the Liberal leaders were not to make lavish promises in their election addresses, because even if they were returned to office, the sovereign was not prepared to give way on certain points. Victoria then showed she was Conservative to the core by obliging Disraeli in all sorts of useful ways. After that her interest flagged. She was taken up with the business of honouring Theodore Martin with a knighthood. At long last he had completed his monumental work, the *Life of the Prince Consort*, and the Queen took a copy of the fifth and last volume with her on a short continental trip while her subjects went to the polls.

It promised to be a delightful spring holiday, first at Darmstadt for the confirmation of poor Alice's daughters; thence to the Baden villa willed to her by Feodore.

At Baden Victoria read and re-read parts of Sir Theodore's excellent work, living in the past and paying small heed to the English newspapers. She attended to the dispatch boxes which came and went with the regularity of a ceremonial liturgy, but otherwise she was largely oblivious of what was going on in Britain. Ponsonby was a Gladstone disciple but he was the Queen's servant first and last and recently she had honoured him with a knighthood. He urged Lady Ely to be bolder and franker. Eventually he volunteered to share the responsibility and together tthey intruded into the Queen's nostalgic privacy. They had to make her aware, they said, that a Conservative victory was by no means certain.

Victoria was appalled as she heard that that impossible, quite dreadful old man W. E. Gladstone had come out of retirement a second time. He could no more be contained by his home in Cheshire than a genie in a bottle. And he had laid all England's past misfortunes, the bad weather and ruined harvests, the foreign upheavals and the financial difficulties, on the head of the Earl of Beaconsfield. From his attitude he made it clear he considered Dizzy was the Lord of Darkness, a man of no scruples, a ravisher of innocence, a beast.

Because Gladstone's own philanthropic interest in metropolitan prostitutes was open to misunderstanding, the Liberal had countered by spreading rumours about Dizzy. In fact, it took some doing to put the mask of a Lothario on the stooping, withered, tortoise-like Prime Minister who was too ill and ancient to walk properly let alone enjoy the pleasures of the alcove. Possibly it arose from a report that a group of chorus girls had been asked which they would prefer to marry, Gladstone or Disraeli, and all had said Disraeli save one who said it would be more fun to marry Gladstone and then run off with Disraeli just to see the look on the old Liberal's face. Dizzy was delighted with this, just as he was with the current scandal in society that Gathorne Hardy had been given a peerage because of Dizzy's liking for Mrs Hardy. It made him, he said, feel forty again to be traduced so. But the rumours did him harm. In London and in the more sophisticated south the rumours were not believed, any more than anything else Gladstone said, but in the wilder, non-conformist, western and northern industrial parts Gladstone was being hailed as a prophet.

Victoria listened white-faced.

Ponsonby warned her that Liberalism would almost certainly triumph. Though a convinced Liberal himself it distressed him to have to upset his mistress in such a way.

As thoughtful and courteous as ever, Lord Beaconsfield telegraphed to Baden:

> YOUR MAJESTY MUST NOT BE UNNECESSARILY HURRIED OR AGITATED AT THIS MOMENT.

Hurried! Agitated! The Queen was almost beside herself. She telegraphed in reply:

> WHAT YOUR LOSS TO ME AS A MINISTER WOULD BE IT IS IMPOSSIBLE TO ESTIMATE BUT I TRUST YOU WILL ALWAYS REMAIN MY FRIEND TO WHOM I CAN TURN AND ON WHOM I CAN RELY.

She was in a fever when Sir Henry Ponsonby gave her the awful warning that Gladstone might well wish to return to office. She had thought herself safe from this threat. It appalled her. Ponsonby regretted mentioning the possibility. The Queen's reactions were so awful. Under NO circumstances, she said, would she have that violent, passionate, ungentlemanly man as her minister. She would abdicate first, abdicate, abdicate. . . .

It took all her Household's tact and skill and patience to mollify her. By the time she returned to England she had persuaded herself that it was out of the question. Hartington and Granville would prevent it. They must.

On April 18th, 1880 Victoria received Lord Beaconsfield and his formal resignation at Windsor.

It was not as sad an occasion as it might have been. Unlike her relationship with Lord M., the Queen's friendship with Dizzy did not depend on them seeing one another very often. She would still be Titania and he Robin Goodfellow even if they were separated by the length of the kingdom. Yet she was upset that the Constitution was once more coming between them. With tears in her eyes she begged him to come and see her often, and to write. He undertook to do so because so far as he was concerned the British Constitution had barely anything to do with the Faery Isle of their imagination; and, he added, they had each other's portraits to talk to, a pleasant practice – he gently teased – because it guaranteed one always got one's own way. His sauciness stopped her crying and he made her laugh by saying it had been clever of the Liberals to saddle him with the responsibility for six bad harvests running. 'Like Napoleon, Ma'am, I have been defeated by the elements.' She dried her tears, and smiled. And then, though he had not really expected it, came the golden offer. Would Lord Beaconsfield please accept an enduring token of her gratitude? She would like to give him a dukedom.

Did Dizzy again hear the echo of his father asking: 'What does little Ben know about dukes?'

He was strongly, strongly tempted. But he cared too much for the Queen. In face of his rejection by the country it would harm her if he accepted. Instead he asked if his faithful Montagu Corry could have a peerage. Corry was *au fait* with everything in international politics and would adorn the House. She was happy to agree and Mr Corry became Lord Rowton.

His final duty was to advise her to send for Lord Hartington, the Liberal leader of the House of Commons. His first thought had been Lord Granville, but perhaps Hartington was better. Dizzy was prejudiced in his favour as he was heir to the Dukedom of Devonshire. He also admired him as the only Member of Parliament ever known to yawn in the middle of his own Maiden Speech. Harty-tarty would do.

He made the last few moments of the audience easier for the Queen by admitting truthfully that at seventy-seven he doubted if he could have carried on. He really pined to rest at Hughenden, to read there and, perhaps, write a little, and, after a lifetime of hectic endeavour, enjoy the tranquillity of angling.

The Queen sent for Lord Hartington. Lord Beaconsfield had recommended it, so had the Prince of Wales, and she was not averse from the idea herself. Officially she felt obliged to disapprove of him because he had had a long liaison with the Duchess of Manchester, but privately she admired his naturalness. Never was there less of a humbug. She could never recall without a chuckle the way he had electrified her Household one evening at a Windsor dinner. It was the footmen's custom to remove dishes when the Queen herself had finished a course. But it was not to Lord Hartington's taste at all. Deprived of his helping of mutton and peas before he had finished, he astounded everyone by saying to the royal footmen: 'Here! Bring that back!' Victoria found this Wellingtonian forthrightness very attractive. Such a man might be able to keep that genie Gladstone inside his bottle. . . .

But it was not to be. Hartington was candid. He was obliged to the Queen for her mark of confidence. He would like to form a ministry to serve her. Nevertheless he thought that it might not be possible. Mr Gladstone was the problem.

Mr Gladstone, said his sovereign sharply, was always the problem.

'Neither Lord Granville nor I believe he could be content with a subordinate position, Ma'am.'

'But Mr Gladstone has retired,' said the Queen firmly. She was hotly indignant because Gladstone had described the election result as 'the downfall of Beaconsfieldism – like the vanishing of some magnificent castle in an Italian romance'. 'Mr Gladstone,' she repeated, 'has retired.'

'With all respect, Ma'am, he is yet an exceedingly active member of the House of Commons.'

'He resigned the leadership of your party and sent word to inform me himself.'

Hartington agreed with her. His own political future was being put in jeopardy by the resurgence of the Grand Old Man. Even now he was back in London, calmly reading – so they said – George Herbert, *Guy Mannering* and a little Egyptology, but, as Hartington well knew, in fact waiting for what he termed the people's call.

Undertaking to do all he could, but feeling unable to promise anything, Hartington returned to consult with Granville in London. He went so far as to visit Gladstone and invited him to serve under him. Gladstone's refusal was categorical. Hartington went back to Windsor, this time taking Granville with him.

In his absence the Queen had lived through old nightmares. To Sir Henry Ponsonby she raved about the wickedness of Gladstone and the impossibility of having a First Minister in whom she had no confidence at all. 'They cannot, shall not force him on me. I told Lord Hartington in the strongest terms my true feelings about Mr Gladstone. They cannot, shall not force him on me.'

But Sir Henry noticed with relief that there was no more talk of abdication.

Both the Liberal leaders were in a state of nervous confusion and very apologetic. Granville kissed her hand twice. Gladstone was being obdurate, he informed her. And that was that. The situation was regrettable, but at present unavoidable.

Victoria was constrained to accept the inevitable. Nevertheless she repeated that Mr Gladstone did not have her confidence and he ought to be informed of it, and she made Hartington and Granville undertake to keep him in control. Only the thought that the Ministry could not last, that perhaps after a coalition the Conservatives would return to office, persuaded her to send for the odious Mr Gladstone.

Not unexpectedly he found her what he called 'natural under effort'. She was too naturally courteous to behave as Queen Elizabeth would have done. She kept her temper and her tongue, but he was aware that he had lost her confidence for ever. It was rather unnerving for a politician of seventy years of age who had been forty years in the public service, and he knew that henceforth he and the Queen would always be at arm's length; but he made the best of a bad job and said he hoped to diminish her cares, or, at any rate, not to increase them. And he offered her what he knew was a consolation by intimating that at his age his office would be brief and his retirement early.

Politically, even constitutionally, it was an extraordinary situation. Without the confidence of his sovereign and unaware that she had requested two of his cabinet colleagues to control him, the Grand Old Man began his second administration.

The Queen, to prove herself independent of the Liberal non-conformists who had the impertinence to name their bigoted morality 'Victorian', thoroughly approved of her Household getting up a Derby lottery and took two tickets herself. In the same cheerful spirit she wrote to Lord Beaconsfield:

> *Mr Gladstone looks very ill, very old and haggard and his voice feeble.*

But it was not the Liberal leader who was to dwindle and rid the world of his presence. Under the outward appearance lay an ox-like constitution. It was Dizzy, seven years older, and not kept in tone by bouts of tree-felling, who diminished and decayed. He was not in the least shocked, in fact was gratified, when Victoria confided proudly:

> *I never write except on formal* official *matters to the Prime Minister!*

Bravo for Titania!

The heaviness and mightiness of the English Constitution sat lightly on Dizzy's bent, fragile shoulders. He did not think that even for the benefit of her country the Queen would listen very attentively to Gladstone, but she would to him. And so, discreetly, he advised her when she asked for it. Only once did he balk and that was when in conversation she required him to define a pro-contraceptionist. She had discovered that amongst the riff-raff elected to that Parliament there was a desperate fellow named Bradlaugh who would not take the oath. It appeared he represented a trinity of villainy: republicanism, atheism and contraception, and she wished to know what the last might be. No one could slide from a question with the dexterity of Dizzy. In his sudden feeling of faintness and complete exhaustion Mr Bradlaugh and his eccentricities were completely and conveniently forgotten.

But, unhappily, his exhaustion was not all feigned. He was growing more and more weary. Six months after his resignation he was even finding it difficult to concentrate on his favourite reading:

the pastorals and songs of Virgil and Horace. Once he had been tempted to turn pagan and sacrifice to the waters which fed the lake at Hughenden just as Horace had thrown flowers and poured wine and the blood of a slain kid into his Bandusian spring. Now he smiled at the memory. He was no bucolic Roman but a Venetian Jew more than three-quarters dead, inconvenienced by imperfect bodily machinery, his mind dulled sometimes by pain or ennui, his silver tongue tied by asthma.

At the end of the year he returned to London. The cold was terrible and he lay all day on a sofa close to the fire. He lay there thinking and remembering, but by no means oblivious to what was going on beyond the sofa. He was vastly amused and so, to do him credit, was Montagu Corry, now Lord Rowton, when they heard the Liberal quip that there had been nothing quite like the ennobling of Dizzy's Private Secretary since Caligula made his horse a consul. He enjoyed reports of the Queen's running battles with the Ministry, especially her spirited plea that English beer drinkers should not be taxed to satisfy those absurd total abstainers who voted Liberal. He was touched when the Prince of Wales defied both the Court and society and attended a Rothschild wedding in a synagogue. He was fascinated by de Lesseps' plan to make a canal at Panama. And he was appalled when news reached England that terrorists had blown the Tsar to bloody gobbets after a military review. With legs pulped, his face terribly mutilated and his belly torn open, the Tsar lived long enough to order his family to take him home to die. It made Dizzy anxious for Titania. The British sovereign was no autocrat but she had some odd and totally unreliable subjects in Ireland. . . .

The Queen was even more anxious for Lord Beaconsfield. Having caught a chill he was driven to his bed and from thence he scribbled her letters in pencil. His medical attendant was an homoeopathist, and therefore to the orthodox medical profession a quack. But the Queen's wishes that he should be seen by a specialist overruled professional regulations. Bronchitis was diagnosed, and asthma. Having suffered from both for a decade and more Dizzy was not surprised. He grew more feeble. Each day Titania wrote to him. Each day she sent primroses and violets. When he was too weak to read her letters for himself he insisted on observing the formalities. A Privy Councillor was sent for to read the Queen's message to him:

Dearest Lord Beaconsfield, I send you a few of your favourite spring flowers....

Lord Rowton went to see the Queen after his master's death in April, 1881. He showed her his will, and told her that Dizzy had not wished for burial in the Abbey. He preferred to be laid beside Mary Anne at Hughenden. Only with the greatest difficulty did he manage to tell her of the end; how, not long before, the dying man had sat up and thrown back his head in a characteristic way as if to make a parliamentary speech. Then, falling back, he had died, without any sort of suffering, and quite calmly, as if he had gone to sleep.

When the funeral was done, and the Queen herself had paid a private visit to the vault where he lay and had laid a wreath of china flowers on his coffin, and when she had taken tea with Lord Rowton in the library at Hughenden and had afterwards said good-bye to Disraeli's faithful valet, Victoria still found it impossible to believe she would never again see his stooping figure beneath the trees, or see his enigmatic smile, or hear his drawling voice making epigrams – all of them studded, like truffles in good pâté, with his habitual and expressive use of the word 'Ma'am'. There never had been and never would be again anyone quite like Lord Beaconsfield.

She arranged for a handsome memorial to be placed in Hughenden Church and she asked Sir Theodore Martin if he would kindly be present at the sale of effects at Hughenden to buy her some keepsakes. And after that she made a determined effort to throw off her gloom.

Deliberately she sought to overcome her private sorrow by immersing herself in the affairs of her family and of the world, and the world and her family at that time were very busy. The Irish were more than usually mischievous, their leader in Parliament being denounced by Gladstone as an unscrupulous enemy of the state. There was rebellion in Egypt, Tunisia and Algeria. And a disappointed place-hunter shot and killed the American President. The affairs of her family were of less moment but no less engrossing. Bertie was dropping Mrs Langtry and taking up with Lady Brook; Leopold was engaging himself to be married to Princess Helen of Waldeck; and Alfred was cruising with Arthur Sullivan on H.M.S. *Hercules* meeting the new Tsar and Willy who made an exhibition of himself by striking attitudes and singing from *Pinafore* 'I polished up the handle on the big front door. . . .'

While the world's hubbub went on, Dizzy and his Mary Anne lay in silence at Hughenden.

PART THREE

1

It seemed to Victoria that there was nothing left to do now except get old and die herself. Yet it was not easy to grow old gracefully. There were too many exasperations.

Though she ate and slept better than most women of her age, the Queen suffered increasingly from rheumatic pains. Furthermore her eyesight was failing, but she was reluctant to admit it. Sir Henry Ponsonby was told that people's handwriting was deteriorating; his own, in particular, was far less legible than it had been. Tactfully he chose the whitest of paper, the blackest of ink, and by sheer will-power he magnified the size of his handwriting. And yet the Queen still had to peer at papers. It vexed her. It vexed her, too, that certain bright colours made her eyes ache. The vivid tartan hangings and carpets at Balmoral were a particular strain. Had they been allowed to fade they would have been far more tolerable, but, a long, long time before, Albert had decreed that wear and tear in the royal palaces should not be seen. Fading tartans were unobtrusively removed and replaced by night. Fortunately, in compensation, the Balmoral walls were still painted in the pale, old-fashioned tints of twenty years before. They were soothing to tired eyes.

But neither poor eyesight nor rheumatism were as bad to her mind as the need to face change. It was this which exacerbated her bad temper and made the prospect of growing older so exceedingly unattractive.

It appeared to her that the things which had been precious to Lehzen and to Albert were not all that precious now. Standards were altering. Self-control was less admired than it had been and self-indulgence expressed itself in a variety of unwholesome ways. The young behaved dreadfully. It was not simply a matter of philandering. That she could understand far better than the majority of her narrow-minded subjects. Nevertheless, while she could tolerate the wildness of the young, she could not abide their lack of consideration for other people, their self-centredness, their abundant greed. But, then, their elders who ought to know better were sometimes a bad example. In scandalized horror Victoria confided to her journal the marriage of the sixty-six-year-old Lady Burdett Coutts to a young person in his twenties. 'Positively distressing and ridiculous,' she commented, and she asked Lady Churchill what the lower orders would make of such an example, so shocking a liaison.

Equally disturbing was the perpetual ruffling of the status quo by acts of violence. The Communists of Paris and the assassinators of Tsar Alexander had revitalized terrorism and socialism. Irish ribbonmen murdered the Queen's ministers in Dublin's Phoenix Park. She herself was shot at; this time near Windsor Station, but an Eton boy gave the villain a sound drubbing with an umbrella and Brown as usual was protective. In an attempt to offer sympathy, the Queen's hated Prime Minister observed that though attacks on sovereigns abroad always had a political motive, in England they were simply committed by madmen.

Victoria was not consoled. Nor did she agree with Mr Gladstone. Socialism was understood even by the meanest intelligences. It had the attractiveness of Christmas tinsel to children. It offered bright prospects. Since the days when Albert had laid down that nothing, however brutal, unpleasant or degrading, be deliberately hidden from the sovereign, Victoria had been kept partially informed of the state of Britain by successive Home Secretaries. She was well aware that many in her kingdom were deprived and neglected and that quite naturally they would be attracted to socialism. Albert's method – which was her method – to combat this threat was to do away with injustice and poverty, and that is what she believed her ministers were for. But the radicals amongst them appeared to think this answer was too simple and that the world could only be put to rights by a transfer of all power to the lower house of Parliament.

Such a doctrine puzzled the Queen. It also frightened her. She was prostrated by anxiety as well as with indignation when her own Secretary of State for War attacked those who imagined that the Army was the Queen's. The soldiers, he said, were not the Queen's soldiers at all. They were members of an Army of the

House of Commons. It was an impertinence to her as Queen, to her cousin George as Commander-in-Chief, and it had not gone unremarked, but the Secretary of State was quite unrepentant, and, to prove his power over the Duke of Cambridge, he forbade him to cross the Channel in a balloon. And what, Victoria asked herself, had this latter-day Cromwell done to put bread in the mouths of the poor or give them shelter and warmth?

The prolific flowering of the three weeds Victoria detested, humbug, self-indulgence, and socialism, gave her no taste for the future. That and her increasing ailments made it difficult for her to grow old gracefully. She was increasingly irritable, increasingly sorry for herself, and, in the middle of her great Court, she felt miserably alone. Now that Leopold was married, only her Benjamin was still at home, and, in any case, like most strong-minded women, she would not have dreamt of using her children as confidants.

There was Dean Wellesley of course, one of her most intimate and confidential friends, but he was ageing and was often ill. He continued to advise her on Church affairs and he looked after her spiritual requirements, but she was diffident about asking for more. Jane Ely was too technical, really too intellectual, to understand her problem. Jane Churchill did, but she herself was inclined to be cynical about both society and politics, and this was of no help to her either. And her other close friends, almost without exception, were too lacking in worldly wisdom and knowledge. Mrs Prothero, for instance, although a constant source of strength and comfort at Osborne, was about as much use as an adviser in great matters as Brown or Maslin; and her devoted dressers Emilie Dittweiler and Annie Macdonald were of no more account than the dear Duchess of Athole who was becoming rather forgetful and thought of nothing but perennial plants.

Once, tentatively, because she presumed he was wise, she tried to talk about socialism with Mr Gladstone. He spoke of democracy. She had heard, she told him (in fact, of course, from Albert) that the Athenians who considered democracy so ideal had only been able to put it into effect because of the huge substrata of slaves in the state. Gladstone simply gaped. Nervous, because of this sudden show of confidence, he found it difficult to pull himself together. When he did and opened his mouth, he went on and on and on and on and on, and Victoria wished she had never mentioned the subject. It had been a terrible mistake to approach him, and she never would again. How much she missed Lord Beaconsfield who would have helped her out of her dilemma with information, encouragement, true understanding.

Her loneliness was deepened when Dean Wellesley died. He had served her faithfully for thirty-three years, in that privileged position as personal chaplain which had brought him closer to her than almost anyone else.

Dulled by grief and a feeling of hopelessness Victoria begged Mr Gladstone not to regard the Windsor Deanery as an ordinary piece of ecclesiastical preferment. Because of its special nature she wished for a clergyman who was especially congenial to her, and she appointed another of her chaplains to the stall: a good, kind man without pride, who would, she was sure, serve the Castle well. But she did not hold out any hope that for her he could ever replace Dean Wellesley, any more than that another Prime Minister could ever replace her dear Lord Beaconsfield.

There was no one left now to help her cope with things. No one at all.

At the beginning of December, 1882 Archbishop Tait lay dying at Addington Park.

The Queen's recommendation that, for his health's sake, he be translated from London to Canterbury appeared to have been justified in fourteen years' active ministry. Dizzy's fear that he was an enthusiast had also been justified. As archbishop he had fired broadside after broadside at the ritualists – the Public Worship Act, processes in the Church courts, sermons and addresses, and speeches in the House of Lords. The High Church barque had not yet foundered but it was considerably water-logged. And, though less forceful with extreme Protestants, he had made it clear that the true cream of Christianity was only to be found in the Board Church party of the Church of England, and, compared with it, all other parties, sects and denominations offered but skimmed milk. This so entirely corresponded with the Queen's own belief that they had become warm friends, and she sent Lady Ely down to Addington Park with a personal message for the dying prelate. In return she received a barely legible scrawl which she found exceedingly touching:

A last memorial of 26 years of devoted service. With earnest love and affectionate blessing on the Queen and her family.

It was the last thing the Archbishop wrote. Two days later he died.

The Queen recorded in her journal what she and the Church and England owed to him. She recalled in her mind's eye the splendid figure he made in rochet and billowing lawn sleeves, his hair worn long and with a centre parting, his demeanour always grave but kindly. She considered him a true prince of the Church, and thought it likely that he, too, would be difficult to replace. She asked for a lock of his hair.

In connection with the Archbishop's funeral, and afterwards with regard to his known wishes about a successor, the Queen was brought in contact with his son-in-law and chaplain, a young clergyman named Randall Davidson.

She was at once impressed.

In her journal she noted:

Was seldom more struck. . . . I feel that Mr Davidson is a man who may be of great use to me, for which I am truly thankful.

Victoria never allowed herself to be hurried into anything important, least of all in the choice of a confidential adviser. She subjected him to a number of tests. He was sent, on her behalf, to talk discreetly with the two bishops recommended by the dead Archbishop as possible successor to the throne of St Augustine. His reports were enlightening and extraordinarily helpful. Next, through Mrs Prothero and Dean Wellesley's widow and other clergymen's wives, she found that everyone had a particularly high regard for Mr Davidson. The politicians of both parties agreed. The seal was set by the new Archbishop, Dr Benson, who appointed Davidson his senior chaplain. And Sir Henry Ponsonby, whose judgement of character the Queen greatly respected, was already an admirer of the young man. He approached the Queen about the desirability of establishing a short cypher code with Mr Davidson so that he could be referred to hurriedly for his advice on Church affairs.

The Queen was pleased to consent. She was very pleased. From all she had heard and seen she believed she might have been fortunate enough to find already a successor to Dean Wellesley as her counsellor and friend. Something told her also – though some time passed before she actually admitted it to herself – that he might even be a successor in understanding and affection to her dear Lord Beaconsfield.

Mr Davidson, whose background was Scotch and decent though not grand, was at first frightened by the prospect which royal favour opened up before him. He was already shy of preferment though marked out for it by his own considerable ability and his position at the very centre of ecclesiastical patronage. As son-in-law and Senior Chaplain to the Archbishop of Canterbury it was inevitable. But his ambitions had always been modest. For most of his life he had been regarded as delicate. Shot at and almost mortally wounded by a careless cousin in his 'teens, and thereafter subjected to illness after illness, he had learnt early about pain and his own limitations. Only with some difficulty had he overcome his serious doubts that he had the strength to act as an ordained clergyman and though, since his priesting, his health had improved and he was now able to enjoy country sports and walking tours as well as many of his fellow clergymen, he still shrank from heavy responsibilities. Unlike Malvolio he did not want greatness thrust upon him. Nor did he wish to excite unholy envy amongst his brethren who would talk, he was sure, of a second Elizabeth and Essex.

Moreover the Queen herself alarmed him. She was tiny and oddly shaped yet, by her manner, her voice, her way of moving, she dominated any assembly. In a private audience she was less formidable, but no one, least of all Victoria, ever forgot that she was Queen-Empress. Davidson was dismayed by the unsought and unwished-for honour which had suddenly descended on him. At first he considered it proper to communicate with the sovereign only through Sir Henry Ponsonby. But, gradually, as he became more sure of himself, he discovered that Victoria's charm was not a myth put out by loyalists but a fact. She really did wish to be friendly and she encouraged him with her confidence. In a moment of candour she confessed she needed his help. After that he recovered his self-confidence and became her spiritual adviser as well as her adviser on Church affairs.

His small, slim figure, the sombreness of his clerical black strongly contrasting with his wistful, cherubic features, was not often seen at Court, but letters passed to and fro with increasing frequency. Their relationship budded into a respectful friendship.

All Davidson had heard or read about Queen Victoria was now dismissed from his mind. The more he came to know her the more he admired her, and he was gratified by his success in understanding the contradictions in her make-up.

The Queen, on her part, appreciated his affection and his frankness and his dependability. Her courtiers and her children also approved. Leopold, not at all meaning to be unkind, made a light-hearted remark about Mama falling for the curate – and quickly had his head snapped off by other members of the family. This was not merely the romantic affection of a woman in her sixties for a good-looking young clergyman. At another level, it bore no resemblance at all to the squalid affair of Elizabeth and Essex. Rather was it in the pattern of other great friendships in Victoria's life, and her family and her friends were well aware of her constant need for a close adviser in great affairs as well as small.

John Brown summed it up, as John Brown frequently did. 'The minister's shrewd,' he said. 'And with it he's kind and he's good and he's true. He'll not harm her Majesty.'

Had she heard this blunt appraisal Victoria might have rebuked Brown by saying that no Highlander was a judge of Edinburgh clergymen. But in her heart she would have agreed.

She was grateful that her loneliness was lessening.

2

At a critical time, when sedition in Ireland reached a fresh peak and ribbonmen plotted daily against the Crown, the government, the landlords and each other, Mr Gladstone was taken ill.

To the Queen's dismay he left the country to recuperate on the French Riviera. To her further astonishment and alarm she heard he was attempting to hasten his recovery by walking long distances uphill in pouring rain. Anyone else, she remarked to Mr Davidson, would have died on the spot. But not Mr Gladstone. He actually recovered from his punishing cure and returned to deal with the Irish.

Unhappily he was no more successful than anyone else. He and his ministers were not even able to protect those few loyal Irish who worked for the government or who gave information about terrorists. A gang called the Invincibles was formed with the sole purpose of murdering officials and informers. Its reach was long. One of its victims – though in heavy disguise and under the special protection of the government – was shot to death before the eyes of his terrified family on board a ship sailing between Cape Town and Natal. Then a fresh wave of terrorism spread through Britain.

With his gentle manner Mr Davidson diffused calm where otherwise there might have been too much nervous excitement if not real fear.

Victoria bravely faced up to the Fenian threats against her own person, but she could not help expressing the opinion in public that it was monstrous she was required to do it so frequently. She showed great courage, but she did not enjoy being such an obvious target. Without Mr Davidson to soothe her and good Brown with his loyal muscles ready to defend her, she would think her case very different. . . .

Public and private buildings were being regularly blown up. A large Irish nitro-glycerine factory was discovered in Birmingham. No one felt safe, and nerves were rubbed raw by advertisements in the American newspapers of exactly where and when the next outrage would take place.

The Queen was particularly angry with the Americans. She had created a precedent and honoured the republic by putting her Court into a week's mourning when President Garfield died; but British government protests against the unrestrained activities of the Assassination Societies of American Fenians met with hardly any response.

When, after an inexplicable and unexplained ten-month delay, the United States Government did reply, their tone was unfriendly. The Queen thoroughly approved of her Home Secretary's published criticism of America:

No other civilized country in the world does or would tolerate the open advocacy of assassination and murder.

Meanwhile portmanteaux full of dynamite were being found at railway stations and in docks, property was being destroyed, and her subjects killed and maimed.

In the March of 1883, when there was an attempt to destroy the premises of the Queen's old adversary *The Times*, a tin bonnet box was found full of unexploded dynamite and from this the government was able to discover that it had been sent from America. The Queen was shocked. She asked Sir Henry to go up from Windsor and make a report on the damage done, and she brooded sadly on the deterioration in the relations between Britain and the United States. Another protest was to be sent by the Cabinet. The Irish had a great deal to answer for.

On the very next afternoon, as she was leaving by the private entrance to go for a drive, she slipped on the stairs and missed the last few steps. She did not actually fall, but she landed with her full weight on one leg which gave her considerable pain. She sat down on the bottom step.

With the immediate irrationality that sometimes follows a sudden shock, her first thought was to blame Beatrice. If Beatrice had been there she would not have fallen, but Beatrice was away for the first time in her life. She had gone to Aix-les-Bains for a cure for her neuritis.

Brown came running to pick her up. He was as fussy and anxious as an old hen. Asperously she told him so. He paid no attention. Could she move the leg? Could she bend her knee? Did she wish to go back to her apartments? Or go out for a drive? Did she want a glass of water? Sal volatile? Whisky? 'But she said not a word,' he told the postilion afterwards. 'And gave me her look. The look. You'll know.' The postilion did. 'So I gathered her up and brought her to the carriage. A bit of fresh air's the thing.'

It wasn't quite enough. That evening the knee was greatly swollen. Dr Reid prescribed rest. Her Majesty must put the leg up. This did not suit. Sir William Jenner was sent for. His diagnosis and prescription was the same. If only Beatrice was not gallivanting in Aix.

The Queen sent to Cumberland House for her daughter Helena, adding hastily that there was no need to trouble Prince Christian. Jenner smiled behind his hand. In the Queen's mood Prince Christian was better out of the way. When Helena arrived she found it was to support her mother in to dinner and hear all about the accident, and for a dozen times at least all about Beatrice and Aix. It was odd, thought Jenner, that someone who was so fearless about the Fenians' threat to her life and safety could be so put out by a fall on the stairs.

It turned out to be rather more serious.

Victoria had a series of excruciating rheumatic attacks which severely lamed her. For a week she spent most of her time prone on a sofa. Then, to walk at all, she required the aid of two sticks and she quickly exhausted herself with pain and with the effort. Mostly she was carried by Brown, who paid small attention to her moods and deposited her in a little pony chaise which had not been used for years. He was worried about the threats of the Robbonmen and was often with the Queen. Every evening after dinner he combed the grounds searching for terrorists. Mr Davidson's advice was sought. What he gave was good and accepted with perfect politeness – but afterwards ignored. Sensibly he let Princess Beatrice know the plain facts.

When Beatrice returned from Aix, she was very much the better for her cure, and appalled by her mother's pitiful state. Her pain, she said, was worse than ever, and there was no Brown now to pick her up and carry her. He had caught a chill on one of his prowls round the Castle and was being nursed for erysipelas in his rooms in the Clarence Tower.

Beatrice did what she could for her mother. Surely massage would be good for her? In Aix she had heard of a Madame Charlotte Nautet. Would it not be a good idea to send for her? It would not, said the Queen. Thoroughly depressed, worn out by pain, constantly agitated by the reports of Irish terrorism, and upset because Brown, too, was ill and could not help her, Victoria found the thought of Madame Charlotte Nautet intolerable. A little hurt, Beatrice went to discuss the idea with her brother Leopold who was at the Castle. The Queen had bought Claremont House from the state as a private acquisition, and Leopold now lived there with his newly-acquired wife. It was conveniently near to Windsor and so he was able to continue as extra Private Secretary to his mother. He was as worried as Beatrice about her. Both regretted that Mr Davidson's work as Senior Chaplain to Archbishop Benson kept him so far from Court. His presence now would be invaluable to the Queen. . . .

. . . . .

A very few days later Leopold went early in the morning to the Queen's dressing-room. Her toilette was not complete because her lameness and rheumatism slowed everything down. Emilie and Annie were gentle and deft and patient but they could not help hurting her as they assisted their mistress to dress. She was white-faced with the pain, and she seized on an opportunity to rest for a moment. Yes, she would see Prince Leopold.

He had still kept his good looks, she thought in an absent way as he approached her, the good looks of his beloved father. Her other sons had lost theirs, except perhaps Arthur. Yes, Arthur too had the same striking features. . . .

He kissed her hand and said something but she did not take it in. A stab of pain set her knee on fire. It clouded everything. Clouded everything.

But then, abruptly, she heard the same words repeated.

She stiffened. Her hand flew to her mouth. The pain was forgotten. The misty, dull lethargy scattered by what Leopold was saying . . . was it for the third time – or the fourth?

John Brown was dead.

3

Those in the Court who expected a repetition of 1861 were put down by Lady Churchill. Did they really think, she asked, that to the Queen the loss of John Brown could be compared with the loss of the Prince Consort? Did they really believe that her perpetual mourning, her order that the Prince's rooms and clothes be kept clean and neat as though he were still alive, her careful observance of his birthday and death-day and their marriage anniversary, were nothing but window-dressing? Chilly in her anger, Lady Churchill begged everyone to understand that there was only one person at the core of the Queen's heart. Abashed, they were careful not to discuss the matter in front of her again.

She was equally indignant with those who made light of his death, for she knew that the loss of Brown was a real tragedy to the Queen.

The long panegyric which Victoria caused to be published in the Court circular, her ordering a coronach at Brown's funeral as though he had been a distinguished chieftain, her commissioning of a statue from Boehm and an inscription from the Laureate Tennyson, all exposed her to ridicule. But no one sneered, no one dared to, when Lady Churchill was there.

Even Lady Ely – normally so gentle and composed – showed her contempt for a member of the Household who made a joke of Tennyson's couplet in honour of Brown. In an exaggerated manner this gentleman quoted:

Friend more than servant, loyal, truthful, brave:
Self less than duty even to the grave.

'The poetry is deplorable,' said Lady Ely stiffly, 'but the sentiments are sound.'

She also plainly showed her disgust with Lady Errol who was pleased to criticize the large statue of Brown set up at Balmoral. Being a Presbyterian Lady Errol said she did not hold with statuary – though it was noticeable she had never condemned the statues of Albert the Good which had proliferated in the royal palaces – and she acidly likened the Brown statue to Nebuchadnezzar's graven image. Lady Ely turned sad grey eyes on her and said she herself did not approve of either over-strict Calvinism or of impoliteness.

Both the Queen's intimate friends mourned Brown. He had been rough but superbly loyal. And they were profoundly sorry for her.

She herself made a brave showing.

Still unable to walk properly and often in great pain, she submitted to Beatrice's suggestion and Madame Charlotte Nautet was sent for from Aix. At once she felt the benefit. The masseuse, swiftly nicknamed 'the Rubber', manipulated her limbs, kneading her joints and muscles, and wrapped her in a specially treated flannel for regular periods of time.

But undoubtedly her greatest solace was a sudden and quite unexpected adjustment of fate which enabled her to place Mr Davidson where she most wanted him. Almost a month to the day after the death of John Brown, the Dean of Windsor died. He had been in office less than a year. The Archbishop agreed with the

Queen that Randall Davidson would make an excellent dean. Mr Gladstone was also agreeable. He might, he said, have demurred just a little on account of this clergyman's extreme youthfulness had it not been for the Queen's wish. 'Extreme youthfulness!' exclaimed the Queen when she read this letter. 'Why, he is surely thirty-three or thirty-four! By the time I was his age I had been ruling the country, let alone a deanery, for sixteen years.' She was delighted for him to be at Windsor and he showed himself extremely understanding about poor Brown.

Poor, poor Brown. How she missed him. He had always been there. Now there was no strong arm to lean on. No one to defend her. She told Davidson that strong John Brown had in a sense become her best and truest friend, as she was his.

The new Dean was touched by her naïvety. She showed him a number of greetings cards which Brown had treasured and which had been returned to her by his brothers. They expressed her sentiments exactly. Davidson was still touched by her obvious affection for the dead man, but he was also just a little anxious about her exuberant frankness. He turned the cards over and over. On one she had signed herself Brown's 'true and devoted one'; on another as his 'devoted grateful friend'; on the reverse of a third was the ingenuous, almost schoolgirlish declamation:

To my best friend J.B.
From his best friend V.R.I.

The new Dean advised the Queen to lock such treasures away. It would be cruel and futile to say much more. It could only cause her great pain.

The Queen then showed him the proofs of her latest selection of *Leaves* which was soon to be published. He had already read most of them and had heartily approved her stand against those who had advised her to cut out all references to toasts and drinking to please the total abstinence movement. She had called it humbug and would not have it at any price, and the Dean was sure she had been right. But now he noticed that she had written a startling dedication: it was to the memory of her faithful Highland Servant. The Brown scandal had foundered on the Queen's implacable refusal to see anything wrong at all in their strange relationship.

Innocence had shone and had won. But even now the press could so easily stir up trouble.

Dean Davidson mentioned his private doubts to Sir Henry Ponsonby. He in turn spoke to Lady Ely and Lady Churchill. In the end they came to the conclusion to leave things as they were. A risk must be taken. It would hurt the Queen unbearably to recommend that she alter her dedication on the grounds of discretion.

Sir Henry hoped that the public would see it simply as an endearing eccentricity of their sovereign. Much, he pointed out, was permitted to eccentric monarchs. The present King of Portugal was obsessed with Shakespeare and after heavy banquets would pin down ambassadors and recite whole plays to them with his views on plot development, characters, the use of imagery and staging. Because of this he was forgiven much else.

Unfortunately for their peace of mind, the Queen was already devising an enterprise so indiscreet that it could never be passed off as a harmless eccentricity. She was engaged upon writing a memoir of John Brown.

Two deeply troubled men, Dean Davidson and Sir Henry Ponsonby, were in the Dean's library at Windsor. They had left their wives drinking tea in the drawing-room. Sir Henry was in a state of agitation because of the Queen's declared intentions. The Dean was alarmed because everyone now looked to him to do something about it. Owing to the Rubber's good work, and her sensible advice, which apparently had not occurred to the Queen before, that it was unwise to picnic on wet grass, Victoria could now get about again without the aid of her pony chaise. Unfortunately, as her mobility increased so did her plans to immortalize Brown in print.

Now that Sir Theodore Martin's magnum opus on Albert the Good was done, she asked him to write a life of John Brown. To her chagrin he slipped away from the honour by declaring that his wife was unwell and he would not have sufficient time to devote to the work. She then contemplated writing it herself, aided by a Miss Macgregor who would smarten up her prose style, and when she had an outline planned and had written up the first sixteen years of the friendship, she sent the manuscript with Brown's own diaries and a covering note to Sir Henry for his opinion.

Had a vulture from a Parsee tower of silence dropped a corrupting limb into his lap, Sir Henry could not have been more horrified. He begged permission to send the manuscript on to the Bishop of Ripon and a Scotch divine, both of whom he claimed were men of letters and better able to advise her on authorship. Their reports confirmed his own opinion that it would be lunacy to publish a record of a relationship so open to misunderstanding. At the Queen's request the manuscript was then shown to Lord Beaconsfield's friend and secretary, Lord Rowton. He was aghast and wrote to Ponsonby that if the project could not be stopped it must be delayed. At all costs it must be delayed. He urged Ponsonby to be frank with the Queen.

Frank! The Queen's rheumatism had made her increasingly cantankerous, so much so that, in deference to her known dislike of meeting anyone when out driving, grown men would dive into bushes and climb trees as soon as they saw her carriage on the horizon. Ponsonby had had to deal with Prince Albert and Palmerston and John Russell in foul tempers, and he had fought the Russians in the Crimean War, and he had never been found lacking in courage, but he quailed at the thought of being frank with the Queen in her present mood.

Eventually he took a considerable risk and expressed one or two of his doubts in a letter to the Queen. He warned her that she was, in effect, doing something which in the end would only cause her distress and pain.

She took no notice. None whatever. Except to remark that she intended the biography to be for private circulation in the first instance.

Appalled by her plan, exhausted by her obstinacy, and at an end of both patience and courage, Ponsonby had begged for the Dean's help.

Davidson had done his best. In a letter he had put the matter squarely to Victoria. Much as he appreciated the copy of the newly-published *More Leaves* he hinted that any more leaves would be less welcome.

'And here,' said the Dean unhappily, 'is her reply.'

In it the Queen had shown her surprise and her great displeasure.

'And clearly,' continued the Dean, 'the Queen has no intention of taking either my hint, or any of yours.'

'She must!' exclaimed Ponsonby. His voice was touched with panic.

'Sir Henry, you yourself have said that the Queen can be obstinate.'

'That is beside the point. She must be made to see that if her book on Brown is printed, by however reliable a printer, a copy will get out. It is inevitable. And equally inevitable would be a throne-rocking scandal throughout the kingdom.' The Private Secretary tried to calm himself. He stopped walking up and down before the fire. He looked Davidson full in the face, and eventually he said: 'Mr Dean, I should not ask you to expose yourself to her Majesty's displeasure if the matter was not so urgent. But I am obliged to ask because I believe at this juncture you have the greatest influence on the Queen.'

The Dean walked directly to his desk. He took a pen from the standish and, after a moment's thought, began to write. When the letter was finished he read it through, signed it, blotted the signature and handed it to Sir Henry.

'That, I feel certain, will do.'

He reflected, as Sir Henry read the letter, that it was almost the equivalent of resigning his deanery. Sir Henry evidently thought the same. He grasped his hand. 'There really is no other way, but I regret having to lay it all on you.'

The Dean tried to make light of it, but, when Ponsonby had gone, he sat at his desk again looking mournfully out of the mullioned window. It was a view he had already come to appreciate. He sighed. Then he decided he ought to confide in his wife, Edith.

The Queen's reply arrived two hours later. It was in Lady Ely's handwriting. She had been commanded to convey her Majesty's order that the Dean withdraw what he had written and apologize for the great pain he had caused his sovereign.

Edith Davidson smiled nervously at her husband. The words command and order had never been used before in a letter to the Deanery. Davidson went to his desk and wrote the required apology, but said he could not withdraw what he had previously written for the good of the Queen's happiness. He then offered to resign.

. . . . .

No word came from the Queen that evening or the next day.

His nerves racked with anxiety, the Dean judged it better that someone else should preach at St George's on the following Sunday. If he looked at the Queen's letter once, he looked at it a score of times. Eventually the wording itself, as no doubt Lady Ely had intended, gave him some comfort. The Queen was imperious but, though she had used the language of the Tudor despots, she had too kind a heart to share their ruthlessness. He sensed that she was trying to bring herself to forgive him for his salty outspokenness, and that it would take some time. During that time he hid his feelings as best he could from everyone except his wife and the Ponsonbys. He pretended an insouciance he did not feel, was infrequently on his knees, and endeavoured to avoid feelings of self-pity or self-righteousness. He was often in the Ponsonbys' home in the Norman Tower. Sir Henry was often at the Deanery.

'The Queen,' encouraged Sir Henry several times, 'does not bear grudges. She does not bear grudges.'

Ponsonby was right. Victoria managed to swallow her pride. But it took two long weeks which were painful for everyone. Yet if anything the Queen and the Dean were drawn still closer together. He was thankful and grateful that she had been able to humble herself in such a fashion. And she, as Sir Henry had undertaken, bore no grudge to the Dean because high motives had made him candid.

The memoir was laid aside. It was never heard of again.

4

Prince Leopold died suddenly in Cannes in March 1884 leaving his widow carrying her second child.

The Prince of Wales at once went out to bring his brother's body home to Windsor. People said that because Leopold's life had always been in hazard it had been time borrowed from the grave, but this did not lessen his mother's grief. Temporarily she was distraught. Only three people brought her any degree of consolation: Lady Churchill with her close but quiet understanding;

Dean Davidson, whose personal knowledge of suffering made him acutely sensible to the pain of others; and the Princess of Wales who had always loved her rather odd and unattractive young brother-in-law and fully appreciated the Queen's feelings. It was 'Dear Alix, so kind and helpful', who encouraged her to pay attention to the Dean's excellent advice and for a time leave Windsor and all its sad associations.

To the Court's amazement Victoria said she would go to Darmstadt for the wedding of Alice's daughter. She had been expected to remain cloistered in deep mourning for months but she was determined to use all her great influence as Queen and doyenne of European sovereigns to champion her grand-daughter and namesake's marriage to Prince Louis of Battenberg.

It was an unpopular match in the courts of Europe because the Battenbergs were children of a morganatic marriage and not considered matrimonial catches. But the eldest brother was elected Prince of Bulgaria and Louis himself had become a naturalized British citizen and served in the Royal Navy. That, to Victoria, made them sufficiently respectable, and she was satisfied that her grand-daughter was in love. By giving her blessing to the marriage, Victoria silenced a good deal of criticism, and, on being given a warm and tender welcome by her son-in-law to Darmstadt, she delighted him by saying it did not matter in the least that the Battenbergs' great-grandfather had been a pastry-cook. Her own had been very little better, that strange flute- and cricket-playing Prince of Wales known simply as 'Poor Fred'.

Louis was touchingly grateful that she had come so soon after Leopold's death and tried to make her comfortable.

Darmstadt was, of course, too small. Accustomed to strict privacy and as much space as she wished, Victoria found her son-in-law's capital city restricting. She preferred, for instance, to breakfast out of doors in April – and in England nowadays in small revolving huts mounted on turntables – but it was impossible in Darmstadt. Even suites were out of the question save for herself and the grandest of the guests. For everyone else the accommodation was modest and there was talk amongst lower courtiers of the horrid necessity to share apartments. Nevertheless Victoria was determined to show no sign of discontent for the sake of dear, dead Alice.

All Europe had come to the wedding. Darmstadt was bright

with bands, buntings, banquets and balls. Greater and lesser royalties mingled and quarrelled. They were all related by blood or marriage and all looked up to the Queen of England who, far more than the bride or the ruling Grand Duke, was the focal point of that picket handkerchief Court. Even Vicky's mother-in-law, the exalted Empress of Germany, deferred to the Window of Windsor. Victoria reflected that the marriage game, as she and Albert had called the founding of their dynasty, had proved successful beyond their dreams. It helped to soothe the ache in her heart for Leopold. So, too, did the excitement of the approaching wedding.

She was very affectionate to her grand-daughter Victoria who soon would be her subject. She and Liko, as Louis was nicknamed, were to live at Sennicotts near Chichester. And she was nostalgic with her son-in-law the Grand Duke who had, she noted, a far-away look in his eyes.

Lady Ely, whose serene beauty had already caused heart-flutters in the Hessian capital, and whose finger was already on the pulse of Hessian affairs, was perfectly aware that the Grand Duke's look was not caused by the recollection of the dead Alice but by thoughts of a very much alive Polish countess. She had run off from a Russian diplomat and had been divorced, yet Grand Duke Louis was determined to marry her. Nevertheless, when pressed by the Prince of Wales and his sister the Crown Princess of Prussia to pass this information to the Queen, she gently refused. It was not, she claimed, her place to do so. In the end Vicky did it herself. The doyenne of European sovereigns must be made aware of what was going on beneath her nose.

'And so, you see, Mama,' she finished, 'it is essential that we all combine together, to prevent . . . to make Louis appreciate . . . to bring about a rupture. . . .' Her voice trailed off.

Her mother was nodding and had the strangest of strange smiles on her face.

Tentatively her nervous daughter continued: 'You do not appear to disapprove, Mama.'

The head immediately stopped nodding. 'Disapprove!' Of course I disapprove. Yes, something must be done. Bertie will help. From his own experience he will have shrewd advice on the unravelling of indiscreet entanglements.'

Vicky was amazed. She was forced to conclude that her

mother's well-known strict views about remarriage had been greatly modified. In fact, for widows they had not been modified in the least, but, having seen Lord Beaconsfield trying to manage without his Mary Anne, Victoria had decided there was perhaps a different case for widowers. Louis was still young and he was lonely, and she believed that a second marriage in his case would be no betrayal of his first because he had so obviously loved Alice, but this Polish divorcee would never do. She would be quite unacceptable from every point of view. She told Vicky that she would not join the conspirators to foil the Grand Duke in his foolish design, but they had her general support.

They were all too late. Even while his guests were plotting, Louis forestalled them. Barely an hour after the civil marriage of his daughter, he was married to the Countess by his own Prime Minister Starck in the presence of two witnesses.

The secret wedding shocked Darmstadt. The Prussians were ordered home by the Emperor. The remaining royalties gathered in conclave under the presidency of the Prince of Wales to issue a joint protest to their host against his marriage. Lawyers were commissioned to find good reasons for annulling so hasty and unwise a marriage.

Victoria remained apart. Yet she was not indifferent. She made it plain to her son-in-law that she believed he had made a mistake; worse, that he had made a fool of himself. Louis would, of course, have to give way to the wishes of the family. The Prince of Wales had warned him : 'We are a very strong family when we all agree.' Nevertheless she was not openly censorious.

Louis was deeply moved by her tolerant attitude. Everyone else was so hostile. When she left Darmstadt and he went to see her off at the railway station, he told her that he had agreed to an annulment.

'Much better so, much better,' she said.

'It was you who persuaded me, Mama,' he said. 'You saved me from myself.'

Victoria was not fond of emotionalism on railway platforms and she disliked seeing a sovereign Grand Duke weeping openly before his gaping subjects. Moreover his sobs were noisy. Yet saying anything at all would only make him worse. She simply nodded and patted his arm.

He kissed her hand, climbed down from the platform of her royal carriage, wiped his eyes and saluted.

There were whistles, orders, the crash of a military salute, and a red-uniformed band played *God Save The Queen*.

Victoria's face set in the fixed familiar smile of a thousand royal departures. But she was worried by Louis' tears, and because her collie puppy chose that moment to tug at the hem of her skirts. Without being bidden, Lady Churchill swept the puppy up into her arms.

After a long shudder and a jolt, the train crawled from the station. The Queen sighed with relief and sat down. She was not sorry to leave the quarrels and romantic intrigues behind.

At home in England there was the sadness of visiting Leopold's fresh grave. He had expressed a curious wish to be always within the sound of sweet singing and had been buried in St George's Chapel. Then the Queen went to Frogmore to the mausoleums of her mother and beloved Albert. Afterwards she fell gratefully into the routine of Windsor. She was at home, secure, content.

On that first evening she expressed her feelings to Beatrice. They did not often talk privately together although Beatrice had taken her brother's place as extra Private Secretary, but occasionally Victoria felt neglectful of her daughter and made a real attempt to share her most intimate thoughts. She spoke frankly of Louis' disastrous marriage, speculated on the possibility of a more satisfactory marriage later, and contrasted the bustle in frivolous Darmstadt with the grave tranquillity of Windsor.

Beatrice surprised her by saying that she, personally, had very much enjoyed the bustle.

Her mother eyed her. It was unlike Beatrice to be contradictory. She decided to leave the subject and talk of other things, but Beatrice was still inclined to be touchy. Quite mystified, her mother tried flattery. She spoke of her approaching old age. What a comfort it was to have the assurance of Beatrice's loving company until God should choose to reunite her with beloved Papa.

Again Beatrice surprised her. Instead of instantly agreeing and saying that yes indeed she would be the staff and stay of her poor old mother, Beatrice looked down, and bit her lip, and said nothing.

'Try a little sewing, dear,' suggested the Queen rather snappily. 'It will calm your nerves after our long journey.'

But Beatrice made no move to pick up her frame from the table. Instead she swallowed and suddenly announced that she was in love. The Queen gave a little shriek. 'In love!' she repeated; and then, again, in a higher key, 'in love!'

'Yes, Mama,' murmured Beatrice. She nodded. She was determined to be firm. She had already planned so carefully what to say and how to say it, and to choose exactly the right opportunity for doing so, but her feelings got the better of her and it all came out in a rush. With a sinking heart she realized it was not the right time at all to blurt out that she and Prince Henry of Battenberg had fallen in love in frivolous Darmstadt, and that in the course of time they hoped to become officially engaged, and —

'Beatrice!' The Queen held up her hand. 'You are overwrought. Our travels, the wedding, the unfortunate contretemps with your brother-in-law, have combined to upset you. Maslin shall ring for your dresser.'

Before she went to bed that night the Queen quarrelled with Jane Churchill.

She had at once sent for her and confided the dreadful news. In agitation she walked up and down her sitting-room, begging that someone open the windows, ordering wine to be sent in, and hot chocolate, and literally wringing her hands at the thought of losing her Benjamin. It was unbearable. Beatrice's great blunder must somehow be rectified. She only imagined herself in love and she had to be made to see reason. Could she have been deranged by the goings-on at Darmstadt? . . .

When, at length, she did leave a pause in her outpourings for Lady Churchill to put in a word she did not in the least like what she heard.

Love, warned Jane Churchill, be it imagined or real, had a great strength of its own. From now on the Queen could be certain that her usually docile and malleable Benjamin would be made obdurate by love.

'She will develop,' said Jane Churchill, 'a will of her own.'

Victoria did not miss the hint. It led to an explosion of indignation.

She said many regrettable things until her friend's patience was quite worn down and she boldly remarked that not even Victoria of England had the right to hold a daughter in perpetual subjection for her own selfish ends.

No one had spoken to the Queen so frankly for a very long time. She turned to the mantelshelf and said angrily: 'Jane, you have put a strain on our friendship, a very, very serious strain.'

'I should not be your friend, Ma'am,' returned Lady Churchill, 'if I kept the truth from you.' She asked permission to return to her apartments.

Fortunately their love for each other survived the quarrel, but each was determined not to give way.

Lady Churchill was demonstrably right in one thing: Beatrice remained obdurate. She would not be persuaded, bribed, or browbeaten – although, in her agony at the thought of Beatrice leaving her, the Queen did not hesitate to try all three. Very well, she decided, if it were a case of will-power she would win. She put both Beatrice and Lady Churchill into Coventry. She would only communicate by means of written orders passed over the breakfast table by a footman.

News rapidly spread through the family that Mama was being difficult and unreasonable. Pressure was put on her. Victoria, a supremely happy bride as Princess Louis of Battenberg, begged her grandmother that Aunt Beatrice should be allowed a taste of such joy. The Grand Duke Louis, now fully restored to favour in the family, urged the same. Vicky wrote letter after letter from Germany in favour of the marriage. Leopold's widow produced a posthumous Duke of Albany and, fresh from her lying-in, she spoke movingly of the romance of young hearts. Alfred, whose own marriage was dying, said that Beatrice should be given her chance. Alix pressed as urgently as anyone. . . .

In all the family only Christian and Helena and Arthur and his wife kept silent, Christian and Helena because they were Christian and Helena, and Arthur because he was so like his father that he never dreamed of testing his mother's fury unless it was vitally necessary.

The loudest complainant of them all was Bertie but he made the least impression because he was temporarily out of favour. Not only had he criticized *More Leaves* by saying that sovereigns ought not to share their secrets with subjects, but he had actually complained because his own name had not once appeared in the book and the omission gave a bad impression. Victoria had had the satisfaction of proving he had never read the book at all by referring to his name on pages 1, 5, 8, 331, and 378; but his criticism still rankled and, when he tried to bully her about Beatrice, she sharply told him to attend to his own business.

In the end Victoria had to give way. But there were conditions. Beatrice and her husband were to live constantly within reach. They should have apartments at Windsor, Osborne and Balmoral, and Beatrice was to continue to be her extra Private Secretary.

Prince Henry of Battenberg agreed at once to this formidable proviso, and, though it caused Prince Christian to shake his head in a reflective, melancholy way, the plan turned out well and neither he nor Beatrice nor the Queen ever regretted it.

Victoria's capitulation to her Lady-in-Waiting was superbly characteristic. 'Jane,' she said, 'you were right and I was wrong, but we will say no more about that, if you please.' Then she added after a reconciliatory kiss: 'Wilful I was as a child; wilful I was in middle age. And, regretfully, and I fear there's not the slightest doubt, I shall be perverse and stubborn to the end.'

5

The Queen now shuddered when she thought of Mr Gladstone.

That evil, evil man had defied her will and the will of her subjects in not saving poor General Gordon from the spears and swords of the rebellious Sudanese in Khartoum. A stronger force, sent out more swiftly, would have made all the difference, and Victoria blamed Gladstone, making it abundantly plain in a telegram sent not in the customary cypher but *EN CLAIR*.

The Prime Minister was angry to receive a public rebuke, but his sovereign was unrepentant and unforgiving. Her chin was set in a little round of disapproval for at least a week. He deserved it. True, George Cambridge had said there was something odd about General Gordon – slaves, or brandy, or too much Evangelical ardour, she could not recall which – and she knew he had behaved very curiously in China where he put up notices forbidding the peasants to drown unwanted girl children in his troops' water supply, but, eccentric or not, he had deserved his country's support. She had no qualms about making her opinion public, and when Gordon's sister sent her one of his well-worn Bibles as a gift the Queen had it exhibited in the south corridor at Windsor. There it lay on a white satin cushion in an enamel and crystal case beside a bust of Gordon and, on the rare occasion when he was her guest at the Castle, she liked to walk Mr Gladstone past it.

Gladstone was aggravated. He was also hurt and bewildered. What, he asked his wife, had he done to deserve such treatment? She knew, but she considered it prudent to pretend that she had no idea. Gladstone consulted the Prince of Wales. They were very friendly. Indeed Gladstone had once amazed society and proved his fondness for the Prince by paying a call on Mrs Langtry when that lady was the acknowledged *maîtresse en titre*. But the Prince could not help a great deal. Though he liked Gladstone as a man, he shared and understood his mother's political prejudices. Both wished that the Liberals would do more for under-privileged subjects and spend less time on promoting individualism. Gladstone then asked for the candid opinion of his colleagues. None was encouraging. Thereafter he determined to do his duty and try, if possible, to put the Queen out of his mind. He might as well have tried to forget rain or thunder or any other force of nature. He had to be in frequent touch with the sovereign, and though he could never recall vexation making her actually discourteous – and to Mrs Gladstone and their children she was invariably friendly – he was sensitive to her continuous hostility.

It had seldom been Victoria's habit to find fault, but in the case of Mr Gladstone it almost became a compulsion. She blamed him for leaving the country without her permission and enjoying a semi-royal progress at the Scandinavian courts accompanied by the Poet Laureate. She blamed him for making public speeches not far from Balmoral – 'practising his odious stump oratory on my own doorstep!' She blamed him for failing to control his radical followers. She even blamed him directly for the faults of his colleagues in the Cabinet. When Hartington showed an increasing tendency to follow Lord Palmerston's maddening habit of acting independently, she pulled him up sharply – and promptly blamed Mr Gladstone for corrupting a Cavendish with his notions of democracy. When the execution of a convicted murderer was botched at Exeter, and, owing to a fault in the drop, three attempts to hang him failed, she insisted that the Home Secretary commute his sentence and was inclined to blame the Prime Minister for not having better hangmen. When Sir Henry received a stony letter of complaint because in *More Leaves* the Queen had described Tomintoul as a dirty town, she refused utterly to retract, insisting that it *was* a very dirty town, and that the complainant was doubtless a friend of Mr Gladstone's. And as for Ireland. . . . Words hardly ever failed Queen Victoria, but what she considered the Prime Minister's ineptness in the Irish tragedy rendered her speechless for seconds at a time.

The problem of Ireland grew worse each month. Gladstone kept the Queen informed of the succession of outrages, and the feeling of the Irish and the English, but his heavy, detailed memoranda failed to convey how serious the situation had become. She discovered it herself by accident when, after a month as Minister in Attendance at Balmoral, Lord Hartington casually wrote to ask for a forgotten revolver to be sent on. It appeared that because of the constant danger from ribbonmen he always went about armed. The Queen was indignant at not being given a full picture of the situation. Then she was angry with Mr Gladstone for recommending that a royal visit by the Prince and Princess of Wales and their elder son to the seditious Irish might be useful. Lord Beaconsfield had, of course, recommended the very same thing seventeen years before, but he had been right. It had done good. The Irish had been welcoming to Bertie and Alix. Yet Victoria doubted if anything in the least Gladstonian could do good, and her solemn prophecy was fulfilled. The royal party met with insolent hostility. The Prince's senior equerry wrote to the Queen a description of their reception in disaffected areas like Cork. There they were booed continuously and pelted with onions as they drove through the streets. On all sides were

> *sullen faces – hideous, dirty, cruel countenances, hissing and grimacing into one's very face, waving* black *flags and* black *kerchiefs – a nightmare!*

The letter was refolded and sent on to Mr Gladstone. What, asked the Queen, was he intending to do now that his dangerous experiment with the members of her family had proved a failure? To her horror she heard that Gladstone's apparent aim was to let these fearful rebels rule themselves. She was appalled. So was the Prince of Wales who had been deeply hurt by his reception in Ireland.

But there was consolation after all. Gladstone's Home Rule policy was not drastic enough to satisfy the Irish members of the House of Commons and they defeated the Liberals in a budget bill.

The People's William was forced to resign.

Victoria was overjoyed, but found fault with his method of resigning. It ought to be done personally and not by telegraph. With his unhappy lack of tact, Gladstone excused himself by saying that evacuating Number 10 Downing Street was consuming all his time.

That nice Marquess of Salisbury who looked so like a minor prophet and who had gone to Berlin with dear Lord Beaconsfield was now the Queen's First Minister. Her delight was tempered by Lady Ely's prophecy that the Liberals were simply biding their time, and that the official residence of the First Lord of the Treasury was the box and Mr Gladstone was Jack. And she was quite correct. After only nine, agreeable Conservative months Jack was back in his box once more, forming a third Administration and concocting a far more drastic Home Rule bill. The Queen showed an independent spirit by refusing to accept its title 'for the *better* government of Ireland'. The word 'better' must be struck out. Mr Gladstone was no better than a conciliator of Irish desperadoes. Trying to remain calm, the Grand Old Man put his bill to the Commons, but trying to balance the Irish members and his radical supporters was his undoing. Barely six months after its formation, the Ministry fell.

It looked as though this time Mr Gladstone really was out. It really did. But the Queen refused to believe it. Wicked genies are not easily contained in Cheshire bottles. He would escape again. And, as it happened, she was, of course, correct.

. . . Sometimes, during the lengthy, exhausting, nerve-fraying war with her own First Minister, Victoria would visit the Carnivorous Plant House at Frogmore where, in an atmosphere which accurately simulated the steaming heats of a Siamese jungle, pitcher-plants and other horrors grew. When she was feeling particularly spiteful it gave her great satisfaction to imagine the People's William being offered up piecemeal to these uncanny, smelly plants.

6

By now it was believed in the family that the Princess of Wales had more influence on the Queen than anyone. Therefore it was she who was deputed to make their request that she appear in regal splendour for the Golden Jubilee Service of Thanksgiving. It was a very short interview. It seemed to those of the family who were waiting in the Prince of Wales' apartments that Alix had barely gone before she was back again. Her cheeks were pink. She always spoke English with a strong accent. In excitement it was even more pronounced. 'Never,' she said, pronouncing the word *neffa*, 'never, never, never, never was I so snubbed in my life.'

Mama had refused point blank to drive in robes of state in a golden coach to Westminster. She would wear mourning and ride in an open landau. There was no question of wearing her crown. A bonnet was quite good enough. 'Do you think,' she had snappily asked Alix, 'that I shall not be recognized?'

The Prince of Wales was put out. No game-cock was fonder of colour and display. It seemed a great pity to waste such an opportunity, and prefer a bonnet and walking stick to the crown, sceptre and orb of royalty. But Mama had been in a curious mood for months. She would not have her decisions questioned. In fact this decision, made because she disliked fuss and preferred to be comfortable, was an unconscious master-stroke.

In June, 1887, on the forty-ninth anniversary of her coronation day, a bright cavalcade left Buckingham Palace for the Abbey. There were separate processions of visiting sovereigns, the Queen's Household, and the princesses, and then, after a detachment of Life Guards, came the Queen's carriage escorted by Indian cavalry and guarded by her sons and sons-in-law and grandsons. At the centre of so much colour and glitter and splendour, with Alix and

Vicky facing her, the tiny Queen, bonneted and dressed in black, drew all eyes by her regal simplicity.

Inside the Abbey, to trumpet fanfares, the roll of kettle-drums, and the peal of the organ, she walked up to her place, leaning a little on a stick. Her eyes swam with tears when Albert's *Te Deum* was sung, and when afterwards, she received the homage and kissed all the members of her family. People noticed that she was also crying as the procession wound its way back to the Palace. She was seated on a cunning revolving stool, hidden by the folds of her black satin dress, which made it easy for her to turn from side to side. As she turned the diamonds of her tears shone in the afternoon sunlight, and, believing she was touched by the affection of her subjects, they cheered themselves hoarse. In some degree this was the reason, though by now Victoria was well aware of the fickleness of British mobs. Less than a month before she had opened a People's Palace and had been booed en route by people she preferred to describe as 'the low, bad Irish who abide in London'. But her real reason was because, though surrounded by hundreds and thousands of well-wishers and by all of her large family who were still alive and could be present, she yet felt low.

To look back, and the whole day was aimed at looking back, was to grieve for her precious dead, for dear Lord M., for Uncle Leopold, for her half-brother and half-sister, for Alice and Leopold, for dearest Lord Beaconsfield; above all, of course, for Albert. Poignantly, the day which should have made her so brisk and alive and happy only served to make her long desperately for Albert.

Events were pressing on her more than ever before. There was trouble amongst the Powers because Russia had forcibly removed Beatrice's Battenberg brother-in-law, Sandro, from the throne of Bulgaria. There was trouble in the family because Bismarck and the old German Emperor would on no account allow Vicky's daughter to marry Sandro; and there was trouble because Beatrice's little daughter had been christened by a Presbyterian in the Balmoral drawing-room. Worst of all was Fritz's illness. Her son-in-law was ill, very ill, although he looked so handsome in the procession with his golden viking beard and uniform of white and gold. He had a terrible disease in his throat.

She turned from right to left and back again, smiling to her people, her hand upraised. In Piccadilly between Venetian masts there was a decorated banner which caught her eye:

PICCADILLY RINGS WITH CHEERS,
TELLING THE LOVE OF FIFTY YEARS.

Humbug! How many times in these fifty years had these same people or their fathers shown her any sort of love?

She turned left and right and left again, smiling, and reflecting that in Jane Churchill's long residence at Court she had caught a little of her dear friend's cynicism. And the thought made her realize how much she owed to those who were closest to her. Except for Beatrice and her husband Liko and their children she had no family around her any more, and they, naturally, put their love for her second to their love for each other. She had already written that morning in her journal:

The Day has come and I am alone, though surrounded by many dear children.

It made good sense. For her daily comforts and joys, for the little things which made all the difference between living and existing, she had to thank her closest friends and servants: faithful Lehzen and good John Brown who had done so much and Lady Lyttleton, and the Duchess, and Maslin who had just retired, and wonderful Miss Skerrett who at that very moment lay dying at the great age of ninety-four; and all those who were still alive and with her.

Turn right, turn left. There was dear Vicky opposite making the small and secret family sign used to warn her that her face needed seeing to. She lowered her aching arm and, with a wisp of a handkerchief, dried her eyes. Probably her eyes and nose were red. Well, it couldn't be helped.

The procession had gone far along the Mall. She was pleased to be close to home again. After her coronation forty-nine years before she had had the energy of a girl and had gone home to bath her spaniel Dash. She smiled at the recollection. Nowadays her energy was less boundless. Indeed of late she had been falling asleep at her desk for no apparent reason. It was extraordinary, really, that there was a connection between that young girl on the brink of everything and she who was on the brink of nothing save the expectation of a long banquet, a march past of bluejackets, a reception of the Corps Diplomatique, and a good deal of formal talk before she could have the rest she longed for.

Turn right, turn left. And now that clever revolving seat had somehow stuck. It was as well they were so close to the Palace. And Vicky was making the same sign. Red nose and eyes. Nothing could be done. How they cheered. What enthusiasm! Lord Beaconsfield had not cared for enthusiasm, but he would have loved this display of imperial pomp. And how he would have relished the astounding manifestation of loyalty in Sind where, to mark the year, the authorities had opened THE QUEEN VICTORIA JUBILEE BURIAL AND BURNING GROUND.

The Queen smiled and raised her hand for what seemed the thousandth time. Tonight there would be firework displays all over the kingdom, and bonfires on the hills....

Then came the crashing of salutes, the sound of bands in unison. George of Cambridge, her own age and a great hulk of a man, was helping her from the carriage. By the look of him he was feeling his responsibility, the heat, and his age. She determined not to do so herself.

She walked on alone again, leaning on her stick.

7

After the Jubilee Fritz was persuaded to remain in England for his health's sake. He and Vicky had taken a house in Upper Norwood, but they were invited to enjoy the tranquillity of Osborne. His mother-in-law assured him that there he would not be pestered by anyone. She had been outraged to discover that the illness of a German Crown Prince had political aspects and that the choice and actual practice of medical attendants were the subjects of court intrigues in Berlin.

Fritz enjoyed a quiet rest at Osborne, having a conducted tour of Mrs Prothero's garden, walking out with his glaucous Italian greyhound, Bijou, and watching Vicky play tennis very badly with Mrs Prothero's son. Eventually, on the advice of a Scotch consultant, they moved to Braemar, taking a suite at the Fife Arms. The Queen naturally invited them to stay at Balmoral, but she did not insist, and it suited Fritz not to be under the immediate eye of his mother-in-law.

No one admired Victoria more than Fritz. He considered her a marvel, but her indomitable spirit was wearing. So was her recent experiment in having Indian servants about her person. Fritz found the smell of Indian cooking objectionable and remarked that their apartments in the royal palaces were reminiscent of old Bombay. The Queen's dogmatically expressed views were also trying to his liberal mind. She could be surprisingly progressive, especially with regard to the coloured races and the welfare of her own underprivileged subjects, but, generally, she was reactionary. For instance Lord Salisbury had persuaded her to admit divorced wives, if innocent, to her Drawing-Rooms – something of which the progressive Fritz naturally approved – but she had given way only under protest. When the subject was mentioned, and it was, frequently, she had a habit of asking rhetorically, 'but *can* a divorced wife be innocent?' All in all, Fritz felt it was wiser to visit Balmoral on regular occasions but to have their holiday headquarters at the Fife Arms.

In her heart of hearts the Queen would have agreed with him. Her routines were now as firmly established as the liturgy of the Church, and she did not care to have them upset. Moreover it distressed her greatly to see Fritz in pain and to hear his hoarse whisper. Her doctors were not over-sanguine. The majority diagnosed the disease as cancer, though some claimed that the successive growths in the Crown Prince's throat were not malignant. She felt sure herself that the disease was mortal, and she could tell from poor Vicky's manner, from her expression when she believed no one was looking at her, from a dozen small, insignificant things that she thought so too. And what would happen when she was a widow? What would happen to Germany when the old Emperor died? For the first time Victoria found herself in accord with Bismarck. The old chancellor described her impossible grandson Willy as being like a balloon. 'If you don't keep hold of the string, you never know where he will be off to.' Just so.

They all wore brave faces. It was the only thing to do.

Fritz and Vicky drove out with the Queen, though Fritz excused himself from the picnics. He confessed to Vicky that he could not bear the gnats nor tea made from tepid water.

They played croquet together. 'Such a malicious game,' exclaimed the Queen every time she knocked an opponent off the lawn, and, for her age, she wielded so vigorous a mallet that Fritz called her Thor.

They went to the shrines made sacred by statues and memories of Albert and John Brown, a process which Fritz thought grotesque though politely he said nothing. He and Vicky exchanged glances when invited to commend one particular Indian servant, Abdul, whom the Queen said was wonderfully quick at helping with the drying of her signatures. They hoped Mama was not going to choose another unsuitable friend but it rather looked as if she might be. Vicky had told Fritz that one of her father's first tasks on coming to England had been to help blot the royal signature. It was a task which invariably fell upon carefully chosen intimates. Mama gave them to understand she was also learning Hindustani from Abdul, a necessary qualification, she thought, for an Empress of India. She underlined the point by using a welcoming phrase taught her by Abdul when the Rau of Kutch and his brother came to luncheon.

Fritz was there to help her entertain the Indians who had taken a grouse moor for the season, and he was amused by the contrast between the Queen-Empress, who was dressed as if about to open a bazaar in Ballater, and the oriental splendour of the princes who arrived in silks, rubies, diamonds and sapphires. There was the same contrast in diet. Despite the summer heat, the Queen took thick soup, a wedge of salmon, boiled fowl and a heap of potatoes, while the young men toyed with string beans, some sort of marrow dish, salad and fruit.

When the time of their departure drew near the Queen became more and more nostalgic and dejected. Vicky and Fritz had been happily married for some twenty-nine years and it seemed to her that there was a quality in their relationship which set them apart from the rest of her children. So far as she was aware both Arthur and Beatrice were content enough, but their marriages were decorous, tame, entirely lacking the intensity and fire of true love-affairs. As for the others. . . . Poor, deaf Alix had so much to put up with from Bertie, and Alfred's marriage to his proud Russian Grand Duchess was breaking down. Loosy was completely disenchanted with her Lorne. She had left him in Canada to seek medical treatment, and, ever since, had been wandering round Europe incognita as 'Mrs Campbell' and sculpting under the guidance of Boehm. Then there was Helena trying to lose herself in a quantity of good works and a school of needlework, leaving stodgy Christian to his shotguns and cigars and mild melancholy. Fritz and Vicky were so very different. They made a handsome, affectionate couple. It appalled her that sickness would soon separate them just as she had been separated from Albert.

She cried on the day they left. They all did. And they had determined not to show their feelings.

'I shall come to see you both in Germany,' sobbed Victoria, embracing her son-in-law. 'I promise to come and see you.'

Not long afterwards the royal physicians and surgeons finally agreed on their diagnosis of the Crown Prince's affliction. He was operated on for cancer and sent off to San Remo for a period of convalescence.

Dreading the outcome his mother-in-law in England watched and waited and prayed and wrote long and encouraging letters to Vicky.

By degrees Fritz's condition perceptibly deteriorated. And then one day in March, 1888, he found himself German Emperor. His father had died at the age of ninety-one, and he was now the Emperor Frederick the Third. But he could barely find the strength to dress and receive the ministers who came officially to acclaim him.

When he was able he returned to Germany to show in a rule of only ninety-nine days, and from a painful death-bed, the promise of what might have been done for the benefit of Germany and Europe. Conservatives, led by Prince Bismarck and by his own son Willy, were antagonistic to his dream of a liberal, progressive German Empire. They conspired to invoke the ancient law of Prussia which declared that no one who was mortally sick could succeed to the crown. Only by a great effort could Fritz keep them at bay but in his weakness he made a grave mistake, giving way to Vicky's pleading that their daughter Moretta be allowed to marry Alexander Battenberg, the banished Prince of Bulgaria.

Though she really approved of the marriage herself, Queen

Victoria had a wide political experience which told her it was folly to overrule the old Emperor's objection and enrage Bismarck and Willy. Privately she begged Vicky not to press the marriage.

Publicly she announced her intention of paying a visit to Berlin.

Lord Salisbury was both startled and worried. The time, he warned the Queen, was not really opportune. Prince Bismarck might be rude to her. Almost certainly the German press would be hostile to any sort of visit from the English Queen.

Victoria was unperturbed. She amused her Prime Minister by saying that, after years of experience with Mr Gladstone and the Liberal press, Berlin reporters and the panjandrums of Prussia held few terrors. It was arranged that she should make a state visit to the Emperor and Empress Frederick after her spring holiday in Florence.

Karré, her courier was unwell, but his deputy made the necessary arrangements. So that there could be no mistake that her visit was official, and no hole-and-corner affair, Victoria travelled in state from Italy as Queen of England and not as the Countess of Balmoral. It meant that she had to be formally received en route by fellow sovereigns or their envoys, a piece of protocol she would happily have avoided although it gave her the opportunity to encounter two particularly interesting monarchs.

The Austrian Emperor came himself to meet her at Innsbruck. He had travelled seventeen hours in order to do so and looked exhausted. Poor man. Victoria regarded him with sympathy. He called himself a *peckvogel*, a bird of misfortune, and really there was something in it. His only son was a scamp. His brother had been the unfortunate Maximilian whose murdered corpse had been sold off in lots as souvenirs. His wife Elizabeth was always away searching for fresh and shocking experiences. In fact, his only consolation – so Lady Churchill informed the Queen – was a robust, retired actress named Schratt who doted on hot chocolate and operetta. Unhappy Franz Josef. He was indeed a *peckvogel*. They had luncheon in a room three-quarters filled with flowers. 'Just like the dear Mausoleum', was Beatrice's *sotto voce* comment until an acid look from Mama told her she was being particularly stupid. And when they left, the Emperor stood stiffly to attention at the salute. The Queen bowed from her carriage window. Poor *peckvogel*. Later she had quite a shock when, by a quick calculation, she realized this unfortunate old gentleman was, in fact, eleven years younger than she.

At Munich there was another royal *peckvogel* to meet her. The Queen Mother of Bavaria was on the platform with a bouquet of roses. They smelt curiously of earth and scent, and were very pale; not so pale, though, as the tragic Queen Mother who still mourned her drowned husband and mad son. Victoria was very affectionate with her, admiring her royal management of grief. It was an example she hoped to emulate in Berlin. Vicky and Fritz's widowed mother would need all the strength she could give them.

Lord Salisbury need not have been over-anxious. The Queen of England was not all that popular a figure in Germany, yet the legendary Victoria was someone to be admired.

The people literally threw flowers into her carriage. The Queen nodded to them, rewarding them only occasionally with a smile. Another mob. Fickle. The flowers might so easily have been brickbats.

The press was less welcoming but, having been the prey of newspaper men most of her life, she had the poorest sort of opinion of them and she cared not a rap.

As for Prince Bismarck, she conquered him at a stroke. When she received him on the second morning of her visit he was glowering and suspicious. Indeed he so feared her approval of the marriage which he himself hated that he had said so publicly.

'The old lady,' he growled, with a studied lack of respect, 'is capable of bringing the fiancé and a parson with her in her carpet-bag.'

But there was nothing so sinister in Victoria's carpet-bag and she immediately disarmed Bismarck by saying that of course such a marriage was quite out of the question.

Afterwards the British Ambassador remarked with pride that only Queen Victoria could have made the irascible old Chancellor gape.

In the darkened rooms where Fritz fought with pain and the frustration of being unable to speak, Victoria strove to hide her feelings. Hard experience had convinced her that a dying man needed to be in ordinary surroundings. Neither sobbing women, nor the brave women who bite back their tears and say he will be up and well again in no time are of much help. She herself tried to be ordinary, and Fritz clearly appreciated it. She talked briefly about his wishes for Vicky and the children and then let him rest. Sitting by his bed, she took his hand and told him there was a saying in the Highlands that touch spoke more wisely, more truly, and more beautifully than any words. Mostly in her short visits she simply sat there holding his hand.

Victoria called on the old Empress Augusta to comfort her and found her deathly pale and crumpled up with sorrow. With palsied hands she gave Victoria a macabre photograph of the late Emperor's corpse. Soon, she said, she would be sending a similar photograph of the body of her only son. Victoria chose to be silent. She kissed the grieving Empress.

If only for Vicky's sake she was glad to be in Berlin. In the privacy of her mother's apartments the young Empress of Germany could be her natural self. Vicky was encouraged to cry and found relief in shedding tears which had been suppressed for far too long. Her suffering was deeply moving. Even Sir Henry Ponsonby found himself close to tears at the sight of her grief. The horror of watching her adored husband dying in the agony of a loathsome disease, the strain of having to fight political squabbles over his death-bed, and the dread she already had of the uncertainties of the future, could have unseated the reason of many women. But Vicky had her mother's toughness and drew great strength from her encouragement in the two short days of her visit.

Before Victoria left her she made her daughter promise to tread gently with Willy. He was not an agreeable person but soon, far too soon, he would be Emperor. She also extracted a promise that, after Fritz's death, Vicky would pay a long visit to England. Karré – she was beginning to say – would arrange anything; but she left the sentence unfinished. A telegraphic message had just been sent to her that Karré had had a relapse and died. Yet another sorrow. . . .

Vicky insisted on saying good-bye to her mother at the station.

She held herself very well, and Victoria was proud that her daughter had so royal a presence. But when the train whistled and the carriage began to glide away Vicky's face creased and puckered. To Victoria's dismay her last sight of dear Vicky was in that moment just before an explosion of grief. She sat back in her chair clenching and unclenching her fists. At last she had found a grief quite equal to her own in 1861. Darling, darling Vicky.

• • • •

Fritz died at 11.15 a.m. on June 15th.

No sooner had the Queen received the news at Balmoral than she asked Sir Henry to send a telegram to the new German Emperor.

> I AM BROKEN-HEARTED HELP AND DO ALL YOU CAN FOR YOUR POOR DEAR MOTHER AND TRY TO FOLLOW IN YOUR BEST NOBLEST AND KINDEST OF FATHER'S FOOTSTEPS
>
> GRANDMAMA V.R.I.

Already she realized the hopelessness of trying to urge Willy in any direction at all, and her worst fears were soon realized.

A fortnight after his father's funeral Willy was showing a marked reluctance to be generous to his mother with regard to her future home. He offered her a little villa and his grandmother swiftly wrote to suggest that Friedrickron or Sans Souci would be more appropriate. 'An Empress could not well live in a little villa.' The new Emperor slid neatly out of the difficulty; but his subsequent behaviour was still displeasing to his grandmother. He was not disposed to mourn for his father, and, though Victoria approved of honesty, she still thought that he ought to be more polite and considerate for the feelings of those who did mourn. Fritz had barely been buried a month and there was his son parading up and down both in Germany and out of it at banquets and reviews in a multitude of uniforms. Victoria considered it 'very indecent and very unfeeling'. Then Willy made an unreasonable fuss because a part of his father's diary had been published by a devoted but injudicious friend without his permission. He blamed his mother, although she was as surprised and as angry as he. After that he turned his back on a British ambassador, and was extraordinarily rude to his uncle, the Prince of Wales, insisting that if he was to make a formal visit to Vienna, the Prince of Wales, who happened to be there then, would have to leave first. Finally the German Ambassador in London produced a list of imperial grievances for Lord Salisbury to forward to the Queen. Amongst them was the complaint that the Prince of Wales was treating the Emperor as an uncle treats a nephew.

When she read this document the Queen was livid. Using the royal plural she wrote a letter to the Prime Minister which, in parts, betrayed the state of her fury:

As regarding the Prince's not treating his nephew as Emperor; this is really too vulgar *and too absurd, as well as untrue, almost* to be believed.
We have always been very intimate with our grandson and nephew and to pretend that he is to be treated in private *as well as in public as 'his Imperial Majesty' is* perfect madness! . . . If *he has* such *notions, he had better* never *come* here. The Queen will not swallow this affront.

Lord Salisbury chuckled when he read her letter. He had heard it whispered at an ambassadorial dinner that the Queen of England was a little passé, certainly feeble, not at all her old vigorous self. He thought it a pity that he could not produce this indictment of the Emperor William as proof to the contrary.

Victoria continued to be a fiery critic of her wrong-headed grandson and a champion of her wronged daughter. She would not hear of the suggestion that it might be more politic for the widowed Empress Frederick to postpone her promised visit to her homeland.

IT WOULD BE IMPOSSIBLE HEARTLESS AND CRUEL [she telegraphed Lord Salisbury] NO USE AND WOULD ENCOURAGE THE EMPEROR AND THE BISMARCKS STILL MORE AGAINST US YOU ALL SEEM TO BE FRIGHTENED OF THEM WHICH IS NOT THE WAY TO MAKE THEM BETTER PLEASE LET NO ONE MENTION THIS AGAIN

That autumn there was a ghastly series of murders in Whitechapel. The murderer was nicknamed Jack the Ripper.

The Queen grimaced when she heard the name; then she smiled to Lady Ely who had been reading out the report. 'They would do better to call him Bismarck,' she suggested.

When Vicky did come to England with her daughters her mother gave her unprecedented honours. She sent the royal yacht, *Victoria and Albert*, to meet them at Flushing, and welcomed her personally on landing in England. Lord Salisbury thought it mildly provoking of her. She had never before gone farther than her own front door to meet any guest. But Victoria was determined to honour Vicky as a widowed Empress. They travelled to London together and not to Windsor, the Queen insisting that her daughter precede her everywhere.

There were hosts of tears. It hurt Vicky most, she said, that on first speaking to his parliament Willy had made not a single mention of his father. He had undertaken to 'follow the same path by which my deceased grandfather won the confidence of his allies'. And, naturally, he had instructed his sister Moretta to abandon any thoughts of marrying the deposed Sandro Battenberg. Vicky told her mother it was, perhaps, as well. Sandro had already consoled himself with an Austrian actress and it was whispered that he was in love with her. But what was she to do with Moretta? ...

The tragedy of Fritz's early death brought mother and daughter together in a very special relationship. Just as Vicky had best understood her mother's tragedy in 1861 so, in turn, her mother now best understood hers. But whereas the chief battle in Victoria's mourning had been between grief and public duty, and she had thought at the beginning that the battle would unseat her reason, Vicky was faced with a different, even bleaker future, deprived at one stroke of the man she adored, her place in the framework of German society, and denied by Willy the support and sympathy and understanding which a woman naturally is entitled to at a time of sorrow.

Neither mother nor daughter had any taste for the gruesome German deathroom, embalmed in dust and cobwebs for decades. Both preferred the simplicity of the Blue Room at Windsor which was regularly supplied with pictures and fresh flowers and clean linen. They preferred to have bright memories of their beloved dead. The Queen confessed she was not all that certain nowadays of the usefulness of mausoleums. She went of course on daily pilgrimages to the Frogmore Mausoleum whenever she was at Windsor, but she felt as close to Albert in other ways and at other places. Still, a mausoleum was an essential and Vicky naturally wished for one for Fritz.

The third day of her visit was Vicky's forty-second birthday. Amongst the many presents she was given, she received from her mother a small posy of flowers and a very large contribution towards the cost of a mausoleum.

8

In the majority of cases the Queen would tolerate no nonsense from her grandchildren.

When Moretta pined because Sandro had renounced his title and actually married his beloved actress, she was told to look alive. When she then decided that a gaunt appearance was appropriate for a grief-stricken princess, and she refused all food save apples and match-box-size helpings of meat, she was invited to stay in England where her plot to waste away was scotched by doses of lemon juice and whisky – pressed on her regularly by Grandmama – and where she was kept so busy with amateur theatricals that she had no opportunity to pine.

When Alicky of Hesse refused to consider marrying Bertie's elder boy Eddy she was told by everyone in the family, and several times by its head, that by refusing so great a position she was being wilful – but Grandmama really admired her decision. Eddy was not a grandson to be proud of: lamentably stupid and self-indulgent, inclined to effeminacy and with so faulty a sense of dress that his attempts at dandyism had earned him the nickname of 'Collar and Cuffs'.

But in a few cases the Queen was less peremptory about her grandchildren. Surprisingly, she abruptly altered her attitude to Willy. The reason was plain to everyone except Willy who believed that his personal charms were irresistible. It was, of course, for his mother's sake that, having said the German Emperor could never come to England again, his Grandmama relented and invited him to Osborne. She even accepted from him the Honorary Colonelcy of the 1st Regiment of Dragoon Guards and gave him in return the rank of a British Admiral. It was a small sacrifice to make for Vicky's benefit and indeed for the benefit of Anglo-German diplomatic relations.

> *Fancy* [wrote Willy] *wearing the same uniform as St Vincent and Nelson. It is enough to make one quite giddy.*

'Ridiculous boy!' said the Queen to Beatrice and Liko.

Willy was still more ridiculous when his sister Sophie, who had married the Crown Prince of Greece, decided to adopt the Greek Orthodox religion. He was so angry that he banned Sophie from visiting Germany. Their mother tried to interfere but had little success. Willy was eventually persuaded to reduce the sentence of perpetual banishment. Sophie reported this in an open telegram to her mother:

FIXES IT TO THREE YEARS MAD NEVER MIND SOPHIE

It was not calculated to soothe Willy. Nor did it. It was said that on hearing of the telegram he jumped up and down violently in his saddle (sitting at his desk he disdained the civilian's chair for an adapted cavalryman's saddle). His grandmother's remark this time was : 'Foolish boy!' But all the same he went up in her estimation when he quarrelled with Prince Bismarck and deprived him of his chancellorship.

She discussed the implications of this tremendous step with Lady Churchill. By custom of course such a political conversation would not have been conducted with her but, by awful chance, Lady Ely's only son, the fourth Marquis, had died, and, thoroughly crushed by the event, she had felt obliged to resign her place as Lady-in-Waiting. To a meticulous observer of routine like the Queen this was a severe blow. Because she dearly loved Lady Ely and sympathized with her misfortune, she had schooled herself to make the parting as painless as possible, but she felt it keenly, and, still hoping that she might one day return, she would not admit her successor to the privileged post of intimate adviser which her friend had enjoyed for so many years.

It was not to be. Barely a year after her retirement Lady Ely died. Only those who had resented her punditry and her position as political intermediary failed to mourn. Everyone at Court grieved, members of the Household and the servants alike; the Queen and Lady Churchill most of all. A fortnight later they went in a closed carriage to see her grave in Kensal Green. They placed wreaths. It was the Queen's first visit to the cemetery which had particular associations with her family. Her uncle, the eccentric Duke of Sussex, lay there beside his second morganatic wife, the Duchess of Inverness. George of Cambridge's Mrs Beauclerk lay there, and only recently Mrs Fitzgeorge had died and been buried in a vault draped with evergreens and covered with a massive marquee. Jane Ely lay in good, family company.

Now only one of the Queen's two Janes remained, and she complained that she was seriously feeling her years. The Queen endeavoured to encourage her. 'Naturally,' she said. 'We all do.' In a moment of frankness she confessed her own limitations. She at last admitted that her eyesight was weakening. But, she said, one had to keep up one's spirits: 'And so I tell poor Sir Henry that his handwriting is getting crabbed, and I blame the river fogs at Windsor when we have lighted candles on the luncheon table.' Lady Churchill was touched by this admission. Her husband was dead by now and her son married, and she had no close contact with her family. She really wished, she explained, to stay with the Queen but she feared that growing infirmities would make her a burden. The Queen quickly reassured her: 'Promise me, Jane, that you will never leave Court.' Lady Churchill did so, and they kissed. 'With our dressers and maids to look after us,' continued the Queen, 'and the dear Munshi to look after little details, and the dear Dean to help keep us sensible, we shall have a comfortable old age together.'

Lady Churchill was touched and grateful, but, being an inveterate cynic, she permitted herself to question the Queen's receipt for a comfortable old age. While the dressers, maids and Dean Davidson would undoubtedly be a comfort in old age, it was problematical that the Munshi would be.

The Munshi was Victoria's favourite Indian servant, Abdul Karim. What Fritz and Vicky had feared was becoming an accomplished fact. Mama's 'brown Brown' was being more demanding. Already he had set the Court by the ears. He had pleaded for a different station from his fellows. He claimed that in India he had been a clerk, a Munshi, and to please him Victoria had nominated him the Queen's Munshi. Instantly there had been rows amongst the Indian servants who did not wish to wait on Abdul Karim, and rows amongst the Household who refused to admit him to their number. They were absurd rows which accomplished nothing. The Empress of India was not going to be denied the right to appoint a Munshi to blot her signature and teach her the rudiments of Hindustani.

Inevitably the Queen's family disapproved. It was not because the Munshi was an Indian. . . . All her children and the majority of her grandchildren inherited her unprejudiced view of coloured people and would never have permitted people to refer to blacks or niggers in their presence. Nor did they object to the Munshi being a servant. Royalty by necessity often had its closest friends amongst servants. But they drew the line at the Queen Empress choosing such a slippery customer as her confidenial clerk. The Prince of Wales was now willing to admit – though very grudgingly – that, apart from a brusqueness of manner which appeared to lack in respect for the Queen's children and apart from being the innocent cause of a huge amount of unsavoury speculation and scandal, John Brown had had his integrity. He had never knowingly misused his great influence. But Abdul Karim was a different matter.

When the Queen honoured Sandringham by a visit – the first since the Prince of Wales' severe illness – and enjoyed watching Irving playing in *The Bells* and then he and Ellen Terry in the trial scene from the *Merchant of Venice* – her family's enjoyment had been spoilt because of the Munshi's prominent place in her suite. And when that summer the Queen had bad rheumatism and had to be wheeled in a chair about Balmoral, who did the wheeling but the Munshi. The Prince found himself in some agitation about Abdul Karim. Soon he reckoned he would be in a position of considerable influence. He began to make plans for the family to close its ranks in a concerted attack on Mama's Munshi.

But the Prince's plans had to be abandoned. His own unhappy penchant for attracting disaster demanded all his attention for a very long time. What he called 'the hounds of self-righteousness' were loosed upon him, and, for a year and more, he was in serious trouble with the government, the press, the public, and his wife and sisters – but never with his mother. Temporarily the Munshi was saved. The Prince had a proper sense of gratitude. Because she was consistently loyal to him he felt it would show ingratitude to conspire against the infuriating Indian.

The scandals which centred on the Prince of Wales were in the usual run.

The first was concerned with other men's wives and a compromising letter. In this case, though, the letter was not written by the Prince himself but by his current mistress, Lady Brooke, whom he called affectionately his darling Daisy. It was written to the wife of one of the Prince's oldest friends Lord Charles Beresford.

What followed was like a game of chess played badly and headlong in the public eye. There were threats of duels, thrashings, publication of the compromising letter, and social boycotting. Lord Salisbury was dragged into the game and moved a piece or two.

While all this was going on a second scandal broke.

The Prince had been at a week-end party at Tranby Croft near Doncaster where baccarat was played for high stakes and where Lieutenant-Colonel Sir William Gordon-Cumming, Baronet, of the Scots' Guards, was caught manipulating a sleight of hand trick known as *la poussette*. The combination of illegal baccarat, cheating, and the Heir to the Throne was irresistible to the press. When, eventually, an action was brought by Gordon-Cumming against his accusers the Prince was subpoenaed to give evidence. This he discovered was worse than appearing in the Mordaunt case. Gordon-Cumming's counsel claimed that his client was being victimized to save the honour of a Prince who habitually encouraged an illegal game. The press made the most of it. Though Gordon-Cumming lost his case, was dismissed from the Army, expelled from his clubs, and socially annihilated, he quickly married a very rich young American girl and retired happily to his Scotch estates. The Prince who in theory was an innocent bystander in the affair became the target for a typhoon of obloquy. *The Times* had the impertinence to express a wish that the Prince of Wales would sign a pledge never again to play cards for money. A group of great ladies begged the Archbishop of Canterbury to remonstrate with him about his private life; and, when he refused, they asked him to devise a series of penitential services in the chapel of Lambeth Palace which they attended with regularity and high satisfaction.

The Prince of Wales was suddenly very unpopular indeed. The Princess of Wales was so distressed by the Beresford scandal that, instead of returning home after her annual holiday with her parents in Denmark, she went off to stay with her sister the Empress of Russia, and refused to say when she was returning to England. She would not return when Sandringham House was badly burned, nor for her husband's fiftieth birthday which perforce he had to spend alone in fire-blackened Sandringham; but a telegram saying Prince George had typhoid brought her quickly back from the Crimea. Her son was soon out of danger but the

Beresford scandal dragged on until its energy was spent, wounding the Princess and bringing satisfaction to no one except the hounds of self-righteousness. By the end of the year the people of Britain had been given the impression – correct as it happened – that the Prince of Wales and his associates were reckless gamblers and extravagant roués.

Through all these emotional scenes the Court was silent. The Liberal non-conformists who expected the Queen to condemn frivolousness in high places were disappointed. The Prince of Wales was so unpopular that Dean Davidson was seriously concerned for the monarchy, but he wisely advised the Queen to maintain a dignified silence. Lady Churchill's advice was the same. Since he had been a good-looking boy of eighteen she had always championed the Prince of Wales. And it was also the Queen's own inclination to serve her heir best by keeping silent. She knew his faults, no one better. He was no less greedy and self-centred and vain than he had always been and as the head of smart society – the Marlborough House Set, or Hauterie de Juif – he was showing an increasingly poor taste. She had shuddered on reading the report of his glee when given a fiftieth birthday present of hideous vulgarity by actors and theatre managers. Yet out of the public eye she worked indefatigably for Bertie, consulting with her ministers and the Archbishops and other advisers as to the wisest courses of action; doing her best to soothe Alix in her great hurt, and not hesitating to speak her mind when members of the family were unhelpfully critical and censorious. It was to be expected that Willy was the rudest of the critics. He had the effrontery to protest that Uncle Bertie's behaviour was intolerable, and to say it was improper for the Honorary Colonel of the Prussian Hussars to be embroiled in a gaming squabble with men young enough to be his children. The Queen wrote three replies in varying degrees of chilling indifference to her grandson's unctuous sermonizing, but by the advice of both the Dean and Sir Henry none was sent. They said, and rightly, that to a sublimely self-centred creature like the Emperor William the worst sort of punishment was to be ignored.

Only to Vicky was the Queen entirely frank, confessing that it had been a terrible humiliation for Bertie to be subpoenaed in a second law case, and that his prestige had undoubtedly suffered.

But there was a chance, she said, that this second, hard lesson might have an effect and make him more circumspect.

Her son was deeply grateful. Through all his trouble – and ever afterwards the Prince of Wales was to claim that those fifteen months or so had been the worst in his life – his mother stood by him. It taught him to love her at last with real affection. Before that his love had been filial in quality and small in quantity. He had always been afraid of her since the time she had appeared in the nursery to mete out royal justice with her own hand. He had always blamed her for allowing his father to prepare him for the throne cocooned in isolation and fed on a diet of scholarship far beyond his capacity. And like many self-centred people he resented the fact that his mother had invariably preferred her husband to her children. He still held her in awe and she still profoundly irritated him by not letting him have any knowledge of or say in public affairs. But her loyalty to him could never be questioned and gratitude made him think of her so kindly that for the first time he saw her many virtues. He greatly admired her contempt for humbug, her refusal to give in, her candid admission of her blind spots, and, though he and his friends were often its target, he even admired her outspokenness. Suddenly he became very fond of her, not simply because she was all he thought a sovereign should be, but also because she was a character in her own right. From that time he took pleasure in repeating her latest exploits to carefully chosen intimates: of her delight at being wooed by a sentry in the Windsor courtyard who, seeing a figure at a darkened window, mistook his sovereign for a housemaid; of her splendidly typical remark when *Truth* published two cartoons to suggest that the Queen preferred Scotch and foreign servants to English ones – 'Of *course* I do!'; of her sulphurous reaction when the Conservative President of the Local Government Board threw out the novel suggestion that the gardens of Buckingham Palace might be opened to the public ('He might as well ask her to dance the fandango!' was Sir Henry's tart comment); and her even more sulphurous reaction when that abominable Liberal Labouchere suggested that Buckingham Palace itself should be turned into a home for fallen women.

9

The Queen and the Prince of Wales were as one about Prince Eddy. He had been created Duke of Clarence and Avondale in 1890 but the dignity suited him less than the sobriquet of 'Collar and Cuffs'. His private life was reprehensible and appallingly public. He fell easily in love, or claimed that he did, and involved everyone in endless trouble while he gave his heart in turn to his cousin Princess Alicky, who would not have him, to Lady Sybil St Clair Erskine who would undoubtedly have had him had he not been whisked away from her, and to the daughter of the Comte de Paris, claimant to the French throne, who could not have him because she was a Roman Catholic.

Something had to be done.

His father and grandmother had a confidential *tête-à-tête* about his future over a substantial luncheon at Buckingham Palace. It was served in a pavilion in the garden and, thoughtful of Bertie's fondness for rich sauces, the Queen had ordered some of his favourite dishes. She herself dealt manfully with soup, turbot, a cut or two from a roast of lamb, potatoes, and pudding. When the covers had been removed the Prince gave the Queen his arm and they walked to a shady place beneath a cedar tree where chairs had been set out. An Indian attendant placed footstools. Another brought a tray of coffee. There was also brandy, but the Prince refused. Indulgent in almost everything else he was abstemious with drink. A glass or two of champagne, hock, claret and seltzer water were all he drank. In this he was unlike his elder son. The latter's habit of sipping was becoming well known. It provided a suitable jumping-off ground for the conversation.

'Dalton, the boys' tutor, has it that drink's the solace of frustrated people, Mama.'

The Queen considered this. 'Probably,' she said, 'he is right. Though I would add that it is also very cheering to those who are not in the least frustrated.' She intimated that drinking was the least significant of her grandson's problems. 'All young men, at some time or other, and especially young officers, drink far more than is good for them. But they do not necessarily become drunkards.' She put down her coffee cup. 'It seems far more serious to me that Eddy is so immature, so incapable of exercising some form of self-control.' She made an expressive gesture. 'We all know, of course, about his self-indulgence, his horses, and his cards and his young ladies. . . .'

The Prince of Wales steadily regarded the lower branches of the cedar. He hoped very, very much that Mama was not going to say that she also knew about Eddy's young gentlemen. But either she was ignorant of it, or – more likely – because she thought she ought to appear to be, she did not add them to the catalogue of her grandson's more reprehensible failings. She continued to list them, telling them off on her fingers. 'He is extravagant, and inclined to be unkind and rude to his inferiors, and sulky when rebuked.'

The Prince acknowledged ruefully that all this was true.

His attitude made the Queen suddenly feel contrite. Her analysis of Eddy's weaknesses could have been a just estimate of his father's. Embarrassed, she strove to cover the awkward moment by adding: 'I will say this, dear, in your youthful scrapes and escapades you were usually amenable to reason, but darling Eddy isn't.'

'No,' said the Prince. 'Alix and I are at our wits' end.' He mentioned his physician's advice and the tutor's: Eddy would have to be managed and told what to do for the good of the country. Marriage obviously was desirable to calm him down. And, for the present, there were two alternatives: either he would be stationed permanently in Ireland, cut off from London vices and yet within reach of his father's control, or he could travel abroad.

The Prince himself thought that foreign travel would be better, although it seemed to be making the Heir Presumptive into a remittance man, and the Queen agreed. But she did not approve of sending Eddy to the farthest ends of the Empire. The boy needed polish, she said, and polish was not the sort of thing one found in Canada or Australia. He ought to go the rounds of the courts of Europe.

'A prince should be cosmopolitan,' she declared. 'Willy is as he is largely because he has not travelled sufficiently.'

The Prince considered. He himself was cosmopolitan and it was true that Willy, the most detestable member of the family, was exactly the opposite. He was inclined to agree with his mother.

But perhaps, he suggested, Eddy's quickest cure would be affected by an immediate marriage?

'Immediate?'

'Immediate,' he repeated.

'And now,' said his mother testily, 'you will propose May of Teck?'

Yes, he said, he would. May was intelligent and pretty. If she could be persuaded to take Eddy, she would make him a very good wife.

The Queen reflected. She liked Princess May well enough. Her mother was her gigantic cousin Mary of Cambridge, but her father, the Duke of Teck, was a soured, touchy old gentleman, not entirely in his right mind, with the nickname of Bif-teck. Nevertheless Eddy himself had considerably shortened the list of potential brides by refusing to marry a Prussian. Perhaps May could be persuaded to look reasonably on the prospect of marrying so unappetizing a prince simply because of his prospects. Her own were very small. Intelligence could never make up for what she lacked in worldly riches and rank. Victoria rather thought that May would take him. Nevertheless she would not herself make any decision. From the country's point of view any of the three alternatives for Eddy's future would do, and she felt something was owed to Alix's privileges and feelings as a mother.

To Bertie's surprise she suggested that the decision be left to Alix.

'To Alix?'

This time the Queen's eyes sought refuge in the lower branches of the cedar tree. 'She has, poor darling, a very great deal to put up with from us all.'

Bertie had the grace to flush. 'As you wish, Mama,' he muttered.

She nodded. 'But I make no doubt she will choose an immediate marriage with May of Teck.'

Her son brightened. 'You do?'

'I do. I am sure she will choose May.'
'Excellent, Mama.'

And Alix did choose May.

The Princess of Teck and the Duke of Clarence and Avondale became engaged to be married four weeks before Christmas in 1891. But early in the new year he caught influenza. It became pneumonia. For seven hours Princess May stood beside his death-bed with his father and mother, his brother and his three sisters, listening to the rattle in his throat, watching the nurses put ice to his head and wipe the sweat from his face until he died.

Queen Victoria received the news with the grief suitable to the grandmother of a difficult child. He had been totally unfitted to be Heir Presumptive and therefore, for England, his death was a fortunate dispensation, but she had also had a natural affection for her own flesh and blood, and she mourned.

Prince George was now in direct succession. He was a good boy. A little dull perhaps, but steady and reliable and with a strong sense of duty, inherited, the Queen liked to think, from his grandfather Albert. He had been kept straight by his devotion to the Royal Navy, shooting driven game, and stamp-collecting, occupations which appeared to leave him little time for anything else. And he had been kept from the clutches of designing women by his devotion to Julie Stonor, the daughter of one of his mother's ladies-in-waiting which, because it was an impossible match – she being a commoner and a Roman Catholic – gave him the melancholy thrill of an adolescent idyll and immunized him from spreading wild oats on foreign service. A momentary fancy for his cousin Marie, daughter to the Duke of Edinburgh, was settled by her refusing to have anything to do with him. This suited his grandmother who, when a decent interval had elapsed, put forward the idea that he should step into his brother's place at the altar as well as on the throne.

The Prince of Wales was not averse from the idea. The Duke and Duchess of Teck were enthusiastic about it. Princess May probably found the exchange something of a relief. Prince George was mildly alarmed. May was so bright. She was taller than he. Her mother was agreeable but vast, a giantess. Her father was dotty. But duty came first. He was willing to marry anyone for England.

Only his mother, with whom he had a particularly close relationship, could not bear the thought of the inevitable. She was sure that May would make him a good wife, but to her the betrothal and marriage were heavy blows.

10

Dean Davidson was too precious to the Church to stay at Windsor for ever. The Queen's own sense told her that it was wrong to keep a young man back when he so obviously had the mark of Canterbury upon him. In March, 1891 she had to let him go to Rochester as Bishop.

In all other aspects the month was a good one. The D'Oyley Carte company delighted her with a performance of *The Gondoliers* in the Waterloo Gallery at Windsor. The dear Dean sat next to her. She found these private performances so entertaining, she told him, though in her prominent position immediately in front of the performers she was subject to some hazards. At one concert an operatic tenor had literally blown off her widow's cap with the force of his singing. She hoped that the massive Mr Richard Barrington would not do the same that evening. The lights were lowered. After a stirring overture the comic opera began and was greatly appreciated, especially the 'regular, royal Queen' song. Victoria tapped in time with the music, both with her fan on her chair and with her shoe on the floor, as the chorus sang:

Oh! 'tis a glorious thing, I ween,
To be a regular Royal Queen!
No half-and-half affair, I mean,
But a right-down regular Royal Queen!

But then her foot and her fan stopped. She had remembered the Dean was leaving. Everything was overshadowed by the coming departure.

After his last service they said good-bye. The Queen gave Mrs Davidson a brooch as a memento. The Bishop elect undertook to be at Court as often as possible and to keep in constant touch either directly or through Sir Henry. Rochester was a large diocese, but the work was not onerous.

That evening she wrote in her journal 'I grudge him going very much.'

Nevertheless Davidson was as good as his word. He did maintain close contact. After the strangeness of having a new dean at Windsor had worn away she barely noticed the difference. Bishop Davidson continued as before to be her intimate friend and adviser.

He was an astute, kindly man, still young but very wise. He was familiar with the Queen's personal history as no one save Lady Churchill was privileged to be. He knew about her regrets, her longings, her fears, her changing sense of values as she grew older. He understood her spiritual needs even better perhaps than Dr MacLeod or Dean Wellesley had done. He had an exact appreciation of her abilities and her virtues as well as her rather obvious faults and limitations. He was not wasteful with sympathy so that it could be used to good effect when it was really needed; for example he was far more prodigal with consolation when Prince Louis Hesse died in April, 1892 than he had been three months before at the death of the Duke of Clarence; and that August he appreciated that, to the Queen, the retirement of her dresser Emilie Dittweiler was as upsetting as the resurgence of Gladstone.

Just as she had feared, the old genie slipped from his bottle again, but it could not be for long, whereas dear Emilie's departure, after thirty-three years of service, was dismally final.

Bishop Davidson urged the Queen to be less rigid with her ancient Prime Minister but not even his persuasion, added to that of Lady Churchill, could make Victoria pretend that she was pleased to see Gladstone back at Downing Street. She wrote to Lord Lansdowne, her Governor-General in India, that once more the affairs of the country and the empire had been

> *entrusted to the shaking hand of an old, wild and incomprehensible man of 82½.*

However bitter her hostility to Gladstone the statesman, Victoria considered that personal and family matters fell into an entirely different category. There could be no doubting the sincerity of her sorrow when his eldest son died. She remembered William Henry as a little boy playing with Betrie at Osborne, and she grieved for his parents. She was quick, too, to send her condolences when, less than a month after forming his Fourth Administration, old Mr Gladstone was chased and knocked down by a mad cow in Cheshire. She was glad to note, she said, that the Prime Minister had consented to go to bed and be bandaged, and that the cow had been shot.

She was ever courteous, but in the vast majority of matters she was unapproachable, disapproving, invariably discouraging to the People's William. 'And why not?' she asked the Bishop. So eccentric a Liberal needed to be discouraged, besides which she did not like him. She quoted a saying of the betrayed General Gordon, 'We are all pianos, events play on us', and she pointed out that Gladstone's atrocious policies were constantly playing shattering arpeggios all over the keyboard of her nervous system.

The Bishop noticed that in fact the return of Gladstone had put warrior blood back into the Queen. She was considerably more lively than when Lord Salisbury had so benevolently legislated.

She faced Tennyson's death with aplomb, and thought his end appropriate for a bard:

> *He died with his hand on his Shakespeare and the moon shining full into the window and over him.*

Telegrams of condolence poured in because he had been her Laureate. Amongst them was a hand-on-heart 'deeply deplore' message from Willy in Germany, and a telegram in French from a Comtesse Pierrefonds in Farnborough, a name she was struggling to put a face to when Lady Churchill suddenly reminded her it was the Empress Eugénie, incognita when travelling in Europe.

'But she is at home in Farnborough! And to send a condolence in French! How odd!' commented the Queen.

Bishop Davidson was quickly at her side when other deaths weighed her down. There was a calamity at Whippingham Rectory when Mrs Prothero fell out of a window and lived for only an hour afterwards. Then came the news that Ernest Coburg had died. His life had hardly been a model for virtuous and progressive princes but he was Albert's brother and therefore had a special place in Victoria's world. There followed the deaths of the Comte de Paris, and Alix's brother and the Russian Emperor, and, in the same month, when Windsor was surrounded with floods, there was another Prothero calamity. The canon himself, enfeebled with age and grieving for his wife, slipped in his own hall at Whippingham and never recovered consciousness. Only three weeks later the Queen received the Canadian Prime Minister and heard him sworn in as a Privy Councillor and, at the Household Luncheon a quarter of an hour afterwards, he dropped dead on the table scattering spoons and knives and forks.

Inevitably such shocks distressed the Queen. But Bishop Davidson calmed her and encouraged her with his wisdom. Had he not been able to help her put death into perspective, its regular attack upon those she knew and loved might have made her give way, perhaps, to the depression which had so often engulfed her in middle age. As it was she developed a healthy resilience, a capacity to see death as a friend as well as an enemy, and sometimes even as a jester.

When there were less mournful challenges to meet, the ageing queen was positively spritely.

She campaigned energetically against the Access to Mountains Bill which she believed would ruin the privacy and the sport of the Highlands, and insisted on what she termed:

a close *time of* six weeks against tourists.

She had her own way.

She also had her own way in the running battle with the Munshi's detractors. They were many and they were in earnest. They resented the fact that privileges and cottages had been showered on to him. They disliked the importation from India of his wife, nephew, and aunts – and Dr Reid remarked that every time a Mrs Abdul Karim fell ill a different tongue was put out for him to examine. It was claimed by the Household that the Munshi was a low-class imposter who was furthering the career of his particular friend Rafiuddin through whom he provided state secrets to the Government of Afghanistan. The complaints were many and various. The Queen's spirited response was to promote the Munshi. Henceforth he was to be the Queen's Indian Secretary or Hafiz with his own office and clerks. So that his feelings should never be hurt, all photographs which showed him waiting at table were to be destroyed. The Household conspirators, led by Sir Henry's assistant Colonel Bigge and Dr Reid, promptly sent her a report from India which contradicted the Munshi's pretentious claims about his social origins. What of it? retorted the Queen. She as good as told Sir Henry that he should keep the Household under better control and teach them that she did not favour discrimination of any kind. Bishop Davidson encouraged her. He was entirely with her in this crusade and greatly amused when, as if to clinch her argument, the Queen wrote to Ponsonby:

> *. . . to make out the poor good Munshi is so* low *is really* outrageous *& in a country like England quite out of place. . . . She has known 2 Archbishops who were sons respectively of a Butcher and a Grocer. . . .*

Like other old ladies the Queen and Lady Churchill took a delight in treats, enjoying their self-indulgence as much as the event. They relished that extra potato or extra chocolate forbidden by Dr Reid. A picnic was enjoyable in itself, but best of all at Balmoral when the presence of gnats guaranteed an excuse to smoke cigarettes. Lady Churchill disapproved of the Queen's apparent liking for driving out in rain and even drizzle, but both took pleasure in sight-seeing and liked to drive out to look at things.

And the Queen had what Bishop Davidson considered a charming habit of sharing her enjoyment. Lady Churchill told him the story of a young Englishman in Florence, who, noticing the Queen holding something up at the unveiling of the west front of the Duomo, had concluded it was some sort of reliquary and that his sovereign was a secret convert to Roman Catholicism. The truth was simpler. She liked to share her pleasures and ingenuously was holding up a locket of Albert so that he could see the unveiling. She also shared her pleasure with members of the Household and her personal servants. In late middle-age she had had a reputation for parsimony which was mostly undeserved, but no one now could accuse her of meanness, and especially in the precious gift of sharing pleasure. In this she was liberal. If she found anything beautiful or wonderful or exciting or even ordinarily interesting her pleasure was generously passed on.

But sometimes she could not share her feelings. Politeness, circumspection and custom obliged her to wear a sovereign's mask of inscrutability. It would never have done, for example, to have betrayed her relief and jubilation when Gladstone once more resigned office. What is more, she dared not encourage him by pleasantries in case the incorrigible old man took fresh heart and returned to plague her as Prime Minister. And so she was very ordinary at his last audience on March 3rd, 1894. She knew, she said, there was no point in offering him an earldom. She had done so before and he had refused it. They talked of trivia, amongst them of occulists. The Queen mentioned a Professor Pagenstacher from Wiesbaden whom she proposed to consult herself. She said something gracious about Mrs Gladstone. And that was that. The audience and Gladstone's sixty years in public life were at an end.

The old man was hurt that she had not said a single syllable about the past and he was not entirely mollified when she wrote to wish him 'peace and quiet with his excellent and devoted wife in health and happiness'. He wrote in a secret memorandum 'which will stand alone, and will never pass the door of my lips on its passage to the ear of any human being' of his awareness of the great antipathy the Queen felt for him. Aloud he repeated his observation on the Queen's longevity:

> *Parliaments and Ministers pass, but she abides in lifelong duty, and she is to them as the oak of the forest is to the annual harvest in the field.*

'Stuff!' said the Queen when she heard this, but she was not displeased.

She sent for the Earl of Rosebery to form a new government.

By an inexplicable and quite awful mistake, his political rival who hoped to be Prime Minister was ushered into the Queen's presence instead. Seeing immediately what had happened the Queen remained unruffled and, with great graciousness, got the wretched man out again with the least possible hurt to his feelings.

When Rosebery did arrive he agreed to carry on as Prime

Minister of the Liberal Government. It was a relief for the Queen. She wanted to get away for her spring holiday and a dissolution and general election would have meant a postponement, and Rosebery was the sort of man she felt she could depend upon. He had his romantic side, too; being Scotch, exceedingly noble and youthful-looking, and a desolated, very rich widower, with exactly that wistful glamour which the Queen as an old lady found particularly attractive.

11

'It seems as if my right hand had been cut off,' wailed the Queen.

Sir Henry Ponsonby had suffered a stroke at Osborne. He was paralysed and rendered speechless. Certain that he would have wished it, the Queen replaced him by appointing his assistant Colonel Bigge, and she was a little comforted because his son Fritz was one of her Equerries. But it was a very, very sad time for Victoria. Unfortunately Bishop Davidson was far away in Edinburgh and so could not stop her brooding on this misfortune. As it was, though she attempted to busy herself with affairs, the affairs themselves were a constant reminder of Sir Henry's faithful work and noble support. She grieved constantly for him lying there immobile in his bed, almost a vegetable, awaiting the end.

Dear Sir Henry, he had had no outstanding or spectacular talents, but in loyalty and discretion he had never once failed her. He had been eminently sensible, always so sensible. She smiled sadly at the recollection of him once taking the crown from the Tower to Westminster, declaring a royal carriage and an escort of elderly beefeaters were bait for all the cutpurses in England, and that the crown was far safer in a bandbox and a hired four-wheeler. She smiled, too, at the recollection of his charming apology when on one occasion at Aix she had been awakened by terrifying regular rumblings which seemed to threaten an earthquake and an investigating footman had reported it was Sir Henry snoring in the room below. And not very long before he had given a splendid example of humility and imperturbability. The German

Emperor had been given the Colonelcy of the Royals, and, typically, he had caused a fuss on his first visit to Osborne soon afterwards by insisting on reporting himself to the senior Army officer at Court. It happened to be Sir Henry who had left his uniform at Windsor and was wearing what the Prince of Wales called a dreadful old frock coat. The Prince set great store by such things and was appalled. He personally rushed off to find something more suitable. But he was too late. The German Emperor arrived, uniformed as a British colonel, and reported himself to Sir Henry with a dramatic salute. Quite unabashed, and still in his dreadful old frock coat, Sir Henry shook him warmly by the hand and welcomed him in the name of the British Army.

The loss of such a faithful friend and servant was a great blow to the Queen and fate decided that, in the remaining months of his life, she had to face many special problems.

Lord Rosebery, the Prime Minister, fell ill. Severe insomnia and a racking bout of influenza left him seriously debilitated. Deprived of his moderating influence his colleagues considered the extraordinary notion that Members of Parliament might be paid. 'Paid!' exclaimed the Queen, when she read a memorandum on the matter, and, for a day or two, her private apartments echoed with sporadic outbursts of the word. To her it was an atrocious idea because she believed that the essence of good government was that it involved some personal sacrifice and was voluntary. Where in any case would the money come from? She was as indignant with a Liberal plot to prune the powers of the House of Lords and drive the Duke of Cambridge from his appointment as Commander-in-Chief. Cousin George tugged one way, the government another. Victoria would have minded George's virtual dismissal less if her son Arthur could have replaced him. But the Liberals had done with royal dukes at the head of the Army. Then, suddenly, at a snap division, they were defeated and the Ministry resigned. Lord Rosebery, romantically young-looking but wan, was replaced by Lord Salisbury who more than ever resembled a minor prophet.

Victoria was surprised to find she rather resented the change and supposed it was because the Liberals were not so offensive to her now that they were shorn of that ogre Gladstone. But, on consideration, she thought it was perhaps a good thing after all. Lord Salisbury had been a friend of Lord Beaconsfield. He was so safe.

Moreover he had a house in the French countryside conveniently near to Cimiez where she had formed the habit of going each spring, and Lord Rosebery's villa was far, far, too far away – in Naples of all places. And Lord Salisbury was very accommodating. He was entirely in accord with her plan that summer to offer the Diocese of Winchester to Bishop Davidson.

The Bishop's translation to the diocese in which Osborne lay was the one real joy of that perplexing time. Otherwise there seemed to be little save anxieties.

The Queen was troubled by rheumatic pains so severe that for days at a time she had to remain in her wheel chair.

She was troubled, too, because the old Duke of Argyll had engaged himself to marry one of her younger ladies. Of course, there was nothing she could do about it, but really a man of seventy-two who had been twice a widower ought to know better, and it was so embarrassing for Louise who was his daughter-in-law.

Louise herself was also causing anxiety. She was hardly ever with her husband. Her sculpting lessons with Boehm had come to a drastic end when, on lifting a piece of Carrara marble in his studio, he had had a heart attack and dropped dead literally at the Princess' feet. When not travelling abroad as Mrs Campbell she was at Court and the Queen's sharp eyes quickly detected that boredom, or Liko's undoubted good looks, were making her set her cap at her brother-in-law. This would never do. Beatrice was already jealous enough. When Liko had gone for a holiday *en garçon* with his brother Louis in Corsica, Beatrice had suspected the worst and asked Sir Henry to send a naval warship to get him away from the temptresses of Ajaccio. Now she was glowering at Louise. Happily a solution offered itself. The government planned an expedition to quell the kingdom of Ashanti or the Land of the Golden Stool and when Liko asked to go the Queen quickly agreed. It would get him out of Louise's way. Helena and Christian's son. Prince Christle, were to go too, so he would not lack for royal company. . . .

Mercifully for him Sir Henry died on November 21st, 1895. It ended an era for Victoria.

She wrote to Lady Ponsonby who had been one of her most gifted Maids of Honour thirty-four or -five years before:

Dearest Mary, It is very difficult for me to find words to express how deeply grieved I am. . . . He was always so kind & so fair & just that I miss him terribly – his memory will ever be gratefully remembered by me & mine.

She laid down the pen. A train of ghosts walked before her. Henry Ponsonby, she recalled, had been a nephew of Lord M.'s awful wife – the mad one who had gallivanted with Byron. And he had been Albert's closest friend after the death of George Anson. She smiled to herself. She could see him now, virtually telling her not to upset his master who had met with an accident in Coburg and to go away. And then he had married, and learnt from his uncle, General Grey, how to be the Private Secretary of a monarch. Her eyes filled with tears. No one, no one, no one could have done it better than he. She picked up the pen again.

It is a comfort to have one of his sons with me & keep up a tie with you & your children.

She hesitated. What more? Nothing. Nothing could be said, except maybe by a poet. The formal Court Circular announcement had lacked all feeling. Some things could not easily be put into words.

She concluded the letter and signed herself 'very affectionately, V.R.I.'

Willy had surpassed himself.

Jameson had made an abortive raid into the Transvaal in the hope of forcing President Kruger to grant the English Uitlanders political rights. But as the English authorities denied all foreknowledge of the raid they were understandably incensed when, quite unasked, the German Emperor poked his finger into the pie. He sent a telegram to Kruger which said virtually that he would not permit England to bully the Transvaal.

When it was published the telegram excited a great bout of enthusiasm in Germany and an equally great bout of indignation in England.

The Prince of Wales, tired of his nephew's arrogance and folly, called it 'a most gratuitous act of unfriendliness' and said it was particularly reprehensible for an Admiral in the British Navy and a Colonel in the British Army to behave in such a caddish way. The Marquis of Salisbury was disturbed. Not severely so. But he did not care to see the people so bellicose and full of animosity towards Germany. A strong note of protest would have to be sent to Berlin.

But the Queen said she would prefer to deal with the German Emperor herself. Would the Prime Minister and Foreign Secretary please hold their hand?

They did. There was still a force in the tiny half-blind Queen in which Salisbury had great confidence. Dealing with the Emperor William as a grandson was more likely to be efficacious than treating him formally as a foreign sovereign.

It turned out that Salisbury was right to trust the Queen. She wrote a grandmotherly letter to Willy and he was instantly deflated. He referred no more to Jameson or Kruger.

The fuss in Germany simmered down. In England only the press and the Prince of Wales continued to demand some sort of atonement. Neither Victoria nor her ministers paid the slightest attention to the fuss; though the Queen did attempt to cool down her son.

> *William's faults come from impetuousness (as well as conceit) and calmness and firmness are the most powerful weapons in such cases.*

It was a lesson he remembered in later years when as King he had to deal with his obstreperous nephew.

Victoria was wretched with anxiety and totally incapable of being calm and firm with herself when she heard that Beatrice's husband had been stricken with fever on the Ashanti expedition. Acting as the Commanding Officer's military secretary, he had ridden a donkey deep into the Land of the Golden Stool, protecting himself from the sun with a white parasol. But he never reached the objective and missed the farcical ending of the expedition when the British forces, after a ghastly trek through tropical jungle, stumbled into the capital to the strains of 'Home Sweet Home' to discover all their endeavours had been quite unnecessary and the native chieftains were only too happy to submit. Word came that the unfortunate Liko was to be invalided home and for days Osborne was in a state of anxiety. Then the anxiety turned to despair. On shipboard off Madeira the Prince had died.

Princess Beatrice was in a dreadful state. In calm moments she repeated again and again that no one was to blame, and she was sure it had been right for her husband to risk his life in Africa, but, at other times, the Queen felt she herself was being held personally responsible for allowing Liko to go to Ashanti. Fortunately Louise was not at Osborne or there might have been words between the sisters. Equally fortunately Prince Arthur and his wife were there, and they were of great assistance in looking after Beatrice and making the necessary arrangements. Liko was to be buried in Whippingham near Sir Henry and the Protheros.

Her son-in-law's death frightened the Queen because it struck at the roots of her security. Not only did she sincerely mourn him because she had grown to love him, but she feared that coming so soon as it did after Sir Henry Ponsonby's his death would alter the routine to which she had become accustomed. She trembled from head to foot when she was wheeled on board the royal yacht *Alberta* which had brought Liko's body from Madeira.

Lady Churchill was at her side. She took her hand and squeezed it. The minute guns boomed, the ship's bells of the escort tolled. Helped by her son Arthur and by Lady Churchill, Victoria climbed to her feet and walked to lay a wreath on Liko's coffin. It was guarded by his three brothers and a nephew. Beatrice, entirely veiled in black, stood weeping at the head of the coffin. Her four children were also there.

Later that afternoon Victoria sat in the window seat in her private sitting-room and confided her fears to Lady Churchill. 'With Sir Henry gone, with poor Liko gone, everything will alter. It must. You will see, Jane. The young people do not understand us any more. Even, in this short time, Beatrice is different. She talks of going directly to Cimiez with her children. Without me. Before the arranged date. Jane, Jane, everything is altering. Changing. Breaking.' She put her head in her hands. 'Poor Liko. Poor Beatrice. Poor Sir Henry. Poor Mary Ponsonby. Oh, Jane!'

Lady Churchill rang for a page and asked that tea should be made. When she had poured two cups she added a little whisky and she pressed one into the Queen's hands. She arranged the screen and put a rug over the Queen's knees. Then she sat beside her on the window seat.

They would have been far warmer closer to the beechwood fire but outside it was a beautiful winter's evening. The sun was setting and making the waters of the Solent sparkle. They sat quietly together, sipping their whisky and tea, saying nothing, watching the sunset.

12

It was 1896. From January onwards the Queen was frequently seen taking in deep breaths. She was practising, she explained to her ladies, for the rigours that lay ahead.

There was still some doubt as to what the anniversary should be called: the Queen's Year, or the Diamond Jubilee or – ugly word – Jubilissimee. But, whatever its title, the event was bound to be exhausting, and the Queen was quite often heard to say that the sooner it was over and done with the better. Secretly she was rather afraid of accidents. The summer before the Tsar had died and at his son Nicholas's coronation a stand had collapsed killing three thousand spectators. If that sort of thing was to threaten the ceremonies in London, she far preferred not to have them. But she knew they were inevitable. She had already received a multitude of congratulations because she had reigned longer than any other British sovereign, and the gifts were pouring in. They varied from exotic beasts sent by oriental autocrats to a ribbon, a watch, and a bicycle from the Mayor of Coventry. But her heart was touched by a great famine in India and she insisted that no collection of any kind should be taken for the celebrations which might divert money intended for famine relief. She also categorically refused to allow Willy to be in England for the event. The Ministry had decided that, unlike the Golden Jubilee, this commemoration of the Queen's sixty-year reign should be an imperial celebration. But the German Emperor took no notice of the decision to ban the Heads of Foreign States and announced his intention of being there. Once more a stern grandmotherly warning produced the desired effect.

Victoria's breathing exercises became more frequent. It was

important to be prepared. There were other exercises, too, devised by Professor Pagenstacher to improve the Queen's eyesight. He had helped her a great deal and made her marvel at what could be done in these scientific days. How interested Albert would have been in everything. She had proved her own modernity in allowing herself to be photographed at Balmoral by the new cinematograph process, though when she saw a performance of the moving pictures she was dismayed. She told the Prince of Wales that everyone appeared to strut like Willy. She had not gone so far though as to brave a ride in a motor carriage. George Cambridge had taken the risk and had ridden in a stately Bollée over a snowy road. He told Victoria with some pride that he had actually controlled the machine and made a little run on his own account. She was astonished.

By the beginning of March the Queen was delighted at the thought of getting away to Cimiez for a rest before the great strain began, and, as so many Indian princes were to put in an appearance at the Jubilee, she considered it a good idea to polish up her phrases in Hindustani and, for the first time, she decided to take her Munshi with her.

The decision caused the first and only Court rebellion in her reign.

The Queen always took a complete hotel in Cimiez but the accommodation was necessarily limited. If the Munshi was there he would have to dine with the Household, and because of their poor opinion of his trustworthiness they refused point blank to accept him at meals. Harriet Phipps, once a Maid of Honour, now with Princess Beatrice, the Queen's personal secretary, was chosen to put an ultimatum to the Queen.

'Well, Harriet?' The Queen was sitting at one of the two brass-edged writing tables in her Osborne private sitting-room. She was in a sunny mood because she had just heard that old Mrs Symon in the Balmoral shop was less ill than everyone had feared. She smiled on her secretary.

Miss Phipps stared at the clock on the mantelshelf. I supported a copy of Johann von Dannecker's *Ariadne and the Panther*, and she felt exactly like Ariadne.

'Why are you so nervous, child?'

Miss Phipps tore her eye from the sculpture, swallowed hard and denied that she was nervous.

'You have perhaps made a mistake in the letters or to-day's memoranda? Tell me, Harriet. I shall understand. All of us make mistakes on occasions.'

Confronted by the Queen's thoughtful kindness and the terrifying nature of the message she had to deliver, Miss Phipps wavered and stammered and then blurted it out all in one sentence. Because it must have sounded incomprehensible to the Queen she repeated it more slowly. It was expressed in courtly terms but the burden was unmistakable. The Queen had to chose between her Household and her Munshi. They were irreconcilable.

Harriet Phipps quickly regarded *Ariadne and the Panther* as she heard the Queen take a deep breath.

'Kindly look at me, young lady,' said Victoria.

Trembling, she did so.

'Am I to understand that this insolent, defiant, disloyal message is sent by the ladies and gentlemen of the Household to their sovereign?'

'Yes, Ma'am.'

'Harriet!'

For an instant Miss Phipps was tempted to retreat, but she knew it was no use. The others had been so insistent. 'Yes, Ma'am,' she replied faintly.

Then the Queen did something she had never done before. In a lunge of rage she swept everything from the top of her writing-table and the nearby stands. Reference books, stationery cases, piles of black-edged writing paper, rulers and pens and standishes, a vase of immortelles, photographs, miniatures, and statuettes, crashed to the floor.

Without being summoned a dresser appeared from the Queen's bedroom next door. Without being dismissed, Harriet Phipps fled.

By the time Lady Churchill and Princess Beatrice had arrived the royal anger had cooled a little, but it was still too hot for them to find it comfortable. Victoria spoke of betrayals, conspiracies and cabals. She bewailed the passing of Lady Ely and John Brown, dear Sir Henry who would never have permitted such things, and dear Liko who would have championed her. She directed Beatrice to stop grovelling on the floor and call a housemaid to clear up the mess, and only a minute later she dismissed the housemaid who had come running and said her things were too precious to be fumbled over and dropped, and Beatrice had to grovel again.

Lady Churchill did the most sensible thing. She waited until there was less wind in the sail of the Queen's anger. Then, blandly, she suggested that the Prime Minister's advice be sought. Lord Salisbury happened to be at Osborne. He was there in the house. Why not use his talents of counsel and wisdom? An excellent plan, said the Queen. Lord Salisbury would show her ladies and gentlemen how disloyal they were being.

Lady Churchill went herself to summon the Prime Minister. On the way back to the Queen's private apartments she explained the controversy. He was filled with dismay.

'But my dear Lady Churchill. How can I possibly solve such a dilemma?'

The question was barely out of his mouth before he found himself in the Queen's presence. Beatrice had finished clearing the floor. There were ink stains on the carpet and the chintz upholstery near the writing desk.

'Ma'am,' he began. 'Please accept my sincere condolences.'

As he said it he felt a blush of shame for uttering so insincere a sentiment, but it mollified the Queen. The deep red patches on her cheeks became pink. She gave him her version of what had happened. It was lengthy and slightly hysterical, but it gave him time to think. He had a fortunate inspiration.

'The point is, Ma'am, the French are an odd lot.'

She blinked at him.

'You see, the Hafiz has never accompanied you abroad before and so this would be a fresh experiment.'

'I am aware of that, Lord Salisbury,' said the Queen frostily. 'I have already explained that I need to polish my Hindustani.'

Salisbury smiled, and he had a very large and endearing smile. 'In my humble opinion, Ma'am, you are better than any of us at welcoming the Indian princes. And with great respect, Ma'am, I shall have to advise you not to take your Munshi with you to France —'

The Queen opened her mouth to protest and so he hurriedly continued: 'Because the French being, as we know, an odd lot, might be rude to him.'

The Queen's mouth closed. She respected her Prime Minister's knowledge of the French nature. It was a consideration she had not thought of. To subject the Munshi to possible rudeness was unthinkable.

'Lord Salisbury I am very much obliged to you,' she said.

He had offered a face-saving solution. She did not wish to quarrel with people on whom she depnded so much and who in all else were devotedly loyal, and yet she could not let them think they had won their point of view. She herself told the disappointed Munshi that Cimiez was out of the question that year.

Unhappily he paid no attention.

The royal progress had crossed France, the Queen meeting the French President in her railway carriage on the way, and the Court was comfortably settling in the hired hotel when the Munshi turned up. And with him he had his friend, Rafiuddin.

The Queen betrayed no emotion whatsoever, but Colonel Bigge guessed she was probably embarrassed. He and his colleagues gave Rafiuddin forty-eight hours' notice to leave the Court and at the end of that time they sent him packing. The Munshi was displeased, but he realized these normally reserved English gentlemen were potentially dangerous. He behaved himself and kept out of their way.

Lord Salisbury called on a visit from his nearby villa. He was astonished to hear the story. He took Colonel Bigge and Ponsonby's son Fritz on one side to discuss the problem. In the end he was reluctantly obliged to advise them that, though Rafiuddin ought to be kept at arm's length, nothing whatsoever had been found against the Munshi and they would have to tolerate him. The Queen's exotic friendship for John Brown had made her equally impervious to the hostile views of her family, her Court and her people. Nothing could be done. Gloomily the Household accepted his recommendation. No one save the Queen and Lady Churchill was ever kindly disposed to the Munshi but thereafter he was tolerated at Court.

Cimiez put the Queen on her mettle. There was little time to snatch the rest she had come for. People were always calling or asking her to meet them. She saw a good deal of the Salisburys. George Cambridge came to luncheon. The Imperial *peckvogel* of Austria called – sadder than ever because his only son had committed suicide with a seventeen-year-old beauty in a hunting lodge. Down in Cannes she met her cousin's widow the Queen of Hanover with her son the Duke of Cumberland, and on the same day she saw, of all people, the Gladstones:

both looking much aged.

It was a brief meeting. His presence was as abrasive as ever to Victoria. She quickly escaped, pleading tiredness.

At Cimiez she also received Sarah Bernhardt which surprised the sophisticated courtiers who knew that she had been the Prince of Wales' mistress for a time. Bernhardt performed a little French piece at her own request in the drawing-room and the Queen thought highly of her acting. Secretly, though, she was sorry Bernhardt had not chosen to play her famous interpretation of Cleopatra. Victoria had heard of this spirited performance, and the remark it inspired from a member of the audience: 'How different, how very different from the home life of our own dear Queen!' – and ever since she had longed to see it.

At Cimiez she wrote in her journal an affectionate note on her dear Lord Beaconsfield as she had done every year on 19 April, the day of his death. In England now on that day people wore his favourite flower and it was called Primrose Day. The memory of Puck still mattered a great deal to his Titania and always would.

And at Cimiez she refused an offer from Sir Arthur Sullivan to compose a special hymn for everyone to sing outside St Paul's on the great day of her Jubilee. She enjoyed his operas and occasionally delighted her ladies by singing coyly the bum-boatwoman's song 'Dear Little Buttercup'. But people would require, she said, with great sense but small tact, a well-known, popular tune.

The procession halted outside St Paul's.

The Queen did not alight and go into the cathedral. Instead there was a short service of thanksgiving out in the open air.

The Queen's cousin, Augusta of Strelitz, had been shocked at the idea of *al fresco* devotions – 'After sixty years' reign, to thank God in the street!' But Victoria thought it sensible. By a freak of good fortune and, considering the chill and scudding clouds and greyness at daybreak, it really was a freak, there was Queen's weather for the Jubilee.

After the Archbishop's blessing and a singing of the *Old Hundredth*, the order was given to move on. But something quite unexpected delayed the procession. Entirely spontaneously the vast crowd broke into the National Anthem.

Victoria was deeply moved and especially because her family escort of Bertie and Arthur and Cousin George were singing as lustily as anyone and each had unsoldierly tears in his eyes.

The great sound died and was replaced with wild cheering.

The Queen wiped her eyes as the carriage moved on. How much more estimable was that unrehearsed and simple sign of affection than all the elaborately arranged details of her Jubilee celebrations. They had to be, of course, otherwise nothing would ever be done properly or on time, but some she found distasteful. For instance, there had been that peculiar idea of sending an instant message of thanks to all parts of the dominions before she left the Palace. Obediently she had pressed a button which was connected to some sort of telegraph instrument, but privately she had thought it rather theatrical. Yes, theatrical and —

'Artificial?' suggested Helena who was sitting opposite.

The Queen started and gave her daughter a penetrating look. Obviously she had been thinking aloud again. It was becoming a bad habit.

She turned on her revolving stool from left to right and gave Helena a glance of gratitude. It was she who travelled with Alix this time in Mama's carriage because Vicky as an Empress could not sit with her back to the horses and had to have her own carriage. In fact, for some unknown reason, there appeared to be a shortage of carriages and people were riding higgledy-piggledy in some odd combinations. Jane Churchill had told her before they set out that one open carriage carried the Chinese Ambassador and the Papal Legate.

There really was a tremendous noise. The Tower guns were booming downriver as the procession passed down Cheapside to the Mansion House. There the Lady Mayoress presented a silver basket filled with rare orchids. The Queen smiled, put out her hand to be kissed, and said thank you. It was polite, of course, but really she no longer cared very much for orchids. They were the new sign of opulence. That eccentric Birmingham manufacturer who had been a radical and was now Conservative Colonial Secretary always wore an orchid. It suited him. She preferred simple flowers, Lord Beaconsfield's violets and primroses.

Now she was passing the statue of her uncle King William. It brought back memories, but she left them hurriedly when she saw Helena look meaningly to left and right. She must not forget her duty to the crowds. She smiled at them, in a fixed and relaxed smile. She wished she could have brought an old familiar parasol with her. This one, given her for the occasion by the Father of the House of Commons, was of a pretty black Chantilly lace but the ivory handle was studded with diamonds and they felt knobbly. She would have been more comfortable and at ease with her parasol which was patterned with huge chrysanthemums and had a smooth, polished handle, but, then, people might have thought it gaudy.

Crossing London Bridge was a new experience. The girders and parapets were decorated with Venetian masts, festoons of evergreens, and celluloid lamps, and everywhere there were faces – literally hundreds and thousands of faces. The south Londoners were noisier, even more joyous than those north of the river. And back by Westminster Bridge to the Houses of Parliament and the Abbey. As the carriage approached the Members' stand they rose in a body to cheer and wave – Conservatives and Liberals, Unionists and Radicals. The Queen bowed and remembered the disaster in Russia the year before. What if the stand collapsed and destroyed the House of Commons at a stroke. . . .

From Parliament Street to the Mall. Victoria's eyes still sparkled with emotion because the crowds cheered in such a frenzy of loyalty. But she was growing tired and most of the time, such is the way of old people, she was really worrying about Mrs Symon at the Balmoral shop, and about her old dresser Annie Macdonald who was very ill at Windsor. And she was a little anxious about what she called Louise's pulpit. A new church had been dedicated at Crathie and the pulpit was of Highland granite inlaid with pebbles collected by Louise on her mournful wanderings in Iona. It was horrid. But she had to pretend to like it. And to keep on pretending. And when one was sometimes a little forgetful, remembering to pretend was not very easy. . . .

On the day after the procession Harriet Phipps, restored after a long interval to the royal favour, was required to read newspaper accounts of the Jubilee to the Queen. She was chosen because the Maids of Honour who happened to be in Waiting lacked the *savoir faire* to select and omit so that the Queen was neither tired nor bored. Princess Beatrice who was also adept at this amended reading was too busy entertaining family visitors. Therefore it was the duty of Miss Phipps. She had already chosen and marked certain passages, hoping they would hold the Queen's interest, and she was gratified to find that they did.

First of all she read out a selection of editorial comments and the Queen was amused to notice how each newspaper, of whatever political colouring and however ill-tempered and insolent to her in the past, appeared to claim her as their own particular and favourite sovereign. She had not forgotten the past even if some of the editors and proprietors had.

Then Harriet Phipps read reports of the celebrations.

Victoria was touched to hear of the crowds of country folk arriving the day before in omnibuses, brakes and wagons, and sleeping out on a cold and windy night so that they would be able to see the processions. She had a special interest in hearing descriptions of the decorations in London because, despite Professor Pagenstacher's best efforts with eye exercises and belladonna treatment, she had seen very little of them herself. It was out of the question, of course, to wear spectacles in public, although they had handsome silver frames which matched her hair exactly.

Besides these there were amusing little incidents to remember. The Queen particularly enjoyed the *Daily News*' account of the Lord Mayor receiving her on foot at Temple Bar and the poor man's anguish at having to mount a spirited horse, while dressed in his flowing robes of office and nursing a great sword, in order to lead his sovereign into the city. She also enjoyed the account of her great-grandson, David, standing on the balcony at the Palace and saluting the crowds with both hands at the same time. But, most of all, the Queen delighted to hear a detailed description of the Colonial Procession led by Lord Roberts wearing his Victoria Cross and carrying his Field Marshal's baton.

The variety of colonial imperial troops was marvellous: Canadian Mounted Police, in their red jackets, New South Wales Mounted Rifles in slouch hats and buckskin breeches; the Victoria Mounted Rifles with khaki and maroon tunics and twisted suncloths on their hats; the Australian Lancers in scarlet puggarees, the New Zealand Maori contingent, the Cape Rifles, Natal Carabineers, Umvoti and Border Mounted Rifles; Cypriot Zaptiehs in dark blue with red fezzes and sashes, the Chinese Police from Hong Kong, the Malta Militia....

The list was long and not all that easy to read out. Nevertheless Miss Phipps was required to do so twice. More than anything in her life before it gave the Queen an idea of the extent of her domains. It was impressive, rather frightening, humbling.

She begged Miss Phipps to indulge her once again – but the procession of the day before had been followed by a formal banquet and a reception of foreign royalties and their suites in the ballroom, and that day she had received the members of both Houses of Parliament, the Chairmen of County Councils, and four hundred Mayors and Provosts, inspected the Yeomen of the Guard, reviewed ten thousand elementary schoolchildren, travelled to Windsor, received addresses at Eton, and had had a substantial dinner. For a young, robust woman it would have been an achievement. But naturally, by the time Miss Phipps reached the description of the Umvoti and Border Mounted Rifles, the Queen was napping.

Lady Churchill made a little sign to her to continue reading. The Queen was exhausted but, if the reading stopped, she might wake and afterwards be unable to sleep again. Miss Phipps read on. After a few minutes she noticed that Lady Churchill was also nodding.

From the dressing room beyond came small noises of activity. Emilie Dittweiler had travelled from Germany for the Jubilee and was quietly and efficiently inspecting cupboards and shelves. She had sent the new dresser away, and was herself attending to the silver tray which, complete with glass and water carafe, tumbler of milk, biscuit barrel, eau de Cologne, napkin and candlestick and Bible, would be placed as usual beside the Queen's bed. As long as she was in England she was determined to look after her beloved royal mistress.

Harriet Phipps read on while the two old ladies slept.

13

The trivial round, the common task,
Will furnish all we need to ask,
Room to deny ourselves, a road
To bring us daily nearer God.

The Queen's voice was yet strong and clear, but failed on the last line. Ever since Mr Keble had written this splendid hymn she had had difficulty in resisting the temptation to sing 'Goad'.

For years and years Beatrice had played the organ in the Prayer Room at Osborne and each year as her figure rounded and her temper shortened she pounded the organ harder. The Queen peered at her through her Pagenstacher spectacles. How matronly Beatrice was, and the prevailing mode – with which she herself would have nothing to do whatever – made her look even more so. How odd that her little Baby, with the fund of odd remarks, should have a large family of her own, and the eldest already a boy at Wellington.

Only, O Lord, in Thy dear love
Fit us for perfect rest above;
And help us this and every day,
To live more nearly as we pray.

Singing sitting down was not easy, but the Queen enjoyed singing and was sorry that the hymn was over. Now they would all have to listen to Bishop Davidson. They were lucky to have him there, of course, but she hoped he would not be tedious and over-long. Dear though he was – and she knew by now that no sovereign could have a kinder or wiser adviser – he did have a tendency to disregard the understood rule for preachers in the Osborne and Balmoral Prayer Rooms: no aesthetics, no economics, no politics, but a plain exposition of practical truth in exactly twenty minutes.

Beatrice thumped out the Amen. The Household and servants behind sat in their chairs. Louise and Beatrice's little daughter Eva sat down in arm-chairs beside the Queen.

Only she had a table before her chair. On it was a watch. She picked it up, studied it carefully, and put it down again, as a pointed reminder of the Bishop's duty to be brief.

He accepted it with wry amusement because he knew that, within five minutes, the Queen would either be nodding or her thoughts would be far away.

He was absolutely correct. Within five minutes Princess Louise had twice woken her mother, the second time effectively, and she had begun to think about the new Canadian postage stamp which was a map of the world with all British possessions printed in red. Really it was very gratifying to see how large her empire had grown. Then her thoughts wandered in a less comfortable direction. She began to worry about war and the belligerence which was erupting everywhere. The British Uitlanders of the Transvaal were threatening to rebel against Kruger because they were unfranchised. The United States had been at war with Spain about Cuba. Her own Army, under that splendid general, Kitchener, had been fighting dervishes and rebellious fellaheens in the Sudan, and for one terrifying moment there had been a real threat of war with the French over a diplomatic impasse on the Nile. Thank God it had been solved in time. And now the unpredictable French were absorbed in the fortunes of a Jewish artillery captain named Dreyfus.

The Queen's eyes, which had been blank, gradually focused on the table and the watch before her and she remembered where she was. For a moment or two she listened to the Bishop's deep voice.

At luncheon the John Brown salts-cellers were on the table. They were silver and shell-shaped and had been given to the Queen by Brown as a personal gift. They appeared on the Sunday luncheon table wherever the Queen was and the sight of them invariably prompted her to speak about faithful service well and truly done. This Sunday speech, not the Bishop's Grace, was the sign for the meal to begin.

Today it was a family luncheon, the Bishop eating as family and allowed the privilege of initiating a subject of conversation.

He was interested to know, he said, if the Emperor of Ethiopia had yet received the recording of the Queen's voice. Emperor Menelek had begged the Queen to use the new phonographic process so that he could enjoy the bliss of hearing her speak, and the Bishop had been present when the historic recording was made. He had then marvelled that the crowned ruler of millions should tremble when confronted with the recording stylus and cylinder of a phonograph, and that her voice, unnaturally forced, had quavered.

'Yes, indeed, Bishop,' replied Princess Beatrice who, to her mother's increasing vexation, had taken to answering for her. 'The British envoy sent a report of the arrival of the message and its reception in Addis Ababa.'

'It caused,' said the Queen, glancing at Beatrice, 'a great how-d'ye-do.' Deliberately she had chosen an expression she knew Beatrice disliked. She added another. 'A hoo-ha.'

Her daughter looked to the ceiling as if praying for patience, and then snapped at her own daughter Eva for lolling. 'I cannot imagine what Mademoiselle is doing to allow such gypsy behaviour.'

The Bishop coughed, but too late to drown the Queen's provocative remark, 'I can.' Rapidly he returned the conversation to Addis Ababa. 'The Emperor was delighted, Ma'am?'

'Yes,' said the Queen before Beatrice could speak, and she hurried on to describe the cylinder's formal reception. A royal salute had been fired by the Ethiopian artillery and, as a mark of respect, the Emperor had stood to hear the message. Afterwards he had bowed to the phonograph and his Empress Taiton had swept it a deep drawing-room curtsey. It amused the Queen a great deal.

'Just imagine it, Bishop,' she said.

He could and he did and he smiled with her.

Louise looked up from her beef. 'Recent majesty,' she commented.

Beatrice said nothing at all.

After luncheon Davidson decided to have a word with Princess Beatrice. For years she had submitted meekly and apparently lovingly to her mother's domination, but now, as the Queen's force abated, she was showing an independence which obviously puzzled and hurt and angered her mother. The Bishop begged her to be patient and submissive for a little time longer. It would return serenity if not happiness to the family circle.

Beatrice was constrained to consent. She respected and liked the Bishop and she accepted his advice although, she assured him, Mama rode roughly over everyone except her grandchildren, Lady Churchill, and the Munshi. The Bishop did not entirely believe her. Beatrice was inclined nowadays to exaggerate her own humiliation at the hands of the Queen. It was a form of self-mortification. And he wanted to smile when she went on to observe darkly that if Alice had been still alive she would have summoned a family meeting to decide what should be done about Mama. And Mama, thought he, would very quickly have decided what should be done about her rebellious children.

The Bishop was invited to join the Queen for her afternoon drive and guessed that he would hear the other side of the family quarrel. He did. They were well wrapped up, because although the weather was exceedingly chilly the Queen insisted on an open carriage and the drive would be for the best part of two hours. Straight away Davidson heard about Beatrice's sulks, and her occasional bossiness. And he heard too about Louise striking arty attitudes . . . and how poor Vicky in Germany was being treated by her own abominable son . . . and how worried the Queen was about who should carry on at Coburg now that Alfred's son had died and he himself was not at all well . . . and how dull Christian was, for ever smoking and eating, shooting and gardening and yodelling; yes, he had taken to that terrible pastime of yodelling which made visits to Cumberland Lodge a nightmare . . . and how, despite Bertie's fall and knee injury which had laid him up for a month or more and ought to have given him time to reflect and perhaps repent, he was again pursuing his rascally, irresponsible ways. . . .

The Bishop neither agreed nor disagreed. He realized that for the moment he was simply a sounding-board, no more significant, in fact far less so, than the phonograph on which the Queen had recorded her voice for the Emperor of Ethiopia. When she came to the end of her list he pointed out the comfort the Queen was given by other members of her family, and, after careful thought, she agreed and said really she was very fortunate.

Then she stopped using him as a friendly sounding-board and asked his advice on a problem which was making her very anxious.

She felt that she might have been discourteous to the Duke of Norfolk and did not know now to put matters right. It had happened like this. She had been badgered by a petition signed by no less than 336,000 women asking that convents should be brought under public control. The current exposés, true or false, about life in convents had been powder and shot for the Orangemen and Evangelicals and Chapel-goers and No-Popery bigots whose attitudes the Queen herself regarded as thoroughly un-Christian. Nevertheless she had felt it her duty to be properly informed, and she had asked for Norfolk's advice – not as her Postmaster General which he happened to be, but as lay leader of the Roman Catholics in England. In his reply the Duke had made it plain his feelings were profoundly hurt. Two of his own sisters were in convents, the sisters and daughters of many of his friends were in convents. He considered it, he wrote, 'an astounding impertinence' that he and his co-religionists should be thought wanting in proper care for the happiness and well-being of their nearest and dearest, and he described the petition of 336,000 women as 'a cruel impertinence and injury'.

'And since then,' the Queen told the Bishop, 'the Duke has appeared cool.'

It was scarcely surprising, thought the Bishop, though he did not say so outright. Instead he undertook to make the Duke aware of the Queen's opinion of the non-Christian attitude of bigots, and the true facts of the case.

Victoria was grateful.

They drove on for a little in silence until they had reached the lodge gates again. Then, suddenly, Victoria unburdened her heart to him. The decimation of her friends and relations through age and disease was making her desperately unhappy. Since her Jubilee there had been a terrible list. The big deaths, as she put it, were bad enough. The *peckvogel*'s Empress had been stabbed to death by an Italian anarchist while stepping on board a paddle-steamer in Geneva. Then Mr Gladstone and Prince Bismarck had died and caused grief throughout Europe. But she, quite truly, had been more affected by the death of her dear dresser Annie Macdonald, and by the death of Mrs Symon at the Balmoral shop. And Dr Jenner had died, and her grandson the heir to Coburg, and her fat first cousin Mary of Cambridge. . . .

The postilion led them up between the high bay hedges

planted by the Prince Consort while the Bishop consoled Victoria. What he actually said she could not afterwards remember but he certainly soothed her growing panic.

Nevertheless it swelled again when she heard of another death, that of faithful Emilie Dittweiler in Germany, and that evening she tried to describe in her journal her feelings of desolation:

> *All fall around me, and I become more and more lonely. So many sad events have already occurred. . . . It makes one tremble.*

At the time the Queen generally said her prayers the dresser on duty heard her begin to sing a verse from a hymn she had often sung of late:

> *The trivial round, the common task,*
> *Will furnish all we need to ask, —*

But then Victoria stopped. And she burst into tears.

14

It was war in South Africa. There had been nothing like it since the Crimean War. The Uitlanders had to be protected and the Boers disciplined. Troop-ships sailed regularly from Portsmouth. Their ancient Queen was sometimes able to see them off and wave good-bye.

But things seemed to go wrong from the start. There was a black week in which the British met with set-back after set-back, and it was not until Roberts and Kitchener were put in charge that there was a slow readjustment in the field. After that the Boers were no longer in complete charge of events, but clearly it was going to be a longer war than anyone had anticipated.

There were great acts of heroism. The Commander-in-Chief, himself a V.C., lost his only son in a glorious action during which he won a posthumous V.C. The Queen herself sent the award to Lady Roberts.

Victoria appeared to be invigorated by the war.

When Lady Churchill had a heart attack and, for twenty-four awful hours, there was a distinct possibility that she would die, she was able to face up to the possibility with a fortitude she had not possessed before the war. And no reaction set in when the crisis passed and her dearest friend was on the road to recovery.

Within her physical limitations Victoria was more spry than before, and she was very much on the alert mentally. She enjoyed a minor brush with the Lord Mayor who, no doubt out of loyal enthusiasm, chose to offer her the Honorary Colonelcy of the City of London Volunteers. He was thanked but reminded that the Queen, being head of her Army, was already head of every regiment in it. Then, when the Archbishop sent a form of intercession to be used in all churches for her formal approval, he was informed that on the whole it would do very well, but certain alterations, made by the royal hand, would be sent to him later through the Prime Minister. And Victoria was not especially pleased when Lord Roberts ordered that all officers in South Africa should be tattooed with their regimental crests. She regarded tattooing as the mark of the Marlborough House Set. The Prince of Wales was tattooed. So was his son, Prince George. Even Lady Randolph Churchill had submitted. She inquired why Lord Roberts should have given such an extraordinary order. His reply, that tattooing encouraged esprit de corps and assisted in the identification of casualties, was not, she thought, at all satisfactory. Nevertheless she had great faith in his powers as a commander-in-chief and said no more.

For his first Christmas in the battle line each private soldier received a tin of chocolates from the Queen. They were a month late in arriving but this made small difference to the men who consumed the chocolate and then proceeded to use the tins as a form of currency. Because of the aura which now surrounded the Queen-Empress the empty tins became precious relics. Soldiers fought over them. One was willed to a sweetheart in Surrey as the man's most valuable possession. Medical officers in the field certified that No. 4497 Private James Humphrey, 2nd Battalion Royal Lancaster Regiment, was saved from a fatal wound at Groblers Kloof by the Queen's tin of chocolates. Thereafter to the men they appeared to have magical qualities as well as monetary value. There was no doubting the latter. Speculators in war souvenirs made sure of it. Only three months after their arrival in South Africa the empty tins were being offered for sale in London at £15 apiece. The original donor did not know whether to laugh or to be angry.

Apart from the acts of heroism the Queen considered it a degrading, soul-destroying war. It shared the squalor but lacked the compensations of the Crimea campaign. She wondered if the men's spirits were being conditioned by their horrid khaki uniforms. There had been a dash about gold and scarlet and the accoutrements of different regiments which had encouraged their wearers. Now only the Highlanders were military peacocks. And she herself no longer felt martial as she had when Lord Cardigan nonchalantly led his charge right into the Russian battery and out again. She supposed it was because she was now an old, old woman. But, old or not, she was determined that as Head of State she should be kept in close touch with affairs. She insisted that her ministers should do nothing unless she had first been consulted, and she repeated her prudent recommendation of forty-five years before that inquiries into the conduct of the war should not be held until it was over.

Victoria's constant awareness of what was happening in South Africa gave her a proper sense of proportion about her own troubles. It enabled her to bear with Beatrice who seemed determined to sigh right through the war, and to bear patiently with Louise who had organized a military hospital in a set of rooms at the Savoy and, by her attitude, appeared to think that she had already won the war single-handed.

Considering her age the Queen's own contribution towards victory was remarkable. She worked ceaselessly.

Besides holding investitures and receiving the wives and children of the men at the front, she worked indefatigably on woollens and comforts for the Army. She had the bugler boy-hero, Jimmy Dunn, sent to see her and she gave him an inscribed bugle to replace the one he had lost on the field of battle.

She also visited the wounded at military hospitals. To the men it was like the descent of Hera from Olympus, but the Queen was also the Lady of Balmoral who regularly visited the cottagers and took an interest in their lives, and she knew how to put them at their ease. They adored her. She really did seem to care about their discomfort and pain. She was interested in what they had done in

Africa. Royal concern for the troops wasn't, as some of the newspapers were beginning to say, a pretence to keep them going. She gave them fruit and flowers from a basket held by a stately footman, and the men were far more in awe of the footman than they were of the Queen.

Although she knew it would tire her inexpressibly, Victoria made a special journey to London in March, 1900. Her object was to show her personal interest in the welfare of the nation at war, and she was contemptuous of a newspaper suggestion that she had come to rescue West End tradespeople from the depressing effect war had had upon their business. She drove about London, facing cheering crowds as large and as noisy as those at her Jubilee. On her last night in the capital a crowd of thirty thousand marched with flags and banners from Trafalgar Square to the Palace and sang and cheered until at last she made a short appearance on the balcony. The effort drained her of energy for days afterwards, but it had a remarkable effect on her people. Thereafter the majority had a fixed determination to prosecute the war until it was won. At one stroke the Queen had eliminated defeatism. The Earl of Rosebery, still too ill to lead his party, wrote her a sincerely complimentary letter describing it as a matchless epoch in her glorious reign.

The Queen's greatest sacrifice of all was to permit the war to alter her routine. Cimiez in April had become part of the quasi-sacred royal round. But the French were being unpleasant about the war in Africa and she suddenly decided against the alternative suggestion of Bordighera in Italy. Entirely on her own initiative she decided to go instead to Ireland. It was an extraordinarily popular decision. She had not been there since the year of the Prince Consort's death and for years and years the ribbonmen had been threatening her with kidnapping and assassination. But in South Africa loyal Irish soldiers had fought so gallantly that a regiment of Irish Guards was being formed and all Irish troops given the privilege of wearing shamrock in their caps on St Patrick's Day. And so their sovereign decided to spend April in Ireland.

It was with a sinking heart that she arrived in Kingstown Harbour in a deluge of rain. The royal yacht was four hours early and so there was no one to greet her, but people were brought tumbling from their homes when the Channel Fleet lying off Kingstown fired a royal salute.

The Queen went ashore with Beatrice and Helena. All wore shamrocks, and there was a shamrock design worked in silver on the Queen's bonnet and parasol. It was thought wise to warn her that it was doubtful if the Lord Mayor and Corporation of Dublin would give her a civic welcome. She said she knew all about that, but surely they would not be uncivil to an old lady from England who wished to ride into the city?

In the event the nationalists on the council lost the day. The Queen was formally received and afterwards there was no hesitancy.

The people welcomed her with enormous enthusiasm. She rode alone in her carriage for two-an-a-half hours through the slums of Dublin. She reviewed schoolchildren in Phoenix Park where her own ministers had been stabbed to death. She bought lace and Irish embroidery on linen. She visited hospitals and a convent. She held levées and drawing-rooms, held dinner-parties, and attended concerts. And all the time dispatch boxes and telegrams came in reporting on the war.

More tired than she would admit, Victoria returned to Windsor to campaign against defeatism. She received the King of Sweden and Prince Kotohito of Japan, and explained carefully to both the justice of England's cause and her utter determination to win. When news of the relief of Mafeking came through she was so delighted that she consented to hear the Eton boys sing patriotic songs that night in the quadrangle. She sat in a window and listened, saying after each song, 'Thank you, thank you. That was very nice.' During the last song of all the boys were delighted to see an Indian servant appear at her side and hand her a whisky and soda. Their cheers were tremendous.

Her birthday, this was the eighty-first, was spent as usual on Deeside. Six men were sent by the post office to deal with the thousands of telegrams which poured into Balmoral. The Prince of Wales gave his mother the Duke of Wellington's hands in bronze. Willy sent a huge clock with photographs of himself, his wife and children set in the surround. His moustaches, she thought, looked more ridiculous than ever. She ordered the clock to be put away. 'Its tick is too penetrating,' she explained.

15

The Prince of Wales and the Empress Frederick walked slowly through the meadow arm in arm. The mock mediaeval palace of Rosenau where their father had spent his boyhood lay behind them. They had planned to walk as far as the nearest stork's nest and then return, but the Prince was feeling his weight and the heat, and his sister found walking more than difficult. By unspoken consent they stopped at a gate and leant against it to rest.

The Prince wiped his face with a pocket handkerchief. 'When we were here as children, Vicky,' he said ruefully, 'we had abundant energy.'

She nodded. Tears crept to the corner of her eyes – tears for everything that was lost, her health and her youth, her dear father, her darling Fritz, her son's affection, and now her brother Alfred. He had died on July 30th, 1900, in great unhappiness, still mourning for his dead son, estranged from his wife, and in great pain from cancer. She swallowed and touched the corners of her eyes.

Bertie saw the signs of her distress. Sensibly he said nothing. He reflected on Alfred's splendid funeral. Really, for a pocket-handkerchief-size duchy, it had been exceedingly impressive, as had the demeanour of sixteen-year-old Charles, Leopold's son, who had inherited the ducal crown.

After a time he suggested they turn back to the house. Vicky agreed and they set off back the way they had come, melancholy in their certainty that they would never visit the storks' nests of Rosenau again.

Vicky leant heavily on her brother's arm. Very properly, since arriving for the funeral she had been chiefly with Alfred's widow and Bertie had not wanted to add to her distress. But now he had to. She must know how badly their mother had taken the news of Alfred's death. He plucked up his courage and told her. Mama was grief-stricken. Her attendants, and in particular Lady

Churchill, were very apprehensive. Beatrice had not found sufficient courage to warn her that Alfred was so ill, and so the announcement of his death had come as a considerable shock.

Vicky stopped. Her face worked. 'Beatrice,' she said, 'is a goose.'

Though really he sympathized with Beatrice, Bertie did not defend her. He had always been a little in awe of Vicky. 'It was particularly unfortunate that it took place on the same day as the murder of the King of Italy. The shock was doubled.'

His sister looked up into his face. 'So, very soon, Bertie,' she said, 'you will be king.'

'Please.' He was upset. Though the throne had been there before his eyes for so long, he disliked her plain speaking. 'You forget that Mama. . . .'

'Must die first?' Vicky smiled at him, and teased: 'You are as bad as Beatrice.' Then she continued seriously, 'No one, believe me, will miss Mama more than I when she dies, but I love her too well to want her to live on and on, getting weaker, and losing her faculties, and suffering pain.'

Bertie was flustered. He could not bear this outspokenness, but it nerved him to be blunt himself. He asked Vicky what he felt he must ask. She was so close to Mama, closer than any of her other children. Would she consider going to England to be with her at the end?

Vicky's eyes filled with tears. 'If I could. Oh, if I only could.'

'Then do.'

She shook her head. 'I had determined not to tell you, but soon it will be obvious to everyone.'

His eyes were bright with fright. To soothe him she laid a hand on his arm.

But he insisted on knowing. 'Vicky! Vicky! What is it?'

She tried to smile at him. 'This awful thing which killed my poor darling, and which has taken Alfred from us, I have it too.'

16

Lady Churchill had been seeing less and less of the Queen because she had to take care of her own heart, and the Queen insisted on being too active and driving out in all weathers. One day that summer she had actually insisted on taking a drive in a thunderstorm so violent that the postilion had barely been able to prevent the horses from bolting and the Queen's lap had been battered with hail-stones. But when her dear friend began to feel seriously unwell, Jane Churchill was prepared to brave anything. The Queen's illness had its roots in tiredness and anxiety. The prolongation of the war in Africa worried her. The Boxer Rebellion in China and the massacre of Europeans worried her further. The death of her son in Coburg had cast her down dreadfully. But Lady Churchill noticed that she was never really herself again after she learnt of her daughter's incurable cancer. It was this which altered her and took away her sleep and appetite and tranquillity.

It had been kept from the Queen as long as possible and then, when it could no longer be hidden, Vicky herself had written to break the news. The Queen had accepted it bravely, but she broke down when the disease made an unexpected and rapid advance and she received from Vicky the last letter in her own hand. She explained that she had such frequent spasms in the back and limbs and bones that she could scarcely find a pause long enough to write in. Thereafter she would be obliged to dictate her letters. The Queen cried piteously – but, typically, she wrote cheering and sympathetic letters to her daughter.

Lady Churchill was with her mistress as much as possible now that her health showed signs of crumbling. Being constantly with her the Household and servants were not at first greatly aware of the change in the Queen. Even her family was largely in ignorance of her depressions and loss of appetite and general feeling of malaise. At the centre of things Lady Churchill and the dressers watched anxiously, talked fully with the Queen's physicians, and did all they could to ease her discomforts.

The physicians were concerned, particularly Lord James who was in attendance that year at Balmoral both in June and in October. The difference he found in the Queen on the second visit was extraordinary. In three months she had lost a great deal of flesh and her china-blue eyes had lost their lustre. The Queen herself put it down to overdoing things that spring in Ireland. Lord James discovered the real reason in a talk with Lady Churchill. Sorrow and anxiety, on top of her old age, were sapping the Queen's vitality and she had little resistance to ill news. This seemed to be confirmed when news came from South Africa that Princess Helena's elder son had died of malaria and enteric fever. The effect on the Queen was instantly noticeable. She seemed to shrink, to draw within herself. On her last day at Balmoral that autumn she confided to her journal:

> *Felt very poorly and wretched, as I have done all the last days. My appetite is completely gone, and I have great difficulty in eating anything.*

Beatrice and Louise became alarmed. It might have showed and proved infectious in the Household if Lady Churchill had not told them both with great determination that, for their mother's sake, they must control their feelings. Beatrice then wore such a determined air of imperturbability that, when she wanted a little sympathy from her and could not get it, the Queen called her unfeeling. Poor Beatrice. Louise was a better nurse, more attentive and less emotional. They made it clear to the family that Mama was not well and had a great disgust for food.

Slowly, inexorably, the Queen was growing weaker. She still had the strength though to rap the Mayor of Windsor over the knuckles because of the scandalous slums in the borough. And she never ceased to work at her papers and she carried out her duties as Queen-Empress and head of a large family as well as she was able. She received eminent visitors. She condoled with Willy on being attacked by a mad woman brandishing an axe. She attended an Irish Industries Exhibition. On December 14th, for the thirty-ninth time, she and her family went to the Mausoleum to hear Bishop Davidson read prayers and remember Albert. She followed the fortunes of the Boer War as regularly as ever.

But she was running down like an unwhipped top.

Try as she might Lady Churchill could not keep her awake on carriage drives. Nor could anyone else. When she was reduced to riding about Windsor and Osborne in a donkey chaise she slept from the moment the rug was tucked about her knees until it was removed at the end of the drive. One day there was a slight flurry of snow. Queen Victoria arrived home fast asleep with white on her bonnet and her muff.

The royal days and nights turned topsy-turvy. When the Queen wanted to sleep, she could not. When she wanted to get on with her work and daily routine, she nodded. She could no longer eat and lived chiefly on Benger's Food and regular sips of whisky in milk. Sitting at dinner with no appetite and feeling miserable was a daily torment.

Lady Churchill was desperately worried and harassed. Poor, poor Queen. She sat with her, urged her to take the pap she loathed, and talked with her of the happy days which were gone.

Victoria spent a wretched Christmas Eve. She was restless and her dressers gave her chloral. It failed to make her sleep. She considered asking Lady Churchill to come and talk to her, but abandoned the idea. Jane needed her rest like anyone else. She turned this way and that. At length she drowsed until it was time to get up. Christmas Day. Always one of the best of the year, and downstairs there would be *lebküchen* sent from Germany, and a massive baron of beef marked with her cypher in grated horseradish. Christmas. She would ring for the dresser and get up directly. . . . And then, exasperatingly, she fell asleep and did not wake for hours.

When she did get up she still felt sluggish and weak. A good drive in the cold would do her good. And she would ask Jane to go with her so that they could talk of the old Christmas days at Osborne when they had both had appetites and strength and there had been a great deal of fun.

But Jane was not waiting in the hall.

Helena and Beatrice were there. They told her that Lady Churchill had had another of her attacks in the night and her son had been sent for.

The Queen's face whitened. Her hand flew to her mouth. 'They have sent for Victor Churchill?'

Princess Helena nodded. 'It was thought advisable, Mama. But you have no occasion to be anxious.'

'Of course I have occasion,' snapped her mother. 'Naturally I am anxious.' She signed to the Indian servant who wheeled her chair out to the waiting carriage.

Mother and daughters had a silent drive. Afterwards the Queen returned to her bedroom.

No Christmas dinner. Simply a bowl of broth with a catnap between sips. She wished she could go to see dear Jane. Perhaps Dr Reid would allow her to.

But Dr Reid would not, and, when badgered, explained why. As gently as he could he told her that Lady Churchill had died in her sleep the night before.

'Died?'

'Ma'am, you must compose yourself. I beg you.' The doctor ventured to take her hand and stroke it as he had never done before. 'I fear she died in her sleep last night.'

Harriet Phipps was there. She said softly, 'Ma'am, we wished to prepare you gradually for the terrible news. It would not have been kind to tell you this way.'

'Kind!' the Queen exclaimed. She half rose from the sofa at the end of her bed, then she sat down again. 'A happy, happy Christmas.'

Only three weeks later there were many people in that same bedroom: children, grandchildren, the members of the Queen's Household, clergymen. But not dear Jane. Three weeks ago they had taken Lady Churchill's body to the mainland in a terrible storm. It was said there had not been one like it since the day the Queen arrived on the island as a young widow. Dear, dear Jane.

Victoria opened her eyes and peered at the figures round her bed. She wanted to find Bishop Davidson. But her eyes were too weak and no one had thought to put on her silver spectacles. Nevertheless he knew what she wanted for he was there at once, putting his head close so that she could see him.

Her eyes sparkled momentarily. She asked him if this was the end, if she was dying, and he said yes, she was. Well, she decided, that was a relief. It was far better to know.

So softly that she could hardly hear, the Bishop asked her if she was sorry for the mistakes and wrongs of the past. She considered. How could anyone remember so long a past? It stretched on and on right back to Lehzen and Mama at Kensington, even farther, to her father's big pocket watch which had ticked in her bedroom night after night after night. The Bishop was whispering again. She nodded. Yes, she said, surprisingly candid to the last, she supposed so, but she could not be sure.

In the same soft voice he was praying. She could not quite catch what it was. But then, more loudly, he repeated part of *Lead Kindly Light*. How kind. Of course he was aware that it was her favourite hymn, but she wondered if he knew she had once wanted to ask the author to tea, but Albert had said no, palace tea parties were not for dangerous High Church Oxford clergymen like Dr Newman. She listened carefully. The last line was her special favourite.

And with the morn those Angel faces smile,
Which I have loved long since, and lost awhile.

How kind of the dear Dean. No, he was a bishop now. And, unless she was mistaken, one day he would be archbishop.

She smiled at him, dear kind man, wondering if Dr Newman had been right. Jane Churchill had been cynical in some things but not in religion. Would they see each other soon? And would she see the others she had loved so devotedly? Would Lehzen be waiting there? And dear Lord M.? And Lord Beaconsfield? Would Albert?

She opened her mouth. The Bishop leant closer. 'Albert?' she breathed into his ear, making it a question.

'I feel sure of it,' he whispered. He smiled at her. 'Very soon now, dear Ma'am. Very soon now.'

She nodded. Pleased and grateful, she closed her eyes again.

A hand touched hers. She opened her eyes and made out that it was Bertie. He kissed her and she called him by his name.

Then she sank back into the pillows and smiled, though this time it did not show because her chapped old lips were motionless. It was an interior smile, and one smiled because in one sense she had been dead for forty years, and now was about to come alive again. It no longer mattered that her limbs were so helpless and her eyes blind. Soon she would be with Albert.

The Widow of Windsor

concludes Tyler Whittle's trilogy on the life of Queen Victoria. Critics have said of the first two volumes:

The Young Victoria

'The modes and manners of Victoria's childhood are sufficiently remote to be intriguing without actually exotic, and the language avoids tushery and retains that peculiar tartness of flavour which one associates especially with Wellington.' *Sunday Times*

'Here is a well rounded and historically respectable portrait of the Queen as a young girl. The characters are filled out skilfully and the age and society in which they lived and moved is vividly described.' *Oxford Mail*

Albert's Victoria

'The book is highly entertaining and . . . highly instructive. Mr Whittle has most effectually whetted the appetite for the forthcoming final part of the trilogy.'
Guardian Journal

'There are some delightful touches . . . This is domestic historical fiction at its best.' *Sunday Telegraph*

Other books by Tyler Whittle

Common or Garden
The Plant Hunters
Some Ancient Gentleman

George III —m.—Charlotte of Mecklenburg-Strelitz

- George IV
- Frederick, Duke of York and Albany, Bishop of Osnaburg —m.—Frederica of Prussia
  - ⋮ 1. George Noel
  - 2. Ellen Jocelyn Cecile
- William IV—m.—Adelaide of Saxe-Meiningen
  - ⋮ 1. George, 2. Henry, 3. Frederick, 4. Adolphus, 5. Sophia, 6. Mary, 7. Elizabeth, 8. Augusta, 9. Amelia
- Edward, Duke of Kent —m.—(ii) Victoria
  - ⋮ Robert Wood

Francis Frederick of Saxe-Saalfeld-Gotha

- Victoria (i)—m.—Emich Charles, Prince of Leiningen
  - 1. Charles —m.—Marie of Klebelsberg
    - Ernest
  - 2. Feodore—m.—Ernest, Prince of Hohenlohe-Langenburg
    - 1. Charles (disinherited)
    - 2. Frederica
    - 3. Hermann (succeeded his father)
- Ernest I, Duke of Saxe-Saalfeld-Gotha —m.— (i) Louise of Saxe-Coburg-Altenburg (Divorced)
  —m.—(ii) Marie of Württemberg
  - Ernest II —m.—Alexandrina of Baden
  - ALBERT, the Prince Consort
- Leopold, later King of the Belgians —m.— (i) Princess Charlot of Wales
  —m.—(ii) Louise of Orleans
  - 1. Leopold II
  - 2. Charlotte —m.—Maximilian, Emperor of Mexico
  - . . . . and others

VICTORIA—m.—ALBERT, the Prince Consort

- Victoria, Princess Royal (Vicky) —m.—Frederick III German Emperor and King of Prussia (Fritz)
  - 1. William II (Willy) —m.—Augusta of Schleswig-Holstein-Augustenburg (Dona)
    - 1. William, 2. Eitel, 3. Adalbert, 4. Augustus William, 5. Oscar, 6. Joachim, 7. Victoria Louise
  - 2. Charlotte —m.—Bernard of Saxe-Meiningen
    - Feodora
  - 3. Henry —m.—Irène, daughter of Princess Alice
    - 1. Waldemar
    - 2. Sigismund
  - 4. Sigismund
  - 5. Victoria (Moretta) —m.—Adolphus of Schaumburg-Lippe
  - 6. Waldemar
  - 7. Sophie —m.—Constantine, King of the Hellenes
    - 1. George
    - 2. Alexander
    - 3. Helen
  - 8. Margaret (Mossy) —m.—Frederick Charles of Hesse-Cassel
    - 1. Frederick William
    - 2. Maximilian
    - 3. Philip
    - 4. Wolfgang
- Albert Edward, Prince of Wales (Bertie) —m.—Alexandra of Denmark
  - 1. Albert Victor, Duke of Clarence (Eddy)
  - 2. George, Duke of York —m.—Mary of Cambridge (May)
    - 1. Edward, 2. Albert, 3. Mary, 4. Henry
  - 3. Louise, Princess Royal —m.—Alexander, Duke of Fife
    - 1. Alexandra
    - 2. Maud
  - 4. Victoria
  - 5. Maud —m.—Charles of Denmark
  - 6. Alexander
- Alice —m.—Louis IV, Grand Duke of Hesse-Darmstadt
  - 1. Victoria—m.—Louis of Battenberg
    - 1. Alice, 2. Louise, 3. George, 4. Louis
  - 2. Elizabeth —m.—Grand Duke Sergius of Russia
  - 3. Irène —m.—Henry of Prussia
    - 1. Waldemar
    - 2. Sigismund
  - 4. Ernest Louis—m.—Victoria of Saxe-Coburg
    - Elizabeth
  - 5. Frederick William (Frittie)
  - 6. Alix (Alicky) —m.—Nicholas II of Russia (Nicky)
    - 1. Olga
    - 2. Tatiana
    - 3. Marie
  - 7. Mary Victoria (May)